Cross Examined

Cross Examined

An Unconventional Spiritual Journey

Bob Seidensticker

CROSS EXAMINED
An Unconventional Spiritual Journey

ISBN 978-1468011333
BISAC codes: Fiction/Christian/General, Religion/Atheism

Cover artwork by Kyle Hepworth

Follow blog at www.patheos.com/blogs/crossexamined

To Bobby, Genny, and Sandy

Prologue

San Francisco: April 18, 1906

Thena startled awake as her bed rattled beneath her. Outside her room she heard a frantic clamor. She stared into the darkness, trying to make sense of the tempest.

"Earthquake!"

Long seconds passed, and the noise increased, as if a monstrous train thundered by just outside her hotel window. She stumbled out of bed, snatched her Bible from the night table, and opened the door.

The hotel hallway was full of the shouts and cries of bewildered guests. The approaching dawn barely penetrated the blackness, and frightened people hurried past, their faces made ghostly by candles. More staggered along in the dark.

Wearing only her nightgown, Thena moved into the stream of people and almost immediately ran into an overturned piece of furniture. She tumbled to the floor as pain shot through her shin. A man tripped over her leg and swore at her before moving off. She reached down and touched the wound, warm and slippery.

"Someone help me," she whimpered, and after a pause, "Help me, *now!*"

But no one stopped. *This can't be happening.* The wooden floor heaved and the wall smashed against her again and again. She felt like a rat being shaken by a terrier. Timber groaned, and she heard things thudding and smashing in rooms around her—books, lamps, chamber pots. Beds skittered across floors. In the distance were harder crashes—what sounded like masonry snapping and stonework falling.

Thena pushed herself to her feet and gasped in pain. People shoved past. Many called out piteously, and some shouted prayers or asked for forgiveness for the people of the city. Babies cried.

Thena waded through the dark with her hand groping the lurching wall. She stumbled forward until the wall under her right hand ended. Where was the lobby—to the right or straight ahead? She guessed straight and continued as she strained to see in the meager light. Her bare foot kicked an overturned spittoon and she recoiled from the feel of the slimy wood floor.

An old woman's voice called out not to be left behind. She pleaded again and then again, her voice fainter as Thena continued. A broken gas lamp hissed.

After what seemed like many long minutes of blundering through black corridors, Thena reached the hotel lobby. Pale light from the outside illuminated jagged glass on the floor, and the air was cloudy with dust. She saw movement in the street beyond, but the lobby seemed empty of people. The shaking and roar continued. She felt alone in this dying building.

Safety finally in view, she hobbled toward the glassless windows, arms out for balance. Pain flashed with every step, and she worried how she would get over the glass with bare feet. Halfway across the lobby, something hit her from behind, hard. She was bludgeoned to the floor as bricks and wood tumbled around her. She felt an intense pressure on her legs and a blinding pain, and she coughed on the dust.

The shaking stopped—thank God. Thena moaned and called out weakly, but her voice sounded muffled by the rubble around her body. Her hands were empty—the Bible was missing. "Help me!" she called out again, a little louder. The background roar was gone and she heard the distant sound of panicked voices on the street, vague and unfamiliar. She pushed to stand but couldn't move whatever was on her legs, then called out again and held her breath for a reply.

Then she heard a faint shout outside, a single sharp syllable. "Fire!" Others picked up the call. The thought of slowly burning to death terrified her. She clawed for the locket around her neck—still there—and thought of the man who had given it to her. Would she see him again? Or her parents? She had so much to live for.

She coughed again on dust, or maybe smoke. The intense pain from her legs receded as she called out, "Help—I'm here!" She paused, then shouted again and strained against the crushing weight. Immoveable.

Thena mentally groped for what to do. And then she knew. Alone and trapped under rubble far from home, she began to pray. In her own inexperienced way and buried under pain, she prayed for help, for someone greater than her to do what she could not.

Chapter 1

Los Angeles: three days earlier

Paul Winston sat on a church step in the morning sun. The step felt warm through the thin material of his suit pants.

"A pastor who's afraid of speaking? That's an odd ailment." The reporter who sat next to Paul wrote in a notebook. He had a modest mustache and wore a bowler hat and bow tie.

"I'm the pastor's *assistant*," Paul said, his face growing hot. He hated being confronted with his fear of public speaking, which often showed as a discomfort in meeting new people. Before, he might have taught this man some respect with his fists. He pounded one fist into a palm—the closest he could come—and turned back to the man, impatient to be done with this. "What would you like to know?"

"I've heard about your church. Causing a bit of a stir. Your pastor makes prophecies, I hear?"

The reporter was from the *Los Angeles Times,* and Reverend Samuel Hargrove was always eager for publicity for the church. Paul had to make this interview count, and he assumed his best behavior. "Yes sir, Reverend Hargrove says the Holy Spirit just comes upon him. He has made several prophecies, and they've all come true."

"Tell me about them," the reporter said as he jotted in his notebook.

Paul told him how Mrs. O'Brien's consumption had vanished, leaving the doctors baffled. And how a land title dispute had ended in the church's favor, giving the church their current building. Samuel's predictions sometimes extended to the wider community, and he foresaw the current police chief, a dark horse whose appointment surprised everyone. Each issue had resolved as Samuel said it would. And wouldn't you think that someone favored by God with the gift of prophecy might be arrogant or pompous? But not Samuel—Paul told the reporter that he was the warmest man you could meet.

Paul turned to smile at the people climbing the worn wooden steps. Several women stood in the sun, chatting and comparing outfits. A trolley clanged its bell a block away, and Paul knew to expect a small surge of parishioners. He felt remiss for not greeting them, but this interview was important.

"Tell me more about the church."

Paul's anxiety faded as he warmed to the conversation. "The church building was originally a barn. Our members made it useable as a church about fifteen years ago. In fact, we're rather proud of its simple origins. Good things have been known to come from stables, you know."

The reporter didn't acknowledge the subtle reference as he wrote. "Tell me a bit about yourself," he said. "You're a fairly young fellow. You weren't one of the founding members, I take it."

"Not at all. I've been here for just two years. In fact, Reverend Hargrove pulled me off the street. That's a story in itself, because I was headed for life as a thief. I'd be one now—or in jail or dead—if it weren't for him. Cleaned me up and straightened me out. I owe everything to him."

"I must say, you don't sound like a former thief. I would have guessed you to be a college man."

Paul shrugged. "I was a well-read thief." Reading had been his escape from a dark childhood. Before the church, Paul had felt aimless, drifting on the ocean of society, simply marking time. He felt as if he were made for something better, and Samuel had shown him the way.

Paul leaned into the step and looked back at the reporter. "But let me mention another unusual aspect of this church. Making an intellectual defense of Christianity is part of our mission. Reverend Hargrove doesn't just assume the accuracy of Scripture, he proves it."

Paul's head snapped to the side in response to the sound of a faint tap. He was in time to notice the sparkle of a pocket watch fall through the steps onto the dirt below. A man, unaware of his loss, walked up the steps into the church.

The last few people were making their way inside, the men removing their hats as they entered. Paul turned back to the reporter. "It's time. Come in and see for yourself." Paul stood and gestured the reporter up the steps ahead of himself. He bent down, slipped his hand under the steps, and snatched the watch. Real gold, he guessed, as he dropped it into his pocket.

The walls were built of dark and unpainted wood, but windows along the sides let in plenty of light. Sunbeams through the east windows behind the pulpit cast patterns on the wooden floor. The stable odor was long gone, but there was the smell of warm wood and God's flock, which to Paul was welcoming and genuine.

He walked unhurriedly down the aisle, smiling at anyone who looked his way. Close to the front, on the left side, he stopped. He put his hand on a man's shoulder sitting next to the aisle, bent down to the man's ear, and said, "You dropped something, Mr. McFarlane. Better get that watch chain fixed." He held out his hand.

The man patted his vest frantically as if checking for the twin of the watch in Paul's hand, then took it and shook Paul's hand with both of his. "It was my grandfather's," he said.

The congregation quieted as Paul stood at the front facing the crowd. The turnout was good, and that would please Samuel. Paul marveled at the mix of faces. The First Church of God embraced anyone who wanted a relationship with the Holy Spirit—white, black, Mexican, or Oriental. This was unusual barely four decades after the Civil War, where racial roles were assumed in many areas of life in Los Angeles.

Paul signaled for the prelude on the piano. Music echoed off the wooden walls and, after the first verse, Reverend Samuel Hargrove strode down the aisle with brisk, powerful steps. He was a bear of a man and carried himself with confidence. Samuel always seemed energetic and self-assured, but Paul noticed him even more so this morning.

The old floorboards creaked and his open suit jacket flapped as he approached. His graying hair bounced to reveal a bald spot, and his beard, slightly longer than fashionable, gave him the look of an Old Testament patriarch. His face was eager, like he'd solved a puzzle that had bothered him for a long time.

Samuel took his chair behind the pulpit. A brief pause followed the prelude, and then Paul led the congregation in his favorite hymn, *Amazing Grace*. An open hymnal lay in his hand, but he didn't need help with this one. He sang the words, certain that they were written just for him.

"Amazing Grace, how sweet the sound,
That saved a wretch like me.
I once was lost but now am found,
Was blind, but now I see."

He had been that wretch, angry and miserable, and he marveled at the transformation God's grace had made. Coming into the church had been like losing himself in a warm blanket after subsisting for years—no, a lifetime—outside in the cold rain. He glanced over at Samuel, the father he never had, perhaps the father he should have had. Samuel had no reason to select him of all people, a worthless sinner, to salvage off the street, but Paul gave daily thanks that he had.

The first chords of the second hymn had just begun when Samuel stood and motioned for silence. The tune strangled to a stop and the congregation sat. Paul hurried to his seat.

Samuel broke the silence. "Friends, the Bible tells us of great prophecies in the past. Elijah and Ezekiel and Daniel and many others foretold events both great and terrible."

Paul turned to glance at the reporter, who was taking out his notebook.

Samuel continued, his voice rising like an organ crescendo. "But the Bible is not simply a history book of a time long ago with no resemblance to the present. In fact, miracles happen even today, and prophecies are still told." He held up a closed Bible, gesturing with it to mark his words. "In Joel we read, 'I will pour out my spirit upon all flesh; and your sons and your daughters shall prophesy, your old men shall dream dreams, your young men shall see visions.'

"Friends, the Holy Spirit has seen fit to entrust in me His humble servant a prophecy, a vision." Samuel's confident voice was nearly a shout. "I see a great mass of people flocking in a mighty stream to catastrophe. I see people by the millions blaspheming and ignoring the word of God. I see a God whose great patience is stretched thin as it was with Sodom and Gomorrah. And I see the awful destruction of a city unless its citizens are brought to a belief in the Faith."

The rest of the service was joyous and celebratory as usual. Samuel's sermon returned to the role of prophecy, but it was commonplace compared to Samuel's opening bombshell.

After the service finished, Paul bypassed his usual duty of saying goodbye to parishioners at the door and trotted to catch up with the reporter. "What did you think?" Paul asked, smiling. "Can I arrange some time with Reverend Hargrove?" Surely this was exactly what the reporter asked for. A prediction—and a big one.

"I've got my story," he said, and then turned to face Paul as if coaching a child in the deceptions of the real world. "But anyone can make a prediction. It's the coming-true part that's trickier."

Paul felt perplexed as he watched the reporter walk away. He wondered how anyone could have seen such a demonstration and remain unimpressed. Sure, predictions were easy to make, but hadn't Samuel shown that his were real?

Paul forgave the insult two days later when the _LA Times_ had a front-page article about the church, including Samuel's prediction. Paul picked up a copy on his way from his rooming house to the church and showed Samuel, who murmured appreciatively as he read. For Paul, any day that began with congratulations from Samuel was a good day.

But Paul only realized the significance of the prediction the next day, Wednesday, April 18, 1906. A banner headline covered the front page: "HEART IS TORN FROM GREAT CITY." He read with shock and fascination the account of the San Francisco earthquake and fire.

With a fury Paul hadn't imagined, Samuel's prediction had come true.

℘

The next morning, Paul was walking to the church from his rooming house when he heard shouts from a small crowd. He found Samuel at the top of the church steps with six or eight men holding notebooks and shouting excited questions at him. Several more were trotting up the street. Paul guessed that they were reporters, eager to write about the pastor with the direct connection to God. Samuel's expression showed that he felt quite in control of the situation, as if he expected it and this was the inevitable consequence of predicting the future. And perhaps it was. The spectacle brought to Paul's mind a circus lion tamer.

Ten minutes into the group interview, the questions slowed, the energy spent. Samuel said, "You have taken time to see me, and I am happy to provide my time to you." He waved Paul up the steps. "This is my assistant, Paul Winston. Time permitting, I am available for individual interviews. Paul will organize them." He put his arm around Paul, leaned in, and said, "Set up a desk outside my office. Let's schedule interviews half an hour apart. Can you handle that?" Without waiting for a reply, he patted him firmly on the shoulder, smiled and waved to his audience, and walked back into the church. The lion tamer gone, the reporters pounced on Paul, each vying for the first interview.

That afternoon, Paul was at his temporary station in the sanctuary, looking forward to the end of a long day. With no time for breaks, he was tired and hungry. The reporters were comfortable bullying past gatekeepers, and he had already intercepted close to a dozen. He gave immediate interviews with Samuel to several, and a few more had short waits. The rest he told to come back the next day, and they took the news with varying degrees of irritation.

One man scowled as Paul gave him his appointment. "Do you understand what a deadline is?" he asked. Paul could smell his cologne, cheap and strong.

Other reporters had been more than willing to share the importance of a press deadline. Paul said, "We're all busy, fella. I don't have a lot of sympathy."

The man put both hands on Paul's desk and leaned forward to stare down at him. He was not physically formidable and was only of medium height and weight, but he was at least a decade older than Paul's twenty-five years and had made it clear that he thought the stature of the *Los Angeles Record* earned him a place at the head of the line. He acted as if his glare were imposing, but to Paul it looked contrived and artificial.

Paul sized him up. He was no taller than the man but much stockier. Paul interlaced his fingers and squeezed tightly to drain away some of his anger, stared at the reporter, and said crisply, "I'm sorry, sir, but you must return tomorrow to interview Reverend Hargrove."

The man leaned forward, putting his face near Paul's. "That's . . . not . . . good . . . enough!" he said, and Paul felt driblets of spit spatter his face.

Paul's hands unclasped and shot up to the man's lapels. He pulled hard and aimed his forehead at the man's nose. An organic crunch filled the sanctuary. Paul shoved him back upright as the man put his hands to his face. He looked around and blinked and then, groaning, he tottered toward the door.

"*Next!*"

The two other reporters who had been waiting took their appointments agreeably.

This wasn't the first time Paul had lost his temper with a reporter that day. Like a recent immigrant who in a moment of anger swears in his native language instead of English, Paul sometimes fell back on baser forms of communication when pushed. He felt ashamed, especially since he was in God's house, and he could imagine Samuel's reaction. But his patience was thin. This was no mere news story to him— he had heard nothing from his fiancée in San Francisco. The earthquake affected him personally.

The blue sky had faded to pink in the west when Paul finally left the church to return to his rooming house. Both were in the same neighborhood, the industrial section just east of downtown. The city had quieted, most of the businesses were dark, and Paul began to relax in the peaceful silence as he made his way home.

A wind came up from behind him, carrying the odor of the meat packing plants a mile up the Los Angeles River. The smell caught him like an unexpected punch, throwing him back to a hot summer evening five years earlier, to a robbery gone wrong. He remembered for a moment, only a moment, a dark incident that he would have given anything to erase. He squeezed his eyes shut to block out the image, then blinked and took a deep breath. His heart raced as it had that evening, and he cleared his throat and wiped his hands on his pants. He was safe, he told himself.

That was long ago, and yet Paul's heart pulsed with the memory. It still had the power to reach up from his conscience and yank him back to the past. More than anyone in the congregation, he justly deserved Hell.

He pushed the memory out of his mind and walked on, comforting himself that he knew the one Person who could forgive.

ॐ

"She had planned to leave the evening of the earthquake. If the quake had been a day later, she would have been on that train." Paul sat in Samuel's office and wiped his eyes with the heels of his hands.

Samuel sat in the massive straight-backed wooden chair behind his large oak desk, and Paul sat opposite in a smaller chair. The office always felt solemn and imposing to Paul, with an Oriental rug on the floor and busts of great men glaring down from the bookshelf. A triptych of fat candles, arranged to suggest the crosses on Calvary, stood on the sill, dark against the bright window. Their floral scent didn't calm him this time.

"You don't know what happened to her," Samuel said. "No need to assume the worst." He looked dignified as usual this morning, his vest and tie looking as precise as that on a catalog model. Paul sat, elbows on knees, with his jacket discarded and sleeves rolled up.

"I went to the station yesterday afternoon to meet her train. It was jammed with people—I guess everyone who could get out did. But she wasn't on it. I walked up and down the platform for an hour, just in case. If she missed the train, she would have sent a telegram. I talked to her parents and they've heard nothing."

"Maybe the wires are down. Maybe the telegraph office is jammed with messages."

Paul sighed. "Maybe. But what if something's happened to her? I've heard stories that thousands have died. And the fires from the broken gas lines—"

Samuel raised a hand. "Paul, we just don't know. We must be patient and all will be revealed. And besides, there's a reason for this. For all of this. You don't understand and neither do I, but God has a plan. You know that, don't you? Our ability to understand is slight compared to God's. But faith gets us through hard times like these—faith that God knows what He's doing. That's an easy assumption to make, isn't it, that God knows what He's doing?"

"Yes." Paul looked down at his strong hands, empty and idle.

"We've got to get out of God's way and let Him do His work on our lives."

Paul opened his mouth to speak. He closed it and sighed, then shut his eyes. "But it's more than that."

"What is?"

"You gave the prophecy. I heard it. We all heard it." Paul stared at Samuel, his mouth gaping. "And I did nothing! I knew of the upcoming disaster, but I did nothing. I should have warned her."

"The Holy Spirit gave us a clue; He didn't give the headline. You couldn't know the details of the disaster. I certainly didn't."

"But what else could it have meant? Earthquake, fire and brimstone, whatever—the details don't matter. Clearly, we would have a disaster of some sort. I was worried about her going off to that sinful city from the start. But when I heard the prophecy, I was excited, like everyone else. I saw only how it affected us here at the church. What I should have done was consider how it would affect others." Paul paused. "I feel so guilty. I couldn't sleep last night. Maybe this is what I deserve. Things have been going so well for me here, that . . . maybe I just needed a correction." Paul stood suddenly. *I can't wait here—I've got to do something,* he thought as he excused himself from Samuel's office.

Back in his rooming house, Paul held a delicate gold necklace and admired the cross dangling from it. He replaced it in its box and put that in his kit bag, now full of clothes and with his Bible on top. He had bought the necklace to give to Thena on the one-month anniversary of their engagement, which was in less than a week.

Paul was determined to go to San Francisco to look for her, to convert anxiety into action. He was ready to dig through the rubble himself if need be. Bag in hand, he walked in to Samuel's office to make his case. He began to speak, but Samuel's solemn stare stopped him. Samuel slowly handed him an envelope. "This just arrived. It's from Western Union."

Paul hesitated, then snatched it from Samuel's hand. It was a telegram from Thena's aunt in San Francisco, addressed to him. He opened it and read, "THENA LOST IN EARTHQUAKE STOP DEEPEST RE-GRETS."

∞

Paul reread the telegram's few words over and over. Thena gone—how was this possible? In these days of trains, telephones, and electrici-ty, when society had so thoroughly insulated itself from nature, how could it still be this vulnerable to so primordial and ancient a force? He laid the telegram on Samuel's desk. Samuel said something, but he didn't catch it.

He shuffled into the sanctuary, dark and hollow. Nobody was there. Or maybe there was—he didn't care. He sat in a pew, put his face in his hands, and cried silent sobs as he hadn't done since he was in the orphanage.

Thena had gone to San Francisco to be a bridesmaid in a cousin's wedding, but that seemed like such a damnably pointless reason now. She had been his partner when things went well and his confidante when things were difficult, but she couldn't commiserate this time. Thena was gone, and God seemed to have left as well. Paul felt empty and very alone.

Samuel did what he could over the following days—offering biblical rationalizations, a patient ear, or distractions as needed—but he was busy with a church thrust into the national limelight because of the prophecy. Paul by turns wanted to tough it out and have his hand held, and he was occasionally angry at Samuel's inattention. Still, he knew Samuel could do no more and that he had to get through his pain on his own and with the comfort he took from prayer.

Four days after the telegram, Samuel conducted a memorial service for Thena. Thena's father, Mr. Farber, ran a popular grocery store and the family was prominent within the church. The service was well at-tended. It provided a bit of closure for Paul, and he felt buoyed up by the many people who spoke to him, shook his hand, or hugged him. He saw many damp eyes, and it felt as if the entire community was helping shoulder his burden.

Paul stumbled ineptly along, wracked by guilt over his failure to warn Thena of the prophecy. During these periods, he wasted time in his room or moped through his job. At other times, he was furious at the injustice of fate, pounding his bed or channeling his energy into physical tasks. Whenever possible, he tried to lose himself in work, and there was plenty of that.

He also spent time with Thena's parents. Paul had received permission to marry Thena from her father, and they treated him like family. Paul could see through his own grief that they were hurting worse, and he offered what comfort he could. As he did, he began to realize that this tragedy gave him experience that not everyone had and would allow him to genuinely empathize with the grief-stricken rather than offer empty platitudes, not just for this disaster but for the rest of his career. He would be a better servant to the people—and to God. With some coaching by Samuel, he began to see the shadow of God's hand in this, and the expression "God works in mysterious ways" took on a tangible meaning. Perhaps there was a purpose after all.

During the days that followed, Paul saw in Samuel's life a marked contrast to his own. Samuel blossomed under the new burdens brought by the earthquake. He greeted each reporter warmly and treated those from small weekly newspapers with the same patience and attention as those from the dailies in New York and Chicago. The extra work wasn't limited to providing interviews. There were letters and telegrams to answer. A flood of new visitors came to the church, and many of those wanted to talk with Samuel. Some were merely curious, but most said that they were eager to participate in a revolutionary new phase of Christian worship. Samuel increased the number of church services from just one per week, to one on Wednesday evening and two on Sunday, but even then they were packed. He clearly loved the joyous services, with every pew filled and the hymns spilling out through the open windows on the warm spring breeze. The greater the workload, the more energized Samuel seemed to be. He would shout from the pulpit, "I promise a spiritual earthquake to follow the physical one!"

∽

On a Wednesday evening three weeks after the quake, Samuel was the main attraction in an event that would have been unusual, even extraordinary, in most churches. In his church, however, Samuel had made it as important and regular as the Easter service.

The event began as Mr. Paisley, one of the church elders, stepped to the lectern. "Thank you for coming to the First Church of God's annual apologetics debate for the year of our Lord nineteen hundred and six. We've had this debate for eleven years now, exploring the fundamentals of Christianity, exploring the *reasons* we believe. I'm sure you will be as enlightened as I will be by the views expressed by our two speakers."

Sitting behind a table to his left were Samuel and a thin man with glasses. The church was full, and latecomers found standing room against the walls as the crowd quieted. Paul looked around and was surprised at how packed the sanctuary was—another consequence of the church's new popularity.

Mr. Paisley continued. "Representing the Christian viewpoint is our own Reverend Samuel Hargrove, and representing the atheist viewpoint is Mr. Henry Putnam, a professor of Physics at the University of Southern California. We want to thank Mr. Putnam for filling in after we had a last-minute cancellation." He turned with a smile and a nod toward the thin man. The professor's tan hair was parted in the middle and lay tightly against his head, leaving his prominent ears to fend for themselves. That and eyes enlarged by the glasses brought to Paul's mind the image of a rodent.

"My role is that of moderator. As such, I will try to be neither seen nor heard but will keep our speakers on track. I give you now our host and first speaker, Reverend Hargrove."

Samuel stood and beamed as applause filled the church. He was clearly playing to a home crowd. Paul clapped and couldn't resist smiling, just a bit. Beginning months ago, he had eagerly helped prepare for this event. The work had become a meaningless chore after Thena's death, but he had to admit that staying busy helped him get through each day.

As Samuel took the podium, Paul felt a little of the old excitement return, but a new anxiety ate at his gut. For Samuel to win or lose in front of a small crowd was one thing, but the stakes were far bigger now. He had wanted a higher profile, and now he had it. Reporters from every local paper were here this evening, plus reporters from papers in San Francisco, Sacramento, Chicago, and possibly more. The old days of anonymity were gone, and the nation watched. Samuel was well prepared, but in Paul's mind there was still too much chance for failure, for humiliation. Samuel was putting all his chips in as he stepped to the podium.

Samuel's new reputation would be either enhanced or shattered with the next day's papers.

Chapter 2

Samuel began his presentation with a brief prayer and then expressed appreciation for the turnout. "Let me address the curious fact that we're in a church but not for a Sunday service. In previous years, some members of the audience have said that using the church building for a debate was sacrilegious. I must respectfully disagree. The logical defense of Christianity is a vitally important part of Christian life. And there is no better place to defend Christianity . . . than in a church.

"This discipline is called 'apologetics.' As you can imagine, the last thing we do is apologize for Christianity. No, 'apologetics' comes from the Greek word *apologia*, which is a defense of something. For example, a defendant in court in ancient Greece would argue his case with an *apologia*."

Samuel stressed to the audience the importance of understanding apologetics. He listed several Bible verses to support this, with special attention to 1 Peter 3:15, "Be ready always to give an answer to every man that asketh you a reason for the hope that is in you." He noted that Genesis does not begin with an argument for God's existence but instead takes this for granted, and Samuel justified this with another verse: "The invisible things of God from the creation of the world are clearly seen so that men are without excuse."

"You want to see the hand of God?" Samuel said. "Then just look around you. These are powerful arguments, but again they satisfy only believers like most of us. Today we will put those arguments aside. The tools today are reason and logic, but these are friends of the Christian. We have nothing to fear from them. In fact, we invite critique because we must know that Christianity is valid and strong. Questioning is good. The apostle Paul said that if our faith in Christ is misplaced, then 'we are to be pitied more than all men.' So bring on the attack. Our fortress is built on the Eternal Rock."

Samuel wrapped up his introductory remarks by thanking his opponent for participating. He then stated the topic of the debate: "Does God exist?" with Professor Putnam taking the negative position. The professor smiled slightly in acknowledgement and took in the audience with a relaxed face.

If Putnam didn't yet know that he was playing Samuel's game, on Samuel's court, and by Samuel's rules, he found out soon enough. Samuel asked the professor's permission to begin the debate with an informal chat to explore the issues for the benefit of the audience. This was unexpected, but the regulars in the audience knew to expect that. Whether preaching or debating, Samuel was rarely boring.

With both men seated at the table, Samuel began by asking for the professor's agreement to a logical statement. The professor brushed at something on the sleeve of his gray suit and identified it as the Law of Noncontradiction. Samuel threw out another one. Again the professor made a quick identification: this time, the Law of the Excluded Middle.

Samuel looked delighted as if a precocious child had answered a question above his age. "Clearly you are familiar with the laws of logic—surely much more so than I."

"That's only to be expected. Logic is what I base my research on."

"Then let me ask you this: *why* are these laws true? Why should there be a Law of Noncontradiction?"

The professor looked up, then crossed his arms and rocked slightly in his chair. He opened his mouth, paused, and then closed it. Paul slid forward in his seat as he watched the man's unease. Finally, the professor said, "We use logic because it works."

"It does indeed work, but why? Why should the universe be bound to obey these laws? Surely the reason logic is true is not 'just because.' "

Again a pause. The professor, slight and scholarly behind his glasses, made quite a contrast at the same table with Samuel, tall and broad and with a more-than-generous voice. In his modest tone, the professor said, "Well, logic is a convention."

"A convention? You mean like a custom? Are the laws of logic arbitrary so that we might have one set while the French would get along quite happily with a different set—like we measure distances in feet while the French measure in meters?" Samuel turned to the audience.

"Oh, I do so enjoy the spring, when the new laws of logic come out of Paris."

Laughter swept the audience, and Paul leaned back, grinning. Putnam pursed his lips and shook his head, and Samuel raised his hands as if in submission. "I apologize, Professor. We're just having a little chat here, so I thought you wouldn't mind my taking the liberty. No, of course you don't see logic to be as changeable as fashion. We agree that logic is universal. I'm simply saying that if you can't tell me why that is the case, I can."

The professor leaned forward and his voice rose slightly in pitch. "We're in the same boat. Your justification for logic is no stronger than mine."

"Not at all. You deny the supernatural source of logic, but I don't. Logic comes from God; it is a consequence of God. The believer can point to his source of logic, but the atheist has no justification."

The professor swept the crowd with his hand. "Look around you—atheists are logical. Atheists are rational."

"Yes, atheists are rational, but only because they are dishonest to their own professed principles. The irony is that the atheist must borrow from the Christian worldview to reject it. Atheists deny the very God whose existence makes their reasoning possible."

The professor took out a handkerchief and dabbed his upper lip and forehead. "Christianity didn't invent logic. The ancient Greeks preceded the Christians and were pioneers in logic—Aristotle, for example."

"I agree," Samuel said. "But that doesn't change the fact that logic is a consequence of God's existence. Non-Christians are welcome to use it, but it comes from God."

"Why can't we presume that logic is transcendent—that it's always existed?"

"It is indeed transcendent. But that doesn't answer the question *why*. Why has logic always existed?"

The professor glanced up at the ceiling before continuing. "Logic just exists. It has certain properties. It's just a fundamental part of reality."

Samuel smoothed his mustache with the back of his hand. "Oh, so that's how the game is played? All right: *God* just exists. God is just a fundamental part of reality. But can we just define things into existence? Of course not. No, that's not an argument. I apologize for being so persistent, but I must return to my original question, which remains unanswered: why is logic true?"

The professor made a growling "Rrr!" sound and said, "You don't understand." He paused as if collecting his thoughts and then scowled. "Reverend Hargrove, is this an interrogation or a dialogue? Will I get an opportunity to ask questions?"

"I do apologize. I have indeed monopolized the conversation. Please, Professor, go right ahead."

Putnam rummaged through a small stack of papers, putting first one sheet on top and then another. "All right," he said. "Why are there so many religions around the world? Doesn't this say that each culture invents a religion to suit itself?" The audience hushed.

"The world's many religions say that people have an innate urge to discover their Maker," Samuel said. "This universal hunger in every human bosom points to a God who can satisfy that hunger." Paul smiled. Another point scored, and the professor's face showed the hit.

The professor leafed through his papers again. "Well, answer me this. The Christian God is described as a loving god. And yet we have disease and famine and war. Wouldn't such a god put an end to this, if he existed?"

"Who knows what disasters might have happened but haven't because of divine providence? We don't see the headline 'THOUSANDS NOT DEAD BECAUSE OF DISASTER THAT DIDN'T HAPPEN' simply because we don't know what God has shielded us from. Indeed, it is arrogant to imagine that we are smart enough to understand, let alone critique, the actions of the Creator of the universe. And the Fall of Adam and Eve—the original sin in the Garden of Eden—explains the imperfect world we live in."

"Rrr!" More paper shuffling. The professor's voice became somewhat shrill and he spoke more quickly. "Tell me this: why believe the Bible? You don't believe Homer's *Iliad*. You don't believe the ancient books of other religions."

"The story of Jesus was written down just a few decades after the fact, and we have perhaps thousands of ancient manuscripts of the books of the Bible. This lets us recreate the original documents with great precision. And many non-Christian historians of that period document the truth of Jesus's life outside the Bible. By contrast, we might have a biography written centuries after the death of a historical figure such as Alexander the Great, and we regard that as truth. And when you consider that the men closest to Jesus were martyred for their beliefs, surely no one would die to defend a story he knew wasn't true."

"Well, history is not really my area of expertise." The professor tapped a new sheet that he had placed on top of the pile. "All right, the Bible documents slavery among the Israelites, but God does nothing to stop the practice. Given this, how can the Bible be called a book of morality?"

"First, keep in mind that the Bible documents many customs that have nothing to do with godly living; they were simply practices of primitive people in a place and time far different than our own. As for slavery, we'd still have slavery in America today if it weren't for people like Harriet Beecher Stowe, John Brown, William Lloyd Garrison, the Quakers, and others—all Christians guided by Christian principles."

Samuel looked over for more questions, but the professor seemed spent. The silence lengthened, and Paul felt the small man's discomfort. He couldn't imagine being on that stage with hundreds of people staring, waiting for a mistake, enjoying his distress.

Samuel slid his chair back. "With your permission, Professor, shall we begin the debate?" Putnam yielded with a gesture of his hand, saying nothing.

Samuel walked to the podium and began his prepared remarks, a proud oration that surveyed a number of compelling arguments. Instead of doing the same when it was his turn, the professor used his time to rebut Samuel's opening points. *That's a bad move*, Paul thought. *You've allowed your opponent to select all the arguments.* He sensed that the contest was already over and leaned forward with his elbows on his knees. He wondered if the professor had already used up his own points in his questions to Samuel. The result was that the entire debate would be fought on Samuel's territory—and this was terrain that Samuel knew very well.

Paul took a personal interest in the progression of the debate, not just because he was rooting for Samuel, but because he had spent so long helping him prepare. Though Samuel was a natural speaker and an accomplished debater, he still took preparation for each debate seriously and this year had assigned Paul some of the research tasks. Samuel had thoroughly explained the various arguments from each side and critiqued their strengths and weaknesses. "You'll be doing this yourself some day," Samuel had said.

The professor gamely held up his end of the argument, but he was outmatched. His voice became thinner and he didn't use all the time that was available to him. His eyes and gestures often pleaded with the crowd as if to ask for their acceptance of an argument he couldn't quite put into words, one that seemed just out of his grasp. The rebuttals were often little more than "I don't agree with you there" or "You'll have to do better than that."

Samuel wrapped up his final remarks. "Let me return to the original question, which, after all this time, still has not been answered from the atheist position: why is logic true? Professor Putnam says that I have no answer to this question, but I do—it's just that he doesn't like it. God created the world, and logic is a consequence.

"We can agree that logic is universal. It's also abstract—in other words, it has no physical presence like a book or a table. And logic is unchanging, unlike the things we see around us that grow or decay over time. Aside from logic—and perhaps what is built on logic, like mathematics—we know of just one other thing with these properties, and that is God.

"Let me be clear that I respect the professor's logical skill. He's a scientist, and I'm sure he uses logic very well in his work. The only problem is that he must borrow from the Christian position to do so. By his own logic, logic can't exist. In rejecting God, the atheist has rejected his source of logic and has therefore eliminated his ability to use it. Without its Christian foundation, this entire debate wouldn't make sense."

The professor had the last block of time, and he used it up like a football team that knows it's beaten and is eager only to run out the clock and go home. When he finished, Mr. Paisley thanked both participants and the audience applauded. Samuel beamed at the crowd, while the professor collected his papers and stood to leave even before the applause was over.

The reporters left promptly—to file their stories, Paul supposed—but people milled about afterwards, seemingly eager to savor the night.

"Another sacrificial lamb, eh, Pastor?" said one man with a smile.

"I think this was the most impressive debate yet," said another.

"You should call these the 'Loose Canon' debates. You know—'canon,' like scripture," said a third.

Twenty minutes after the debate had ended, the church was still half full of supporters. A few people encouraged Samuel to speak and the call for an encore swept through the crowd. Samuel mounted the podium in response to the curtain call and gave a short epilogue. As the audience took their seats, he emphasized the importance of apologetics to his ministry and encouraged everyone to be an ambassador.

Paul leaned back in his pew and smiled. It seemed to him that no one in the city knew more about the defense of Christianity than this man, and surely none could beat him.

℘

"Paul, do you remember when we prepared for yesterday's debate that I said that I wanted you to participate yourself someday?" Samuel set his briar pipe down in his ashtray. The smell of tobacco smoke was a familiar note in the office.

Paul sat across the big desk from Samuel. He had been staring at the wall across from the bookcase. It showcased a small collection of framed newspaper articles about the church and an award from the mayor. Samuel was very proud of these. A Currier and Ives lithograph added some color with its celebration of a bucolic New England countryside with a hamlet of houses and two tall-spired churches. In the corner hung a list of the Seven Virtues, embroidered by his late wife.

At Samuel's question, Paul looked up. "Me? You don't want me to debate." His hands tightened on the arms of his chair. He had made plain to Samuel his dread of public speaking.

"Not debate, but this might be the first step. I'd like you to go out into the community and introduce people to the church."

Paul stood in agitation. "No. You know I'm not good at that."

"There's nothing to be afraid—"

"I'm not *afraid*. Speaking to strangers is not my strength, that's all. I'd be better used in other areas." He took a step toward the desk.

"Sit down, please." Samuel leaned back in his chair and interlaced his hands over his large belly. Paul paused for a moment, surprised that he had created a confrontation, and took his seat.

"Paul, you have been a blessing to me since the earthquake. The lay volunteers have been a big help, but with all this work, I couldn't have carried on without you. A lot of people have been affected by the quake and we've brought God's comfort and counsel to many—we have much to be proud of."

Paul forced a smile and nodded.

"Your work is all the more impressive given your loss."

"It seems to take my mind off . . . my troubles."

"Work is indeed the best medicine. You've not been yourself lately—quite understandable. But I sense that the worst is over and my old Paul is returning. I think a new challenge is what you need."

Samuel banged his pipe on the ashtray and slowly refilled it. "I've been delighted by your progress these past two years. You have picked up the apologetics arguments very quickly—much faster than I expected. You're an excellent logical thinker, and I couldn't ask for a harder worker. I had hoped to let you grow within the church at your own pace, but we don't have that luxury. Too much work. It seems I'll need an associate pastor sooner than I thought."

The prospect of being an associate pastor intrigued Paul. He was "Assistant to the Pastor" and had calling cards to prove it, but after two years, he was eager for a promotion. He had hoped to postpone the speaking part, however. "What do you need me to do?"

"I want you to introduce people to the church. All this press attention gives us a rare opportunity, and we must make the most of it. Newspaper articles are good, but we need souls in seats. I'll take care of the reporters—the workload has dropped so that I can handle the press. But I need you to convert that publicity into new church members. I want you to get out and knock on doors. Start in neighborhoods nearby. Introduce yourself, tell them about the church, invite them to a service. It will usually be a conversation with just one person."

"I really would prefer to avoid talking to new people. What if they want to argue? What if they want to debate?"

"All the better—you know the issues. You'll convince some people who attend other churches to visit. If we're a better fit for them, then that's great for both us and them, but if you convince a nonbeliever to become a churchgoer, you've helped save a soul. Can you do any greater service for Mankind?"

Samuel leaned forward with his arms on the desk. "Apologetics is our central mission. A questioner is someone who's thinking, and thinking people can be converted. Also, you've had a loss no one should be forced to bear—but how many people in this city have had similar losses? You can speak to them in a way that few others can."

"Writing is different from speaking. I'm fine with writing."

Samuel sighed. "Passing notes through the mail slot in the door won't work. Look, I'm a pretty good speaker, but that didn't just happen. I wasn't born that way. I had to work at it."

Paul was not persuaded. Samuel loved to speak—to friends, to strangers, to individuals, to crowds. He was good because he enjoyed the attention. Paul had survived in life to this point by avoiding attention.

Samuel paused as if inviting a response and then sighed and said, "Paul, this is not optional. I understand that this is difficult, but I'll work with you. Together, we'll make you stronger. Remember when Moses complained to God that he was not eloquent enough? God didn't say, 'Never mind—go back to herding sheep.' No, God gave him the words he needed. With only the two of us, this church is too small to not have everyone giving his all. You need to trust me that this is the best for the church and for you. This may well be hard, but what good lesson isn't?"

Paul exhaled with puffed cheeks and looked down, and then he slowly got out of his chair. "Okay," he said as he turned toward the door.

"I want you to start tomorrow."

෪෭

Dread drained away Paul's strength—he felt like he had a fever as he shuffled home. He mentally stepped through his plans for approaching people the next morning, but even in his mind he saw himself paralyzed with fear when confronted by a strange face.

He unlocked the door to his small apartment, eased himself into his desk chair, and tried to relax his mind. The apartment was simple but adequate for his needs. His few clothes took up half of one shelf of a tall bookcase, stealing precious room from a large collection of books neatly organized. Classics by Homer, Chaucer, and Shakespeare were in one section, American novelists including Twain, Hawthorne, and Melville were in another, and books on science and history were in a third. The desk was next to the bookcase, and a bed lay against the opposite wall.

He stood and paced as he considered how to approach strangers with his message. Back and forth, over and over, he made no more forward progress with his feet than he did with his mind.

Paul told himself that his emotions were driving him and that he needed to rein them in. His unhappy childhood continued to hobble his adult personality. In the orphanage, abuse from older children and neglect by the staff had made Paul wary and defensive. He could blame his fear on childhood trauma, but knowing the cause didn't make it less draining. His dread remained, and he slept little that night.

෪෭

The next morning, Paul muttered to himself as he turned onto the first street, repeating a short set of commands—give your name, the church's name, say where the church is, and ask them to attend service this Sunday. Over and over.

He turned down the walk to the first house. Lilies bloomed in the corner of the yard, fragrant and white, but they only brought to mind a funeral. He had been nervous since he started out this morning, but now his heart raced and he felt short of breath. His deliberate steps clumped hollowly on the wooden stairs, as if he were walking to a gallows. Finally at the door, he held his breath and knocked. The door opened. "Good morning, sir," Paul began as he read from a note card. He looked up to see a middle-aged woman holding the door. "Uh . . . good morning *madam*. My name is Paul Winston," he said, reading on, holding his notes in one hand and offering his calling card in another. He stuttered through the remainder of his brief pitch with his eyes down and was flushed and sweaty when he finished.

"Thank you, but we already have a church." The woman closed the door.

And then he was alone again on the porch.

He trudged to the next house and received "No solicitors!" through the closed door. He opened his mouth to argue, thought better of it, and moved on. At the next, the lady of the house acknowledged that she had read about the church in the paper but said that her family belonged to another church. At the next, another curt "No, thank you" behind a closed door. Paul cheered himself with the hope that Samuel would call off the experiment after hearing how difficult it was and the poor results it had yielded.

And so the day progressed. Some people already had churches. Some cut Paul off, saying that they weren't interested in whatever he was selling. But a few—a tiny handful—let him make his pitch and said that they would consider the offer.

At the end of the day, feeling exhausted and beaten, Paul reported back to Samuel.

"It wasn't pleasant," Paul said.

"Okay, but I didn't promise you pleasant. Neither did Jesus."

"What I meant to say is that it was very hard."

"I understand."

Samuel wasn't taking the bait, and Paul tried another tack. "I really don't think that sales is my strength."

"Sales may not be a strength now, but it will be. It must be." Samuel paused. "You won't be doing this forever. It's training. When you have a pulpit of your own, you will draw heavily on this experience. You'll know what works and what doesn't."

Paul sighed.

Samuel asked if there had been any discussion or debate.

"I spoke to one man—I guess he was about sixty—who said that he fought in lots of battles in Virginia during the war, and he said, 'Given the horror of what I've seen, there is no God.' "

Samuel snorted. "He thinks he's seen horror? Imagine hell. And that's the point—that's why this is important. I don't doubt that this is hard, but you're saving *souls!* Always keep that in mind. There is no more important work."

The next day was more of the same—an emotional wringer that left Paul's white shirt drenched in sweat. He saw a complete slice of society: rudeness at one extreme, a few considerate people on the other, and in the middle, lots of people too busy with their own activities to give much attention to the nervous young man interrupting them. Never was a two-mile walk through a pleasant residential neighborhood during a Los Angeles spring more exhausting.

At the end of the day, Samuel gave him another pep talk and asked to hear Paul's pitch. Paul had been adding to it as new ideas had occurred to him, and he launched into a forced performance.

"Far too long." Samuel cut him off when Paul was only half done. "Try something like: 'Have you been saved?' It's short and to the point, and it gets them thinking. It invites you to offer the answer to the problem—salvation. More importantly, it suggests that there's something to be saved *from.* It points to hell."

Chapter 3

When Paul finished one neighborhood, Samuel assigned a new one and insisted that he knock on every door. Samuel recorded Paul's progress on a city trolley line map, with completed neighborhoods marked with a star.

As the days turned into weeks, Paul had to admit that he was improving, and he felt less anxiety in talking to strangers. Though Samuel didn't say so, Paul thought that one reason for the assignment was to take his mind off Thena. This seemed like relieving the pain of a broken leg by hitting your thumb with a hammer.

Work did indeed occupy his mind, but he still mourned her frequently. He would turn over and over in his mind the question of whether she had died a painful death. He still felt enormously guilty about doing nothing to warn her of the earthquake. Memories often ambushed him as he walked through peaceful neighborhoods, bringing to mind the things that Thena had talked about—what she would make him for breakfast when they were married, her plans to decorate their bedroom, her hopes for children. He walked past the kinds of homes they had dreamed of owning and saw young wives like Thena had dreamed of becoming. And it was his fault. His stressful task was his penance, and he pushed on without complaint.

About a month into his assignment, Paul felt almost comfortable. His anxiety would have returned had he been asked to speak to a crowd or preach from a pulpit, but his door-to-door evangelism worked fairly well. He had even debated a few people and held his own and, in a few cases, he imagined that he made conversions.

He took pride in his success, however small, knowing that it was the result of hard work—and perhaps natural ability, if Samuel were right—rather than luck. Samuel had coached him with increasing intensity over the previous two years, assigning books to read, working with him to analyze and critique all manner of apologetics arguments, and shaping his debate technique.

In early June in the well-to-do neighborhood of Angelino Heights, Paul noted an odd street name that stood out from the many Spanish names: Stageira Street. He turned down the walk of a two-story house covered in white stucco and with a blue-tiled roof. While the house seemed in good condition, the large yard was overgrown. The hedge, possibly trimmed square the previous fall, bore new light green growth sprouting at odd angles, and neglected bushes sagged with big flowers. A burly tree supported a frayed rope without a swing. The neglect couldn't hide the generous and thoughtful design, and Paul imagined a child playing here, safe within its hedge walls.

He knocked on the door and was surprised to see a man open it. Paul rarely spoke to men as he made his visits—most doors were either answered by women or not at all. The man appeared about Samuel's age—maybe fifty. He was of average size, or perhaps slightly smaller, and he wore a jacket but no tie. Stubble covered his cheeks, and he had a bushy Wyatt Earp mustache that overhung his upper lip. He looked annoyed, as if he had been interrupted, and one hand held a book with a finger holding his place.

"Have you been saved, sir?" Paul asked him.

"Saved from what?"

"From the fires of hell. Christianity offers salvation from eternal torment. It worked for me, and if you haven't been saved, it will work for you. Wouldn't you say that eternity in hell is something to be avoided?"

The man considered him for a few seconds as if deciding what to do with this curious annoyance.

"You don't want to talk to me, son." He turned to go back into his house. "I'm an atheist. Your God doesn't exist."

Well, that was different, Paul thought as he watched the door slam shut.

₮›

Samuel always made time for Paul when he returned from his visits, though he was primarily interested in just two things: debates and descriptions of the men that Paul met. Paul kept notes on both to have reliable answers. The debriefing this day proceeded like others until Paul came to the man in the house on Stageira Street.

After several minutes of increasingly agitated questions, Samuel slapped his desk and smiled broadly. *"That's* who you should be talking to."

"But he said that I ought not talk to him. He said he was an atheist."

"That's why you should be talking to him!" Samuel leaned forward and molded invisible clay with his big hands. "An atheist is someone we can work with. He's apparently thought about this subject. He's come to the wrong conclusion, to be sure, but he's a thinker. Someone who refuses to think can be tougher to reach and isn't much of a Christian if they do convert. But a thinker can make a true Christian soldier."

Samuel smoothed his mustache. "From what you've said, this is what we're looking for. A challenge, but not an impossible one. Imagine that you've been training in Reverend Hargrove's Apologetics Field School, and converting this man is now the school's final project. Make this your priority, just this man. Bring him into the church, and I'll have a new associate pastor."

ℂ

The next day, Paul returned to the white stucco house with the overgrown yard. *What if he refuses to talk with me?* Lots of things needed to fall into place for Paul to satisfy Samuel's assignment, and many were frustratingly out of his control.

Paul knocked on the door and pressed his Bible to his chest with both hands. The same man answered, holding a book in one hand as before.

"Again?" He frowned. "I told you that we have nothing to talk about." He stepped back to close the door.

Paul felt his goal draining through his fingers like sand. "Wait!" He raised his hand. "You said yesterday that my God doesn't exist. I'd like to challenge you on that, sir. My God does indeed exist. And if you give me a chance, I can prove it to you."

The atheist stopped, then stepped forward. A few seconds passed as he looked at Paul and then smiled faintly. "Come." He turned and walked in, leaving the door open behind him.

Paul entered and shut the door. He followed the man down a short corridor into a bright living room, though it seemed remade as an office or library. Sun poured through large windows on two sides onto the blue and white Oriental carpet, and more would have done so if not for bookshelves placed up against much of the glass. A sofa, worn but comfortable looking, sat under a window, and every opportunity for a cushion was taken by embroidered pillows. The pale blue wall opposite the window held framed embroidery and samplers. An upholstered chair and a bureau were against the blue wall, and a low table covered with books was pulled close to the sofa as if used as a desk.

Everywhere, Paul saw books. The shelves were crammed with them, and short stacks lay against a wall.

"Take a seat," the man said as he sat on the sofa.

Paul stepped to the chair and turned to sit when the man leapt up.

"Stop!" he said as he pushed past Paul. He was surprisingly strong, or determined, as he reached for the chair's pillow. Holding it with two hands, he carefully laid it on the bureau. "Now sit," he said, his voice annoyed as if Paul had deliberately broken a taboo.

Paul eased himself into the chair slowly, his eyes on this erratic man.

His graying hair reached below his collar and needed a brush. The bushy mustache was long on the sides of his mouth, and his face hadn't been shaved in days. He looked like a prospector recently returned to town and temporarily dressed in city clothes.

Paul leaned forward to better see the man against the sunny background. "My name is Paul Winston. I appreciate your time, Mister . . . ?"

"My name is Jim. You look like a fellow with something on his mind."

Paul noticed Jim wore no shoes, and his socks didn't match. "Yes, sir. I would like to ask you about what you said yesterday—that you are an atheist. Surely you agree you don't know everything."

"I don't know everything, so how could I know that God doesn't exist—is that where you were going?"

"Well, yes." This conversation felt different. The old discomfort of speaking to strangers was returning.

"You don't understand the definition of 'atheist.' A theist has a god belief, and an atheist is someone who lacks that belief."

"I thought that was an agnostic."

"An agnostic admits that he doesn't *know* there's a god; an atheist doesn't *believe* in one. The agnostic also has no god belief, so an agnostic is an atheist as well. But back to the point: I'm an atheist because I don't have a god belief. I'm not certain that there is no god, but that seems to be the best explanation of reality, given what I see."

"I've heard that some atheists are Satan worshipers."

"An atheist couldn't be a Satanist just like he couldn't be a Christian. A Satanist has a god belief; he is a theist."

As lessons go, this one was quick and even appreciated, but Paul was in unfamiliar territory. This wasn't like conversations in the past.

Jim said, "Now, what about this proof of God's existence you promised?"

"The best evidence I can offer you is the person in front of you right now." Paul had been successful with his own story. "I didn't know Jesus. I was a criminal, and I cringe when I think back on the crimes I committed. Terrible, awful things. I spent time in jail. But by the grace of God, I found—"

"Stop, stop." Jim held up a hand. "I have no interest in your personal 'I'm saved, thank you Jesus' story. I want an intellectual argument, not an emotional one. Your own experience may be important to you, but I didn't go through it, so it doesn't mean a goddamn thing to me."

Paul had picked up every bad word conceivable when on the street, but Samuel had wrung them out of his vocabulary. To let this offense pass unchallenged would be to approve. "May I ask you not to swear?"

"Profanity is a useful spice for the English language, and I'll do whatever I want in my own house."

"It's blasphemous. You do see how that is offensive?"

"I do not. Blasphemy is a victimless crime. If it offends God, then let God deal with it. Any god that needs defending is hardly a god."

Paul paused to collect his thoughts. He needed to concede this battle and get back to the war. "Well, let me address your request for an intellectual argument. All around us, we can see God's hand. In nature, I mean."

"You mean through disease and famine? Or did we see God's hand through the earthquake in San Francisco? Or in death during childbirth?" Jim frowned as he leaned forward and jabbed the air with a finger. "Is that the hand of God that you're talking about?"

This was not the way it was supposed to go. Paul licked his lips and said, "Well, no. . . ." The familiar anxiety was upon him again, paralyzing. "The Bible says that. . . ." He groped for one argument, considered it, tossed it away, grasped for another and another, frantic. "I mean, God tells us. . . ." His humiliation seemed to well up like a flood, reaching first his waist, then his chest. Jim looked at him and said nothing—was he enjoying seeing a Christian in distress? Paul's face felt hot, and he wiped his forehead with the back of his hand. Each clumsy phrase only made him more flustered. He felt like he was being strangled from the inside.

"Get yourself some water." Jim's voice was gentle, and he leaned back on the sofa. "The glasses are on the shelf." He gestured toward the kitchen and returned to his book.

Paul was startled at the reprieve. He got up and walked to the kitchen, trying to control his breathing and rein in his panic. He returned a minute later with an idea for an argument that he thought would make progress—he'd use the Argument from Design.

"Tell you what," Jim said. "Go home and think about it, and come back tomorrow with your best argument."

Paul opened his mouth. Now that he finally had something coherent to say, he was ready to say it.

"Think about it and come back." Jim motioned impatiently toward the door and returned to his book.

Paul had hoped for more progress, and Jim's curtness stung. Back at the church, Samuel was eager for every detail—how the conversation went, everything about the man, and even what the house looked like. Samuel seemed pleased.

"You've got an invitation to go back—that's good. This will be a process. It will take some time. This man won't be a pushover, but remember that you know you're right. Your message comes from the Bible, and the Bible is truth. The very words out of your mouth come from the Holy Spirit. You simply need the patience and wisdom to find the right arguments and the right approach."

Samuel leaned back in his chair and smiled. "A famous Protestant leader had a helpful observation for when we feel under attack: 'It is the lot of the Church to endure blows and not to strike them. But we must remember that it is an anvil that has worn out many hammers.' Your lot may be to endure some blows too."

§⊃

Thena's framed photograph was the closest thing to artwork Paul had on display in his apartment. He had laid it face down after the earthquake, but a month and a half after the disaster, he could look at it again without feeling overwhelmed. Her smiling face cast him back to when they were together. He picked up the portrait and imagined the smell of her lemon verbena perfume. He thought of the swish of her skirt as she walked. He remembered the way she would face forward in church and turn only her eyes to him as he faced the congregation, and then after she had made eye contact, she would try various solemn expressions to try to make him laugh. He smiled at the memory.

"Thena, I'm sorry," he murmured, the smile vanishing. "I'm sorry I didn't warn you about the earthquake. But my faith isn't shaken. I know God has a reason." He thought back on things he saw on his walks—houses that Thena might admire or interesting sights he wanted to share with her.

"I never deserved you. That a lady such as you could find a place for me in her heart . . . I'll never find another." He remembered the small gifts she had given him during their courtship—his favorite pen, his fancy cufflinks. Thena was gone, and yet Paul thought of her more than ever.

And that heartless atheist Jim—trying to destroy Paul's faith and wanting to pull Thena from heaven and put her in the ground.

Paul replaced the photo on his desk and saw his hand shaking slightly. He felt drained. He knelt next to his bed with his hands clasped and laid his head on the coverlet. "God, please return her. Let her come back to me. I know it doesn't make sense to ask, and I know I don't deserve her, but . . . I need her." Paul lay in meditation, absorbing strength and calmness.

He awoke some time later, surprised that he'd fallen asleep still kneeling. He turned out the light and climbed into bed with one final thought: *And Samuel, thank you for selecting me, for lifting me up.*

℘

Paul stood at Jim's door, his Bible in hand and his argument shaped with Samuel's help. He leaned forward with his knuckles poised above the door but hesitated. Paul had spent his life learning to stand up for himself, and he hated losing. *I know the truth*, he said to himself, over and over. His confidence stronger, he was no longer on the defensive.

He took a deep breath, held it, and knocked.

Jim answered the door. His face showed little emotion, as if he were about to plod through some mindless chore. Paul followed him to the sun-drenched library and noticed large photographs on the wall of Yosemite and the Grand Canyon. Jim took the sofa and Paul again sat on the chair facing the window. A typewriter on a moveable stand stood at the left side of the sofa. Jim's shoulder-length hair was wilder than last time, and with the bright window behind, he looked like an animal.

"I must say, it certainly looks like a beautiful day." Paul's heart was thumping, and he hoped to ease into this argument slowly.

"I don't have time to discuss the weather," Jim said. One arm lay extended along the top of the sofa, and he gestured impatiently with his free hand.

"Well then, let's discuss the accuracy of the Bible." Paul looked for approval from Jim, saw nothing, and continued. "Many say that the Bible contains the world's greatest literature. It's certainly the world's most influential book—a book that has inspired mankind for thousands of years."

"I won't disagree." Jim picked up what looked like a clumsily wrapped cigar laying on the sofa and put the soggy end in his mouth. It left a small dark stain on the seat cushion.

Paul wanted to continue but was distracted as the end of the thing bobbed up and down under Jim's shaggy mustache while he chewed, making gentle crunching sounds. "Is that a cigar?" Paul asked finally.

"*Cinnamomum zeylanicum*—cinnamon bark," Jim said, his words garbled as he spoke while holding the cinnamon stick with his lips. "It promotes sweating."

Paul had never considered sweating worth promoting.

Now Jim was making a kissing sort of sound, perhaps to keep the saliva from dripping out the other end of the tube of bark.

Paul tried to ignore the noise, deliberately looking down at his note card to avoid the distraction. "So what I'm saying is that the Bible is very accurate. Researchers have found thousands of copies, enough to convince them that errors introduced from copy to copy have been insignificant. And old, too—less than 400 years after the New Testament originals. In other words, today's English translations started with a copy that differed minimally from the original text. Aside from the different language, we read almost the same words as were originally written two to three thousand years ago."

Jim shook his head. "That's a foolish argument."

Paul's jaw went slack.

"I can say the same of Homer's *Iliad*," Jim said. "It's quite long and very old—older than much of the Old Testament. We have many old copies of the Iliad, and today's version may also be a decent copy of the original. Using your logic, must we conclude that the *Iliad* is correct? Must we say that Achilles really was invulnerable, that Cassandra really could see the future, that Ajax really was trained by a centaur?"

"But that's not a good comparison," Paul said. "No one believes the *Iliad*. Biblical fact is quite different from Greek mythology."

"Don't change the subject. You introduced the question of the accuracy of manuscript copies. Does your logic help us judge the accuracy of ancient books or not?"

"I don't think the Bible and the *Iliad* can be compared is all."

Jim sighed. "To your point, no one believes the *Iliad* now, but they once did. Achilles, Hector, Helen, Aphrodite, the Trojan War—the *Iliad* tells much of the history of the Greeks just like the Bible is a history of the Jews. And, of course, many of the places and people in the *Iliad* actually existed. Archeologists have found Troy, for example."

Jim held up a hand as Paul opened his mouth to speak. "Of course I see the difference. While the *Iliad* and the Bible were the histories of their people, only the Bible is believed today. Here's my point. Let's assume that the Bible and the *Iliad* are both faithful copies. That doesn't make them true."

Paul said, "It's not just the Bible—other sources confirm Bible stories. Josephus, the first-century Jewish historian, for example, writes about Jesus." He glanced at a note card in his hand. "Also, Tacitus, Pliny the Younger, and other writers from that time."

Jim jerked a hand as if dismissing a gnat, and his face showed an exasperated disgust. "I've read these sources, and they strengthen your case not a bit. They basically say, 'There are people who follow a man named Jesus' or 'Jesus is said to have performed miracles.' I already agree with that! I'd be interested if an eyewitness from the *Jerusalem Times* newspaper wrote a report the day after a miraculous event, but that didn't happen. You're left with four—not thousands, but *four*—written accounts that summarize the Jesus story after it had been passed around orally for decades, and they're not even completely independent accounts. I need a lot more evidence than that."

Paul thought for an instant how satisfying it would be to take their argument to the street, even though it would be an unfair fight. He rubbed his right fist against his left palm and strained the muscles of his upper body to drain away some rage. In five seconds he might remind this atheist of his manners. But he had to take the high ground and pushed on, using a response that Samuel had given him. "Why do you need more evidence? You never saw George Washington, but you accept the historical account of his life. The Bible has the historical account of Jesus's life—why not accept that?"

Again Jim shook his head. "We have articles from newspapers of Washington's time published within days of events, and there are hundreds of accounts by people who met him. We even have Washington's own journals and letters. By contrast, Jesus left no personal writings, we have just a few Gospels as sources of his life story, and those are accounts of unknown authorship handed down orally for decades before finally being written. They were even written from the perspective of a foreign culture—Jesus and his disciples would have spoken Aramaic, and the New Testament was written completely in Greek."

"You're overstating the problem. If you don't like Washington, take Caesar Augustus—you accept the story of Caesar's life even though he's from the time period of Jesus."

"How can you make this argument? Are you stupid?" Jim leapt to his feet. "The biographies of historical figures like Washington and Caesar make no supernatural claims!"

Paul opened his mouth to protest but retreated as Jim waved his arms as he stalked back and forth in front of the sofa like some hysterical prosecuting attorney.

"They were great men, but they were just men. Suppose you read that Washington was impervious to British bullets during the Revolutionary War or Caesar was born of a virgin—these claims were actually made, by the way. You would immediately dismiss them. Or what about Mormonism: Joseph Smith invented it just fifty miles from my hometown of Syracuse, shortly before I was born. We have far more information about the early days of his religion—letters, diaries, and even newspaper accounts, all in modern English—and yet I presume you dismiss Smith as a crackpot or a charlatan. In the case of Jesus, the most extravagant supernatural claims are made—why not dismiss *those* stories as well? The Bible has tales you wouldn't believe if you read them in today's newspaper, and yet you see them as truthful ancient journalism."

Paul struggled to keep his hand steady as he glanced at his note card. He had no response but was not about to admit it. He decided to try a new line of attack and took a deep breath. "Okay, answer this one. The Bible has stories of fulfilled prophecy. Early books documented the prophecy, and later books record that prophecy coming true. There are hundreds about Jesus's life alone. For example, the book of Isaiah details facts about the Messiah's life, and then the New Testament records the fulfillment of that prophecy."

"Show me."

"Okay, let's look at Isaiah 53."

Jim walked to his bookshelf and pulled off a large leather-bound Bible. A few loose pages and many notes stuck out from its edges. As Jim sat and leafed to the chapter, Paul saw that its pages had notes written in pencil and ink, some in small script and some in big block letters. Did Jim make those annotations, or was it someone else's Bible?

Paul turned to his own copy. "Isaiah says, 'He is despised and rejected of men'—Jesus should have been the king, but He was rejected by his own people. 'He was oppressed and He was afflicted, yet He opened not His mouth'—He could have proven that He was God with a word, but He chose to keep silent. 'He was wounded for our transgressions, He was bruised for our iniquities'—this describes the beatings He endured before crucifixion. 'With His stripes we are healed' and 'He bore the sin of many'—Jesus was whipped and took the burden of our sins when He died. All this was written hundreds of years before the crucifixion."

"Unconvincing," Jim said. " 'He is despised' doesn't sound like the charismatic rabbi who preached to thousands of attentive listeners and had a triumphal entry into Jerusalem on Palm Sunday. And I notice that you've ignored the part of this chapter that was inconvenient to your hypothesis: in the same chapter, God says, 'Therefore will I divide him a portion with the great, and he shall divide the spoil with the strong.' Jesus is counted as merely one of the great ones and must share with them? That's quite an insult to the son of God. And who are these equals? Most important, note that there's no mention of the resurrection here. How can this be a Jesus crucifixion story without the punch line? This chapter is actually a very poor description of the crucifixion because the 'he' in this chapter is not Jesus but Israel."

"But the Gospels themselves refer back to this chapter as prophecy of Jesus."

"I don't give a damn—this chapter isn't about Jesus."

Paul felt blindsided, as if he were lying on the ground, wondering where the haymaker came from. Samuel hadn't told him about this rebuttal. Paul said, "Well, what about Psalm 22? It describes the crucifixion experience and has Jesus's last words, *exactly*. It even describes the guards casting lots for his clothes. And this was written centuries before Jesus's day."

"Come now, think about it! The writers of the Gospels were literate, and they would have read all of the Law—what we call the Old Testament. They could have sifted through it to find plausible prophecies *before* they wrote the Gospels. Don't you see? It's as if they looked at the answers before taking a test."

Paul leaned forward. "You're saying that they cheated? That they deliberately invented the Gospel stories to fit the prophecy?"

"Think of the incredible boldness of the Bible's claims," Jim said, "that Jesus was a supernatural being sent by an omnipotent and omnipresent God who created the universe. That's about as unbelievable a story as you can imagine. Deliberate cheating to invent this story—that is, a natural explanation of the Gospels—is much more plausible than that the story is literally true—which is a *supernatural* explanation. But here's an explanation that's more plausible still: suppose Jesus was nothing more than a charismatic rabbi. The original facts of Jesus's life were then told and retold as they went from person to person, each time getting a little more fantastic. Details might have been gradually changed until they matched a particular prophecy. If people assumed that Jesus was the Messiah, he had to fulfill the prophecies, right? The Gospels were passed along orally for decades after Jesus's death before they were written down, gradually translated into the Greek culture on the way. No need to imagine the deliberate invention of a false story."

"But there was no oral tradition. The Gospels were written by eyewitnesses."

"Prove it."

"Ask any minister!" Paul said with a chuckle that probably betrayed his unease. "It's common knowledge. Matthew was an apostle, he was an eyewitness, and he wrote the book of Matthew. And so on for the other Gospel authors—all apostles or companions of apostles."

"The names of the Gospel books were assigned long after they were written. No one knows who wrote them—each Gospel is anonymous, and the names are simply tradition. No Gospel begins, 'This is an account of events that I witnessed myself.' Even if they did, should that convince me? You take any fanciful account, put 'I saw this myself' at the beginning, and it becomes true? A natural explanation—that the Jesus story is just a legend—is far, far likelier than the supernatural explanation."

Jim had been noisily worrying his cinnamon stick but now set it back on the sofa. "Besides, we have lots of examples of similar things in other religions—holy books that are really just myth. For example, we can probably agree that the Koran, Islam's holy book, is mythology. Muhammad wasn't really visited by the angel Gabriel and given wisdom from God. Did Muhammad invent it? Did a desire for power push him to create a new religion, with him as its leader? Through extreme fasting, did he have delusions that he interpreted as revelations from God? *Any* of these natural explanations and many more are much more likely than the Koran being literally true. Or *Gilgamesh* or *Beowulf* or the Hindu Vedas or the Book of Mormon. They all have supernatural elements and they are all mythology. How can you and I agree that these are mythology and that mankind throughout history has invented religion and myth, but you say that the Bible is the single exception? When you cast a net that brings up Christianity, it brings up a lot of other religions as well."

"You can't lump the Bible in with those books. It's in a completely different category."

"Prove it," Jim repeated, and he slammed his Bible onto the table.

"Why should *I* have to prove it?"

"Because you're the one making the remarkable claims."

"Remarkable?" Paul paused, his mouth open, as he collected his thoughts. "How can you say that? You're in the minority and you reject the majority view. Christianity is the most widespread religion the world has ever seen. Almost everyone in this country is thoroughly familiar with Christianity. They wouldn't think the claims are remarkable."

Jim smiled. "I wouldn't make that majority claim too loudly. Within your own religious community, your views are in the majority, but your flavor of Christianity isn't even in the majority right here in Los Angeles. Even when you lump together all the denominations of Christianity worldwide, the majority of people on the Earth still think you're wrong.

"It's true that the tenets of Christianity are widely familiar, but that doesn't make them any less remarkable. A God who can do anything, who has been around forever, and who created the universe? Take a step back and see this as an outsider might. You've made perhaps the boldest claim imaginable. No one should be asked to believe it without evidence, and very strong evidence at that."

Jim picked up his cinnamon stick and waved it as he spoke. "Suppose someone claims to have seen a leprechaun or a dragon or a unicorn. Next, this person says that, because no one can prove him wrong, his beliefs are therefore correct. And since they're correct, everyone should adopt them. This is nonsense of course. He is making the bold claim, so he must provide the evidence. In other words, we are justified—no, we are *obliged*—to reject extraordinary claims until the extraordinary evidence has been provided."

"I *have* provided evidence!" Paul said.

Jim leaned back on the sofa and looked at Paul, for the first time at a loss for a quick retort. "Son, this is what I expected from you," he said quietly, almost gently. "But this evidence barely merits the name. What you've provided is a flimsy argument that might satisfy someone who wants to support beliefs that he's already decided are correct. But don't expect this to convince anyone else."

Paul sat back in his chair as if hit in the stomach. He had been preparing for a debate like this with increasing intensity for two years, and he thought that he deserved more. He didn't expect accolades for his cleverness . . . but *something?* He tried to salvage the discussion and glanced at his note card, almost used up. His voice felt shrill and unreliable as he began. "But you must adjust your demands given how long ago this was. You can't ask for photographs and diaries when the events happened close to two thousand years ago. It's not fair."

"Not fair? Suppose you come to me and ask to buy my house. I say that it's worth three thousand dollars. You say, 'I'll give you five dollars for it.' I say, 'No—that's ridiculous. I must reject your offer.' And then you say, 'But that's not fair—five dollars is all I have.' "

Jim leaned forward, staring at Paul and with his arms outstretched. "That would be absurd. But it's equivalent to the argument 'since proving the fantastic claims of the New Testament is quite hard, you'll have to accept whatever evidence we have.' No, I don't! I won't accept five dollars for my house, I won't accept pathetic evidence for leprechauns, and I won't accept it for God."

Jim paused and then said, "And while we're at it, neither should you."

Chapter 4

San Francisco: Wednesday, April 18
Four Japanese Buddhist monks left the San Francisco docks before
dawn. Their handcart rattled over the cobblestones, loaded with fresh
fish. They would dry the fish after they returned to their monastery in
the hills outside Sausalito, just across the bay to the north. They made
the trip a few times each year to visit other Japanese citizens in China-
town, consult with the local leadership, collect donations, and buy supplies.

The earthquake caught them in the heart of the city. Suddenly, it was
upon them, pouring down on them through the street in vast, visible
waves. Every cobblestone seemed alive, no longer solid and reliable.
Cracks in the street opened up and then closed. The noise became
deafening. The building to their left suddenly lurched over as if about
to topple on them, and then the building on their right. They moved to
the middle of the street and rode out the terrifying experience, scanning the darkness for falling danger.

After what seemed like several minutes, the earthquake finally
stopped and they moved on, muttering prayers of thanks. They wove
around the fallen walls and decorative stonework, now merely rubble
on the sidewalks and streets. Once-proud cornices, grand and ostenta-
tious when in place high above the street, looked grotesque and out of
scale when seen up close.

The city had always seemed chaotic and foreign, but it had become
more so. Garbage cans and flower pots were overturned and their contents strewn across the streets. Rats flushed from their homes under
apartments and office buildings poked around in the garbage and acted
more boldly and impulsively than usual. Delivery animals pranced
nervously, unfamiliar with a route they might have walked for years,
and power lines lay sparking in the street.

Ahead, the monks heard shouts of "Fire!" They had only a rudimentary knowledge of English, but that was a word they understood.

They came to a brick hotel with empty windows and shattered glass covering the sidewalk, and they heard a woman screaming from inside. Where was everyone else—perhaps frightened off by the fire?

Chiba was the oldest of the four. "Stop here," he said in Japanese. "We must see if we can help."

"We are visitors in this country," Nishimura said. "We must leave women alone. Our actions could easily be misunderstood."

"There is no one else. We must."

The hotel doors were jammed shut, but the monks entered the lobby through the large empty window frame. Using the pale light of the approaching dawn, they picked their way over glass and rubble and found a young woman face down near the back of the lobby with only her head and shoulders exposed. A mound of bricks and shattered pieces of furniture covered the rest of her. She was alternately crying and moaning. The monks hastily removed the debris, alarmed by the cries of fire and thoughts that the building could collapse. Finally her legs were free.

"Horrible!" The monks stared in shock. One leg was bent unnaturally and blood stained her nightgown. She continued to cry out.

Life is suffering, Chiba thought. Only death is painless.

Anxious to get her to safety, they gently turned her over and picked her up. Her whimpering turned to screams. Her screaming continued as they carried her out the window and placed her in the cart, on a blanket tossed over the fresh fish. The fish shifted under her weight to accommodate her. Chiba grabbed the medicine bag, freshly restocked, and took out a bottle of laudanum. He opened it, held it to the woman's lips, and said in English, "Drink." She jerked her head back with a groan in response to the strong smell. "Medicine—drink," he said, enunciating each syllable, and lifted her head. She calmed her breathing a bit, held the bottle and took a swallow, coughed, and returned to loud whimpering. "More," he said, and she took another swallow.

In the pale light outside, the monks could better evaluate her injuries. The bleeding came from a number of deep cuts. The more shocking problem was a broken left thigh. Her nightclothes were pushed up enough to see the end of a bone poking through the skin, just above the knee. For Chiba, the leg brought to mind a butcher's table, with skinned animal parts chopped to show the end of a bone, ragged and pinkish-white against the red of the wound.

But the bone could wait—the bleeding was the urgent issue. Blood very slowly pulsed out of the wound with each heartbeat. Chiba pointed to a bolt of new cloth in a pile of supplies in the corner of the cart. "Cut some bandages," he said. Nishimura cut strips of cloth while Chiba mixed herbs to create an astringent and antiseptic poultice. By the time her wounds had been dressed, the woman had quieted and fallen into a narcotic stupor.

"Look!" A third monk pointed to an upper story of the building. Through a window they saw the flickering light of a burning room. This was not a safe place. The monks hurried on to find a hospital for the injured woman.

The city landmarks had changed with the earthquake, and familiar references were gone. The cobblestone streets were buckled in places and progress was slow, and some streets were impassable. They passed two pale-colored horses still hitched to their wagons, dead under a fallen wall. The eyes of one were open wide, and its body was frozen as if a sculpted snapshot of the terror of its last agonizing moments. The other's neck lay at an unnatural angle, its tongue hung out, and a large pool of dark blood glinted in the morning sun.

Everywhere people cleared rubble, removed belongings, or picked their way through the rubble. Women holding children's hands hurried along, followed by men carrying suitcases, a few simply wearing coats over nightclothes. All seemed too preoccupied with their own problems to notice the four monks moving slowly with their handcart and its curious cargo.

About a mile after leaving the hotel they saw an empty lot with a makeshift clinic. A dozen patients lay on blankets on the ground while relatives or friends tended them, and several more patients approached on foot or horse. Bloody bandages wrapped limbs, torsos, and heads. A surgeon with a blood-stained apron moved between patients. He was an Army surgeon, judging by the tan uniform under the apron and the stacks of identical wooden boxes of medical supplies on the ground. A sheet strung up as a curtain shielded the surgeon's work from view, and amputated limbs lay in a pile.

Nishimura went to the side of the cart and grabbed a corner of the blanket. The other two took up their positions, but Chiba held up his hand. "Wait. We can't leave her here."

"Why not?"

"This must be an Army field hospital. For a leg broken as badly as hers, they have nothing to offer but amputation. She'll have one leg for the rest of her life—if she survives the infection."

"She'll be with her people."

Chiba shook his head. "No. We can't do this. She no longer has serious bleeding, and we can set the leg at the monastery. We've treated worse."

"We can't have a woman at the monastery. What will the abbot say?"

"He'll say that we did the right thing. The right action triumphs over the convenient action." He gestured at the patients. "We can't help these people, but there is one person we can help."

A man's screams came from behind the curtain, loud and piteous. The monks moved on.

୪୦

The big chair creaked as Samuel leaned back.

"I could not believe the rudeness of that man," Paul said. He sat in his usual chair, in front of Samuel's desk. No longer constrained by politeness, Paul could vent his anger, and he smacked his fist into his palm. "He rejected everything I said—everything! *None* of my arguments satisfied him. He even compared belief in God to belief in unicorns. He was a complete...." Paul caught himself—Samuel was intolerant of swearing. "He was a complete scoundrel."

"So you found him a tough debater?"

"Very tough, at least for me. I don't know what tricks he used, but he maneuvered every argument so that I couldn't respond."

"Now you see the need for the hard work," Samuel said. "That's why I've pushed you the past year. Desire and a little common sense is a good start, but that won't win debates with experienced opponents."

"I wish you'd been there. I want to see you do to him what you did to that professor from the university."

"I won't need to—you'll be able to do that soon enough." Samuel eased forward to lean his elbows on the desk, a smile spreading across his face. He looked as energized and confident as Paul had ever seen him. "I like a challenge. If this were easy, where would be the sport?" he said with a wink. "Have confidence. You will win—the truth will prevail.

"Now, tell me how it went," Samuel said. "Give me the arguments you made and his responses."

"He accepted the argument that the copies of the Bible are accurate but said that that doesn't make them true," Paul said. "He asked why the Bible should be correct but the *Iliad* not."

He glanced up to gauge Samuel's reaction. His arms were crossed and his lips squeezed together—not a good sign. Paul pressed on. "I told him about Josephus and other sources outside the Bible, but he said that they simply echo the Gospel conclusions rather than provide new evidence."

"Go on."

Paul looked down at his note card and cleared his throat. "We talked about historical figures—Washington and Caesar as well as Jesus. He dismissed that comparison because the Jesus story contains supernatural claims while the biographies of historical figures like Washington and Caesar don't. He said that the Jesus story was legend."

Samuel scowled and shook his head. "How did he respond to the prophecy argument?"

Paul wiped his hands on his pants. "Jim said the 'he' in Isaiah 53 made more sense as Israel, not Jesus, and said that any claim of fulfilled prophecy is suspect because the Gospel writers knew about the prophecy before they wrote."

"And so they cheated?" Samuel snorted. "What a ridiculous claim— the Gospels were written by eyewitnesses!"

"That's what I said. But he demanded that I prove it."

Samuel smacked both hands on the desk so hard that Paul jumped. "How much evidence does this man need? If his mother said she loved him, would he demand a second opinion? It's a wonder he gets through the day—does he distrust the very ground beneath his feet?"

Samuel shook his head slowly and gravely, looking directly at him, and Paul imagined an unspoken *How much worse could this interview have gone?* in Samuel's mind. "Well? Is there more?"

Paul decided that he had dug his hole deep enough and put his card in his pocket. "No, that's it," he said and hung his head to await the ax.

Samuel waited his customary few seconds to let the magnitude of Paul's failing soak in and then lectured Paul on attitude—how he must take the high ground and not yield an inch to any attack. How the truth of Christianity was the most important issue imaginable and had to be defended to the last man. Paul looked down at the thick Oriental carpet, trying to imagine himself safely hidden within the maze-like pattern. He knew from experience that this was not a dialogue—Samuel wanted the floor to himself—so he made the best of the scolding and listened carefully to Samuel's points. Still, he felt stung. He realized that he had lost the last debate with Jim, and badly, but he didn't think that he was at fault. He hated being wrong, and he didn't think that Samuel's rubbing it in was necessary.

After a final pause to let his lesson take, Samuel blew out a deep breath and said, "All right, let's put that behind us. The oral tradition—that's where you must focus. That's the weak part of his argument."

Samuel stood and ran his finger along the spines of his treasured red-leather Harvard Classics that prominently occupied an entire shelf, pushing in several volumes that were out of line from the rest. "In society today, our memory skills are poorly trained. But the memory feats of people in societies long ago were amazing." He pulled a book from the set, laid it on his desk, and tapped it reverently with his finger. "The *Iliad,* the Greek story of the Trojan War, was a poem that took many hours to recite. It was all done by memory—and every telling was identical. In Jesus's day, rabbis and even Jewish students would in many cases memorize entire books of the Old Testament. The error is in assuming that past societies were identical to our own. They were not."

Paul nodded, taking notes. The note card was sweaty and crumpled, and his writing was faint.

"Next, notice how very remarkable the story of Jesus is." Samuel returned to his chair and gazed upward, his fingers steepled together. "I remember events from twenty or thirty years ago with the clarity of a photograph—and these are events from my own poor life. Imagine thinking back on a miracle! Wouldn't the image of something that marvelous be burned into your memory with far greater clarity?"

"Yes, yes, I see your point. The eyewitnesses to a miracle must be reliable. That's good," Paul said as he scribbled.

"The third point is that a false story would be corrected. Suppose you tell a story to a gathering of people and you make a mistake. You're all in the same community, and someone in the audience will know the story and correct you. Next time, you will tell the story accurately. Stories this important don't simply pass a single time through people, with you telling ten people, each of them telling ten different people, and so on. Society is an interconnecting web, and fundamental stories like the Jesus narrative would have been told over and over in the early Christian communities. You would hear the story many times, which would give you a chance to learn it well, and you would have others correct your telling of the story as necessary.

"And remember that the Gospels were written at a time when many disciples—the eyewitnesses—were still alive. If they heard an inaccurate story, they'd say, 'I was there, and that's not the way it happened.' An incorrect version of the story would not have survived."

Paul scribbled notes during the pause.

"I can't stress strongly enough the importance of this battle," Samuel said. "We're fighting for an immortal soul, but God is on our side. Failure is not only unacceptable, it's impossible."

∞

That evening, Paul checked his damp hair in the mirror, threw his jacket over his shoulder, and walked half a mile west to Samuel's apartment. Samuel invited Paul to dinner about once a month. Never a casual chat over sandwiches, Samuel's dinners were formal affairs, and Paul would have worn a tuxedo if he'd had one.

Samuel's building fronted on Los Angeles's one-block Central Park, a single wooded city block west of downtown Los Angeles. As Paul walked through the park, he came upon a tiny stage on a grassy area with children watching the show. It was a performance of *Pinocchio*, with the protagonist as a marionette and the other characters as hand puppets. Paul thought of his own cramped childhood as he watched the laughing children.

Samuel's apartment was small but luxurious, a first floor corner unit with high ceilings and big windows that looked across the street to the park. Every surface that in an ordinary house would have been painted was upgraded in some way. The mantle was gilt ebony and supported an overmantle full of mirrors and shelves holding porcelain figurines. The walls were papered with designs of flowers and feathers, and the tin ceiling was white with an embossed gilt pattern. The Oriental carpets and upholstered furniture with tassels made Paul feel in Samuel's parlor as if he were waiting for an audience with a sultan.

Samuel greeted him at the door and led him into the parlor. "I met a state assemblyman at the theater last night," Samuel said. "He said that he knew Representative McLachlan." He went on to sketch how he might parlay this chance meeting into an audience with the congressman.

He often talked about connections he made at social events. Paul would have liked to have done more with Samuel, but their interests didn't overlap. Paul enjoyed boxing, football, and baseball at the local university, and sometimes cockfights. Samuel had little patience with "philistine pastimes" and preferred the theater and the occasional round of golf.

Seated in the parlor, Paul admired the precise placement of each piece of furniture. He had been a guest here dozens of times and yet never felt comfortable. Unable to relax deep in the puffy chairs, he always sat erect, vigilant against any social error. He felt genuinely welcome, but on Samuel's terms.

Samuel had lived alone since his wife Bea died of consumption three years earlier. When visiting parishioners, Paul had noticed that the women in the church were divided on how they saw Samuel's status. Women in their forties and fifties tended to focus on his being a "poor widower," while older women clucked about the lack of propriety in the first group. And that was probably the main reason Paul was included this evening. One final guest was expected, a married woman, and decorum demanded a third party.

At the sound of the doorbell, both men rose. Samuel warmly welcomed Mrs. Abigail Bradshaw, a fairly new church member. Paul recognized her from the receiving line the previous Sunday—a confident woman in her forties, dressed this evening in a fashionably narrow brown dress that trailed on the ground. Her auburn hair hung in waves in front of her shoulders, and she needed a few moments to remove her substantial hat.

Seated in the parlor, Mrs. Bradshaw adjusted her hair and said, "Reverend Hargrove, I've learned so much from your sermons. Our last church, it was all songs and collections, with a nap in between during the sermon." She looked up at Samuel's impassive face and added, "I'm joking, of course."

"Of course." Samuel nodded. "We're pleased to be able to meet you socially."

"I must say that the reception I've gotten has been delightful. You really make a new member feel welcome." Her floral perfume filled the room.

Paul pushed himself to say something. "When I first came to the church two years ago, I could hardly speak to strangers. Many people in the congregation told Reverend Hargrove to get rid of me, but he stood by me."

Neither Samuel nor Mrs. Bradshaw responded. Paul felt several long seconds slip by, and then Samuel turned to Mrs. Bradshaw and said, "I'm sorry your husband couldn't attend. A business trip, I understand?"

"Harry is in Maine of all places. He's visiting the Electrolytic Marine Salts Company. They have an invention that extracts dissolved gold from seawater, and Harry wants to be the west coast representative."

"I thought he ran a hardware store," Samuel said.

"He runs Union Hardware."

Samuel nodded at this correction. Union Hardware and Metal was not a mere store but a factory in a four-story building that occupied an entire block. "He's a busy man if he can run such a big operation while looking for new business."

Mrs. Bradshaw looked down. "I was hoping to talk to you about that."

Paul felt out of place, as if he were a child eavesdropping on an adult conversation.

After a pause, during which Mrs. Bradshaw made a few attempts to continue, she said, "If he would just focus on the company." Another pause and then she looked at Samuel. "He got gold fever in the late nineties after the big strike in the Yukon. I wouldn't let him go, so he staked claims in the hills around here and panned for gold. He wasted a couple of years imagining himself a prospector, and then it was oil leases. Then it was some crazy perpetual motion scheme in Chicago—'It's patented so it has to work,' he said. And now it's this gold-from-seawater thing."

This was the kind of man, Samuel would say, who had "more dollars than sense."

Mrs. Bradshaw unfolded a fan and beat the air. "Harry's just too trusting. He'll meet someone in a bar with some wild idea for easy money and all of a sudden this strange man is family. Then a month or a year later he's come to his senses, but then he's back in the chase for another scheme, none the wiser for all the money he lost."

"He's providing for you?" Samuel asked.

"Oh, yes. We have so much to be thankful for—the business is doing well enough to support us and his schemes. But it's such a waste."

"Have you asked him to stop these adventures?"

She nodded. "He listens and then he smiles and pats me on the shoulder and tells me that he'll take care of it. But nothing changes. I know he'd respect you—maybe if you talk to him."

"Of course I will." Samuel reached over and patted her tightly clasped hands. "That's what I'm here for."

Samuel continued to assure her that her husband would be in good hands within the church while Paul's mind wandered to his own temptations. The kind of schemes that plagued Mr. Bradshaw didn't interest Paul, but his past showed his own weaknesses—alcohol, women, robbery for easy money. The world was a dangerous place, full of seduction, and he was pleased to have left his old life behind.

Mrs. Bradshaw seemed much comforted by Samuel's assurances.

Samuel stood and guided the party into the dining room. The table was elaborately set as usual—red napkins wrapped around a roll sat on blue and white china plates with Japanese designs. Three forks on the left of each setting balanced two knives and a spoon on the right, all ornate silver. The large and small water glasses were crystal, as were the small bowls of olives, radishes, and salted nuts scattered about the table. A thick white tablecloth hung to the floor, and the centerpiece was four candlesticks surrounding a china vase covered with a colorful menagerie of animals.

Paul took in the display and said nothing. He had once made an ill-advised jest about the grand layout and suggested that reusing utensils and plates would be less wasteful. Samuel had snapped, "Civilization separates us from the animals."

After Samuel seated Mrs. Bradshaw, he laid a Bible from the sideboard on the table. Once everyone was settled, he put his hand on the Bible and gave an elaborate blessing that included Mr. Bradshaw and, as was his habit, thanked God for a compassion great enough to include those who had committed the worst sins.

The blessing over, Mrs. Bradshaw put her napkin in her lap. "It feels so good to find a church home that fits. My soul felt hungry."

"It's a mature person who knows when to rejuvenate his faith," Samuel said.

Paul smiled broadly. "A good church service makes me feel clean, like I've just taken a bath." The comment was ignored and Paul's smile faded.

"May I tell you about something that's been a real blessing?" Mrs. Bradshaw asked. "A few weeks ago, I got a letter from my brother in St. Louis. He was laid off months ago. Well, I had just started coming to your church, and my faith was feeling strong again. I prayed hard for him and felt so good about it that I sent him a telegram that said so. A couple of days later, I get a reply back—he'd gotten a job. His 'perfect job,' he said."

"Prayer does the trick," Samuel said.

"And it's so freeing!"

"Exactly. Mrs. Bradshaw, you understand perfectly—I should have you give the next sermon. You see the relief you get from trusting in

God. You lay your troubles at the feet of Someone who can do so much more than we can."

Samuel hired a cook for these occasions, and she came out of the kitchen with the soup course. The smell of warm potatoes rose from Paul's bowl.

"I'm having one difficulty with prayer though," Mrs. Bradshaw said. "My aunt has cancer. My greatest wish is for her to get well, and she's in so much pain. Prayers have done nothing."

"She takes laudanum?"

"Oh yes, but it's now either agony or stupor. Neither is the aunt I knew."

Samuel touched her hand again. "All prayers are answered, but sometimes God's answer is No."

Mrs. Bradshaw turned to her soup, and the only sound for a minute was spoons clinking against bowls. Looking more composed, she said, "It's difficult, but my faith is strong." And then, with a big smile, "My friends say that I'm like the White Queen who could believe six impossible things before breakfast."

"That's the spirit," Samuel said.

The conversation paused for a moment as the cook refilled the water glasses.

"I'm sure you heard of the prophecy," Samuel said.

"Of course—the whole city has."

"It's transformed the church," Paul said.

"I'm thinking we may be at a religious turning point," Samuel said. "We've had spiritual renewal in America since its founding, but that hasn't always been for the best. American religious practice fragmented during the last century, and I would love to see American spirituality come back together. I imagine a family that's scattered and wandering the world, and I think that we may have in our church the spiritual home that will bring them back."

Paul thought how Samuel's vision made his own seem pathetic. Samuel was on a mountain, shouting out what he saw to Paul stuck in the valley. Would he ever have Samuel's reach, his vision, his ambition?

The future that Samuel described seemed to excite Mrs. Bradshaw as much as it did Paul. Samuel continued as the courses were served, talking about what this might mean to the church, to Paul, to the parishioners, and to himself. According to Samuel, Paul was already a significant historical footnote. Growing up, he had always felt that he was made for something more than life on the street. What could be more noble than being a founding part of the movement that restored America's spiritual unity?

As a slice of warm peach pie was placed in front of everyone, Mrs. Bradshaw took hold of the conversation again. "I wonder if I could ask something else about Harry," she said. She turned to both of them, and Paul felt pleased that he was included.

"He's taken up some rather odd beliefs. It started because of the epilepsy he's had since he was a child. He gets episodes every few months, and they terrify him. He's been searching for cures, and I support that, but this has made him vulnerable to every charlatan in the state."

"They're selling hope, not a cure," Samuel said.

"Yes, that's it. There's one on every street corner and a dozen in every magazine. They've turned Harry into a hypochondriac. He hasn't met a cure he didn't like. I know he'll return from Maine with a satchel full of whatever patent medicines they sell there that he hasn't seen. He already has cabinets in the kitchen full of useless medicines—nerve bitters, Chinese snake oil, St. Jacobs Oil, liver pills, mandrake pills, Indian root pills, homeopathic pills. He has syrups and liniments and plasters. He's had chiropractic treatments and electro-magnetic treatments and water therapy and seawater injections. He's getting sick from all this medicine." She took a handkerchief from her purse and squeezed it. "And now he's getting into mesmerism and spiritualism and even the occult."

"Now calm yourself, Mrs. Bradshaw," Samuel said. "Coming to me was the right thing—the church can help. Society is full of dissipations like these, and a man of a certain disposition can easily get caught up in them, especially a man who may have too ready access to money, if you'll excuse my saying so."

"Of course, Reverend. My father built the company, and Harry succeeded him as president when he died about ten years ago. I think if

Harry had built it up himself, he would have a different attitude toward money."

"Now tell me," Samuel said, "what does he say when you try to reason with him?"

"He just digs in his heels and becomes more convinced of the rightness of his position. Any criticism just makes him more obstinate, so I've stopped arguing."

"I've seen this many times," Samuel said. "The problem is that reason won't get a man out of something he didn't use reason to get into. To change would be to admit an error, and Man's pride forbids this. In my experience, the smarter the man, the better and more energetic the intellectual defense he makes for any opinion, whether well-founded or groundless."

"I'm so glad you're experienced with this." A smile flickered on Mrs. Bradshaw's face. "It's like he's drowning, looking for something to keep him afloat. When a pill or potion or easy-money scheme sinks, he abandons it without embarrassment or a second thought and flails around for another to support him."

"What he's looking for is hope."

She looked as if groping for something to keep afloat herself. "But what can be done?"

"You know the answer, dear lady," Samuel said, "it's the church. Think of a fireplace. Take a hot coal out of the fire and set it to the side. What happens? It turns black; it gets cold. But when you put it back in the fire, it glows red and becomes alive again. That's what the church community does. We need to get Harry into the warmth of the church."

"Yes, that sounds just right. I expect him back from Maine in about ten days. Will you talk to him?"

"The minute he walks into my office, I'll drop what I'm doing and we'll have a talk. That's a promise."

After a few minutes, Samuel suggested that they return to the parlor, and the conversation turned to lighter subjects.

The evening was winding down when Samuel said, "Mrs. Bradshaw, I wonder if you've considered a donation to First Church of God."

"I'm always generous when the collection plate comes around."

"I've no doubt about that, but I was thinking about a special donation. We're looking for the Lord's help to expand."

This was the first that Paul had heard of a fund-raising campaign or any expansion of the church.

Mrs. Bradshaw's eyebrows raised. "Well, I don't know. I've only recently become a member."

"Of course, and let me apologize if I was abrupt. It's just that we're going out to some of our stronger members to offer them the opportunity to take the lead in this project."

"I am a little preoccupied with worry about Harry just now."

"Do you mind if we pray about it?"

"Why no, not at all." Mrs. Bradshaw covered one hand with the other.

Samuel put his elbows on his thighs, interlaced his fingers, and bowed his head. "Dear Lord, you have been so generous with what you've given Abigail and Harry Bradshaw. Please give them the wisdom to invest your money wisely. Help them see the life of noble charity that you have chosen for them. Lord, please guide them past the difficulties in life, and give special attention to Harry, who's in a rough patch right now. Help him turn toward the love within his family and the church and away from worldly temptations and dissipations. Amen."

Mrs. Bradshaw looked up. After a pause, she smiled and said, "We'd like to help. I'll talk it over with Harry when he gets back."

A few minutes later, Mrs. Bradshaw thanked Samuel and stood to leave, and Paul followed. Samuel's cheerful face showed that the evening had been a success, both socially and for the church.

The sky was darkening as Paul accompanied Mrs. Bradshaw to the taxi station. He saw her onto a taxi and waved as it moved off. He crossed the street to the park and was drawn to the sound of three boys running and shouting in a gravel clearing. As he came closer, he saw that each boy carried a hobby horse between his legs. Lines made in the gravel from the ends of the horses' stick bodies traced the progress of an elaborate campaign. Paul wondered if the boys were jousting or reenacting a skirmish from the Civil War or perhaps accompanying Teddy Roosevelt up San Juan Hill.

And they imagine that the horse is carrying them, Paul thought with a smile.

$$\wp$$

Paul made the trolley ride to the blue-tiled house on Stageira Street the next day. The dinner with Samuel had given him a clear view of the world and buoyed his confidence, and it reminded him that he had truth and God's guidance on his side. He told himself that when besieged, he would let God provide the words. Nevertheless, he still felt anxious about facing this unpredictable man.

"Come," Jim said in response to his knock. Paul entered the house and walked down the hall to the library. He noticed for the first time a chessboard on the bureau. The board appeared to hold a game in progress, with the white pieces against the wall.

Jim motioned for him to take his seat and said, "Paul, I think I was a bit rude in our last encounter."

Was this the same man? His speech was as direct as before, but this was Paul's first sign that Jim had any awareness of, let alone concern for, anyone else's feelings.

"You'll have to excuse me," Jim said. "I'm an old man and rather set in my ways."

Paul took the "old man" reference as a deliberate exaggeration—Samuel was 51 years old, and Jim must have been within a few years of that. Though unkempt and pale, Jim seemed fit and carried himself with a young man's energy.

"I usually don't care much for social custom," Jim said, "and I've become a bit housebound. A guest, particularly one who wants to engage in intelligent debate, is a welcome surprise. I won't apologize for arguing with intensity, but I must be civil or I'll scare you away." Jim smiled. "So let me begin again, but with respect for the social niceties. Good afternoon, I'm Jim Emerson." He extended his hand.

Paul stood to reach across the low center table and shook it. "Paul Winston. Nice to meet you, Mr. Emerson." This seemed rather like sharing a beer with someone you've recently had a bar fight with.

"Please call me Jim. Tell me about yourself, Paul. What drives you to get out and spread the Good News?"

Paul hesitated. "Do you really want to know, or is this simply more respect for social niceties?"

"No, I honestly want to know. It may surprise you that I went through a strong spiritual period when I was about your age. Perhaps we'll get to that."

"I've been a part of the First Church of God for two years now," Paul said. "The truth of the Message is very important to us. We don't say 'Jesus is Lord' simply as a custom. We prove it, and we're eager to share that with our neighbors."

"And before that? Have you lived here long?"

"I was born in Los Angeles and have lived here all my life. I grew up in an orphanage near Elysian Park."

"I'm sorry to hear that," Jim said. "Did you know your parents?"

"No, the orphanage was the only home I ever knew. I knew nothing about my parents—whether they died or if I was just unwanted, I never found out. It was a rough place to grow up."

"I can imagine."

Paul usually resisted inquiries into his past, but Jim seemed genuinely interested, and sharing a bit of himself somehow seemed right. He leaned forward. "I learned no trade, so I picked up odd jobs once I was on my own—mostly around the docks and train yard, but nothing steady. I fell in with some street thugs. I didn't benefit much except that I got better at fighting and stealing. I never felt comfortable with them—the other fellows saw me as too bookish. They were only interested in getting money, getting girls, or getting drunk."

"And you? What were you interested in?"

"I was an impressive failure in school, though the one subject I did excel in was reading. As soon as I understood what reading provided, I learned quickly. It became my escape."

"Your diction betrays your passion," Jim said. "You have a mature command of language."

"Not everyone was impressed. After the orphanage, it was clear that no one shared my interests. I kept to myself and read a lot, on just about every topic, and I went to the library often. My friends called me 'Professor.' But in my mind, I traveled to places and talked to people from history that they never dreamed of. I don't read as widely now, though."

"Why is that?"

"My pastor says that our ministry is of the here and now. He sees excessive learning in areas that don't glorify God as a distraction. I focus now on the Bible and apologetics."

"We'll have to see if we can't re-broaden your focus," Jim said, smiling. "Tell me—how did you get into the church? It doesn't sound like you were particularly religious growing up."

"No, religion was hardly a priority. About two years ago, I needed some money, so I was out one night looking for someone I thought wouldn't mind exchanging wallets with me. Some people I knew, once they picked someone to rob, they wouldn't let up until they had what they wanted. That was just a principle with them. I was the opposite—I would give it five seconds or so, and I was intimidating enough that that was usually enough. Then I left, whether I had what I came for or not.

"But one night, the man I picked fought back. He held me up long enough for a cop to whack me with his nightstick from behind. I woke up the next day in jail with my head throbbing. That was my first time in jail, but it turned out to be my last. Later that day, the jailer brought this big guy who said something like, 'Hello, Paul, I've been looking for you. You're coming with me.' He said this in a cheerful voice, with a wide smile, as if the idea were nonnegotiable. I wasn't in a cheery mood, but I understand power, and this man had it. The jailer let me out and said how lucky I was and how attempted robbery should have gotten me six months. The man turned out to be Reverend Hargrove, the pastor of my church."

"Stop—Reverend *Samuel* Hargrove?"

"Yes, that's right."

"So Sam is a proper minister now, and with his own church—I guess I should read the papers more. Not surprising, I suppose. He got what he wanted, usually."

"You know Reverend Hargrove?"

"I met Sam shortly after I arrived in Los Angeles in '76. I was twenty-one, the same as Sam. We met in church—the Trinity Methodist

Episcopal Church. I was new in town and far from home, the church provided a strong and supportive community, and I believed the Christian story. Seems hard to imagine now, but it formed a big part of my life. Jesus died for my sins, I was going to heaven, God was looking out for me—all that.

"Sam and I did some street preaching to pull more young people into the church. We were a good team." He paused. "He was my best friend during that time. We were inseparable, but that didn't last—pity." Jim's voice faded as he looked blankly at the wall behind Paul.

After a long pause, Paul felt obliged to revive the conversation, but gently, as if rousing a dozing uncle for dinner. "Tell me—what brought you to Los Angeles?"

Jim turned back to him and needed a moment to return to the present. "Well, I'd just graduated from Boston Tech as an engineer. The family business in Syracuse was in rifles, and we did very well during the Civil War. I was only ten when it ended, but that's not something that I'm proud of—that my prosperity was built on weapons sales. My father had to scramble after the war to find new work for the factory, and he licensed a typewriter patent. The typewriter was not new at the time, but it had never been a successful product before our version. We were just starting to see sales of the new typewriter when I graduated."

Jim turned to his right and pulled toward him the typewriter on its rolling stand. He idly pushed on a key, not to strike the platen but as if to admire its smooth and silent action. "I arrived here from Boston, and my job was building and selling typewriters to customers in the new cities in the West. Even in the commercial centers like New York and Chicago, people didn't know why a typewriter was an improvement over a pen, so I had a hard time at first. Now, typewriters are all we sell."

Jim waved his hands, erasing an imaginary blackboard. "But enough about me. You came to discuss the truth behind Christianity."

"Yes, that's right." Paul felt that his position had strengthened since he and Jim had shared some background. More importantly, he realized that Jim was simply a lost sheep. Jim had understood the truth of the Bible, and he could be reminded of that again. Paul felt confident and enthusiastic as he began. "You argued yesterday that oral tradition is unreliable and that we can't trust the Gospel story of Jesus."

"I argued that the evidence the Gospels provide is paltry compared to what is necessary to justify such amazing claims."

"Yes. I'd like to challenge that—"

Jim held up a hand. "Before you begin, let's try an experiment. You think that oral tradition is reliable. Let's simulate a step in that process. I'll tell you a story, and then we'll see how well you remember it."

Paul didn't expect a quiz. "I suppose, but remember that I'm just an ordinary person. I'm not trained in memorizing stories."

"And neither would have been an ordinary citizen in Palestine who heard the story of Jesus and passed it along. From Jesus's death to the first Gospel was thirty or forty years. The story wasn't confined to scholars—it was passed through ordinary people."

"I suppose so," Paul said. Samuel had talked about trained scholars memorizing the story, but the story passing through common people made sense.

"Do you know the story of Circe from the *Odyssey?*"

"No—I've only read the *Iliad.*"

"Then you know the context." Jim got up and walked to the book-case on his left. The bookcase was densely packed with no apparent order. He ran his fingers across the spines of the books on one shelf, muttering titles to himself. After a few moments, he pulled off a book and leafed through it as he returned to the sofa. "The *Iliad* is about the Trojan War, and the *Odyssey* is the story of the Greek hero Odysseus and his ten-year trip home.

"Here's the story—pay attention." Jim looked down at the book as he spoke. "Odysseus and his men were lost and they landed on the coast of a strange land. After a few days of rest, Odysseus sent Eurylo-chus, a trusted friend, with a party of twenty-two men to explore. They found a house in a clearing guarded by lions, wolves, and other animals but were surprised to find the animals tame. They approached the house, and a woman named Circe invited them in. The men were delighted to find so beautiful a hostess and accepted the offer—except for Eurylochus, who suspected a trap. Circe showed the men a banquet and they ate enthusiastically, but she was a witch and the food was drugged. She turned the men into pigs and locked them in pens. The wild animals were men from other expeditions that Circe had also transformed."

Jim looked up at Paul and then continued. "Eurylochus saw all this and hurried back to tell Odysseus. Odysseus was determined to rescue his men and went alone to Circe's house. On the way, he met the god Hermes, who wanted to help. He gave Odysseus an herb that would protect him from Circe's magic, and he told Odysseus that the threat of his sword would beat the threat of her wand. The encounter went as Hermes had predicted—Circe was no match for Odysseus, and she returned the men to human form. Odysseus and his men enjoyed Circe's hospitality for a year, and she and Odysseus became lovers."

Jim looked up and set the open book on the sofa. "That's long enough. The Jesus story is far longer, of course, but let's see how you do with that. Make sure you got it right—are you unclear on anything?"

Aside from Hermes and Odysseus, the names in the story were new to Paul, and he asked to have them repeated. He checked on the number of men, the kinds of animals in the clearing, and other details.

"Okay," Jim said after Paul was satisfied, "let's sit on that for a bit and return to what you were saying about oral tradition."

"My point is that if the Gospel story was wrong, there would have been people who said, 'Hold on, now—I was there, and that didn't happen' or 'I knew that fellow, and he didn't do that.' A false story wouldn't have survived."

"Have you thought this through?"

"Sure," Paul said.

"I doubt it."

Paul again felt the punch in the stomach.

Jim frowned. "Think critically about claims like this. You're smart enough to demand the truth, not just a pleasing answer. First, let's get an idea of how few potential naysayers there could have been. I'm guessing a few dozen."

"But there were thousands who saw the miracle of the loaves and fishes. And that's just one miracle—there were many."

"That doesn't help us. A naysayer must have been a close companion of Jesus to witness him *not* doing all the miracles recorded in the

Gospels. He would need to know that Jesus *didn't* walk on water and *didn't* raise Lazarus. Seems to me that a naysayer must have been one of Jesus's close companions during his entire ministry. No, there's no reason to imagine more than a few dozen."

Odysseus, Eurylochus, Circe, Hermes, Paul thought to himself.

Jim looked up at the ceiling and counted off numbers with his fingers. "Two: the naysayer must be in the right location to complain. Suppose he were in Jerusalem, and say that the book of Mark was written in Alexandria, Egypt. How will our naysayer correct its errors? Sure, Mark will be copied and spread, but there's not much time before our 60- or 70-year-old witnesses die. Even if we imagine our tiny band of men dedicating their lives to stamping out this false story—and why would they?—believers are starting brush fires of Christian belief all over the Eastern Mediterranean, from Alexandria to Damascus to Rome. How can we expect our naysayers to snuff them all out?

"Three: remember that two thousand years ago, you couldn't walk down to the corner newsstand to find the latest Jesus Gospel. How were our naysayers to learn of the story? Written documents at that time were scarce and precious things. The naysayers would be Jews who *didn't* convert to Christianity, and they wouldn't have associated much with the new Christians and so would have been unlikely to come across the Jesus story.

Twenty-two men, the food was a drug, the men became pigs, Paul thought.

"Four: there was another gulf between the naysayers and the early Christians. The Gospels were written in Greek, not the local language of Aramaic spoken by Jesus and the naysayers. To even *learn* of the Jesus story in this community, our naysayers must speak Greek. How many could have done this? And to influence the Greek-speaking readers of the Gospels, a rebuttal would have to have been written in Greek—not a common skill in Palestine.

"Five: suppose you knew the actual Jesus, and you knew that he was merely a charismatic rabbi. Nothing supernatural. Now you hear the story of Jesus the Son of Man, the healer of lepers and raiser of the dead. Why connect the two? 'Jesus' was a common name. Your friend Jesus didn't do anything like this, so the story you heard must be of a different person. So even when confronted with the false teaching, you wouldn't raise an alarm."

"Six: consider how hard is it *today* for a politician or business leader to stop a false rumor, even with the press to get the word out. Think about how hard it would have been in first-century Palestine. How many thousands of Christians were out there spreading the word for every naysayer with his finger in the dike?"

Magic plant for protection, sword beats wand, Paul thought.

"Seven: you say that there were no naysayers, but how do we know that there weren't? For us to know about them, they would need to have written their story *and* have some mechanism to recopy the truth over and over until the present day. Just like Christian documents, their originals would have crumbled with time. What would motivate anyone to preserve copies of documents that argued against a religion? Perhaps only another religion! And it's not surprising that the Jesus-isn't-divine religion didn't catch on."

Jim let out a sigh. "That's a longer list than I expected. I hope you can see that naysayers could hardly be expected to stop Christianity."

"A lot to consider," Paul admitted. "But I still think the oral tradition preserves the truth."

"That's a poor rebuttal!" Paul looked away as Jim glowered at him and continued. "Think about it—you're smarter than this. I hold you to a higher standard, one that doesn't abide by sloppy thinking. Does God exist? If so, he gave you that mind to *use*. Your mind is an engine to be harnessed, not a vessel to be filled. You must be a truth seeker; don't blindly follow someone else's thinking."

A soft metallic clap came from the hallway. Paul appreciated the break in the scolding as Jim walked to the door. He returned holding a postcard, dropped it in a trash can, and stood over the chessboard.

"You must read awful fast," Paul said.

"It was a short message: 'Knight to king's bishop three.' I'm playing chess through the mail with an old friend from college. He still lives in Boston, so this will be a long game." He moved one of the white pieces. "Do you play chess?"

"I know the rules for how the pieces move, that's it," Paul said. "Do you know how you'll respond?"

"Yes. The early moves in a game are rather predictable, but still interesting. They're the foundation on which your position rests."

Jim gazed at the board a few moments, then slowly walked back to the sofa and sat. "Do you eat nuts every day?" He pushed a bowl of shelled almonds across the table toward Paul with a bare foot.

"Uh . . . no, not often."

"You should. Your body is a machine, and it needs lubrication. Nuts provide oils that are essential to good health."

"Well, thank you. I didn't realize that."

"And I suppose you eat meat."

"You don't?"

"I'm a vegetarian—I follow the Battle Creek Sanitarium diet. Whole grains, fruits, and vegetables. And lots of nuts. Nature provides all that we need to be healthy—no need to kill animals for us to live."

Paul said nothing as he wondered how to get this derailed train back on track.

"And do you enema?" Jim asked.

Paul assured him that he did not.

"You should, every day. And drink lots of water." Jim described in unnecessary detail how the colon works and the benefits of daily cleansing. "You'd be shocked at what comes out," he said.

Paul felt vaguely ill as he agreed.

Jim moved on to how to avoid mucus and the need to chew food so thoroughly that it slithered down the esophagus by itself, but this was mercifully interrupted by a knock on the door. "This should only take a moment," Jim said.

"Groceries," he said as he walked into the kitchen carrying a small wooden box. "I get a delivery every day."

Home delivery seemed to be an extravagance when there was a grocery store two blocks away. Paul mused that the rich lived quite differently than ordinary folk.

When he returned, Jim picked up his copy of the *Odyssey* as he sat and thankfully dropped the topic of healthy living. "Now, pretend that I'm someone who hasn't heard the amazing story of Odysseus and Circe and that you're eager to pass it along."

Paul said a little prayer as he slid to the edge of his chair. He gestured as he spoke. "Odysseus and his men walked into a strange land. Odysseus stayed behind and Eurylochus took the remaining twenty-two men to investigate. They found a witch named Circe in a house in a clearing, surrounded by wild animals that were actually tame. She invited them in for a banquet. All entered, but Eurylochus refused. One of the foods was a drug, and the men turned into pigs after they ate it."

"Go on," Jim said, his left index finger tracing the story in the open book.

"Eurylochus went back to Odysseus and reported what happened. Odysseus went to the house to free his men, and on the way he met Hermes, who gave him a magic drug to protect him. When he met the witch, they fought, Odysseus using his sword and Circe her wand. Odysseus won, and he forced her to release his men. She became nice—though I'm not sure why—and they stayed with her for a year."

"Not bad," Jim said. "The basic story is correct, but you changed a lot of details. First off, Odysseus and his men were sailors—they didn't come marching in overland."

"I didn't hear 'sailors.' "

"I said that they landed on the coast," Jim said, looking down at the book. "These are minor changes, but multiplied with the retelling, they soon turn into big changes. You forgot that they rested first . . . the party of men who went to the house was just part of Odysseus's crew, not all of it . . . you forgot the kinds of wild animals—lions and wolves . . . Eurylochus stayed outside, he didn't refuse to enter . . . you said one food was a drug, but I said 'the food was drugged' . . . the food didn't turn the crew into pigs, Circe did . . . the wild animals were also men . . . Odysseus and Circe didn't fight." Jim looked up. "Well, how do you think you did?"

"Okay, I guess. That's a lot to remember in a short time. But the early church was a web of interconnections. If one person is telling the story to a group, another person in the group may well have heard it before. He could correct any errors."

"Based on what?" Jim asked. "When I corrected your story just now, I was reading from a book—that's our authority. There was no book when the Jesus story was oral tradition. When two people's memories conflicted, whose was right?"

"There were scholars who memorized whole books of the Bible. They would have been an authority."

"Are you saying that the Jesus story went from scholar to scholar, with a student sworn to secrecy until he could flawlessly repeat the story? That's not how it was told." Jim gestured impatiently as if unable to contain his amazement at Paul's stupidity. "It was a dramatic and exciting yarn that went from fallible person to fallible person, just as stories do today. Society has changed since then, but the basics of storytelling haven't. When you see two women gossiping over the back fence, you're seeing something that hasn't changed in thousands of years."

Jim leaned back into the sofa, and his voice softened. "You did pretty well, but now imagine that the story was far longer, and you waited days instead of minutes to retell it. Such a story can change dramatically after decades of retelling over and over. What better explains the supernatural elements of the Jesus story—that they actually happened that way or that the story is legendary? Sure, the supernatural claims could be accurate, but why think that? You've got a long way to go to show that that's the best explanation." Jim grabbed a handful of nuts and ate them one by one. "I'd as soon believe that you could turn me into a pig with magic."

Paul felt emotionally drained. Empty. His intellectual arsenal was spent as well. He could only pray that Samuel had more ammunition.

Chapter 5

Pain met Thena as she slowly returned to consciousness. She opened her eyes expecting to be in her canopy bed with its colorful crazy quilt, to see the walls papered in blue acanthus leaf, and to have her mother hovering nearby.

Instead, she awoke alone in a small room lined with pale wood. Light filtered through moving leaves outside the window to scatter on the walls. She lay on a thin mattress on the floor. No bed, no wallpaper, no mother—just a small and plain wooden room. Though she was very sore in many places, her left leg hurt the most. She lifted up her blanket and patted the leg, wincing at the pain. A thick layer of cloth bandages wrapped the leg as far down as she could reach, and two sticks were bound into the wrappings, keeping the leg immobile. She groaned as she shifted to get more comfortable.

Footsteps outside creaked on the wooden floor, and a small man opened the door, bowed politely, and smiled. He wore a short gray robe that came to his knees. Under that he wore white leggings. He was perhaps thirty years old and seemed to be Chinese or Japanese, and he looked faintly familiar.

"Hello, please stay," he said in a clumsy accent before leaving, and Thena wondered groggily how she could do anything else. And wondered where she was. She touched vague, fuzzy memories of being crushed and unable to escape the approaching fire, and she recoiled as she had with her leg.

Thena heard returning footsteps. The small man brought an older man, also Oriental. A little taller and maybe sixty years old, this man walked with a confident grace. Their clothes were the same except that his robe was white.

"My name is Tanaka," he said. "This is Chiba." The small man bowed slightly and smiled as the older man continued. "You were trapped in a building in San Francisco. He is one of the men who rescued you yesterday." Tanaka's English was accented but excellent.

"Where am I?"

"This is the Daitoku-ji Buddhist monastery, just north of San Francisco. I am the abbot."

Thena pushed herself up on her elbows. "But why am I here?"

"The monks who found you tried to take you to a hospital. You would likely not have your leg if they had left you there. You are here to rest."

"My leg. . . ." Thena grimaced as she touched the bandages.

"Your leg is broken, but it should heal well. We will give you medicine to help the pain."

She looked around the room. "Where are my things? My clothes?"

"They rescued you, not your clothes. The hotel probably burned."

Thena looked down at the nightgown she wore, shocked at the loss, at the realization that this was all she had left of her best clothes. "But what about my clothes? They should not have left them. Your man can go back to get them."

"We are needed here."

This was harder than it should have been. "I would like to be taken to the San Francisco train station." She spoke slowly and plainly so there would be no confusion.

"You cannot travel with a broken leg. You may stay with us until it is healed."

Thena pushed her lip out slightly, looked directly at the abbot, and said a little louder, "But I want to go home. My father will pay you."

"We are needed here. We cannot take you." The abbot smiled. "We come from Japan and are far from home ourselves. Perhaps you have a purpose here just as we do." He turned and walked away. Thena realized her mouth was open and closed it. She couldn't remember when she had been talked to so abruptly, but by the time she had a response, he was gone.

Chiba knelt next to Thena, lifted the blanket, and inspected her bandage. She was horrified to realize that she wore only her nightgown, and she put her hands on her upper thighs to keep the nightgown in place. She rationalized that having this man see more of her than usual was tolerable because he was a servant.

Chiba seemed to care little for Western propriety. He unwrapped the bandage, and Thena's modesty was shoved aside by new pain and revulsion at the red gash in her leg. Rewrapped with a new dressing, the leg throbbed.

Over the next few days, Chiba tended Thena's injuries and brought her two meals a day. The meals were simple and repetitious but filling. She grew frustrated with Chiba's demonstration of the chopsticks and ate with her fingers, though he was eventually able to convince her to use them as a shovel. He gave her laudanum that dulled the pain but made her sleep a lot. He also gave her a monk's robe to wear. It was a man's outfit, but she reasoned that it was more dignified than the nightgown. A wooden chair had been fitted with a bedpan. Though she was familiar with chamber pots, she was accustomed to indoor toilets and looked down on those who made do without them.

Once a day, Chiba helped her get to the washroom down the hall. He demonstrated how a small square of cloth could be used as a washcloth or, wrung out, as a towel. Her leg prevented her from using a bath, but the improvised arrangement was a tiny but welcome element of civilization. Thena's hair combs were lost in the hotel, and she considered using clean chopsticks as a substitute to pin up her long brown hair but settled instead on twists and a tuck to hold it up.

She slept far more than usual and spent much of her waking time agonizing about her parents and Paul. What were they doing now? They must be worried sick. Did they know that she'd been rescued? And her aunt and uncle and all the wedding guests back in San Francisco—were they safe? She banished these thoughts with prayer as best she could.

So much had changed in her life. Her trip to San Francisco had begun two weeks earlier when she boarded a first-class train car in Los Angeles and waved goodbye to her parents and Paul. She had been planning this trip to the big city for some time. She was to be a bridesmaid in her cousin's wedding, but the fact that this was her first long-distance trip—and that she was making it on her own—was a step toward independence that thrilled her even more.

The wedding events proceeded as planned. Athena's aunt fretted about the flowers, the food, and the changeable spring weather while Athena made herself comfortable and socialized with the other young people. Pretty and popular back home in Los Angeles, she soon became an eddy in the stream of well-dressed guests.

A horse-drawn cab took her on her daily commute between her hotel and the event of the moment, with a spinster aunt as her chaperone. She would have been welcome to stay with her aunt and uncle, but other guests filled their small house. With the festivities finally over and the happy couple seen off on their honeymoon, Athena returned for a final night in the hotel and prepared for the return trip. Then the earthquake, and now this strange place.

At times the laudanum brought to mind bright and realistic images, and she often daydreamed. She thought back to when she and Paul were first courting. Clean-shaven and neatly dressed, he impressed her as a serious and pious man. She first saw him in church, and he had soon shown a shy interest in her. She worked in her father's general store, and Paul seemed to patronize it much more than necessary. He had a childlike wave that melted her heart. Eventually he became bold enough to ask her to social events. First, it was the weekly church suppers, and then it was walks through the neighborhood and parks.

After a few months, he told her how inadequate she made him feel and contrasted his own desperate early life with her high school education, finishing school, and middle-class life of privilege. He admitted his prior life as a criminal. But to her, his new responsibility in the church showed a serious frame of mind. She had known other boys, but they were shallow, and Paul's increasing stature within the church showed her an honest, hardworking, and moral man who had overcome his background.

They talked about everything—their past, their fears, their dreams, their faith. Paul was more intense about Christianity than Thena, and that was another attraction in her eyes. He said that they were like two jigsaw puzzle pieces that had been tried for a long time against many other pieces without success, only to find a perfect fit with each other. He told her, "Only God could have made such a match."

&

When Chiba was in the room to tend to Thena, she sometimes spoke to him simply for the pleasure of talking. Chiba's English skills limited his replies, and she played both roles in the conversation. "Don't you have any different food?" she might say, and then share her favorites. "Where are you from?" would be followed by a summary of her own past. "I'm bored," and then her pastimes. She wondered aloud if tending to her was a privilege or a punishment—was she a guest or an obligation? She heard people talking in nearby rooms, though she couldn't understand them and gave a prayer of gratitude that she had not been put with strangers.

On the fourth day, the abbot returned. "How are you feeling?" he asked.

Thena was lying on her mattress. "My leg hurts a lot. And the medicine makes me sleep."

"Yes, I understand. The pain should be better soon, and then you will need less medicine."

"Now see here," she said, sitting up. "I need someone to take me to the train station so I can go home. This man would be fine." She gestured to Chiba. "I have a family worried about me. My father will pay you." Thena had been taught that firm words were usually the best approach in situations like these.

The abbot studied her for a moment. He turned and walked toward the door, leaving with a short sentence in Japanese. Chiba bowed, took Thena's crutches from the corner, and helped her stand. With small painful steps and Chiba beside her, she hobbled out of the room. She had never been beyond the washroom—at least not while conscious. A few hallways later, she found herself in a large courtyard, more than large enough to hold an entire floor of Bullock's department store. The courtyard was full of people. Chiba eased her onto a bench in a sunny corner and walked away.

She wondered if they were getting a carriage. As she waited, she idled away her time watching the activity. It seemed rather like a small town square, with a wide assortment of people—young and old; parents and children; Japanese, Mexicans, and Americans. Monks served food in a corner, distinctive in their knee-length gray robes and white leggings. More were sprinkled through the crowd. She watched the people with increasing interest and curiosity.

The sun was beginning to get uncomfortably warm when whimpering from behind caught Thena's attention. She turned and saw a Mexican boy about three years old on the raised wooden walkway several feet behind her. His face was a dirty gray, and wetness from his eyes and nose had rinsed away small patches of dirt, showing his brown skin underneath. A tan diaper bulged out of the top of his ragged shorts, and he wore no shoes. Thena took one crutch, hobbled to the other side of the bench to see him better, and groaned as she sat. The laudanum was wearing off, and she ached all over.

"Mama," the boy said repeatedly, and he wiped one eye with the back of a filthy hand. He tottered unsteadily along, though Thena could see no obvious mother where he was headed. In fact, she was the only adult nearby. She watched the boy take a few more steps, suddenly realizing that he was at the edge of the walkway and more than a foot above the hard-packed ground.

Before she knew what she was doing, she stood, supported by her right leg, and caught the boy as he stepped over the edge. With the boy in her arms, she fell back hard onto the bench. He was heavier than she expected. Pain jolted through her bad leg, and she clenched her teeth to hold back a scream. She reopened her eyes to see the boy safe in her arms, but he had contorted his face in the buildup to crying.

"Don't cry, little fellow," she said as she hugged him and patted his back. "Don't cry." Her shushing held back the tears.

"Pedrito!" A woman's voice came from the left. Thena looked up and saw a brown woman with a long black braid running toward her on the walkway. She wore a floral print dress and was also barefoot. When she got to Thena, she scooped up the boy in her arms. Chattering in Spanish, she spoke first to the boy and then to Thena. Thena couldn't understand a word, but the way the mother kissed the boy and smiled at Thena, she must have been conveying an effusive "Thank you."

When they walked away, the mother waved the boy's hand and Thena waved back. Just then the abbot sat silently next to her.

"I didn't know about all these people," she said. "Why are they here?"

"Most are from nearby. Their homes are destroyed or unsafe from the earthquake. Or they are here because they are hungry. Many stores are out of food. Some became empty on the first day as people bought all they could carry."

"The stores can just get more."

"Not since the earthquake. We are remote, but we have still heard news from travelers. Railways are broken, and there is damage in San Francisco."

"How much damage?" Thena asked.

"We do not know. Some food is coming in to the city, but distant places like ours cannot expect help."

"Do you have food for all these people?"

"We depend on the generosity of others. Now it is our turn to give."

"But what if you don't have enough?"

"We share what we have. If we don't have enough, we will be hungry with our neighbors."

Thena pointed to the blankets and other belongings piled under the eaves. "Have they been sleeping out here since the earthquake?"

"Yes."

"But you should put them inside!"

"Inside is full of people. You, for example."

The words stung. "Well, what about that man?" Thena pointed to a wrinkled and bent old man sitting at the edge of the courtyard, one of the people she had stared at in fascination. He held a walking stick and surveyed the activity as she had. She had never seen anyone who looked as wrinkled and had no way to judge his age. Maybe . . . a hundred years? She said, "Can't you find somewhere for him?"

"He is a farmer who lives about an hour's walk from here. He prefers to stay outside."

"And them?" She pointed to two people under the eaves. She had noticed them when one vomited noisily onto the wooden floorboards. They still occasionally made disgusting noises. "Can nothing be done?"

"The earthquake broke many water pipes, and they became sick from drinking bad water. We gave them medicine. They will be well in time."

"And . . . what about that man?" She pointed to an old man lying in the shade but wouldn't look at him again. He had a blanket pulled up to his chest. His skin was pale, his head was tipped back, and his mouth was open. No one was around him, and he wasn't moving.

"He arrived here sick. The effort of traveling here may have been too hard. He died about an hour ago."

"But what are you doing about it? Something must be done!" Thena had never seen a dead person before. She'd heard of remote family members who had died, but the details of death had always been in some faraway city, some distant relative's problem.

"We are searching for his family, and we are preparing a funeral."

Thena took in the community with her hand. "Why didn't you tell me about all these people? I didn't know you had so much work." The abbot turned to her with a patient face, saying nothing.

After a long pause, she looked at the abbot and broke the silence. "I'm not going home today, am I?"

"We are needed here," he said. "We cannot take you."

She surveyed the different people in the courtyard—each one displaced and eager to return home, each one hurting, each one the same. She said to the abbot, "Can I help?"

ℐ

For the first time, Paul doubted. Samuel's apologetics weren't as ironclad as he had thought. He trudged from Jim's house back to the church, bypassing the trolley to give himself time to analyze the debate.

Jim was right that he had occasionally argued for his recollection of an event, only to be forced to admit later that he had remembered wrongly. And since he was fallible, why imagine that the authors of the Gospels were not? It did indeed seem far-fetched for a story to move orally through a community for decades without significant change. He kicked at a rock—he hated being wrong.

What did all this mean? Was it a serious obstacle? Samuel could help. But he found Samuel busy in his office, and that discussion would have to wait.

Later that afternoon, Paul left the church to visit Mrs. O'Brien, a devoted long-time parishioner. The church was a short walk from her house, but that distance had been increasingly isolating as her rheumatism had worsened. She lived alone, childless and a widow of three years. Solitude burdened the gregarious woman, and Samuel encouraged Paul to visit regularly. Visiting church members was an important and enjoyable part of Paul's job.

Mrs. O'Brien had married in Illinois, just after her husband-to-be had returned from service in the Union Army. Farming had drawn the young couple to California in 1868, but they soon moved on to open a successful shoe store in the new city of Los Angeles.

She always seemed genuinely appreciative of Paul's visits, and he enjoyed them as well. Sometimes they were even therapeutic. On an earlier visit, Paul had told of his childhood in the orphanage, and her honest sympathy emboldened him. "They wouldn't even give us cake on our birthdays—nothing to make one day any more special than another," he once told her. " 'Too expensive,' they said. 'That would teach the children to be greedy.' "

Mrs. O'Brien had looked as if she were hugging him with her expression. "There must have been some good people?"

"There were a few matrons who were patient and kind. But, of course, they could go home to their families. The good ones never stayed long. The only consistent support I ever received was from a storybook—one particular book."

Mrs. O'Brien's smile encouraged him to continue.

"It's childish, I realize," he said, suddenly aware that he had overcommitted himself. This was more personal than he was comfortable discussing, but he pushed on. "Someone read to me a story called *The Devoted Princess*. It was about a young princess who had a baby boy." He glanced briefly up to see Mrs. O'Brien's supportive expression and continued. "An ogre stole the baby and demanded a ransom to keep the boy safe, but each year the ogre increased his demand. This taxed the kingdom's treasury and, of course, the princess was worried over her son. After ten years, the demand was more than they had in the entire kingdom. The princess decided that the young prince must not be sacrificed to the ogre's greed, so she sneaked into the ogre's castle, poisoned the ogre, and freed her son. They returned home dragging huge bags of gold from the castle and lived happily ever after."

He looked up. "A silly little story—"

"No, that was the perfect story."

"Well, it was that fairy tale that drove me to learn to read. I read that book over and over, long after I'd memorized it, and then I moved to other books. Reading was my one success. I did poorly in school, but I read everything."

With the story out, his anxiety left him as well, and he felt safe enough to volunteer one more confidence. "I imagined my own mother worrying about me and wondered when she would rescue me. I would sit by the window, the book in my lap, imagining the day when she would walk up from the street. But she never did."

"Did you ever know your mother?"

"My earliest memories are of the orphanage."

Mrs. O'Brien's eyes were red and wet as she embraced him.

To the orphaned young man, Mrs. O'Brien was the caring grandmother he never had. But on this visit, with the fresh memory of his discussion with Jim, Paul was driven by more than devotion.

Paul sat with Mrs. O'Brien at the table on the small patio in the back. The house shaded them, and a light breeze carried the citrus smell from the lemon and orange trees in the backyard. Mrs. O'Brien always seemed dressed for an outing, ready for an invitation that could arrive at any moment. This time she wore a high-necked frilly pink dress. Her elbow-length puffy sleeves gave her an old-fashioned look.

"I picked the lemons this morning," she said, gesturing to her pitcher of lemonade.

Paul was not clever at small talk but was a patient listener, and that seemed to suit Mrs. O'Brien. She began with a commentary on her small orchard's growing season, as concerned and protective as a mother discussing the ups and downs of her third grade child's school year. Paul poured two glasses of lemonade. A chunk of ice rattled in the pitcher as lemon slices danced out of its way.

The agricultural report complete, Mrs. O'Brien moved on to the gossip pages, updating Paul on the neighbors with her critique of their activities. She dismissed one neighbor's occupation and concluded, "That's just an excuse to avoid a real job, if you ask me." She turned to Paul and patted his hand. "Not like you. Everyone knows what a hard worker you are."

Paul smiled and pulled his hand into his lap.

Mrs. O'Brien moved on to tell how Teddy Roosevelt should be running the country when Paul cleared his throat.

"Mrs. O'Brien," he said and paused to be sure he could take a turn. "You've been part of the church for a long time, haven't you?"

"Of course, dear. Henry and I were some of the first members. Reverend Hargrove started the church in the fall of . . . it must have been '82."

"But you knew Reverend Hargrove before."

"That's right. We were all in the same church for years before then, the Trinity Methodist Episcopal Church. It was rather like our church now, though he wasn't in charge back then. Samuel was such a precocious young man—so energetic, and so filled with the Holy Spirit. He always seemed bursting to tell you about it." She smiled and leaned an arm against the edge of the table as she reached for her lemonade.

Paul said, "I wanted to ask you about someone—someone you may have known back then. Did you know Jim Emerson?"

Mrs. O'Brien's posture straightened. "What do you know about him?" she asked and turned to face Paul.

"Not much, really," he said, his hands waving away any contrary notion. "I've met him recently. I've been trying to evangelize to him, and I was surprised when he said that he and Reverend Hargrove knew each other."

"Oh, they knew each other. That man was a member of our church. He and Samuel were friends for a while, but there was girl trouble, if you know what I mean." She turned slowly to look at her orchard.

"She hurt Samuel," she said finally. "I never forgave her for that. I don't think anyone did. Her name was Jenny, and she was also in the church. I suppose she was pretty, in a plain sort of way. Samuel and that typewriter salesman were both stuck on her, though I never thought much of her. She was too willful, too headstrong."

She turned back to Paul. "Anyway, one day she and that typewriter salesman were out of the church—expelled. I never saw either of them again. I told Samuel that she would never have made a good preacher's wife, and I think that was a comfort to him."

She leaned toward Paul with her voice lowered. "Everyone knew she was in a family way, and that wicked Jim Emerson was the father!"

℠

Paul walked slowly home late that afternoon, hands deep in his pockets. Getting a girl pregnant—Jim was quite a rogue. He thought of Thena, pure and innocent Thena, and he couldn't imagine forcing her through that humiliation. Had Jim then discarded Jenny after she became inconvenient, with her reputation ruined?

But the conversation with Mrs. O'Brien also meant that he needed to reevaluate Samuel. If Jim and Samuel knew each other decades before, finding Jim must have been Samuel's goal. Why had he not made that clear from the beginning? Had Samuel been pulling his strings to maneuver him into debating with Jim? Why the secrecy?

The next morning, Paul found Samuel in his office writing.

"I'm following up on a request from a big Chicago newspaper," he said, tapping a telegram. "They're doing a story on the church."

Samuel picked up a large roll of paper from the floor. "And look at this." He stood and spread the stack of sheets across the great desk. The top sheet had a background of mottled blue—majestic in some places and pale in others. Strong white lines showed the skeleton of a building, and the paper gave off a slight smell of ammonia. "It's a blueprint for our new church." Samuel stroked his mustache.

"New church?"

"God's hand is plain. Church membership has jumped by thirty percent, and four times as many people attend services now compared to before the prophecy. We finally have the income to fulfill our dream. Our little barn is bursting, and it's time we moved up. I'm negotiating to buy a piece of land on Garey Street, a fifteen-minute walk away, so we'll still be the neighborhood church for our members."

"It seems sudden."

"God has acted boldly, and we must fall in behind Him. I just got these today." Samuel poked at the blueprint to point out the various features of the design—its stone foundation, wooden walls with stained glass windows, a huge arched ceiling like an inverted boat, and massive wooden doors behind thick stone pillars.

"It's huge," Paul said.

"Only from our cramped perspective." Samuel rolled up the drawings and returned to his chair. "I'm giving this to the church elders this afternoon, and I'll announce it to the congregation on Sunday. We'll need to begin a fundraising program."

That explained Samuel's request that Mrs. Bradshaw donate. Paul dropped into his chair. The new building was an exciting project, though far more ambitious than he could have conceived. Was this a lesson? Perhaps he needed to be more aware of clues to God's wishes, like Samuel.

"I wanted to ask you," Paul began, flipping his note card over and over. "I understand from Mr. Emerson that you and he knew each other long ago. I wonder—was it just a coincidence that you asked me to focus on him, or did you know who he was?"

"Sure, I knew who he was from your description."

"I was a little surprised that you didn't tell me that."

"You didn't need to know," Samuel said with a hard look, leaning back into his chair. He studied Paul for a moment and said, "I'll tell you a story. This must have happened forty years ago. A prospector was crossing the Mojave Desert about eighty miles east of here. He was out of water and desperately thirsty when he saw a hand pump with a note attached. The note said, 'This pump must be primed to work. If you start pumping now, you won't get water—you'll just get tired. Under the white rock is a jar of water. Pour half of the water into the top of the pump, and wait five minutes to let the leather valve soak. Then dump in the rest and pump hard. You'll get plenty of water. Take what you need, then fill up the jar and put it back under the rock for the next fellow.' So what do you think the prospector did—drink the little water in the jar or trust the pump?"

Samuel paused, eyebrows raised. "He followed his instructions, the pump worked as promised, and he got all the water he needed and more. In the same way, I trust the Lord to guide my hand, and you trust me. And you see that it all works out."

"But don't I deserve your confidence?"

"You're the apprentice here, not the master," Samuel said, his voice now severe. After a pause, he continued in a gentler voice. "Anyway, there's very little to tell. Mr. Emerson and I attended the same church a long time ago. I believe he was from Boston. He had a fancy college attitude, and he wasn't an especially good fit for the church. We did a little debating back and forth. He seemed to delight in taking the atheist position, just for fun. I suppose I have a debt to him because it was those conversations that showed me the need for the apologetics ministry I've built here."

"How did you know where to find him?"

"I didn't. I thought he might still be in town, but I didn't know where—he's something of a hermit. He's not in the telephone directory. I wanted you to find him, and I knew he'd make an excellent project for you. And it wouldn't hurt to add a wealthy man to our congregation. Does that satisfy you?"

Paul nodded. "Yes, sir."

"Trust, my boy."

Paul wondered what more Samuel could tell him of the Jim/Jenny relationship. Mrs. O'Brien's story was reliable, of course, but he was curious to learn more. But no—this would be simply wallowing in gossip.

Samuel put the blueprints on the floor. "Now, you're off to see him again today, right? Tell me how it went last time."

"Oh, pretty well." Paul was accustomed to Samuel's interrogations. Since his first anxious trip into local neighborhoods a month before, Samuel had insisted on hearing the details of each of Paul's encounters, and Paul had been eager to comply. With his years of experience, Samuel spotted errors and found ways to improve the arguments that Paul would never have figured out on his own. But this time he felt overwhelmed. His arguments had left no more impact on Jim than arrows on armor.

"He said that if the Gospels were wrong, there would have been very few naysayers, and that they wouldn't have been able to stop the Jesus story," Paul said.

"Ridiculous!" Samuel shouted. "It's simply common sense. I hope you told him so."

"Oh yes." Paul consulted his notes. "And . . . he said that the Gospels weren't written by eyewitnesses."

"The very names of the books are those of Jesus's closest companions! I'm really not impressed by the depth of this man's thinking. Did you point out that the memory skills of the people of that time far outshone our own?"

"He wanted to do an experiment. He read a passage from the *Odyssey* and asked me to repeat it a few minutes later."

"But you had no time to memorize it. And no one was there to correct any mistakes. I hope you told him that."

"Yes I did," Paul said, pleased that he could give one answer with confidence. "But my arguments weren't very effective." He glanced up at Samuel, who was scowling.

"Practice," Samuel snapped. "That's what you need."

"I think I know the arguments well—"

"The arguments aren't at fault! I know because I've used them myself, for years. And theologians have used them before me, for centuries."

Paul stared at his notes, unseeing. "Yes, I'm sure you're right. I'll practice more." He looked up at Samuel's stern face, and then he looked back down and repositioned himself in his chair.

After the uncomfortable penalty of silence that Paul had expected, Samuel continued his critique of the last battle. He insisted that various points be made, while Paul struggled to portray his performance in the best light.

"Don't be too polite about this," Samuel concluded. "Don't avoid saying what needs to be said because it might be unwelcome or even rude. The Word gets top priority.

"Now, let's talk about today. I want you to bring up Pascal's Wager. This was proposed by a Frenchman named Pascal who was a scientist and mathematician during the seventeenth century. He should be someone Mr. Emerson can respect."

Paul took a clean note card from his pocket and readied his pencil.

"Pascal concluded that it simply makes sense to bet that God exists. If you assume that God exists and live your life accordingly, and you're right, you go to heaven. If God doesn't exist, then nothing is lost. But if you're an atheist and you bet wrong, you go to hell. The enormous consequences of heaven and hell mean that you must bet correctly."

Paul nodded in recognition of a familiar apologetic. He couldn't have worked with Samuel for these two years without hearing these arguments, but now he would be using this one himself.

Samuel said that this had been effective in converting many people. He had Paul practice his pitch several times and added his corrections. Finally satisfied, Samuel said to Paul as he walked out the door, "Practice. Remember that it's simply foolish to bet against God. A man's immortal soul sits in the balance."

℘

"Come!"

Paul found Jim where he always seemed to be, in the library at the end of the hall, but this time the clutter on the floor was not from books but from a pile of machine parts arranged on a towel stained with grease.

Jim sat on the floor at one end of the towel, a compact dark lump in one hand and a screwdriver in the other. "Just fixing this fan," he said. "The weather's getting hot, and this thing needs cleaning." He gestured at the parts.

Paul saw that it was indeed a table fan as he noticed a two-bladed brass propeller and a wire cage.

"Playing with new machinery is an obsession of mine. I'm used to steam power and levers and I still find electricity a little miraculous, although I use electricity in the project I'm working on." He gestured at the light fixture in the ceiling. "I got electric lights about ten years ago. And I couldn't live without my fans."

He ticked the metal lump with the screwdriver. "This one's a changeover. It was originally direct current, and I had to replace the motor when Edison Electric finally switched to alternating current."

Paul had no idea what he was talking about. "I'm sorry to interrupt."

"That's fine—we can talk while I finish." Jim gestured for him to sit in his usual chair. "What's today's subject?"

"Well, before we begin, I thought a change of scenery might be nice. It's a bit hot inside—how about a walk?"

"The fan will be working soon."

"Let's go out. A change in scenery might be nice?"

"No." Jim's voice was louder than seemed necessary. "I'm not leaving." He looked down at his work.

This was clearly an argument worth abandoning. Paul cleared his throat and began. "Okay, I'm sure you'll agree that you possess only a tiny fraction of all knowledge."

"Of course."

"Then isn't it possible that there is compelling evidence that God exists, but you just don't know it? Doesn't this throw great doubt on your belief that God doesn't exist?"

"Great doubt? Hardly," Jim said as he strung the power cord through the fan's base. "I'm also not certain that leprechauns don't exist. No good evidence argues that they do exist, so I assume they don't. By this logic, I also think God doesn't exist. Give me the information that would convince me otherwise. If he exists, that fact is apparently not well publicized or not convincing."

"Evidence for God's existence is both well publicized *and* convincing," Paul said. "The Bible tells us, 'Since the creation of the world, God's invisible qualities have been clearly seen, so that men are without excuse.' "

"How can his invisible qualities be *seen?*"

"What I mean is, the majority of your fellow citizens believe in God."

"And the majority of *people* don't. The preponderance of evidence says that there is no God, so that's what I believe. That's what I *must* believe. If I stumbled across new information that showed my position was wrong, I should indeed change it."

Jim mounted the motor on its base. "You raise a dangerous challenge. Turn it around: given the tiny fraction of all knowledge that *you* possess, how can you reject the hundreds of belief systems that exist today and have existed through history? Aren't you concerned about being a bad Muslim? You don't want to spend eternity in Muslim hell. Or a bad Buddhist? I've seen pictures of the hell of Tibetan Buddhism, and you don't want to go there either.

"We're *both* atheists. We agree that the thousands of gods in history are fiction, with the single exception of the Christian god—you think that particular god, out of all the others, actually exists. I rejected the Christian god with much more deliberation than you used when you rejected all the others. If you think that I'm obliged to consider Christianity's claims, surely you're obliged to consider the claims of the other religions."

Paul said, "I consult my feelings and know the Christian path to be the true one. Faith is believing what you know in your heart to be true."

"That's something a believer from any tradition could say. What religion would you claim if you grew up in Egypt or Morocco or the Ottoman Empire? If you were of a spiritual bent, you would almost surely be a Muslim. You'd be a Hindu if raised in certain parts of India, a Confucian in China, and so on. Were you just extraordinarily lucky to have been born in a place and time in which the correct religion happened to be dominant?"

Jim poked his screwdriver toward Paul. "Why are you a Christian? Not because Christianity is the truth. It's simply because you were raised in a Christian community. It's the same with language—you speak English because you were born in America. You didn't evaluate the world's languages and rationally decide which one to speak—it was a decision made for you by society. You're simply a product of your culture."

Paul squeezed his hands into a fist so hard that he could feel his fingernails digging into his palms. "Then how do you explain the hundreds of millions of Christians? Christianity is the most popular religion the world has ever seen."

"Truth is not a goddamn popularity contest." Jim slashed with the screwdriver to punctuate his words like a manic orchestra conductor. "*Some* religion will be the most popular—does that make it the correct one? And how do you explain the hundreds of millions of Muslims? Or Hindus? Or any of the other religions that have been around for centuries and seem to satisfy the spiritual needs of their adherents? Is it delusion? Superstition? Custom? Indoctrination? However you explain the success of those religions should answer your question about why Christians believe. Look at the new variants of Christianity that have sprouted in this country in just the last century—Mormonism, Christian Science, Seventh-day Adventists, Jehovah's Witnesses. Why is your flavor of Christianity not invented just like these were?"

Sweat tickled Paul's skin as it ran down his sides. He couldn't control this slippery conversation. *Now would be a good time to help, God,* he thought as he launched into Samuel's approach to Pascal's Wager.

"All right, let's think of this like a bet," he began, "the most important bet imaginable. Suppose your concerns are correct and there were just one chance in a hundred that Christianity is correct. Let's suppose the time, energy, and money you would invest in the church amounts to ten thousand dollars over your lifetime. For it to be an even bet, the return on a win—Christianity being true—must be a hundred times your expense, or a million dollars. That is, you wager ten thousand dollars for a one-in-a-hundred chance to win a million dollars. Would you say that that's a fair bet?"

"Yes, that's a fair bet," Jim said, smiling.

"But wouldn't you also say that the prize of eternal bliss instead of torment is much more valuable than a million dollars? Doesn't that make betting on Christianity the obvious choice?"

"Sam and I came up with that argument on our own. We were quite pleased with ourselves—only later did I discover that Pascal had beaten us by 250 years." Jim wiped his hands with a rag as he stood and walked to the bureau holding the chessboard. "I don't know about Sam, but I've thought quite a bit about these arguments over the years. What seemed very compelling to us long ago has a lot of holes under close examination. If all you've got is Sam's arguments from twenty-five years ago, then I'm afraid he hasn't armed you very well." He pulled open a wide drawer, poked through its clutter for a few moments, and returned to the sofa with a deck of cards. The low table in front of the sofa held several open books, which Jim closed and dropped with a thump on the blue and white Oriental rug.

"Since we're talking about betting, let's simulate your argument with cards," Jim said, as he held the cards face down in one hand and fanned them with the other. "What card shall we use to represent the Christian jackpot?"

Paul groped for a symbol, and the image of the princess mother from the fairy tale came to mind. "How about . . . the queen of hearts."

"Okay, and let's improve your odds. Let's say that you must pay just a thousand dollars for the privilege of picking a card, but if you pick the queen of hearts, you get a million dollars. That's about what you're saying, right?"

"Sure."

"But is that really analogous to our situation?" Jim turned the cards over and leafed through them until he found the queen of hearts. He put that card face up on the sofa beside him and fanned the remaining cards as before, offering them face down to Paul. "How about now? Would you pay a thousand dollars to play now?"

"Of course not," Paul said. "There's no chance of winning."

"Right. So which game are we playing—the one with the winning card in the pack or the one with no winning card?" Jim looked at Paul for a moment before slapping the cards onto the table. "There's no winning card here! Show me why that's not completely analogous to your wager. If you said that you worshipped the sun, at least I could know that what you worshipped actually existed. And this wager applies to you as well. You can't offer this wager to me without making a similar bet yourself with a thousand other religions."

Jim returned to sit on the floor in front of the fan and pushed the blades onto the motor shaft. "Another thing: I can't *choose* to believe. I won't pretend to believe either—I don't respect hypocrisy, and if God exists, he doesn't either. I can't choose to believe in God or Jesus just like you can't choose to believe in Zeus or Hercules. Christians seem to imagine faith in Jesus like a plate of sandwiches passed around at supper—I can take or not as I choose. But belief doesn't work that way, so don't imagine that your religion has provided eternal salvation for the taking."

"But what if I'm right?" Paul asked.

"And what if *I'm* right? Then you will have missed seeing your life for what it truly is—not a test to see if you correctly dance to the tune of an empty set of traditions; not a shell of a life, with real life waiting for you in the hereafter; not drudgery to be endured or penance paid while you bide your time for your reward. But rather the one chance you have at reality. We can argue about whether heaven exists, but one thing we do know is that we get one life here on earth. A too-short life, no matter how long you live, that you can spend wisely or foolishly. Where you can walk in a meadow on a warm spring day, and laugh and learn, and do good things and feel good for having done them. Where you can strive to leave the world a little better than you found it. Where you can play with children, and teach someone, and love."

Jim gestured with increasing vigor until he sprang from the floor and paced like a preacher, looking at Paul as he did so. "There's simply no reason to imagine that there's a beneficent Father in the sky to lean on, to take care of us, to clean up our mistakes—the evidence says that we're on our own. That reality can be sobering, but it's also empowering. We're the caretakers of the world, and if we blunder, we pay the price. But if we create a better world, then we and our descendants get to enjoy it. This is no hollow philosophy. It's joyous and empowering—and it's reality. I would rather live in reality than in a delusion, no matter how delightful. I don't want my mind clouded by superstition just like I don't want it clouded by opium. And making the most of today is better than living for an imaginary tomorrow in heaven." Jim stared at him with his hands on his hips.

"Well. . . ." Paul stared at his note card, looking for his next move. "Well, let me ask you this: what would you say if you died and found yourself standing in judgment before God?"

"I would say that I followed reason, not faith," Jim said as he walked back to the towel and set the brass cage in place around the blades. "That I didn't allow superstition to govern me and saw no sin in being intellectually honest. That I tried to lead an ethical life driven solely by my love of my fellow man, not by fear of punishment or desire for reward in the afterlife. And what about you? If there is a God, maybe he will say to you, 'You had no evidence to believe and yet you did. Is that what I gave you brains for—to follow the crowd? You had a powerful tool that you didn't use. I gave you brains for you to *think*.'"

Jim set the rebuilt fan on the floor next to the bureau. He plugged it in and the blades swung into motion with a hum, sending a cool breeze across the room.

"Remember the story of Jack and the Beanstalk?" Jim asked as he returned to the sofa, wiping his hands. "Jack sells the family cow for five magic beans. His mother throws out the beans and scolds the boy. But the next day they find an enormous beanstalk. Jack climbs up, finds an evil giant, takes all his treasure, and kills him—a happy ending."

He threw the rag onto the center table. "But is this good advice? Should we all be like Jack? Would you recommend that someone trade his most valuable possession for some magical something, with no proof?"

"But look at what happened," Paul said. "Jack made the bet and won. He took the leap of faith, and things worked out well for him."

"It's a *story!* It's just pretend. Is Christianity compelling in the same way—because it's also a story?" Jim jabbed his finger in the air to punctuate his words. "You should not . . . take your life lessons . . . from a fairy tale. You should not trade a cow for 'magic' beans, and you shouldn't trade away *your* most valuable possession, your life, on a mythical claim without evidence."

"My life isn't my most valuable possession—my soul is."

"Show me that your soul is any more real than magic beans and I'll see your point."

Chapter 6

Thena sat on the floor in a corner of the monastery kitchen removing the bones from dried fish held in two large wooden bowls. Sitting didn't hurt much, and, clumsy though her bandaged leg was, she was grateful that it was almost free of pain. Her leg limited the kind of work she could do, but in the two weeks since she had arrived, she had become fairly dexterous at preparing vegetables and dried fish for her new community.

Staying busy occupied her mind. She accepted the fact that she wasn't going home soon, but she thought frequently about her parents and Paul and wished she could get word to them that she was safe. The monastery was still full of refugees, and the monks were busy tending them. They could neither get her to a train station nor carry a message to a telegraph office. Once people began to leave, she would send a letter with one of them.

She looked up from her work. Five monks were preparing the afternoon meal, and Thena enjoyed watching their precise movement. The big iron stove seemed to be constantly burning, cooking food or heating water, and the kitchen was always warm and busy. She wore her monk robe and had braided her hair, finding that more practical than trying to keep it pinned up. Comparing her one bandaged leg, wrapped in tan fabric, to her good leg, covered in the white leggings of the monks, she amused herself to imagine that she looked like half a monk.

As she worked, Chiba came up to her with his usual smile and said, "Come, please." He put her bowls of fish on the table as she got to her feet. Chiba was still her guide through this curious Buddhist world, and she followed him to the abbot's small office. He bowed to the abbot and left.

"Hello, Athena," he said. She had told him her nickname several times, but he never used it. Only when in trouble with her parents had she heard her proper name before, but it seemed to make sense in the formality of the monastery.

"Hello, Teacher," she said and tipped her head as much as her crutch allowed. She took the stool he indicated. The abbot sat at a desk with writing tools arranged neatly to the side—two brushes on a jade rest, an ink stick, an ink stone to hold the ink, and paper. A tiny black metal teapot sat next to an empty handleless cup. The desk and chairs looked homemade but sturdy, and she wondered what other parts of the monastery were built by the monks themselves. Trees swayed outside the window, making a kaleidoscope of shadows on the wall.

"I think you do not have enough to occupy your mind," the abbot said. Always active but never rushed, he usually got to the point immediately. "We have a small library," he said, indicating the packed bookshelf on the wall opposite the window. "You may read any book here."

Athena took up her crutch and walked closer. One section held Japanese books, but fully half of the books were in English, perhaps a hundred or more. This contrasted with her own church, which contained no books except Bibles and hymnals. The exception was Reverend Hargrove's office. She had peeked in once and had seen a bookcase with a modest number of books neatly arranged, but Paul had said that he never consulted any but a small stack of apologetics books.

In addition to the large number of books on the abbot's shelves, she was also surprised that they were on a wide variety of subjects—not just Buddhism but literature and art, as well as a survey of the world's great religions, including Christianity, Hinduism, Judaism, Islam, and a few religions that she had never heard of.

There were several Bibles, and he walked over and selected one. "You said that you are a Christian. Perhaps this will comfort you."

"Actually, I've read very little of the Bible," Athena said. "But I've been hoping to," she added quickly.

"Perhaps when you have much free time?" He smiled and held the book out to her.

Athena returned to her small room and found her new roommates absent. She had asked that her room be used to help with the people sleeping outside under the eaves, and she now shared it with a woman and her three-year-old daughter. The woman spoke only Spanish, and

Athena never discovered her history or what happened to her husband. They cheerfully got through their few communication tasks with pantomime plus the few words each knew of the other's language. Though living conditions had become more chaotic than before, Athena could usually find a quiet place during the day when her kitchen duties left her some free time.

For the past few years, Athena had tried to carry her Bible with her, though that Bible was now entombed in the rubble of San Francisco. She thought this might make her more pious or at least give that impression. But in truth, her Bible was more amulet than book, no more significant to her than the cross around her neck, and the only verses she knew were those that had been taught to her. Before being trapped in the hotel, she had never prayed for anything more profound than a new dress—she had never had a reason to.

She sat in her room and opened the Bible to the first verse in Genesis. The archaic style made the reading slow going, but she was fascinated to encounter so many stories that she had heard before: Adam and Eve, the Garden of Eden, Cain and Abel, Noah and the Flood, Abraham and Isaac, Sodom and Gomorrah.

Questions came to mind as she studied the Bible. It made many demands about food—an ibex was fine to eat, but rabbit was unclean, for example. But where was the concern for clean water? Athena had lived through major upgrades to the Los Angeles water and sewer systems and had heard stories of city life before clean water. It would have been simple for the Bible to include some healthy rituals such as "ye shall not discard wash water into a stream" or "dig your privy fifty cubits from your water source to keep it pure" or "boil your drinking water to avoid sickness." Wouldn't those have saved thousands of lives? And why was there no recipe for something as simple as soap? Was Mankind disobedient for inventing it? Or for delivering clean water with modern plumbing? Or for inventing medicine?

The Bible's authors didn't know that the earth moves around the sun (and not the other way around) and that the earth's rotation makes day and night, or at least the Bible didn't show this. She wondered if *any* truth of modern science came first from the Bible. Were the fanciful stories like polar bears and penguins getting to the Middle East to board Noah's Ark intended to be just that—stories, like Aesop's fables?

Reverend Hargrove said that the earth was just 6,000 years old, but she knew that science said that it was much older. When science contradicts the Bible, which one prevails?

Athena knew of another man within the monastery who might help. Father Mondegreen was a Catholic priest whose adobe church had collapsed in the earthquake. His flock had come to the monastery for food and shelter, and he had followed.

Two days earlier on Sunday, he had held a Catholic service in a corner of the courtyard. Athena was curious about the service and watched from under the eaves. There were no pews, and everyone stood. Worse, rain began halfway through the service. Father Mondegreen, wearing his colorful vestments, ignored the rain and persevered, partly shielded by a parishioner's umbrella. His congregation gradually dissolved away to watch from the dry periphery, leaving him to finish alone, shouting his florid Latin message over the sizzling sound of rain on mud.

The sun had returned and the mud dried when Athena knocked on Father Mondegreen's door. She carried her Bible.

"Yes, enter," came a frail voice.

She pushed open the door. The room was little larger than hers. Two large trunks formed a table against the right wall, a neatly made bed lay against the left wall, and the priest sat at a desk under a window. Assorted church clutter—large brass candlesticks, an embroidered wall hanging with a stained-glass design, books, clerical clothes, and so on—filled a corner next to the trunks.

Father Mondegreen turned to face her. He looked sixty or seventy years old, thin and gray. He wore a long black robe, and a broad-brimmed parson's hat with tassels sat on the desk.

"I'm Athena Farber. I'm not Catholic, but I was hoping to talk to you about the Bible."

"Yes, my child. What do you want to know?"

Athena took the chair he indicated and summarized the Bible's odd stance on food and water—obsessing over the ceremonial purity of one but ignoring the safety of the other—and asked what he thought of it.

"What an extraordinary question from a young lady." He moved gingerly, as if spending his energy carefully. "Why do you want to know that? That's my job."

"I've started reading the Bible," she caught herself and worried that she might be crossing a boundary, "and, well, some of the rules seem a bit severe."

"One really must be trained to interpret the Bible. If it had been my decision, the Bible would never have been translated into English. There are better ways for women to serve the Lord than fretting over biblical hermeneutics."

His reluctance to discuss the Bible and his vague condescension surprised her, and her project to understand the Bible suddenly seemed inappropriate and overwhelming and perhaps even rebellious. "I apologize for disturbing you," she whispered as she stood.

Athena returned her Bible to her room and hobbled slowly to the kitchen to find work to keep her busy. She wanted something to occupy her mind. But as she peeled vegetables in the corner, she mentally kneaded the conversation with the priest. Was it appropriate for the average person to study the Bible? Was she crossing the line, as a woman, to ask these questions? Two bowls of peeled parsnips later, she decided that she must stay the course.

The next day, Athena returned to her reading and began thinking about morals. Was there one fundamental set of absolute morals that applied to everyone at all times? That was the message from the Ten Commandments. Yet even they didn't seem fundamental. Why did the Ten Commandments have room for "thou shalt not covet" but not "thou shalt keep no slaves"? Slavery was acceptable in the Bible but not in America. Half of the old men in the church had fought in the Civil War, which had been, in part, over slavery. Why did Mankind have to battle this out when the answer could have painlessly come from God?

The Israelites felt it immoral that they were held as slaves in Egypt, but why was it then moral for them to enslave other people when they reconquered Canaan? Slavery in Israel was so commonplace that it was even regulated. And why was it moral to kill so ruthlessly? In the cities that resisted the Israelite invasion, Deuteronomy said, "Thou shalt save alive nothing that breatheth, but thou shalt utterly destroy them." What had those tribes, including the children and babies, done to deserve slaughter? She could find nothing except that they happened to belong to the wrong tribe.

Even people whom the Israelites allowed to live didn't have a pleasant life. In Numbers she read, "Now therefore kill every male among the little ones, and kill every woman that hath known man by lying with him. But all the women children that have not known a man by lying with him, keep alive for yourselves." So the virgins were merely property? She imagined herself in that situation. If Father Mondegreen didn't want women to read these kinds of verses, she could understand why.

The second of the Ten Commandments talked about "punishing the children for the sin of the fathers to the third and fourth generation." Is that moral—to punish someone for the crime of an ancestor? The punishment for violating almost all of the Commandments was death. She wondered if morals were relative, and something could be moral in biblical times but immoral now. The alternative was unthinkable—that the biblical conditions were actually the moral ones, meaning that keeping slaves, treating women as property, and punishing someone for a crime they didn't commit were moral now.

Athena decided that she would try Father Mondegreen one more time. Two days after her first encounter, she stoked her courage and knocked on his door again.

"Father Mondegreen?" she said as she opened his door. "It's Athena. I was hoping we could talk again."

"Certainly, child. Come in." His face held an element of sadness, and he motioned for her to take a chair next to his desk.

"I was sorry to see rain ruin your service on Sunday," she said.

His face brightened. "Yes, the conditions are frustratingly primitive here. I asked Mr. Tanaka if we could hold the service in his meeting hall, but he refused."

"I think it's a Buddhist temple."

"I don't care what it is. Don't they realize this is a Christian country? And that they are guests here?"

Athena owed her life to these "guests" and tried to refocus the conversation. "I was hoping we could talk about the Bible. Perhaps you could teach me a little of how you interpret it."

"We can try."

She took a deep breath and summarized the moral questions that worried her as she read the first few books of the Bible. She tried to keep the summary brief, but the concerns kept spilling out—how women were treated, polygamy, slavery, the savage conquest of Palestine.

Father Mondegreen was silent for many long seconds. This seemed a natural consequence of his deliberate style. "In the Gospel of Luke, Jesus says 'I thank thee, O Father that thou hast hid these things from the wise and prudent, and hast revealed them unto babes.' The Bible itself tells us that it is difficult to understand; indeed, it *celebrates* that fact."

"Do you use the verses that I mentioned in your sermons?"

"Of course not—why trouble people unnecessarily?"

"But aren't all verses valid? Don't they all have lessons?"

"Not lessons that I want to convey. I'm the Lord's shepherd, and a wolf running through the flock is not helpful. You mustn't think so much—a great deal of the Bible applies to a different time and culture."

"Then why are those books still in the Bible?"

"Because the Bible has timeless wisdom."

Athena paused to understand what the priest was saying. "So a person must just believe because you say so?"

"I've been trained in interpreting the Bible, and ordinary people have not. I have the church's wisdom, and it's my job to give it to people like you who need it."

It was clear where Athena stood in Father Mondegreen's hierarchy. She excused herself from the conversation, the first time she had ever discarded the advice of a spiritual leader.

Father Mondegreen had not been helpful, and a few days later, she tried the abbot. "Christianity is a religion of love," she said as she sat in his office. "But I don't know how to square what I've been told with what the Bible actually says."

"The Bible contains more than love, as you have seen. Many Christians have not read the Bible. Deciding for yourself is a necessary step. I could tell you that the Bible came from a god or that it didn't, but that would not satisfy you. More study may give you the answers."

"Have you read the Bible?" she asked.

The abbot nodded.

"But why? You're a Buddhist."

"I read Christian literature for the same reason that you should know something about Buddhist or Muslim or Hindu literature. I seek the truth. But few people do this.

"Let me tell you a story. In some parts of Asia, hunters build an unusual monkey trap. They hollow out a coconut and tie it to the ground, then they put rice in the coconut. The monkey can reach in through a hole and grab the rice, but the hole is carefully cut so that it is big enough for the monkey's empty hand to go in but too small for his fist to come out, full of rice. When the hunters come, the monkey refuses to release the rice, and he is stuck. He traps himself."

Athena nodded and the abbot continued. "Preconceptions are like the rice. They are attractive, but we must let go to find the truth. To release what we were taught as children can be frightening, but it is the path to wisdom. If the lessons from childhood are true, we will find them again. And we will be more certain about them when we uncover them ourselves rather than when we take them because someone told us to."

No one had given her this before—more than information, it was permission. Maybe no one had trusted her to take this odyssey. "How should I proceed?"

"Do what you are doing—read and think. My answers won't be your answers. Just remember that you are on an important journey."

⅋

Paul settled into his usual chair in Jim's living room for another chat.

"You've provided a few discussion topics," Jim said from his sofa. "Now let me offer one. Have you thought much about how prayer works?"

"The Bible tells us how: 'Ask and ye shall receive.' "

"Does it really work that way? You just ask for things and then you get them?"

Paul breathed deeply to focus his mind. He had to think clearly. Jim's arguments always seemed to trap him. "Well, no, of course not. And that frustrates some Christians. They don't understand that they need to let God's plan unfold for them. It may simply not be part of God's plan to give you what you ask for right now. You can't treat God as an all-powerful servant always at your elbow, fulfilling every whim that comes to mind. God isn't a genie."

Several white chess pieces—three pawns, a knight, and a bishop—lay on the center table. Though the table was not marked with a chessboard, Jim leaned forward and set them up on the table in their beginning positions. "Perhaps not, but 'ask and ye shall receive' is pretty straightforward. It makes God sound like a genie to me."

"But that's clearly not how prayer works."

"I agree, but the Bible doesn't. It makes plain that prayer *is* supposed to work that way—you ask for it, and then you get it. Prayer is a telephone call to God, and he always answers your call."

"No—you're misreading the Bible. It doesn't say *when* you get it."

Jim shook his head. "But it does say that you'll get it."

Paul tried another tack. "God answers every prayer, but sometimes the answer is No."

"That's not what the Bible says. Jesus said that if you have faith as tiny as a mustard seed, you will be able to move mountains. Jesus said that prayer offered in faith will make the sick person well. Jesus said that whatever you ask for in prayer, believe that you have received it, and it will be yours. Jesus said that all things are possible to him who believes. Jesus said, 'Whatever you ask in my name, I will do it.' No limitations or delays are mentioned."

"Fine," Paul said, clenching his teeth. "Fine." He hated conceding ground, but he had no response.

"Okay," Jim said, "let's look at another aspect of prayer. When you pray, are you telling God something he doesn't already know? That is, is prayer important because you're informing God of some news, like 'I've lost my job' or 'my brother has consumption'?"

"Certainly not—God is all-knowing. Obviously, he already understands your situation. It's the asking part that's important."

"So you need to change it to 'please help me get this new job' or 'please cure my brother's consumption'?"

"That sounds better."

Jim leaned forward. "But even this doesn't make sense. God knows what's best for you. For you to ask God to change his plans is presumptuous. It's like an ant giving an engineer tips for designing a bridge. Will God think, 'It's best that you *not* get the new job, but since you asked nicely, I've changed my mind'? And maybe it's simply part of his plan that your brother die from consumption."

"But prayers are answered all the time! Lots of consumption patients can point to God as the reason they're alive now."

"Not with any justification. Let's say Aunt May has an illness. She and her family pray, and then she gets well. She concludes that it was prayer and God's intervention that cured her. But obviously there are other explanations, such as, that her treatment saved her. And if she had no treatment, perhaps it was simply her body healing itself."

"And perhaps it was God!" Paul ached to pace around the room to burn off some of his tension, but he was a guest and thought better of it.

"Perhaps so, but you're basing that on no evidence. I agree that we can't rule out that it was God—or Vishnu or Osiris or a four-leaf clover. But we have no evidence that any of them did anything." Jim was quickly running through different opening moves for his five chess pieces—*tick, tick, tick* as the pieces quickly struck the table, then a pause as he set them up again.

Paul wondered if his responses were so bland that Jim needed to play chess to keep his mind occupied.

Jim looked up and said, "The attraction of prayer in many cases is that it's easier than doing the hard work yourself. Praying for a promotion is easier than doing what's necessary to deserve a promotion. But let's look at this from another angle. God has cured zero cases of birth defects—say, mental idiocy. We know this because zero cases have been cured by *any* cause, natural or supernatural. Millions of mothers have been devastated by the prospect of their children growing up with a disability or even dying an early death. Has God found none of their prayers worthy of an answer? Or amputations—there are probably men in your own church who have lost limbs due to war or injury. Has a single limb ever grown back? No. And since God has cured zero of these, maybe he has intervened in zero illnesses. That is, since God hasn't performed any visible cures, maybe he hasn't done any invisible ones, either.

"And think of the millions of people around the world who are starving. Prayers or no prayers, God apparently can't be bothered to help them. If God is going to set aside the laws of physics and perform a miracle, is he to put my needs at the top of the list? If he won't save a country starving during a famine, why should I think he'll cure my rheumatism?"

Jim expanded his diversion, adding opposing black chess pieces to his imaginary board—three pawns and a knight from the other side of the table. He alternated moves from each side and held the captured pieces between his fingers so that the round bottoms embellished his hands like fat wooden rings.

"Consider smallpox," Jim said as he set up the pieces for another mock game. "We don't think of it much now, but it has been one of civilization's most deadly diseases. In fact, the last smallpox outbreak in this country was here in Los Angeles, about thirty years ago. Suppose you have a large number of people who are vaccinated against smallpox and an equally large number who aren't, and both groups are exposed to smallpox. Those who were vaccinated will do far better than those who don't—regardless of who prays. You can look at this from the other direction—the high death rate from smallpox suggests that God's plan is for it to be deadly. That is, vaccines *interfere* with God's plan. Maybe we shouldn't be using them."

Every confident tick of a chess piece was a goad to Paul, a reminder that he was the novice in this discussion. *Tick, tick, tick* became "i-di-ot." He said, "Maybe God doesn't need to focus on smallpox anymore because science has stepped in. Maybe He's focusing His miracle cures on diseases like consumption or cancer because that's where the need still exists."

"Did God *ever* focus on people with diseases?" Jim tossed away the chess pieces, and they clattered on the table. "Before vaccines, smallpox was life threatening. It killed hundreds of thousands of people every year. But in America, it's now just a nuisance. Science has improved life expectancy; prayer hasn't."

Paul clenched the arms of his chair. "You can't judge prayer with science," he said, probably louder than he should have. "You can't expect God to perform like a trained monkey at your command. It's not our place, nor is it even possible, to judge God's work. I agree that there are aspects of God's actions that we just can't explain. But I have the patience and the humility to accept God's wisdom and wait for understanding. Perhaps I won't understand until I get to heaven."

"Fine, but if your argument is that you don't understand, then say so. When asked, 'Can we say that prayer gives results?' the correct answer must then be 'No, we cannot because we don't understand.' God might answer every prayer as you suggest, but we have no reason to believe that. A sufficient explanation is that prayers don't appear to work because there is no God to answer them. The invisible looks very much like the nonexistent. Which one is God—invisible or nonexistent?"

Paul had no clever rebuttal, so he treated the question as rhetorical. "You've ignored praise," he said. "That's a vitally important reason for prayer. We humble ourselves before God and acknowledge that He can do what we can't. It's only appropriate to give thanks and praise to God."

Jim snorted. "What's the point in praising God? Surely *God* doesn't need to hear how great he is. Is he that insecure that he needs constant reminding? Put this in human terms—do we curse insects for not acknowledging how important we are? Suppose we built a race of mechanical men. Would our first command to them be that they need to worship their human creators?"

"Are you unwilling to humble yourself before a greater power?"

"I'll consider it when I know that such a power exists," Jim said. "The picture of God that the writers of the Old Testament painted for us is that of a great king—a man with the wisdom of Solomon, the generalship of Alexander, and the physical strength of Hercules. And he apparently needs the fawning and flattering of a great king as well. You would think that God would be a magnification of all good human qualities and an elimination of the bad ones. But the small-minded, praise-demanding, vindictive, and intolerant God of the Bible is simply a caricature, a magnification of *all* human inclinations, good and bad. As Man becomes nobler, he loses these petty needs. Shouldn't this be even more true of God?"

Jim leaned down and picked up a rumpled copy of a newspaper from the floor. "Let me show you something I read in this morning's paper," he said as he noisily flipped through a section. After a few moments he laid the newspaper on the table. "Here it is. It's about a train accident in which eight people died. A woman was just released from the hospital, and here she says, 'The doctors told my husband that I probably wouldn't make it. But he prayed and prayed. And his prayers were answered—it was a miracle.' " Jim looked up. "So according to this, prayer works. But I must wonder if I understand the meaning of the word 'works.' Imagine if the utilities that we use so often— electricity, clean water, trains, mail delivery, and so on—worked no more reliably than prayer."

"You're mixing two different things," Paul said. "You can't judge the Almighty's response to prayer in the same way that you judge something as artificial and profane as electricity."

"Then don't use the same word to describe their reliability. Prayer clearly does not 'work' as electricity does. And to compensate, the rules are rigged so that success is inevitable—if I get what I pray for, that's God's plan, and if I don't get what I pray for, that's also God's plan. When a train crash kills eight people, and it's called a miracle, how can God lose?" Jim slapped his hand on the newspaper. "But this makes praying to God as effective as praying to an old stump."

Paul's rebuttal lay scattered about him like a division of troops overrun by Jim's argument. His fists were clenched, but he felt defenseless. "Are you saying that prayer has no value?"

"Many spiritual traditions across the world use meditation to clarify the mind or relax. Christian prayer can have these same benefits. A mature view acknowledges what you can't control and can be an important part of facing a problem, but to imagine an all-powerful benefactor helping you out of a jam is simply to ignore reality. None of prayer's benefits demand a supernatural explanation, and to imagine that prayer shows that God exists is simply to delude yourself. The voice on the other end of the telephone line is your own."

Chapter 7

Paul walked into the office to see Samuel put on his suit jacket.

"Are you ready?" Samuel asked as he repositioned the ink well at the corner of his desk blotter.

"I have paper," Paul said.

"Good. I want you to take notes of the meeting."

"Should I look for something in particular?"

"No, just take notes. Try to record as much as you can. And you'll need to straighten that tie before we get there." Samuel walked out as Paul held the door and then followed.

"We're going to meet with Representative James McLachlan." Samuel said the name with deliberate pauses. "Write that down. He's our representative to Congress in Washington. He thinks I could get the Republican nomination for the California House from our district. He contacted me about it yesterday."

"That's fantastic." Paul felt a surge of admiration. Was nothing beyond Samuel's reach?

"I try to know people in government. I know the mayor. I have friends in the police department."

"Didn't you run two years ago?" Paul asked as they turned a corner.

"I did, but that was before the prophecy. Everything's different now. The prophecy has given me a lot more stature."

"What if you win? What happens to the church?"

"Nothing." Samuel stopped, turned to face Paul, and put a hand on his shoulder. "The church comes first—don't worry about that. The legislative session in Sacramento is only two months long. We'll arrange for a temporary pastor during that time—maybe you," he said with a squeeze of his hand.

They heard the trolley bell around the corner and hurried to catch it. Climbing aboard, they dropped their nickels into the fare box. Samuel settled himself in his seat and lit his pipe.

"This Assembly seat would be my next step in serving people. I've been doing it all my life. I don't think I've told you about my work in Iowa," Samuel said as smoke wreathed his head.

"I thought you grew up in Ohio," Paul said. This seemed an odd tangent.

"I did, and when I was twenty, I struck out on my own and found a utopian community."

Paul absorbed the words hesitantly. That didn't sound like the Samuel Hargrove he knew. "Something like the Amana communities?"

"Amana is German, and you need to be born into that one. But there were many separate societies like that back in the seventies. Some were religious like the Shakers and Amana. Some were anarchist. The one I was drawn to was a utopian community—Harmony, Iowa. We were trying to show the world how to get along. Everything was owned in common, men and women were given equal status, we shared the work equally, and decisions were made by consensus."

Paul leaned forward with his hands on his knees to hear Samuel over the clatter of the trolley.

"I loved it and hated it—often at the same time. It was a noble experiment, but it failed all the same. We rotated leadership positions so that everyone had a turn. Unfortunately, some folks just aren't good leaders. So after three years, I left."

"What brought you into the church?" Paul said.

"Leadership was one of God's gifts to me, and the church gave me opportunities to use it. I'd been raised in a strongly Christian household, and when I came to Los Angeles, God made positions in the church open to me."

The trolley bell clanged at another stop.

"Now, back to the seat in the state Assembly. This is not a career change for me, and I'll still be the pastor. My life has been an exploration of ways to serve. The Harmony community was first, the church is how I do it now and, God willing, I'll be able to expand that with political office."

"We'll need you in that big new sanctuary," Paul said.

"To be sure."

The trolley into downtown took ten minutes, and a short walk brought the two men to the Security building and then to Congressman McLachlan's sixth-floor office. His secretary announced them.

"Ah, the famous Reverend Hargrove!" McLachlan said as he stood from behind his desk. Samuel introduced Paul as his assistant with handshakes all around.

The congressman looked to be well over sixty years old, though still tall and powerfully built. Even during summer recess his attire reflected his position, and he wore a high white celluloid collar with a tie, vest, and jacket. Paul was relieved that he had worn his best clothes.

The congressman motioned for Samuel to sit in an overstuffed brown leather wing chair in front of his desk. Paul found a straight-backed wooden chair against the wall. Diplomas, awards, framed newspaper articles, and photographs sprinkled the patterned red wall-paper above the dark wood wainscoting. One photo showed the congressman in front of the Capitol building in Washington, another had him with President McKinley, and another shaking hands with President Roosevelt.

A squat brass spittoon sat in the corner, and the sight of it brought back memories for Paul. Chewing tobacco had been a pleasant vice when he'd roamed the streets, but Samuel had insisted that he stop.

"I was delighted to get your letter," McLachlan said to Samuel. "I'm part of the Republican nominating committee for the seventy-second Assembly district. We're finalizing our list of candidates, and let me say that you look to be the best by far." McLachlan leaned forward slightly and said, "This must be formalized by the committee, you understand."

"Of course."

Paul looked up to see Samuel beaming.

"But given what I've read about you, I'm optimistic enough to proceed on the assumption that you will be our candidate in November—congratulations." He opened a large inlaid wooden box on his desk and turned it to Samuel. "Cigar?"

"Thank you, Congressman."

"Take two."

The two men were silent as they lit their cigars, and white smoke rose to the ceiling.

"There will be candidates from the Socialist and Prohibition parties, but we won't worry about them. Your challenge will be the Democrat. He is Frank Henderson, and this is a first run for him as well. You will need close to two thousand votes to win, but with the publicity you've been getting, you're halfway done before you start."

Paul's pen scratched as the two men talked strategy—public appearances, advertising, newspaper coverage.

Perhaps thirty minutes had passed and the conversation mellowed. McLachlan stood from his desk and said, "I think we have our plan." He picked up a crystal decanter from the table behind him. "Drinks, gentlemen? I'd like to propose a toast to the next representative of California's seventy-second district." He poured the whiskey. "To Representative Samuel Hargrove!" The three clinked glasses.

The conversation turned from business to celebratory small talk. After a few minutes, McLachlan said to Samuel with a smile, "I probably shouldn't give you ideas, in case you come after my job. But if you take my advice, you'll begin considering your next step. You have a story that would play well on the national stage."

Paul and Samuel returned to the church on foot, walking leisurely. Samuel's mood was buoyant, and he continued to toss out ideas as Paul took notes. Samuel talked about using some of the church's free press to boost his candidacy and finding volunteers within the congregation, and then he mused on campaign issues that he might want to champion. "You could visit in Sacramento—for the swearing-in ceremony, say," he said to Paul as he pulled out McLachlan's cigar and lit it.

"But let's talk about your project. How was your progress with Mr. Emerson last time?"

Paul felt his gut tighten. "Good. Better than before, I think."

"Great news. Practice does wonders, doesn't it?"

"Yes. Yes, it does. That must have made the difference." The desired answer was easier than the truth. Or at least safer.

"So is he still game?" Samuel asked.

"He hasn't converted yet."

"Then try the design argument next. Let me tell you."

Paul had heard the story before, but he knew not to interrupt.

Samuel took a deep pull on the cigar and exhaled a cloud of smoke. "William Paley, writing in about 1800, imagined walking in a meadow and coming upon a rock in the path. Nothing surprising here—that's what you'd expect." Samuel reached into his vest fob and pulled out his watch. It lay in his hand, gleaming like a golden egg and wobbling as he walked. "But suppose he came across one of these lying in the path. Is this just part of the landscape like the rock? Surely not—as I study the watch, with its many tiny gears and parts that fit intricately, I must conclude that there is a designer. This is not like the rock—the complexity and order of the watch demand a designer.

"We see the same thing when we look at nature. The human body, for example, with a heart like a pump. No—a heart that *is* a pump and arteries that are pipes and eyes that are cameras. The world looks designed because it *was* designed! It's the simplest explanation. Design must have had a designer. And that Designer was God."

℘

Later that day, Paul strolled to Jim's house, absorbed in thought. The trees along the street gave shade, though on this cool and overcast June day, Paul walked in the sun where possible. He replayed the facts, trying to fit together the pieces of the puzzle. He was still a Christian and he was still fighting for Jim's soul. He needed to satisfy Samuel and he needed to place Thena and his mother in heaven—that was clear enough.

He slowed for a moment. That was clear, but it was not enough. He felt a piece fall mentally into place, then he straightened and walked briskly forward.

A few minutes later, Paul walked up the steps to Jim's house and was about to knock when he was surprised to hear through an open window Jim talking to someone inside.

"This is really going to do it," Jim said. "This is damned powerful—surely he will see the value in it."

Paul didn't know that Jim kept any other company. He knocked. He was probably intruding, but he could at least find out when to return.

"Come," said the familiar voice.

Paul closed the door behind him and walked down the hall to see Jim in his usual spot on the sofa, alone. A stack of magazines sat on the floor and individual copies lay on the low center table—*Scientific American, Electrician and Mechanic, Popular Science Monthly.*

"Ah, my Christian antagonist," Jim said with a smile.

"I heard voices," Paul said. "I hope I'm not interrupting."

"No, that was just me talking to myself—I do that sometimes. This is good timing." Jim closed a few magazines and neatened the stack on the floor. "Have you seen this?" He pushed a magazine across the table. The cover showed a thin vehicle, rather like an inverted canoe with four fat bicycle wheels. "It's the Stanley Rocket. It just set a speed record of more than 125 miles per hour."

"I didn't realize that motor cars could go so fast. Is this what you work on during the day?"

"Not really. I'd love to own one of those Oldsmobiles, though, mostly just to dismantle it to see how it works."

"And drive it, too. A motor car that goes by itself, without a horse, and never gets tired—they're amazing."

"Well, I probably wouldn't drive it. I'm more the tinkering sort."

Paul tried to imagine someone buying a six-hundred-dollar machine only to take it apart. "May I ask what you do work on? Are you still with your typewriter company?"

"I retired about ten years ago. It was time to turn leadership over to more energetic hands. I'm still the largest shareholder—an inheritance from my parents—and I have a seat on the board, so I stay involved by mail."

"These motor cars might be a new product for your company."

"I thought about that, but I have a better idea—something that should be revolutionary, something that I've been working on intensely for about six years. It picks up on the work of Nikola Tesla, but I can't tell you more than that. It will likely be public in a year or two. In fact, the chairman of the company will be here in a few weeks for a demonstration. I think he'll be impressed." Jim leaned back into the sofa with a comfortable smile.

Paul was eager to get to business. "I'd like to talk about evidence of God's hand in the design of the world."

"Okay, but I've already told you what I think of it." A tea kettle whistled. Jim walked into the kitchen, and returned with a tea tray and set it on the center table.

"The world has some marvelous things in it," Paul said. "Rainbows and sunsets, laughing children, spring flowers, warm beaches, love. It's a beautiful world."

"True. But the world also has some terrible things in it. Earthquakes, droughts, famines, parasites. Take Guinea worm—it's a parasite that's common in Africa. It grows in people up to three feet long, eventually living just under the skin. When the mature worm is ready to lay eggs, it burns its way through the skin. Very painful, I hear. To extract the worm, it's wound up on a stick, which is also a painful process. It takes days. In fact, you've already seen this. You know the doctor symbol, the snake twisted around a pole? That symbol came from this remedy."

Paul grimaced and pushed himself back into his chair. "How do you get infected?"

"By drinking contaminated water. Nature has many kinds of diseases—some that kill you, and some that just make you wish you were dead. For every laughing child, I could find a child who no longer laughs, dying of dysentery or smallpox or even measles. Or an old man slowly dying of cancer. Or . . ." Jim inhaled noisily as if he were coming up for air. "Or a young mother dying in childbirth."

Jim cleared his throat as he stood and walked to the wall opposite the window. At the bureau, he paused before a large framed portrait of a young woman. As Jim leafed through a drawer, Paul thought of the needlepoint pillows and framed samplers. The vacancy left by a woman was now obvious. He was surprised he hadn't noticed before.

"How old are you?" Jim asked.

"I'm twenty-five."

Jim returned to the sofa holding a newspaper clipping. "This is a list of major natural disasters from recent history. We can date them by your life. The earthquake in the Himalayas last year was much deadlier than the one we just had in San Francisco—20,000 people died. When you were twenty-one, a volcano in Martinique killed 29,000, and when you were two, Krakatau killed even more. A cyclone in Bengal killed 150,000 people when you were sixteen, and one in Vietnam killed twice that in the year you were born. When you were six, a flood in China killed as many as 2,000,000. And years of drought in India caused a famine that killed 10,000,000 when you were about twenty."

"Yes, I've heard of some of those."

"There's a hell of a lot of pain and suffering in the world to go along with the good things."

"Perhaps God has a reason."

"To teach us to be humble? To count our blessings? To not get cocky? Those are some heavy-handed lessons. Let me propose this explanation: there is no reason at all. Our earth looks just as it would if there were no purpose, no design, and no wise designer."

This was another Jim onslaught to which Paul had no rebuttal. "Well, let's approach this from another angle," Paul said. "You're familiar with the Paley pocket watch example?"

Jim dismissed the notion with a wave of his hand. "That argument has been around since Cicero. What's amusing about Paley's watch argument is that it defeats itself. Let's imagine his original situation. He's walking in a field and discovers the watch. It looks out of place, different from the plants and rocks. But if it looks different from nature because it looks designed, then nature must *not* look designed. You can't argue on the one hand that the watch looks remarkable and stands out from the natural background, and on the other that the watch looks similar to nature, so both must be designed."

"But nature does look designed. I've seen close-up photographs of insects like fleas. If God puts this amazing detail into insects, He must care far more for humans."

"We marvel at God's handiwork only after we know that he exists." Jim leaned forward. "The design argument simply takes a childish view of the world. Does the world *look* designed by an omniscient and benevolent god? Go to the freak show at the circus—it's a museum of nature's poor design. Siamese twins, two-headed pigs, bearded ladies, the Lizard Man, hermaphrodites, dwarves, giants. Monsters like the Elephant Man and unfortunates with all manner of birth defects. Deformed babies floating in formaldehyde. Is this the best that God can do?"

"Maybe birth defects are meant to test us, to teach us to be better people."

"That's quite a barbaric test. Isn't it ironic to imagine God teaching us to be kind with the cruelest test imaginable? Think of the parents every day who are told that their newborn has some hideous defect and will live a short, painful life. And why are there birth defects in animals? Do they need testing too? A natural explanation works best. 'God is testing us' is not where the evidence points."

Jim poured tea from the pot into two delicate white china cups on saucers and pushed one toward Paul. "And there are examples of inept designs. One of the best examples is in a whale—I saw a few whale skeletons when I lived in Boston. Many species have small bones as remnants of their nonexistent rear legs, and their flippers have all the joints of a land animal's hand but no reason for that flexibility—very different from a fish's fin. If the whale had been designed, it would have been tailored to life in the ocean with no wasted bones."

Paul set his Bible on his knee and opened it to a bookmark. "When Job questions God, God replies, 'Where wast thou when I laid the foundations of the earth? Declare, if thou hast understanding.' Maybe it's presumptuous of us to judge God."

"Once again, that assumes God, the very thing we're trying to establish. Maybe I'll avoid judging God once I know that he exists. Let's approach it this way: if you were God, would you design the earth with volcanoes and hurricanes, plagues and famines?"

"Maybe those are necessary features of the earth," Paul said. "Maybe hurricanes distribute rain or heat; maybe volcanoes relieve pressure underground. We just don't know."

Jim reached for his tea cup. "You're God, infinitely smarter than the smartest human, and that's the best you can do? 'Sorry about the volcano—I had to relieve some pressure.' You can't argue strong evidence for design at one moment, but plead ignorance at another when it suits you. Take your pick: does the earth look designed or not? It could indeed have been designed, but it's not designed in a way that any human designer would have used. A loving and omniscient human designer wouldn't have created earthquakes, plagues, legs for whales, and Guinea worm. Therefore, the design metaphor, which says the earth looks as it would if designed by a human with the ability, fails."

"Maybe God didn't *want* a perfect design," Paul said. "Genesis says that Creation was perfect, but it is now imperfect because of the Fall—the sin of the apple."

"If we live in a fallen world, then don't argue that it looks perfectly designed. You can't argue for an imperfect fallen world and a perfectly designed world at the same time."

Paul took stock of his position. His argument was eroding, but this didn't feel like earlier conversations. It wasn't really *his* argument, and he could view its strengths and weaknesses dispassionately. This objectivity was the new piece to the puzzle that he was trying out. "I'm trying to be open minded about this, but I still think that the earth and life on it look designed. Think of the complexity. Don't you see that, too?"

"Many undesigned things have interesting properties. Snowflakes are complex, crystals have order, rainbows are beautiful. By contrast, many things that we know were designed *don't* have these properties."

"But a snowflake is hardly as complex as, say, a flea. When you get to a human, the complexity is overwhelming."

"Complexity is weak evidence for design. A clumsy sock puppet or a childish clay sculpture are designed, and an intricate crystal or snowflake with trillions of precisely placed atoms is not. Which one is more complex? Mere complexity is deceiving. Atoms obey simple rules as they lock into place, one by one. From simple natural rules can come complexity."

Jim drank from his teacup. "But the Design Argument forces you to come at this from the other direction since designers are always more complex than what they design. If a complex world must have been created by an even-more-complex God, then what created God?"

"Yes, I see that, but I think the argument makes an exception for God."

"So 'simple things must come from complex things . . . except for God' is your argument."

"Well, it's not necessarily *my* argument."

"Ah—good to see that distinction."

And that distinction was quite plain to Paul, too. Samuel's arguments had been a part of him like a suit of clothes, and critiquing them was like judging his appearance without a mirror. For the first time he could see this argument separate from himself, as if displayed on a mannequin. Looking at it objectively, he had lost faith that its strengths outweighed its weaknesses.

"You know of things that might look designed but aren't," Jim said. "The English language, for example. It's very complex, but it wasn't designed—it just happened. Or Adam Smith's 'invisible hand' that controls the marketplace."

Jim set his cup on the table with a clack. "Even if I found the Design Argument compelling, this mysterious Designer is unidentified. Is it the God of Christianity? Or is it Allah or Osiris or Zeus or some other god? And it doesn't explain anything. 'God did it' simply replaces a mystery with another mystery. Who is this God? Where did he come from, how did he do his designing, and what natural laws did he break? A true scientific explanation is quite different—it adds to our knowledge. No scientist, deciphering some puzzling aspect of nature, would ever say, 'God did it, you say? Well then, nothing left for me to do here—I'll just go home.' "

Paul had never been a tea drinker. Without sugar the tea was harsh, but it had a kind of intriguing charm. "I'm beginning to see your point, but science doesn't answer everything," he said.

"True. I don't suppose it ever will. But adding God to the explanation doesn't help, it just complicates. Believers tie themselves in knots trying to rationalize why God allows bad things to happen and why he doesn't provide the relief himself. The convoluted rationalization vanishes when you simply realize that you have no need of the God hypothesis."

"You use the word 'rationalize' as if it's a bad thing."

"Not all rationalization is bad. If you knew for a fact that God existed, then you would want to rationalize or justify any apparent contradiction with that fact—to reinterpret new clues to fit the known facts. But God's existence is exactly what we're trying to establish. Rationalization parries an attack, nothing more. It is very different from giving evidence to *support* a position."

That made sense to Paul. "Giving evidence strengthens your position, and rationalizing avoids the weakening of your position," Paul said. "They're almost opposites."

"Exactly. Rationalization starts with God's existence: given Christianity, how can I square it with the facts? Reason starts with the facts and follows them where they lead."

Paul wanted to return to an earlier point. Acting on his hunch, he gestured at the portrait on the bureau and said, "I was wondering about that photograph. Was that your wife?"

Jim stood and walked to the bureau. He picked up the photograph and brought it to Paul, holding it out with both hands. "This was Vive when she was twenty-three, just after we were married." The picture was a formal portrait, though the woman's lips seemed only just under control, as if she were about to break out in a smile. Her head was crowned with a generous coil of hair ringed with a ribbon.

"Vive is an unusual name," Paul said.

"It was her nickname. It fit her perfectly—it means 'lively' in French. Her full name was Genevieve."

"She's beautiful," Paul said. Though her hairstyle, clothes, and jewelry looked old fashioned, she had a natural grace and elegance that spoke timelessly through the photograph.

"Three years after we were married, she died in childbirth," Jim said as he replaced the portrait and returned to the sofa. "I lost a wife and a daughter in one day—what should have been the happiest day of my life was the worst. We'd just bought this house, with room for a big family, and now it's only me. It's been over twenty years, but I can still hear her singing softly as she worked around the house, or imagine her walking through the door with coffee when I work late. I tried to lose myself in my work, and that helped, but I really haven't gotten past it."

Paul leaned forward. "And is that why you hate God? Because He took someone you loved?"

"Someone I *love*," Jim snapped. Anger burned in his face as if a switch had been flipped.

Paul had meant to prod, not provoke.

"That's a stupid question," Jim said. "Have you not been listening? I'm an atheist! I can't hate something that doesn't exist."

"I'm sorry," Paul said. "You're right—that was a stupid question."
Jim's stern look slowly faded. "I went through a phase where I hated
God for taking Vive, but that was when I was a believer. Then I accepted the loss, again as a believer. Finally, I decided that God was just
a story, and the hatred evaporated."

Paul thought of his own loss. Turning around the pen in his fingers,
he said, "Thena gave me this." He held out the pen for Jim to see and
immediately felt foolish and exposed, but he continued with his point.
"Thena, my fiancée. We became engaged in March. I lost her. I lost her
in the earthquake." Paul focused on his breathing, slow and deep, to
stay in control. "It's been months, but I think of her constantly."

Jim shifted forward on the sofa. "I'm so sorry to hear that. How did
it happen?"

Paul told him in halting words how Thena had gone to San Francisco for a wedding, about the aunt's telegram, and about a letter from the
aunt with more details—that the hotel had collapsed, that it had been
consumed by fire, and that Thena was the only hotel guest unaccount-
ed for. If she had somehow slipped out safely, surely she would have
sent a message by now.

The account began as almost an admission, something to be
ashamed of, but as Paul told the story, he felt increasingly at peace. As
a gentle surprise, he slowly realized that he was safe with Jim.

Chapter 8

Ten weeks had passed since Athena had been brought into the monastery, bloody, drugged, and cushioned by a cartload of fish. It was now the last week of June, the weather was warm, and Athena had helped prepare the monastery's first fresh carrots earlier that day. Chiba was removing her splint, this time for good. The cuts had healed weeks ago. Her leg was thin and pale, but she could feel the straight outline of her thighbone. She felt free.

So much had changed in her life. She winced as she remembered the terror of the shaking and the pain and helplessness of being trapped. And then waking in Wonderland. That felt so long ago, and she had explored so many new ideas since. Athena had come to enjoy her frequent discussions with the abbot, and he clearly delighted in the intellectual challenge of discussing the attributes and merits of different belief systems. She knew that her time in the monastery, with him as her mentor, would soon end.

"You could have sent a message with the group that left yesterday," the abbot said. "They could have sent a telegram to your family."

"Yes, I thought of that." Athena and the abbot sat in his office. "I've sent two letters home already, close to two months ago, but I've gotten no reply. I'm not sure what that means. I mentioned my doubts about my faith, and I'm worried that the lack of a letter is the reply. My parents are quite devout, and I can only imagine what they might be thinking. But I've changed. I can't revert to my old life, focused on clothes and parties, and I can't go back to church in the same way. I'm a different person—how will they take me?" The gate to home was finally open, and yet she hesitated to go through it.

"Some people go to a monastery and stay," said the abbot. "Others learn and grow, and then they return to life."

"I've learned so much."

"And now you must return to your life."

"Yes." She turned her engagement ring around her finger. Its little opal was up, then down, then up. It brought to mind a game she had played with daisy petals as a child. He loves me. He loves me not. He loves me. "I believed Christianity simply because I was taught to believe, but I can't call myself a believer now. I like your term—truth seeker. But I don't know how I'll fit in back home."

The abbot smiled. "Truth is not always convenient. You must first be true to yourself. But surely your family loves you and will accept you as you accept yourself."

Athena looked down at her left leg, broken but now healed. Leaves scratched at the window in a soft breeze. She raised her eyes to the abbot. "I'd like to leave tomorrow."

ⅎ

Paul sat on the bed in his small apartment in the rooming house. He needed to catalog all that drew him to Christianity. It gave him a home, of course—a warm and welcoming community of good people. It gave him a job and a purpose in life and the good feeling that came from helping others. It gave him his sense of right and wrong, which had changed his life since his time on the street. It gave him heaven for the two most important people in his life, Thena and his mother. And it gave him a ticket out of hell with absolution for his own sins—and God certainly knew he had sins that needed absolution.

He couldn't discard any of that. Nevertheless, his discussions with Jim had undercut much of Christianity's logical foundation that had been so important to him. He had to go where the logic pointed. An argument that was wrong but satisfying was still wrong.

But was this disloyal? What would Samuel think of his doubt? He owed his very life to Samuel, a debt that weighted him with a profound feeling of obligation. He flopped back on the bed and imagined a life without Samuel—easy to do, because he'd lived most of his life without him.

He thought back on an incident in the orphanage when he was about ten. He'd had some kind of argument with the warden, Mr. Dammer. He told Paul to apologize, but Paul felt that he was the injured party and refused. Mr. Dammer told the staff not to give him any food. They made him sit at the dining table during meals, but his bowl only had water. On the second day, one of his friends tried to slip him some bread, but they caught the boy and gave him a beating.

Paul convinced himself that he didn't want to eat. The clawing hunger made him dizzy, but he thought that he could turn the tables on Mr. Dammer—show him how wrong his punishment was and make him change his mind. Slowly he realized his mistake—the warden couldn't back down. That would undermine his authority both with the boys and with the rest of the staff. Anyway, Mr. Dammer just didn't care. A boy could die and he would simply blame it on some illness. Paul had wagered his life, but that wasn't high enough stakes. The warden could always call his bluff. Paul realized then that his life wasn't worth much.

After four days he did as Mr. Dammer commanded—he came crawling back and apologized, in front of everyone. The warden sat like a king in his big chair at the front of the room. He condescended to let Paul eat, and then he told Paul to say, "Thank you, Mr. Dammer," so he did, and the warden laughed. When Paul ate too fast and got sick all over himself, he laughed again.

That chapter was over, as were the empty years on the street, and life was civilized now—even joyous. Samuel was the cause.

ဆာ

Later that day Paul knocked on Jim's door.

"Come."

Paul walked to the living room and found it empty. The room held its usual tidy clutter, and another postcard with a chess move lay on the bureau. "Hello?"

"In the kitchen."

Paul followed the voice further down the hall to find Jim filling the kettle from the kitchen faucet. Paul was surprised that the kitchen wasn't messier—Jim's appearance showed that he didn't care about convention, at least in his own house. And yet the counter was clear, with tidy shelves of glassware and dishes above. An icebox stood in a corner. Opposite the counter were a gas stove, sink, more counter space, and a wide window onto the sunny backyard with grass as high as hay. An overturned pan was drying on a dish towel, and dishes from a serving for one sat in the sink. Dusty plaid curtains framed the window.

Jim said, "How are you doing?" He turned off the water and set down the kettle. His face showed a generous concern.

Paul considered the question for a moment until he realized that Jim was referring to his recovery from Thena's death. "I'm doing well," Paul said. "Thanks." It had been a while since he had been asked that question.

"I was hoping you'd come by today," Jim said.

"It's lucky that I always find you in. I must be more clear about when I'd like to stop by."

"That's all right. I'm always home." Jim turned back to the sink and finished filling the kettle.

"You must go out sometimes."

"No, never. I don't like to leave the house."

That choice was at least in keeping with his attire, Paul thought. This time, Jim wore crisply pressed gray suit trousers with a striped cotton pajama top, and his feet were bare.

"What about groceries?" Paul said.

"Food, milk, ice—they're all delivered. Errand boys do anything else that I need—fetch books, deliver laundry. Some stores are getting telephones, so I might need to get one soon."

Paul absorbed this doubtfully. That someone would deliberately live as a hermit in his own house made no sense, but it felt rude to pursue the issue. "You said that Reverend Hargrove and you had worked together, and I mentioned this to Reverend Hargrove."

"What did he say?"

"That you and he debated a lot. He said that that's where his passion for apologetics came from."

"We did debate a lot. Sam liked to win. I took that as a challenge and learned more about apologetics to present the atheist counterpoint. Perhaps I played the role of the freethinker a little too energetically—I like to win as well."

"But you were a believer then."

"Yes, but that doesn't mean that you can't argue from the opponent's side. You must know his position. Until you do, you don't completely understand your own." Jim dried his hands on a towel. "I met a woman in Boston once. The conversation turned to travel, and I asked her where she liked to go. She said, 'Why should I travel? I'm already there!' Extraordinary—and yet that's the way many Christians think. 'Why should I critique my position or evaluate someone else's? I'm already there!' "

"I've been thinking a lot about my own position. It's hard to admit this, but I've been having some doubts." Paul looked at the floor as he smacked his fist against his thigh. "Just a little." He looked hard at Jim. "As an atheist, I guess that must please you."

"Not really." Jim set the kettle on the stove to boil and walked past Paul to the living room. "I care about the truth." Jim sat and motioned Paul into his chair. "If you think you have it, I want you to argue as convincingly as you know how. On the other hand, if you find my opinions convincing, you're welcome to them—they're free. And if neither of us changes but we can live in a civil manner with each other, then that works as well. Thomas Jefferson said, 'It does me no injury for my neighbor to say there are twenty gods or no god. It neither picks my pocket nor breaks my leg.' "

Jim walked to a bookshelf and pulled off his Bible. He returned to the sofa, set the Bible on the center table, and slowly flipped through the pages so Paul could see. "This was my approach to truth." There didn't seem to be a single page without a handwritten mark. Some notes were small and dense while others were scrawled in large block letters. Some notes were in pencil while others were in various and seemingly arbitrary colors of ink. Some pages had margins full of comments with more on scraps of paper.

"Wait—what did that page say?" Paul pointed at a page.

Jim leafed back, page by page.

"There!" Paul said. In the outside margin of the page, with a dark pen and in capital letters, was written the word "Nonsense."

"Oh, that," Jim said. "That's the book of Job."

What was next—shopping lists? Drinking songs? Bawdy limericks? "Why would you deface a book of Scripture? And why Job? It's the book where we see God's consistent love during hardship."

"Indeed? Then let me suggest you read that book more closely. God says that he ruined Job without reason—took away his health and money and killed his family. Why? Because he could. That's not a very helpful book if you're trying to find God's love."

"That's not what I remember from the book."

"Sermons rarely tell the complete story of Job. Read it and decide for yourself."

Paul resolved to do exactly that, but there was a more immediate problem. "I must say, you seem to have treated your Bible rather harshly."

"I critique what I read, and whether something is wicked or noble, I write what I think."

"But you can't treat the Bible that way. It's a holy book."

"Who cares? If it's the truth, then surely it isn't so fragile that it can be damaged by a nasty comment in the margin. The truth can take whatever punishment I give it. If it can't, then it's not worth my regret—or yours."

"It just seems disrespectful."

"I treat the claims of Christianity as if they can be tested against logic and reason. I can't give a philosophy any more respect than that."

The kettle whistled, and Jim went to the kitchen. He returned with the tea tray and set it on the center table.

"Tell me about your change—how you became a freethinker," Paul said.

Jim eased back into the sofa. "I left the church in about 1885."

"Why did you leave?"

"There was a falling out in the church. I wound up on the losing end, and Sam was part of the group that forced me out."

"That must have been devastating."

"I felt betrayed, but that's another story. A few years later, Vive died—it's been over twenty years now. I was still a Christian then, but struggling. How could God have taken Vive from me? Every Christian who endures the death of a loved one asks the same questions, of course, but it was especially tough since I didn't have the church community for comfort. I felt very alone.

"Then I began noticing natural disasters that God apparently felt were necessary to impose on his favorite creation. One year, a blizzard in the Midwest killed hundreds of people, many of them children. It was called the Schoolhouse Blizzard. There was one Nebraska school—when the stove ran out of wood, the teacher led her students to another building less than a hundred yards away. The blowing snow made visibility so poor that they didn't make it, and all the children froze to death." Jim swallowed hard and faltered.

Jim ticked off other disasters that had made an impression, making clear that this wasn't a period of unusual tragedy, just unusual awareness on his part. "These disasters prodded me. What explained natural evil? I called out to God and got no answer—as if there was no one on the other end of the telephone—and that was when I made those notes in my Bible. I felt abandoned, in agony."

Paul often felt privileged when parishioners confided their difficulties in him, but he had rarely heard so personal a story.

"Then I began to take seriously the objections from the atheist side," Jim said. "I knew them well, but I had always assumed that they were wrong. I had never given them a chance. But when I did, I noticed something surprising. The difficult questions in Christianity fell away when approached from the atheist viewpoint. Why do natural disasters happen? Because they just do—there is no conscious cause, no particular message behind them. Why does God answer my prayers but let millions of people die every year from malnutrition or disease? Because there is no God, just an unfeeling and indifferent Nature in which people are hurt sometimes. Why does God answer some of my prayers but not others, even the unselfish ones? Because there is no God to answer prayers, and I just imagined answers. Why is there support for slavery and barbarism in the Bible? Because it was written by ordinary men thousands of years ago and is a reflection of their primitive attitudes, nothing more."

Jim set the cups on their saucers and swirled the tea in the pot. "It was a revelation—all the convoluted and flimsy rationalization that had been necessary before just vanished. My God hypothesis was a poor explanation of reality, and when I no longer insisted that it was correct and simply followed reality where it led me, things made vastly more sense."

"Moving from love to nothing is a harsh change," Paul said. "You must at least agree that the atheist position repels many people."

"Some do feel that way, but that has nothing to do with whether or not God exists. I have no use for the happy explanation but quite a bit for the correct explanation. You can't be arguing that it's disagreeable to imagine that there is no God, so therefore he exists—surely we have higher standards of evidence than that.

"Many Christians admit that the problem of evil is the most difficult problem for Christianity—why God lets bad things happen to good people," Jim said. "The Greek philosopher Epicurus had an excellent way of putting it. He said that if God is willing to prevent evil but not able, then he is not omnipotent. If he is able but not willing, then he is malevolent. If he is both able and willing, then why is there evil? If he is neither able nor willing, then why call him God?"

"Well, difficulties build character," Paul said. "My own life started out pretty bad, but it made me who I am."

"That's just what an atheist would say—we don't seek out misfortune, but good can come of it. It's a simple and workable understanding of the world, and it doesn't need a supernatural element. But the Christian's challenge is to make sense of evil permitted by a supernatural being who could stop it in an instant if he wanted to—a tall order."

"Here's how Reverend Hargrove explained it to me," Paul said. "Free will is mandatory in a good world. God could have created us like machines without choice so that we would always do the right thing, but then we wouldn't be human." He remembered a metaphor from one of Samuel's sermons. "What's the point in walking a maze if there's a sign pointing the correct direction at every junction?"

Jim dropped the Bible onto the carpet and put his bare feet up on the table where it had been. They were practical feet, ugly with calluses, and they looked like they were rarely confined in shoes. His feet made a sharp contrast with his natty gray trousers. "If God cares so much about free will, I wonder why he allows the free will of the victim to be trampled by the thief or murderer," Jim said. "And tell me this: does free will exist in heaven?"

"I would think that it must."

"And does it cause the same problems in heaven that it does here on earth?"

Paul swirled the tea in his cup and watched the dark bits of leaves make patterns in the liquid. "I suppose the spirits in heaven are enlightened. They'd have no desire to do bad things. Otherwise, heaven would have the problems we have here."

"Then God could give us that enlightenment now."

"God can't just *give* us wisdom. Then we'd have no opportunity to learn. My point about the maze was that a lesson learned is more powerful than a lesson given. Wisdom is more valuable if we earn it."

"Why is that?" Jim asked. "God could enlighten us with the same lessons as profoundly as if we'd learned them through experience, and no trials would be necessary. If free will is mandatory, why was the enlightenment needed to properly use it reserved for the spirits in heaven? Why would God shortchange us like that? It's like an automobile without an instruction manual. The God hypothesis is unnecessary and it complicates the explanation. And why does God not show himself? Why not make clear his purpose? Why the mystery, why the test, when he knows the outcome already? Why not just tell us?"

"He did tell us. He told us through Jesus's ministry."

"That's a story, not concrete evidence. What we see, including the legend of Jesus and the emphasis on faith instead of reason, is exactly the kind of thing primitive people would give us. The natural explanation is far more plausible than the existence of a divine maze maker."

Paul leaned back in his chair. The defensiveness of the past was almost gone. Instead of focusing on his own crumbling argument, Paul reflected on the construction of Jim's. He tried for another analogy. "I think of life as a school. We learn and then we graduate into heaven."

"But some fail and go to hell. It's a poor school that fails such a huge fraction of its students. Isn't God a skilled enough teacher that everyone could pass?"

Paul fingered the seams on the arm of the chair as another avenue came to mind. "I've always found comfort in everyday miracles—not parting the Red Sea, but a child rescued from a fire or a miraculous recovery from illness. Don't events like that make you stop and think?"

"Good news pleases me as well, but let's be clear about what causes it. I read in the paper a few weeks ago about a woman whose home was destroyed in April's earthquake. She lost everything, but charities and the government have given her food, clothes, and a temporary place to live. Do you know what her reaction was? She said, 'Thank you, Jesus.' "

"And you say that it wasn't Jesus who helped."

"Exactly. Give thanks to those who provided the help—the people who have opened their homes to the homeless or fed the hungry. It doesn't happen often enough, but it happens. People from as far away as Idaho and Washington are still sending bread by train to feed people in San Francisco. The prayer 'give us this day our daily bread' is being answered, but by people, not God. We don't need to invent supernatural beings to explain what we see."

Paul had seen enough callousness to last a lifetime—and yet, he had seen plenty of generosity, too. "Some would say that Jesus caused those people to do good, that He worked through them."

"Right, and Santa Claus works through parents. 'God will provide' really means that *people* will provide. It's amazing how far Christians will go to rationalize a positive role for Jesus. The Creator of the universe apparently stands by to let disaster consume a city, and then his apologists want to credit him with the people cleaning up afterwards. No—I'd rather give people the credit they earned."

"Many would say that disasters are part of God's plan—a short-term loss for some greater gain in the future." Paul surprised himself as he shored up the Samuel side of the argument. He didn't think it the stronger position, but he wanted to hear Jim's response.

Jim said, "People don't say, 'This disaster must be for the greater good' and sit back to watch dispassionately. They help where they can. We don't say, 'Smallpox is supposed to be deadly and to change that would interfere with God's plan'—we create vaccines. We don't say, 'Injuries are supposed to hurt' or 'Bones just break sometimes'—we create laudanum and splints. People talk about how there must be a greater good behind God's plan so they can salvage the claim that God is good, and yet they don't hesitate before using modern medicine to help the sick and injured or using charity to help people displaced by a natural disaster. They don't hesitate a moment before interfering in 'God's plan.' "

Paul sipped from his cup as he considered Jim's argument. He was beginning to enjoy this tea—harsh but with a sweet aftertaste. "I heard a story about a woman tending her garden." Paul wasn't much for telling jokes, but this one took on a new meaning. "The pastor walks by and says, 'Isn't it marvelous what God can do in a garden?' She wipes the sweat from her forehead and says, 'You should have seen it when He had it all to Himself.' "

Jim stood and let out a whoop. "There's hope for you yet!" He picked up the tea tray. "Let's continue in the kitchen."

Paul followed Jim. "What about the miraculous recoveries from illness? I suppose luck or coincidence or legend explains them."

"If there is a remotely plausible natural explanation, that is far more believable than a supernatural one. Just take the facts for what they are and don't force them to fit a Christian presupposition. The Bible was written by a tribe of people thousands of years before modern science. Supernatural explanations were the best they had. Religion is a cultural fossil from a time when society had nothing better."

Jim showed Paul where he kept the tea. Paul put two fresh spoonsful in the pot while Jim refilled the kettle and set it on to boil.

"I'm impressed by how tidy you keep things," Paul said. In truth he'd seen only the kitchen, the living room that Jim used as his office, and a hallway with several closed doors, but he was curious about this grand house.

"I maintain things the way Vive liked. She was content for me to keep my office as I wanted, but the rest of the house she kept pristine. Our neighbors had maids but Vive insisted that keeping the house in order was her job."

Paul felt a wave of sympathy with a bit of pity for this sad recluse. He was keeping his house in order so Vive could return at any moment and be satisfied. Locked away in his luxurious hermitage, this man with his savage intellect and mismatched socks was living in a world of the mind, shielded from outside emotion. But Paul felt strongly drawn to this eccentric man and realized he now thought of Jim as a friend.

Jim stared out the window. Paul shrugged off the weight of the silence to restart the discussion. "What do you think of the other attributes of God—that He's merciful, just, loving . . ."

"*Loving?* Ha! Imagine a man saying to his wife, 'Darling, I love you more than words can express, and I want you near me forever . . . but if you ever leave me, so help me, I'll hunt you down and kill you slowly!' We are told that God's love is infinitely deep, far greater than that of a parent for a child, and yet if we don't believe the right thing, into hell we go for a jolly and exhilarating carnival of torture forever."

Paul remembered a frequent subject of Samuel's sermons. "The book of John says, 'For God so loved the world, that He gave his only begotten Son, that whosoever believeth in Him should not perish, but have everlasting life.' A father offering up his child—it's the ultimate sacrifice."

Jim smiled and shook his head. "Jesus's sacrifice—hugely important to the Christian, but it now seems to me a rather small matter."

"No!" Paul had listened in awe to too many sermons in which Samuel paid loving attention to the details of Jesus's death to let this stand. "Jesus died by crucifixion—a horrible, humiliating way to die."

"And I might die from cancer," Jim said. "I might suffer from six months of agony before I finally die—agony so great that I would wish I were dead. Six hours of pain on the cross might seem the easier route."

"You may not understand six hours of pain from crucifixion."

"And you may not understand six *months* of pain from cancer." Jim ran his fingers through his long hair. "Now let's imagine I go to hell to suffer an eternity of torment. That makes Jesus's six hours of pain insignificant compared to mine."

"Still, His death was the height of sacrifice. He's God. It's like a human sacrificing himself to benefit an insect."

"Not a good analogy. Jesus is supposed to have infinite love for humanity, but I don't see any human having much love for an insect." Jim placed two clean cups on the tea tray. "The absurdity of the story, of course, is the resurrection. If he died, there's no miraculous resurrection, and if there's a resurrection, there's no sacrifice through death. Miracle or sacrifice—you can't have it both ways. The Gospels don't say that he died for our sins but that he had a rough couple of days for our sins. And if we must bear Adam's sin no matter what we do, why don't we benefit from the sacrifice that removes it no matter what we do?"

"But the Christian story is unique. Where else do we have a god dying for the benefit of humans?"

"Christianity is unique, just like every religion," Jim said. "And what about Prometheus?"

Paul had read quite a bit of Greek mythology, but he let Jim continue.

"Prometheus stole fire from Olympus and gave it to humanity. Zeus discovered the crime and punished Prometheus by chaining him to a rock so that a vulture could eat his liver. Each night, his liver grew back and the next day the vulture would return, day after agonizing day. Now *that's* a sacrifice for humanity. Jesus is crucified once and then pops back into existence—rather weak by comparison."

Prometheus was fiction, of course, but Paul had nothing to argue that the miracle stories of Jesus were anything different. "But if the sacrifice saves you from hell," he said, "maybe we should appreciate it and be grateful for it, even if we can't understand it."

"Do Bronze Age customs persist so that we need a human sacrifice? If God loves us so deeply and he wants to forgive us, couldn't he just . . . forgive us?"

"God can't just forgive us."

"Why not? That's how you do it."

"What I mean is, He's the judge, and to forgive us, to let our sins go unpunished, would bypass His perfect justice."

"Then I don't think much of his 'perfect justice.' It's certainly not the lesson we get from the parable of the Prodigal Son where the father forgives the son even after being wronged by him. If that's the standard of mercy, why can't God follow it? And maybe I'm old-fashioned, but I'd prefer to see punishment in proportion to the crime. The person whose crime was a white lie shouldn't get the same punishment as Attila the Hun. No crime deserves an eternal stay in hell.

"And I find the logic behind Jesus's sacrifice especially opaque. God made mankind imperfect and inherently vulnerable to sin. Living a sinless life is impossible, so hell becomes unavoidable. But God sacrificed Jesus, one of the persons of God, so mankind could go to heaven instead. That is, God sacrificed himself to himself so we could bypass a rule that God made himself and that God deliberately designed us to never be able to meet? I can't even understand that; I certainly feel no need to praise God for something so nonsensical. We can just as logically curse him for consigning us to hell from birth."

Paul leaned against the counter and stared at the floor, absorbing these ideas and taking stock of his position. He had crossed a boundary, gradually. Like a wagon almost imperceptibly cresting a large and gently rounded hill, things felt different, and he now realized that he was on the other side. Two drops of rain can land near each other on a mountain ridge, the first flowing down one side, and the second down the other. One eventually finds its way into the Atlantic Ocean and one into the Pacific—a slight initial difference with vast ultimate consequences. He had been on one side of the ridge, and now he was on the other. He had assumed that God existed, and any evidence to the contrary he had reshaped to fit that assumption. But he could do that no longer.

The kettle whistled. Jim filled the pot and carried the tea tray back to the living room with Paul following.

"How's your chess game?" Paul asked.

"It's still early, but I'm gaining the upper hand."

The two men sat and drank tea and traded pleasantries as the afternoon light faded. But as congenial as the environment was, Paul couldn't relax. He fidgeted in his chair, feeling distracted as he gave increasingly curt responses to Jim's comments. Finally he turned the conversation to the issue that had been nagging him. "I don't think I believe anymore." There—it was out. "I can't force myself to believe— I need reasons. That's why I was a quick convert to Reverend Hargrove's way of thinking—he promised those reasons." His thoughts seemed muddled, but the words tumbled out more easily now. "I thought that he delivered on that promise . . . but I don't think so anymore. If the reasons aren't there, I can't believe, can I?" Maybe it wasn't advice he needed as much as support. He didn't mention that he could never admit this to Samuel. Samuel would be furious.

"You gave up childhood things once you'd outgrown them."

Paul felt doubtful and said nothing. While in Samuel's orbit, his belief had kept him in a safe place—confining but comfortable. Jim's new thinking took him out, away from those confines. He felt as if he were squinting in the bright sun, breathing invigorating but unfamiliar air. Old constraints now appeared ephemeral, even imaginary. There were many possibilities, but it was all so new.

Jim leaned back with his arm on the top of the sofa. "Imagine that a man goes to a doctor. He has been crippled for his entire life and uses crutches. The doctor examines the man and says, 'Good news—I've seen this problem before, and I know how to fix it. After a couple of months of treatment, you'll be able to walk normally. No more need for those crutches.' The man hugs his crutches and says, 'Don't throw away my crutches, Doc! I couldn't get along without them.' But the doctor has no intention of doing so. He heals the patient, and the crutches become unnecessary. The patient throws them away himself."

"But who are you to say what my crutches are?"

"No one at all. If you think you don't have crutches, then that's fine. If you think you do, then you're the one who will need to discard them. It's all up to you. Don't replace Sam as your authority with me. The authority is you."

Chapter 9

Christianity was false. Paul had pushed this idea away for weeks, but it would stay down no longer. He savored it like a bitter candy.

The intellectual focus that Jim championed, with no quarter given to sloppy thinking, felt right. It was an honest outlook on life. But what was he losing in the process? Who was he betraying? The magnitude of Paul's conclusion sucked the air from his apartment.

He grabbed his jacket and left. The evening air was warm and the streets quiet, and brisk walking calmed him. He walked aimlessly at first but then found himself in the Dresden neighborhood, an area he tried to avoid but knew well. Obeying his feet, he soon found himself at an apartment building he hadn't visited in a year.

Virgil Maynard lived here, and he had grown up with Paul in the LA Boys Home. Virgil was a little older but had always been smaller, and Paul often stepped in when Virgil was bullied, taking the punishment meant for his friend. A strong bond developed between the two, as if they were family.

The environment that taught Virgil that success came through kindness and accommodation taught Paul that it came through strength and intimidation. Samuel stressed that he needed to unlearn that lesson and stay away from harmful influences from his old life. Paul followed Samuel's dictate, mostly. His rare and clandestine visits with Virgil were the only connection to his past life.

Paul walked up to the third floor, found the door with the smudged calling card tacked to it that read, "V. Maynard, Esq.," and knocked.

Virgil answered. "Howdy, little brother," he said, though there was no actual relationship. "It's been a while. Are you here to have another go at salvaging my soul?" When Paul first joined the church, his exuberance with his new life had pushed him to evangelize to Virgil a few times.

"Definitely not. This is a social call."

"The best kind. Come in."

Virgil's apartment was similar in size to his own. It was a small room with a bed that doubled as a sofa, a kitchen table with two chairs, a sink, and a bureau. An open window looked out at a brick wall on the other side of a narrow alley. The table was covered with dime novels, thick copies of *Argosy* and *The Popular Magazine* with gaudy color covers, and a copy of the *Union Labor Record*. A parakeet cheeped occasionally from a small cage in a corner, and the place smelled of fried food.

"Staying busy?" Paul asked.

"I've got work at the refinery—assistant boilermaker." Virgil's greasy overalls without a shirt fit the job.

"Steady work?"

"For now." His hand swept the apartment. "Keeps me in my swanky digs. But I guess envying my job isn't what you came for."

Paul poked through the magazines. "I need someone to talk to."

"I'm good for that." Virgil gestured to one of the chairs and took the other.

Paul seated himself and sighed. "Since Reverend Hargrove rescued me a couple of years ago, it's felt right being a Christian. I know that doesn't work for you, but it convinced me—mostly because he had a *reason* for the belief. It wasn't just 'believe because I said so.' I need that logical foundation. And it's been like a family—there are people who care about me and need me."

"Yep, I know all that."

"Well, it's coming apart."

"Been fired?"

"No, nothing like that. I just don't believe anymore—or I don't think I do."

"I can see how belief might be a job requirement," Virgil said. "Wish you did?"

"Sort of. I don't know."

Virgil stood up and squinted, looking like a doctor critiquing a patient. "I know what your problem is. You need a drink. Or maybe several."

Paul waved his hand. "Drinking's off limits."

"You had no aversion to liquor a few years ago." Virgil took a white shirt off the bed and put it on. "Get up—we're going out."

"If Reverend Hargrove found out, he'd kill me . . . and *then* fire me."

"And where's the safest place, the place where the good reverend will never find you? In a bar."

"I might be seen."

"For a smart guy, you're pretty stupid. Anyone who sees you in a bar can't tell your reverend because that would prove that he was there, too." Virgil lifted Paul from his seat and guided him to the door. "Tell yourself that you're just going to keep me out of trouble. Or that you're old enough to make a decision on your own."

Paul's anxiety had drained him, and he let himself be guided. A few minutes later, they walked into the Carronade, one of Dresden's larger bars. It was early on this Saturday evening, but the bar was already busy and noisy. The patrons seemed to be mostly roughnecks from the oil rigs near Echo Park, but a few working women were laughing loudly at the bar. Paul and Virgil found a table near the back.

With beers before them, Paul opened up about Jim and how convincing he was, how sensible Jim's demand for solid arguments felt, and how useless faith seemed to be in reply. When he got to his third beer, he moved on to Thena and how much he'd missed her the previous two months.

Paul listened closely to Virgil's news of friends from the past. Most of it was bad. One friend was dead. Another had started a long stint in prison and wasn't adapting well.

A fresh glass in front of him, Paul said, "Reverend Hargrove would kill me if he caught me here."

"You told me."

"Let me tell you what he did to the Evans family." Paul took another drink of beer. "Young Mr. Evans is a little older than me. He and his parents were church members from way back. So young Mr. Evans decides he wanted a different church—bigger, smaller, more women, I don't know why. So he leaves First Church of God and somehow the story of what he didn't like gets back to Reverend Hargrove, and he goes off like an oil gusher. Like I said, I don't know what Mr. Evans left for or didn't like, but I wasn't going to get in the middle it to ask.

"Reverend Hargrove was mad for a couple of days and then calls the Evans parents into his office and tells them that they weren't members anymore. They're gone, just like that. He was real polite to them, and after they left, he was whistling for the rest of the day."

"Gosh, is there a job for me, too?" Virgil clinked his glass against Paul's.

"I'm serious. He's furious when you cross him."

"So leave."

"I can't. Reverend Hargrove demands loyalty, but in this case, he deserves it. He saved me, from this." He gestured at the room. He was rejecting Virgil's life, but he knew Virgil felt the same way and would take no offense. "This is where I'm from, but growing up I always felt that I was made for something better." Paul shook his head. "But it's more than that." He thought back to an evening five years earlier, to the memory that still haunted him.

Peeking out from an alley, Paul had selected his victim—a man about his height but thinner and about forty, walking alone. The rancid smell of the meat packing plant was almost visible in the hot summer air. Paul reached out, dragged the man back into the shadow, and demanded his wallet. Incredibly, the man fought back and gave Paul a feeble smack in the chest. Paul reacted instinctively and punched him solidly in the jaw. The man's head hit the stone wall behind him and then, instead of easing down into a heap, he toppled over stiffly like a tree. His head bounced off the cobblestones with a sickening, hollow sound.

He lay there face up and eyes open as if he were surprised, as motionless as a side of pork. A tiny dark puddle spread from under his head, and Paul ran.

That was long ago, and yet Paul's heart raced with the memory. He had killed a man. The police never found him, but his freedom brought torment rather than comfort.

The job, the community, and the respectability had all been important, but absolution—the church's unique power to erase even the biggest sins—had been its greatest attraction. How could he leave?

ॐ

"How is our atheist friend?" Samuel patted Paul on the shoulder as they walked down the sidewalk. Hollow banging from a boilermaker shop echoed from across the street as they passed a horse hitched to a wagon full of bricks.

"Oh, doing well. I met with him two days ago."

"And what did you talk about?"

"The problem of evil."

"We hadn't prepared for that."

"No—he brought it up." Paul's gut tensed as he prepared for the blow—Samuel would surely grill him on his performance.

"And how did you do?"

"Pretty good, pretty good. I think I scored some good points."

"Great to hear."

Paul cowered internally, waiting for more questions, but they didn't come. Samuel seemed satisfied with that summary, or perhaps he was occupied with his own thoughts. The two men walked along for several more blocks as Paul gradually relaxed.

Two mules pulling a dray piled high with straw kept pace with them in the street. The businesses became more industrial—a stable with a small blacksmith shop, a warehouse of building materials, a mason with marble statues and tombstones and the clink of chisel on stone inside. The smell of manure from the stable seemed to follow them.

Paul thought back on his last visit with Jim. He felt a twinge of guilt that he now doubted the bedrock on which Samuel's life was built. The idea that he should leave the church flitted into his mind like an erratic butterfly, but he dismissed it. He knew what life outside the church was like.

Samuel stopped in front of a storage yard. "This is it," he said with a theatrical sweep of his hand. The fenced yard occupied half a block. Inside, Paul could see a few piles of lumber, bricks, and other building materials, and grassless rectangles on the ground showed where more piles had lain. A low warehouse stood on the other half of the block.

"The new church will be built here?" Paul asked as he turned to examine the neighborhood. Warehouses, workshops, stables, and smokestacks were all he could see. Wagons and horses clattered by, and the banging and wheezing of machinery filled the air.

"It'll stand right where this yard is. The land was inexpensive, and building permits are easier to get in this neighborhood. Construction starts Monday."

"It's a bit noisy."

"Not on Sundays. Everything's shut down, and it's as quiet as a meadow. And I'm sure we'll draw new members from the men working here."

Paul studied the weedy lot and tried to imagine Samuel's grand church here. "How long will it take to build?"

"Six months or so. That schedule pushes the builder, but he's pretty certain that he can make it. Certainly by Easter."

"Will we have the money?"

"We hit a peak about three weeks after the quake, but it's steady now. I'm still seeing new faces from all the press back in April."

"God will provide," Paul volunteered.

"Yes, He will."

The platitude slipped out of his mouth easily and was accepted readily, but Paul felt as though he were masquerading.

Samuel showed Paul around. After ten minutes of walking the lot, sketching the imposing building in space for Paul's benefit, Samuel stopped and slapped his jacket pocket. "I forgot." He took out a small cardboard box. "These are for you."

Paul opened the box and saw that it held engraved calling cards. He took one out and, under his name and in an authoritative font, he read "Associate Pastor."

"But I thought you wanted me to convert Jim Emerson first," Paul said.

"It sounds like you're almost there."

"Well, perhaps, but I can't say he's converted yet."

"Maybe you can get back to that later. We've got the election for the Assembly seat coming up and we're working on this new church building—these projects are more important. I think your apologetics work has met its goals, and we need to move on." Samuel smiled. "Congratulations."

Paul thanked Samuel and stared at the card. The promotion was an unexpected honor, but it felt undeserved. He hadn't converted Jim; Jim had just about converted him. Perhaps this closed the Jim issue so that he would no longer need to hide his debating failures from Samuel, but the issue of his crumbling faith remained, hidden and undiscussed. And could he still visit Jim? He enjoyed talking with the eccentric atheist. To take the convenient path and turn his back on Jim . . . no—this was impossible.

He ran his fingers over the card and felt the raised ink. This card ought to belong to someone else—someone who deserved the promotion. He returned the card to the box.

∽

The train lurched to a stop with a final squeal of brakes. Athena looked out the window at the imposing sign on the train station: "Los Angeles." Home! Finally, after nearly three months.

She saw no familiar faces on the platform. The passengers around her stood and stretched and collected their belongings. Athena had none to collect, as if she were returning from a day trip. She carried only the Bible the abbot had given her.

For the entire twenty-hour trip she had puzzled over what to say to her family about her loss of faith, but she was still undecided. She didn't know what to make of the silence that had followed her second letter in which she had tried to explain her new thinking, her questioning of the Bible.

But perhaps this was more worry than necessary. The abbot was probably right—her family loved her and would accept her for whom she had become. This nagging anxiety overshadowed what should be a joyous and well-deserved homecoming. And yet her parents' strong faith wouldn't easily accept dissent, and Paul would feel the same way.

Athena was almost alone on the train when she got to her feet, feeling a little like Alice in Wonderland. This technology-saturated world with its locomotives, smoke, and noise was vastly different than the one she had come from, with the gongs marking time as they called the Buddhists to prayer or meditation, the trees quietly brushing the tops of the light wood walls, and the monks moving about their daily tasks. She had come to cherish each of the monks as well as many of the refugees who had shared the monastery with her as their temporary home.

She stood on the bottom step of the train car and looked out over the crowd of people—all strangers—as steam from under the train boiled up between her feet.

"Thena!" At least one was not a stranger. The voice was indistinct but feminine, and Athena scanned the crowd. After a few moments, she heard her name again and saw her mother, her ruffled shirtwaist and long black trumpet skirt flapping as she ran.

"Thena, it really is you!" Her mother pushed past the last few people to embrace her as she stepped down. The faint German accent that had embarrassed her as a child was now sweet music. Athena hugged her mother tightly, breathing in the familiar, comforting smell of her soap. She looked up to see her father and Paul trotting up, both smiling. Mr. Farber wore a suit and derby, his requisite attire in public. His eyes were red and his voice choked. She gently stroked his lined face.

"Thena . . ." he said as he squeezed her against her mother.

Her mother looked up at her. "We thought you were . . . we thought you were gone, forever."

"Didn't you get my letters?"

Her father showed her a telegram. "We've heard nothing from you except the telegram we got just a few hours ago." His accent, slightly stronger than her mother's, was comforting.

It reminded her of all that she was pulling away from but also all that she had missed. She was home.

"We hardly knew what to make of it—it's been so long," he said.

Athena had sent the telegram from Fresno, a few hundred miles up the line. She hadn't realized—hadn't imagined—that her parents hadn't received her letters, that they didn't know that she had been safe all this time. She thought of what she had put them through and began to cry herself. "I wrote to you . . . I'm sorry . . . I didn't know," she managed. The letters must have gotten lost in the chaos after the earthquake. Squeezed though she was between two sobbing parents, it felt so good to be back home. She kissed first one face and then the other.

"Jesus brought you back," her mother said. "I've been praying and praying!" She repeated her thanks to Jesus several times, her voice muffled against Athena's neck.

There would be time enough later to talk of who had actually saved her, Athena thought as she held them for long moments.

"Thena." She felt a new hand on her back and looked up.

"Paul . . ."

He held out his hands to her, and she turned to him. He grabbed her tight and put his cheek against her hair. After a few moments, Mr. Farber cleared his throat, and Paul took the hint and dropped his arms. Mrs. Farber reached out for Athena's arm and she embraced her mother once more.

Athena slowly released her mother and breathed deeply to collect her emotions. Her parents did the same, wiping eyes and clearing throats. Strangers walked around their reunion, a small but safe pebble in the noisy stream of chattering people, clattering baggage wagons, blowing whistles, and hissing steam.

Her mother looked her up and down. "Thena, whose dress are you wearing? It looks hideous. And what happened to your hair? Dear, you look like a factory worker."

Athena's hands went to her hair, setting it in place with her fingers. She had cut it more than a month earlier and no longer thought of it as a novelty. Without brushes and hair combs, her long hair had been a nuisance at the monastery, and short hair was easier to care for. She had felt liberated once it was gone. "It's much easier this way," she said, feeling compelled to justify herself. "With a trim and a few pins, it will look better." She smoothed the print dress over her legs. "One of the women I knew gave me this dress."

Mother clucked her tongue and shook her head as she looked at the offending dress. "Where is everything? Should we get your luggage?"

"This is it." She held up her Bible. "I was crushed under bricks in the hotel. Some Japanese monks rescued me, and I don't know where my things are."

"Your Aunt Abigail said that the hotel burned," her father said. "Nothing inside was saved."

"All those pretty dresses," Mother said, her face clouded as she rubbed Athena's arms. "But you're here, and that's what matters." She hugged Athena again. "I suppose if everything is gone, a Bible is a good thing to make a fresh start with."

"What happened after you were rescued?" her father asked.

"My leg was broken," Athena said, patting her left leg under her dress. "The monks took me to their monastery near Sausalito, north of San Francisco."

"Not to a hospital?"

"There were so many casualties and things were so chaotic that makeshift clinics amputated for injuries like mine. They set my leg at the monastery, but I couldn't walk without crutches until about a week ago."

Her father bent down to look at Athena more squarely. "But they could have taken you to a proper hospital after that."

"They took good care of me, Daddy. Anyway, they had no carriages to take me."

"Dear, you should have told them that we would pay," he said.

"I did, but money wasn't important to them. They were overflowing with refugees—people from farms whose homes had collapsed. So many people lived in adobe houses, but the wooden monastery survived just fine. Some came because they had no food. Taking care of the survivors was the priority, not getting me to a hospital."

Her father shook his head. "Those inconsiderate heathen—that could explain how your letters got lost."

"No, no—not at all." Athena took her father by the arm. "They took me in and a hundred other people and didn't ask for a penny from anyone."

"Well, I won't be in debt to a Chinaman. You tell me how much it cost and how to contact the head man, and I'll wire the money."

Athena wanted desperately to repay the monastery for her care, but she shrank from her father's harsh language. Still, she knew her parents were good people, and over time she would help them appreciate all that the monks had done for her.

"Let's get you home and cleaned up," her mother said, "and out of that dress." She took Athena's hand and the four of them walked slowly down the platform, the setting sun bright in their eyes.

Los Angeles felt much warmer than Sausalito, and the air smelled like industry. Her bad leg was stiff, and she favored it as she walked.

Athena's parents walked on either side of her, and she missed holding Paul's hand.

"How did you pay for your train fare?" Paul asked. "Or food on your trip?"

"The abbot gave me money."

This set her father off again on indebtedness to "Chinamen."

A yellow car pulled up to the trolley station and they boarded, taking nickels for the fare from Mr. Farber as they stepped in. They rode the trolley home and Athena said little, listening as her mother prattled on about dresses, the goings-on within the church community, and the crush of new people after Reverend Hargrove's prophecy, with occasional interjections from her father or Paul. Athena noted the newly foreign streets and houses as the trolley clattered the three miles to their home in North University Park.

After they got off at their stop, her father said, "Why don't we do this: Mother and I will get Thena her supper and give her a chance to rest, and Paul, you can come back tomorrow after church. I'm sure she won't mind repeating her stories. How does that sound?"

Paul looked doubtfully at Athena, but her return to civilization had been stressful and she was ready for some quiet.

"Would that be all right with you?" she said to Paul, holding out her hands.

He took her hands and looked at her sadly. "I'll come by tomorrow," he said. As he hopped back on the trolley, he turned and smiled. "And I'll see you in church."

She'd forgotten that the next day was Sunday. The days of the week had meant little at the monastery. Several months without church had become a habit she didn't want to break even though it would clash with her parents' ideas of correct living. She didn't want to participate in and support an empty ritual, but she also didn't want to upset her family. As the three of them walked home, she fretted about how she could handle this problem.

At the gate to the small fenced yard, she looked up at the house she had lived in with her parents for a decade. It was familiar and unchanged, and yet she saw its Victorian excesses in a new light. It looked like a gigantic and extravagant jewelry box. A porch wrapped around the right side of the house, and the pediment over the front door and gable on the left side of the second floor were elaborately ornamented. Pale green siding with blue and white trim covered the house, and wooden finery dripped from the edge of the porch ceiling. The generous porch made Athena think of the people crowded with their belongings under the plain wooden eaves in the monastery courtyard.

Her father held the door for the women.

"Sit in the parlor, Thena." Mother steered her to the small, overstuffed room with walls painted a strong red. Everywhere, Athena saw things—framed photos on the mantle over the fireplace, decorative pottery on the chest, figurines in the cupboard, watercolors on the picture rail. It made her uncomfortable, almost claustrophobic, and was quite a contrast with her uncluttered room at the monastery.

"I'm not company," Athena said with a smile. "We don't need to sit in the parlor. Let me help with supper."

Athena put on an apron, and the reunited family spent the rest of the day cooking and laughing and eating standing up as she struggled to tell the story of her rescue and stay in the monastery, what it had meant to her, and how she changed. She spoke of the food, the people, and the living conditions but avoided the abbot's invitation to explore Christianity, Father Mondegreen's inept attempts to shore it up, and her own conclusions—everything superficial and nothing important. Athena regretted holding back, but the rest would come with time.

During a pause in the conversation, her mother stepped in to launch it in a new direction. "I never gave up hope," she said as she held Athena's hand in hers. "I knew that God would see us through. And He did—He saved you, and here you are."

"The monks saved me, Mother. And my leg."

"You listen to your mother," her father said. "She understands these things."

"And it was nice to see you carrying your Bible," her mother said, patting Athena's hand. "Through all your trials, you haven't forgotten what's important. You'll have such fun tomorrow, seeing all our friends at church. They'll think they're seeing a ghost."

Athena sighed and shook her head. It was late and she was tired. She had slept poorly on the train, and she excused herself to get a bath and go to bed. She looked at her parents through wet eyes. "I'm so sorry to have put you through all that worry. It feels good to be back." She held out her arms. "I love you both." The family embraced again.

Upstairs and seeing her bedroom with fresh eyes, Athena was surprised to be looking at a child's room. In one bookcase, china dolls, fashion dolls, baby dolls, and dolls of other sorts packed in as tightly as people on a crowded trolley. Fashion magazines lay neatly stacked on the night table. Clothes filled two standing wardrobes, despite the empty hangers reminding her of what had been lost to the earthquake and fire. These were someone else's belongings, and she would prune away most of what she saw.

One additional element in her life might also need to fall away. Paul was a good man, sweet and sincere, but she had left his simple faith behind and wouldn't be dragged back into it. There was no future for her as a pastor's wife.

Chapter 10

Paul woke early on Sunday eager to tell Samuel about Thena. Dressed and ready to go, he touched his jacket pocket, found it empty, and went to his bookshelf to get more calling cards. His hand hesitated over the full box, and then he opened the old one.

At the church, he found Samuel already in his office, writing a letter.

Samuel peered over his glasses at Paul and continued writing. "Morning," he said. The three fat candles were lit, as they often were when Samuel was writing his sermons, and the room smelled like flowers.

"Thena's back," Paul said with a broad grin.

Samuel took off his glasses and stared at Paul.

"I saw her yesterday! She's back and she's safe and she's home now." Paul related the whole story, bubbling over with the news—how she escaped from the earthquake, spent the previous several months in the monastery, and returned home the previous afternoon.

Samuel, all smiles now, stood and gave Paul a bear hug with a strong slap on the back. He held Paul by the shoulders at arm's length and said, "I guess prayers *are* answered."

It felt to Paul like an imagined Christmas afternoon after he'd gotten just what he wanted. He was floating, powered by the energy of retelling the story and Samuel's excitement. Then the magnitude of Samuel's words hit him—*was* Thena's return an answered prayer? His intellect knew her return was impossible, but he had prayed just the same, and the impossible happened. He had never heard a more powerful testimonial to God's power. Jim's atheism had only just taken hold in him, the superior viewpoint that best explained the world, but now this.

Samuel pounded his desk. "I'll work this into my sermon!" he said as he reached for paper and put on his glasses.

Paul felt full of life as he took a deep breath. Heck—he would be happy to thank *Zeus* for Thena's return. He excused himself to prepare the sanctuary for the service. Half an hour later, he stood outside the church as he welcomed people in. Mr. Farber walked up, alone.

"Where are the ladies?" Paul looked toward the trolley stop to see if they lagged behind.

"Thena said she was tired, and Mother stayed with her, so I'm the family representative today," Mr. Farber said with his German accent. "We've had such a blessing that I had to give thanks."

The service began in the usual way, but Samuel took advantage of the big story once he had the podium. "I understand there is some happy news in the Farber household," he said. "Mr. Farber, may I impose on you to tell us about it?" He gestured for Mr. Farber to stand.

Mr. Farber stood slowly from one of the front pews. With one hand on the pew in front, he turned to face the congregation, shifting his feet as if to get a stable footing. He gave a few sentences summarizing the events from the previous day and Athena's ordeal. Every regular member had known of her assumed death, and many had attended the memorial service several months earlier.

Mr. Farber spoke clearly enough, but perhaps because the news was so startling, the brief statement produced a confused buzzing as people talked among themselves.

Samuel jumped in to regain control. His powerful voice could always fill the church, and he used it now. "Thank you, Mr. Farber." The talking stopped, and Mr. Farber sat. "Friends, our own Thena Farber, a precious child of God, was lost and is now found. Under the wreckage of that satanic earthquake, in a building licked as if by the very fires of hell, she was found by heathen Japanese. And yet almighty God protected her and returned her to us unscathed. The Japanese were prohibited from harming even a hair on that child's head and were turned into instruments for the Lord's work. Surely it can be said that 'though I walk through the valley of the shadow of death, I will fear no evil, for thou art with me; thy rod and thy staff they comfort me.' "

With arms extended and face heavenward, Samuel finished his oration shouting "Praise God!" The congregation burst into applause, loud and long. Paul tried to find Mr. Farber to gauge his reaction, but he sat hidden in the chaos.

Samuel juggled the lineup of hymns to support his new theme of celebration and praise, and his extemporaneous sermon was particularly inspiring. Truly, he had the gift, Paul thought.

Standing at the church door after the service with Paul opposite him, Samuel mirrored the jubilation of the event. The crowd moved more slowly than usual as they paused to praise Samuel for an especially moving service. Several congratulated Paul on the return of his fiancée.

Paul enjoyed a bit more celebratory small talk with Samuel afterward and then moved through the sanctuary to prepare for the second service. The wooden floor creaked, and sunlight streamed in from the south-facing windows. Hymnals lay scattered on the bare wooden pews, and he walked each row, tidying as he went.

The simple task freed his mind to wander, and it goaded him about Thena. He could imagine Samuel's voice warning about being unequally yoked with unbelievers, but this imperiled her, not him. He needed to be open with her about his unbelief, but how? He remembered her walking home the previous night, back from the earthquake with just her life and her Bible. Given her simple and even beautiful faith, was it selfish for him to tarnish it? Was the engagement salvageable? The fairest plan might be for them to go their separate ways.

He thought back to an evening visit, distant in his memory. Three weeks before the earthquake and about a year into their relationship, Paul had stood in the Farbers' parlor. He wore his nicer suit, reserved for special occasions, and he wore new cuff links, a present from Thena. He studied the photos and knickknacks he had seen dozens of times before—figurines from Germany, small formal portraits of Thena as a child and of the Farbers as a young couple, a hand-tinted photograph of the original general store run by the family.

Thena came downstairs wearing a pastel blue dress that brushed the floor with its frills and had lace on the sleeves and collar. Her long brown hair was pulled into a bun on top of her head. Paul greeted her with a smile and a compliment on her dress. It was another new one, a benefit of being an only child.

Paul chose an extravagant restaurant that evening, but he didn't mind the expense. He fingered the hard little box in his pocket. Supper complete, he took both of her hands in his and stumbled through a brief summary of their relationship and its importance to him. She squeezed his hands as a smile broadened across her lips, her expression encouraging him on. When he finally got to the marriage proposal, she giggled and whispered, "Yes!"

He fumbled for the box and opened it to show the ring, gold with a small opal birthstone. A few guests at nearby tables noticed what was happening, and when Thena put on the ring, they applauded. As the explanation spread, applause rippled through the restaurant.

Paul remembered his embarrassment at the attention but also his delight that this angel had agreed to marry a reformed bum like himself. Nothing he'd loved and lost had ever returned before.

The second service dragged as Paul fidgeted in his chair. Samuel recreated the jubilation of the first service, but Paul's thoughts were elsewhere. Images of Thena flooded his mind as he weighed various schemes for resolving the uncertainty in their relationship. He could try to pass as a Christian. He could try to deconvert her, with them running away from the church and living in obscurity. Or he could do the honorable thing and break off the relationship.

Once the last parishioner had left, Samuel patted Paul on the shoulder. "Come into my office," he said.

Paul sat on the edge of his chair, uninterested in whatever Samuel wanted to talk about. He was eager to return to the Farbers' house.

Samuel also sat upright, smiling at Paul. He patted the desk loudly as if gaveling a meeting to order. "I've realized something. I think we're missing an opportunity." Samuel paused like a cat gathering itself before springing. "Thena was lost and now she's found. It's a miracle. Not only is it a miracle, but it was prophesied."

"I don't remember that."

"Think back—we talked about it right here." Samuel smacked his desk with his palm. "We talked about God's mysterious plan, and I said that all would be revealed."

"Is that a prophecy?"

"Sure it is." Samuel spoke with a powerful and confident voice. "We could tell the papers. In fact, we must tell the papers. We can start with your reporter friend at the *Times*—you should contact him."

"I don't know what I'd say. Athena's return seems to us like a miracle, and that would be a great story, but I'd have a hard time making a case for prophecy."

"Paul, we need this."

Paul didn't like where Samuel seemed to be going and said nothing.

"We need the publicity."

"Why?"

"Our donations have dropped off, down quite a bit from the peak a couple of months ago. Publicity got people in before, and it can work again. One more good story making the rounds in the papers might get people in here and keep them here."

"Why do we need to increase the donations? With the new people, I thought we received enough."

"It's the new church building." Samuel's tone made clear his frustration, and he flung out his hands as if at a loss to explain something so obvious. "We're obliged to pay the builder a lot of money, and payments will come due soon. We had enough for the down payment, but we must find a lot more. We need some good press."

This felt wrong to Paul, deceptive. "God will provide?"

Samuel frowned. "He did provide—He returned Thena, and now it's our turn. I can't do this alone. I'll need your help."

૭)

Mr. Farber answered Paul's knock that afternoon. "Come in, Paul. We've set a place for you at the dinner table."

Paul entered and greeted everyone. Thena looked pretty in a simple white dress, perhaps a little thinner than before. Her short hair gave her a less formal air, and her engagement ring was on her finger, where he had put it in March.

The conversation at dinner centered on Thena, and she captivated Paul with more stories of her ordeal—the pain of being crushed in the hotel, her horror at seeing sick and dead people, the kindness of the abbot and the monks.

At the end of the meal, Mr. Farber said, "You two have a lot to catch up on." Mrs. Farber picked up the plates, and Thena led Paul into the hall.

"Let's go for a walk," Thena said as she pinned up her short hair and put on her hat.

Paul brushed past her to open the door. Before, she usually smelled like perfume—lemon verbena, or sometimes rose water—but this time, nothing.

She held Paul's arm and hobbled slowly down the front steps, her left leg held straight. On the sidewalk, he took her hand, delicate as always and yet rougher and stronger than before. For a while, they walked in silence. Paul shoved thoughts about his lost faith from his mind and simply enjoyed walking with her again, holding her hand, and being seen with the prettiest girl in the city. She limped slightly and pushed against his hand with each step.

"The abbot was very formal, and he called me by my given name," Athena said. "I thought it was nice."

"Do you want me to call you 'Athena' now?"

"If you'd like. I told my parents, but they didn't take me seriously."

They walked another block, past ornate Victorian houses with tidy lawns. The sidewalk was shaded by short, bushy pepper trees and towering eucalyptus trees with flaking bark.

"Reverend Hargrove had me knocking on doors over the past few months," Paul said.

"The doors of strangers? But you hate talking to strangers."

"I got a little better at it. He had me find an old friend of his named Jim. He's a freethinker, and we've talked a lot lately."

"Are you trying to convert him?"

"Reverend Hargrove expects me to. And it's let me try out the apologetics arguments that he uses in his debates."

"I had the chance to talk about Christianity with a few people in the monastery. They got me thinking about things I'd never considered. It was a lot more interesting, more *important*, than I expected."

She sounded confident in her beliefs, more confident than before the earthquake, and Paul felt her slipping out of his grasp. "Sounds like you could be a missionary for Reverend Hargrove. You could be out there, spreading the Word."

"Oh, no," she said with a laugh. "That would definitely not be a fit."

"Speaking to strangers is hard for me, too."

He let go and wiped his sweaty hand on his pants. "Sorry about that," he said with an awkward smile. He pulled off a palm-sized piece of bark as he passed by a eucalyptus tree and broke off little pieces as he walked.

"It's more that faith is a puzzling concept to me," Athena said.

"And quite important. Reverend Hargrove celebrates it in his sermons frequently. You'd be an outsider without faith."

"I can believe that."

They stopped as the residential street ended at Adams Boulevard, a busy divided street with landscaping in the center.

It would be wrong to upset Thena's beautiful faith and suicidal to bring up his own doubts. Paul's bark was gone, scattered as fragments on the sidewalk. He turned and took Athena's hand and they walked back.

&)

Samuel wanted to see his prophecy of Thena's return given prominent play in the papers. Paul had to visit seven local newspaper offices, sometimes several times, before he could make his clumsy pitch. Even on his final try, the argument that Samuel had prophesied Athena's return seemed weak, even dishonest. Paul arranged three interviews with Samuel, and was relieved to be done with the painful process.

The results for only one satisfied Samuel—the *Evening Express* had a short piece titled "LOCAL PASTOR DOES IT AGAIN," but they buried it deep in the newspaper, not on page one as Samuel had wanted.

He was enthusiastic about the new coverage though, and he had Paul paint a third Sunday service time on the sign in front of the church. Samuel worried that a burst of new attendees would fill the first two services and didn't want anyone left out.

The November election for the California Assembly seat was four months away, and Samuel treated the race as a formality, with him all but chosen. Nevertheless, he had Paul visit newspapers for endorsements and visit several local companies for campaign contributions.

Paul laboriously typed copies of Samuel's short campaign position statement titled, "Rev. Samuel Hargrove—a Godly Man for Assembly Position 72." Paul's old fear of speaking to strangers resurfaced, especially to those who might be hostile. Compounding the fear was the need to speak to a secretary and then wait for his turn to talk with a busy man who would prefer not to see him. Once inside, Paul felt incompetent and immature as he stumbled through his brief pitch, his eyes glancing down at his script on a note card in his lap and his shirt damp with nervous sweat. And then he moved on to the next one on his list, with a different secretary, a different waiting area, and a different busy man, but the same frustrating feelings of anxiety and incompetence and the same curt and noncommittal reaction. He considered pleading with Samuel to not force him to make these pitches, but the embarrassment of admitting to Samuel how clumsy he felt was the greater fear.

Fortunately, these were short-lived chores compared to the work on the new church building, which quickly grew to consume most of his time. Construction started as planned, and workmen crowded the site as they cleared the remnants of the storage yard and hauled it away by wagon. Carpenters hammered at the old fence to salvage the boards, and the brittle clink of bricks landing on bricks competed with the neighborhood's industrial noise. Stakes and string laid out the perimeter of the building, hinting at the final grand result.

Paul acted as the liaison between Samuel and the foreman—approving materials, recording progress against the schedule, ordering minor blueprint changes, and so on—and he would sometimes make the five-block trip between Samuel's office and the work site half a dozen times per day. He quickly became comfortable with the job, blissfully stress-free compared to selling Samuel to newspapermen.

A new routine overtook Paul's life after Athena's dramatic return from the dead. They saw each other frequently in the evenings and on Sunday afternoons as they rebuilt their relationship.

Athena slipped uncomfortably back into her previous life. She returned to work in her parents' store, managing the books, restocking shelves, and helping as needed, just as before. News of her parents' loss had spread among their many customers, and the story of Athena's miraculous homecoming made her something of a celebrity. She responded to the attention with a forced good humor and was relieved as she gradually regained her anonymity.

§∽

Life had become so busy and comfortable that Paul was startled to realize one day that he hadn't visited Jim for over two weeks, which fired him with an eagerness to share with Jim the news of Athena's return. However, he had some unfinished business from his last visit, and that night Paul reread the book of Job as promised. He had to admit that Jim was right—Job was a good man, but God brought every conceivable calamity on him for no reason but that He could.

But who is the clay to question the potter? Who would begrudge someone the privilege of destroying a sand castle that he built himself? Job agreed: "The Lord gave, and the Lord hath taken away; blessed be the name of the Lord." God could ignore the rules He demanded humans follow, and Job was content with that.

Paul was not. The God he had worshipped had not been so arbitrary—at least not in Paul's mind. More importantly, the story of Job could not justify why evil happened but was just a rationalization that dismissed it. When things are going well, praise God; when things are going poorly, praise God. That might be enough evidence for Job, but it didn't satisfy Paul.

The next day he took the trolley to see Jim. Jim's generous concern for him when he was mourning Athena had touched him, and he was eager to tell him of her return.

At Jim's door he heard the faint sound of gramophone music from inside. The florid and unintelligible singing told him that it was opera. He knocked on the door and waited. No answer, just the music. He knocked again. Nothing.

He tried the doorknob—unlocked. He opened the door a few inches and called in. "Hello?"

"Come." It was Jim's voice, but oddly feeble as if he were an old man.

Paul walked down the hall but slowed at the sight of the library. The room had always had a tidy messiness about it. Anything out of its place never seemed to be far from it, but not anymore. Books were stacked in piles, and many of these were topped with plates holding the dried remnants of half-eaten meals. More plates lay on the carpet. A pillow and blanket were bunched on the right side of the sofa. A Victrola with its lid up and doors open sat to the left of the sofa where the typewriter had been. On the sofa next to the Victrola sat Jim, his white nightshirt spotted with stains and his head leaning on the arm of the sofa. Black shellac records lay scattered about him—on the sofa, on the floor, on his lap—and the music played on. Jim opened his eyes and looked at Paul as he came in.

The house smelled organic and stagnant, like a back alley. Maybe it was the old food, or maybe it was Jim. A bottle of whiskey and a wine glass sat on the center table.

"Jim, are you sick?"

"Have you heard this aria? That's the great Caruso singing in Puccini's 'La Bohème.' Very sad."

Paul knelt down so he could look Jim squarely in the face. "Are you sick? Or are you drunk?"

"A little of both, I suppose."

"Is whiskey allowed in your special diet?"

"I'm off my diet at the moment."

The great Caruso held one final long note and the record ended. Jim reached for the needle and repositioned it at the beginning of the record and the music began again.

"I thought we might just talk. With no music."

Jim gestured at the Victrola. Paul took that as permission to turn it off, and the room became silent. Jim slouched into the sofa with his head fallen back as if exhausted, his face to the ceiling and his Adam's apple prominent beneath his bristly chin.

"Jim, what's wrong? What happened?" Jim was the immovable rock, always in control. Paul couldn't imagine what calamity had caused this change.

Jim lay still, looking up at the ceiling. "Oh, I got some bad news. I was expecting good news, but what I got was bad news." Jim slowly tipped his head upright and looked at Paul. "I told you that I was expecting an important visitor."

"You said that the chairman of your company was coming."

"That would be Mr. Randolph Pierce, chairman of Emerson Typewriter Company, the man my father put on the board. Yes, the thoughtful Mr. Pierce stopped by to see me. He's a busy man—I was honored." Jim sounded as if he were speaking to an audience of children.

"I've been working on a new type of tube lighting for over six years," he said. "It takes about a quarter of the power of regular light bulbs. My workshop's in the basement. I didn't show you or even talk about it much, but there's no point in being secretive now—no one gives a damn and I can't even give it away.

"Anyway, Mr. Pierce saw my demonstration, saw that it works, and then told me that this was not a direction the board felt appropriate for the Emerson Company. It was obvious that he'd made up his mind beforehand and endured my tedious demonstration simply to be polite. The decision wasn't negotiable."

"I'm very sorry to hear that," Paul said as he moved to his chair. "Maybe you could sell the idea to another company."

Jim pulled away from the sofa, making plaintive and feeble gestures. "I built it for *my* company! For my father's company. Selling it doesn't interest me—I already have more money than I need. I spent the last six years doing nothing but creating this light tube, but I guess that was all wasted. I guess I was a fool for speculating, for being loyal, for thinking that a rifle and typewriter company would see any value in a revolutionary new electrical product."

The exertion of telling the story seemed to drain Jim, and now he sank back into the sofa. Under the unshaven growth covering his cheeks, Jim's face looked more gaunt than Paul remembered.

"You could work on something else. The company must have lots of research areas."

"My technology is not supportive of the direction the company is headed, and I'm apparently not either. He asked me to resign my board position."

"But you're the majority shareholder!"

"I'm the *largest* shareholder, and that's not enough when he's turned the rest of the board against me. He said that my ideas and I are a diversion—'an unwanted diversion,' I believe were his exact words."

"You didn't."

"I did as I was told—I resigned. I certainly don't want to stand in the way of a company determined to remain firmly in the nineteenth century." He sighed. "Half of me wants to plead for my position back, and half wishes I never hear the name of that company again. I guess I don't know what to do."

Paul had counseled parishioners before, but his experience was limited. Giving gentle assurances of God's love and reading Bible verses together had been easy, but now he was floundering. He wished he could tap into Samuel's far greater expertise. "I reread the book of Job," Paul ventured.

Jim didn't take the bait.

Paul leaned forward in his chair. "I agree with your conclusion—not a very loving portrait of God."

"No, it's not," Jim said quietly.

The silence slowly closed back around Paul like a suffocating blanket. He almost wanted a return of Caruso. Then he remembered why he came. "I've been waiting to tell you—Thena's back."

Jim lifted his head up and looked at Paul, his hair shaggy and wild. "She is? How?"

Paul told the story and Jim revived a bit.

"I'm very happy for you, my boy," Jim said, putting out his hand.

Paul smiled as he walked over to shake it, noting as he did that Jim did indeed smell worse than the plates of leftover food.

"I wish the loss of my wife Vive had the same ending," Jim said as he slowly sat up straighter. "I certainly prayed for it."

Paul leaned forward to encourage Jim on.

"Even now I have dreams of the day they died—she and my daughter. I didn't want to go on. I felt numb, suicidal. I couldn't sleep. I drank too much. I drove away my remaining friends. And I couldn't leave the house even if I wanted to."

"Why not?"

"Don't you understand why I'm always here? Agoraphobia is the technical term—fear of open spaces. For me, it's really more a fear of places out of my control. I feel safe in here and nowhere else."

"How long have you been like this?"

"Must be more than twenty years."

"Wasn't Reverend Hargrove a friend? Couldn't he help?"

Jim chuckled and shook his head. "Sam was the problem, not the solution."

"You had a falling out, then."

" 'Shunning' is the precise way to put it. The church expelled Jenny and me. Sam was just an ordinary member back then, but he pushed the church leadership to label us bad elements, caustic to the spiritual well-being of the godly members of the church, and everyone was forbidden from contact with us."

This fit what Mrs. O'Brien had told him—that Jim had gotten Jenny pregnant. "But surely Samuel wasn't behind this," Paul said.

"He was. He told me."

No one could begrudge a church for having rules, but cutting someone off from his community seemed cruel. Was Samuel simply a firm moralist or had this been excessive?

Jim rubbed his bearded face with his palms. "The expulsion was a complete surprise. One day a church elder told me that I was no longer a member. Just like that. It made no sense and I told him so, and I thought that laid the matter to rest. That Sunday I went to church as usual. After the first hymn, I was singled out and made to stand in the aisle. The pastor laid out the charges, and I had no chance to defend myself. Everyone else in the church was given an explicit choice—pick me or the church. It was like looking over the edge at the top of a tall building and feeling vertigo for the first time. It hits you, hard."

Jim brushed at his legs through the nightshirt, smoothing the wrinkles. "There I was, alone in the center of the church. My friends wouldn't look at me, and it seemed like everyone else was glaring. It took a few moments to realize that the only avenue left was to walk out the door, to publicly accept their judgment, to admit that I was powerless. It wasn't negotiable. The humiliation, without a chance to give my side—it was completely unexpected.

"After that, I tried to reach out, to correct the wrong, to repair the bridges with old friends, but they mostly did what they were told. They'd walk away, ignoring me as I pleaded my case. I hardly knew anyone outside the church, so my entire social network was gone in an instant. I even approached Sam, demanded that he justify himself. The bastard said something about preserving the integrity of the church."

"That can't be a Christian thing to do." This event seemed inconceivable in the warm family of Samuel's church, or any church of which Samuel had been a part.

Jim reached for the wine glass, half full of brown liquid—whiskey judging by the bottle next to it. He took a generous swallow and grimaced. "There's plenty of support for shunning in the Bible. If my former friends said anything to me at all, it was usually a terse reference to a verse. They'd say, 'I bid thee not Godspeed,' a reference to 2 John 10. Or, I was simply denounced as a 'tax collector,' a reference to the fallen-away man in Matthew 18:17. I had a couple of shouting matches with people, and I must admit that being humiliated in public, with all the charges against me laid out for the entertainment of every passerby, is a pretty powerful punishment. Soon, simply seeing one of my old friends, if only by accident, was enough to bring up those feelings of humiliation again."

Jim stared at the wall behind Paul, his eyes sunken and his face strained. "Once I was incapacitated simply by the anxiety of the situation, not by any insults thrown at me. Drowning slowly would have been more pleasant. An intense unreasonable fear, dizziness, my gut in knots, my heart racing and legs rubbery, unable to catch my breath— the feeling was upon me in two seconds. Then I was on the ground for twenty minutes until I recovered." He took another sip. "I experienced that once more, a few years later after Vive died. I had been rather housebound at that time, but with Vive gone, I tried to reach out to my old church friends. I had no one else to turn to. But again the panic came over me and I was lying on the ground, awash with that drowning feeling. I never wanted to experience that panic again, and I told myself that I'd happily stay in my house for the rest of my life rather than risk it. And so I did."

Paul knew what this felt like. When he was about eleven, he had once confided his complaints about the poor conditions in the orphanage to one of the matrons, someone he felt would be sympathetic. That evening at supper, Mr. Dammer the warden said to everyone, "I understand there's a boy who has recommendations for how we can make this a happier place. We all want this to be a happy place, don't we, boys?"

The words stopped Paul's heart. He hunched over his meal trying to avoid notice, staring at the ripples in his soup as rapid boot steps pounded closer. A hand yanked him to his feet and dragged him to the front of the dining hall.

"Paul can tell us, can't you, Paul?" Mr. Dammer said, his voice echoing off the bare stone walls. "Tell us." He was a tall, thin man who always had a tumorous lump of chewing tobacco in his cheek except for mealtimes. A thin tobacco-colored line stained one side of his stubbled jaw.

Paul said nothing.

"Come on now—give us your advice. Tell us how to make this a happier place."

Paul thought of the poor food, the bullying from the older boys, the beatings for rule infractions, the boredom. He thought of the muffled screams and vague fighting sounds from nearby bunks that sometimes jolted him awake late at night and kept him up for hours afterwards, his heart racing as imaginings ran through his head.

But a reasoned and dispassionate critique was clearly not what Mr. Dammer was after.

"I'm waiting, boy." His tone grew harsher. He bent down to look Paul in the face, and Paul could smell alcohol on his breath. "Tell us," he said, and smacked the back of Paul's head. "Tell us!" Another smack. The cycle repeated, over and over, as the scene swam behind tears. "Tell us! Tell us!" The other boys began laughing.

Paul blubbered out, "Nothing," but the smacks continued. As did the taunts. And the laughter, interminably. A drowning feeling swelled up as he tried to choke out something, anything that would stop the torment.

It only happened once, but once was enough.

Paul breathed deeply as the memory passed. But what could be done for Jim? Paul felt powerless to help. It seemed so unfair. Surely Jim's housebound condition wasn't Samuel's goal. "Could I talk to Reverend Hargrove for you?"

"That ship has sailed," Jim said with a weak laugh. "I have no interest in him or his church or his religion."

Paul realized with a jolt that time was short—in fact, he was already overdue at the construction site. He made his excuses and got up to leave.

It didn't feel right to leave Jim in this state, to not even help tidy up. He felt his own allegiance tested, as if he were in that church twenty-some years earlier, being forced to side with the church, with its community and heaven and Samuel, or with the man standing alone and discarded in the middle of the aisle. Paul slowly turned and walked away, his footsteps loud in the newly long corridor.

At the end of his workday, Paul went to Samuel's office to ask about Jim. Samuel had far more experience, and maybe he could recommend ways to help.

"Tell me what happened." Samuel's face was eager as he lit a cigar.

Paul described Jim's new lighting technology as best as he could, how he'd failed to convince the chairman, and how he'd given up his position on the board.

"What makes you say he was depressed?"

Paul talked of the sad opera music and Jim's demeanor.

"You say the house was messy—in what way?"

Paul told him about the abandoned plates of food, the whiskey, and the pillow and blanket on the floor.

Samuel thought for a moment. "You can have all the money in the world, but without the embrace of the church, you have nothing," he concluded with a smile.

That didn't address the problem. "Can you tell me how best to help him? I have no experience dealing with someone so depressed. I thought I might leave work early tomorrow to visit him."

"Visiting this man takes away from your work. He's a diversion—discard him."

Chapter 11

Paul and Athena walked through Central Park, just west of downtown. Six- and eight-story buildings surrounded the one-block oasis, and the couple went there often. Sunday was the most popular day for couples to promenade, but this was a Thursday afternoon, and the crowds were light. It was late July, the sun wouldn't set until eight o'clock, and the two of them walked without haste.

Paul wore a suit and had a new celluloid collar on his shirt, and Athena wore a high-necked dress with lavender and white stripes that made her look as enticing as a cake. Current women's fashion had a shapeless quality to it, but Paul saw enough curves to give him something to think about.

As captivating as seeing Athena the previous few weeks had been, Paul's mind had become mired in Jim's problem. He felt Jim's anguish as if he were a favorite uncle—in fact, Paul was the closest person to a relative that Jim had in Los Angeles, and perhaps anywhere. Despite Samuel's command, Paul could not abandon Jim—he owed him that much. Jim had given him a new worldview and a bone-deep respect for the truth that shrugged off any inconvenience it might cause. And Jim needed him now.

How to help? He had stopped by for a short visit the previous day, as if Jim had been a sick parishioner, tidying up and talking. He felt useful, but it was only treading water and Jim was still far from shore.

A squeeze of Athena's hand reminded him that he was ignoring his fiancée. He looked down at her. "I didn't see you in church Sunday," Paul said, watching a couple on a tandem bicycle crunch slowly past on the gravel path.

"No."

"I think that's the third time."

She stopped and looked at him. "So you're keeping count too? Sounds like we're about to repeat the argument I just had with my parents."

"Sorry—I was just wondering."

She sighed and they walked on. "That's okay. Things have changed since the earthquake, and everyone seems to want me back in the same spot."

"Maybe First Church of God isn't the right church."

"Maybe." Athena's bad leg had grown stronger, but Paul felt her slight limp through her hand. "I'm doing a little study on my own now. I'm reading the Bible."

"Your parents must like that."

"They'd rather I go to church and do what I'm told than try to think things out myself."

"I'm in the middle of some personal study too." Paul admired her interest but couldn't imagine her approaching Christianity with his skepticism. Athena's miraculous return had breathed new life into his faith, though that was sagging again. He felt like a hypocrite when they said the Apostle's Creed in church, with all those "I believe" statements. It staggered him when he kept rediscovering it, but he just didn't believe.

They sat on a bench shaded by an oak tree. After a pause, Paul said, "Tell me about your suffragette meeting."

"Please—it's suffra*gist*."

"Sorry. I'm still amazed that you wanted to go. That never interested you before."

"It should have since it affects me. Women can vote in four states now. They think that California will be next, and there's a referendum on the ballot this November. They've planned public rallies and letter-writing campaigns. It's all very exciting."

The issue seemed frivolous to Paul. "But when we're married, I'll vote for us."

"Not all women have husbands. Anyway, I want to decide and vote for myself. We may not always agree."

"If we don't agree, we'll have bigger problems than who to vote for. We agree now, right?"

"I suppose," Athena said, "but I expect to learn and grow in the future."

"It's not the natural order for women to vote."

She tisked with her tongue. "People thought that owning slaves was the natural order, but we've moved past that. I think that we also need to get past half our citizens being disenfranchised."

That was a word Paul had never heard from her, and he wasn't quite sure he *liked* hearing it from her. "What do your parents think?"

"I guess they want to know what happened to their little girl who collected dolls and liked parties."

The same thought had occurred to Paul. "Will you meet with your suffrage group again?"

"Oh, yes. We're working on a public rally on September thirteenth, the six-month anniversary of Susan B. Anthony's passing. That will build support for the November referendum. The theme of the rally will be, 'Men, their rights and nothing more; women, their rights and nothing less.' I volunteered to help mail invitations."

Athena let go of his arm and gestured as she spoke. "And I met one woman who said I should go to college."

"But you've already been to school."

"That was finishing school. I want to learn more than how to smile, how to dress, and how to entertain guests. I could take a degree, maybe in English or History or Art."

Paul sat in silence, startled by these new passions and unsure what to make of them. He had expected to take care of her after they were married. But if she could take a degree and then get some fancy job and earn her own money and even vote—if she could take care of herself—what was his role?

This conversation needed steering to safer territory. Paul said, "I think I'll avoid taking you with me when I visit Jim."

"I think he sounds rather interesting, based on what little you've told me."

"The man is a riddle. He's a hermit in his own house, stuck in the past. His wife has been dead for over twenty years, and he's made his house a memorial to her, keeping it the way she liked, with her needlepoint displayed everywhere. And he never leaves—agoraphobia, he tells me—though I'd like to help him get beyond that. He has the quickest mind I've ever seen—as rapid fire as a Maxim gun. Apologetics is some sort of hobby for him. Reverend Hargrove is good but so is Jim, and I have no idea who would win a debate. They were friends at one time."

"Jim and Reverend Hargrove?"

"Yes—they were close friends in the same church, but that was years ago. They fought over a girl, and that ended badly."

"Sounds romantic, at least from the girl's standpoint."

"It wasn't. Her name was Jenny. Jim . . . well, he compromised her, and then they were both expelled from the church. Jim abandoned her and then married another girl named Vive. She died in childbirth a few years later. His devotion to her, all these years later, is touching, but it's also sad. He showed me her photo, with a big brass label that said, 'Genevieve C. Emerson.' He keeps it prominent in his library. He didn't want a future without her, I'm guessing, so he lives in place, in the 1880s."

"Genevieve," Athena said slowly. "Are you certain that Jim abandoned Jenny?"

"Well, he had to drop her to pick up Vive."

"Jenny and Vive are both nicknames for Genevieve. Maybe they're the same person. People are hard on a girl who has a baby out of wedlock, and maybe she came back from her seclusion with a new name."

Paul felt a flush as he considered how he may have misjudged Jim. "I never thought of that. Maybe Jim didn't abandon Jenny. But then I wonder what happened to the first baby."

"She must have given it up. How sad to give up her baby and then die trying to have another."

&

Sundays had become particularly busy since Samuel had added the third service. Samuel hoped that news of Athena's prophesied return would create more demand than two services could satisfy. It hadn't, and the third service had simply become a convenience for members who preferred to sleep late. The inefficient new schedule annoyed Paul. He thought it would frustrate Samuel too, but the pastor didn't seem to notice the extra work and put as much power into the third sermon as the first.

It was the last Sunday in July, and a month since Athena had returned. Once the services were complete, Samuel and Paul walked to the new church building where they could see it unimpeded by the workers. Samuel was happy to see workmen silent and orderly in church, but he had little tolerance for them swearing and unruly on the job.

"How did it go at the Farbers' yesterday?" Paul asked. Athena's parents had asked Samuel to visit and pressure their daughter to come back to church. Paul didn't participate, not wanting Athena to feel ambushed.

"The girl has been through an ordeal, let's acknowledge that," Samuel said. "But it's been a month. She's had her recovery time."

"What did she say?"

"That she's exploring. She's reading the Bible, but based on the comments she made, she's misinterpreting it. Her focus is all wrong. That's why she needs to learn within the church. The Bible is a bit like gunpowder—a powerful force for good but easy to misuse."

"And is she returning?"

"I was frustrated about her not participating earlier in the month. Frankly, for the good of the church, she had an obligation to be seen. Now it's less important, and we can be patient. She'll return with time. But I must say that this empty-headed feminism that has taken hold is annoying. You need to take it from here, and with a firm hand. What are you doing to rein this in?"

"What can I do?" Paul asked. "She's thinking for herself, and she's an adult."

"Not as a girl of nineteen."

"Well, she's independent then."

"Not as your fiancée. Your obligation for her spiritual well-being doesn't begin at marriage. It's not that you would step on her rights if you imposed on her. Rather, it's that you would ignore your obligations if you *didn't*."

Paul said nothing.

"She should act like Bea." Samuel occasionally spoke about his late wife Beatrice, his example of the ideal Christian lady that other women ought to emulate.

Gossip in the community had nicknamed her the Church Mouse. Samuel described her as "dutiful," which from him was high praise. Paul had seen her photo on Samuel's mantle, severe and silently judgmental. Athena had become as unlike Bea as any two women could be.

"I made the family decisions, and Bea ran the house. I had my role and she had hers." Samuel twisted his big gold ring with the blue stone on his finger as he talked.

"Athena won't do something just because I say so."

"Then you need to clarify things with her now. Tell her to attend church, and she'll obey. I'm sure her parents would agree. The problem only worsens if left to fester."

Samuel walked on, catching Paul with an arm around his shoulders and gesturing with his free hand. "Think of a kite without a string. On a windy day, you can throw it up and it'll just fall down. But tie a string to it, and it flies high. Do you see? A kite will soar, but only if you constrain it."

They stopped at a corner to let a hay wagon pass.

"You know what's at stake," Samuel said. "We're talking about a soul here. The Bible makes clear that an eternity in hell is what awaits the person who falls away from the church."

Paul already had a sufficiently vivid image of hell.

"I blame it on the feminism," Samuel said.

"Yes, that surprised me, too."

"Jobs, voting, college—she's giving her parents fits. This is not how society works. It needs to be corrected before the wedding. I brought the two of you together, and I care about this union, but more important to me is your well-being. It's the feminism that's the problem, and steady pressure should bring her back in line. There will be no marriage if she's lost and insists on staying lost."

Samuel's argument seemed clumsily made, but Paul appreciated this validation of his own feelings. This new Athena troubled him. He had expected a subservient wife, and he wasn't quite sure what he would be stuck with now. He felt a surprising warmth toward Samuel.

At the building site, Samuel climbed over piles of timbers and up stone walls like a child on a playground. He paced the rectangular concrete floor, judging his distance from the various walls. "Here's where my pulpit will be," he said finally, looking around. "Stand here." He put his arm around Paul's shoulder, and together they looked out over the imaginary multitude. "Think how grand it will look when it's done."

"It's huge." Every time Paul pictured the finished building, he marveled at its scale and wondered if Samuel were overreaching. "How many will it seat with the latest design?"

"Over eight hundred in the pews. More with chairs in the aisles." Samuel slowly turned in place. "I've been waiting for years for this."

After a few more minutes trying on his new church, he asked Paul for the blueprints. They talked about the schedule, materials, manpower, and other details of the project. Finally out of questions, Samuel took one more tour around the site, and they headed back.

"Now—where are we on the election plans?" Samuel asked as he lit a cigar.

"We have contacts at the *Times,* the *Record,* and the *Examiner,* but the election is still three months away and it's too early to get endorsements."

"And campaign contributions?"

Thunder rolled in the distance, and Paul noticed the sky had darkened. "Nothing from companies, but we've gotten some from church members. Not much."

"God will provide. We may need enough to run an ad or two in a paper, probably the *Times* or maybe the *Evening Express.* But closer to the election. And I want a mailing to everyone in the district."

"What about going door to door, making your case in person?"

"Undignified," Samuel snapped.

Paul wondered why his own dignity counted for nothing when he suffered through weeks of door-to-door agony before he met Jim. "Not even a few neighborhoods?"

"It would hurt my chances. That's not the image I'm trying to create. Impractical, too. No, what I'd like to do is arrange a debate—you see, you build on your strengths. Contact the Democrat, Henderson, and say that I challenge him to a debate. With the right reporters in the audience, I can't lose."

Samuel puffed on his cigar as big raindrops fell.

∞

The next day was another busy one. The concrete foundation of the new building had set, and the masons had almost finished with the low stone walls. Stacks of timbers and planks lay around the site, and workmen moved through the clutter in ways Paul was becoming familiar with.

Paul's mind was elsewhere, however, and he slipped away just before lunch when he thought he wouldn't be missed. He rode the trolley to Stageira Street after first detouring to pick up something from a friend, something he hoped would be a tonic for Jim. He rang Jim's doorbell, relieved that the opera records weren't playing this time.

"Come." Jim's voice still sounded weak, though perhaps more confident.

Paul let himself in, carrying his present. Jim sat on the sofa. Plates of food remained, but he wore new pajamas, and the whiskey and pillow were gone—small but positive steps.

"I've brought you something."

Jim stared. Paul counted it a triumph that Jim couldn't find his words, if only for a moment.

Finally Jim said, "I don't want a damn *dog* in here."

"You two get acquainted," Paul said as he put the puppy on the sofa next to Jim. "Here, she likes these." Paul handed Jim several small pieces of jerked beef. At the smell of the meat, the puppy, short-haired and tan with a white splotch on one side of her face, wagged her tail so energetically that her rear wagged as well, and she dropped her ears and looked up at Jim.

Jim held out one piece of beef and the puppy snatched it. Jim yanked his hand back as the puppy swallowed and stared back expectantly, her eyes moving eagerly between his face and hands. Jim fed the puppy the remaining snacks and leaned away slightly as the puppy edged closer, still eager.

"Sit," Paul said sternly to the puppy, pointing his finger. She looked at him and sat. "That's the one command she knows. Sometimes you need to push her rear down. But the lady who gave her to me said that she should be very smart, able to learn quickly."

Seeing no more food from Jim, the puppy eyed the leftovers on the center table.

"I'd better take care of these," Paul said as he stacked plates. He looked at Jim, who had his hands on his thighs as he stared at the dog.

"You're not allergic to dogs are you?"

Jim shook his head.

"Then pet her. She likes that."

Paul took a stack of plates into the kitchen. When he had first tidied up two weeks earlier, the counter had been strewn with pots with caked-on food, plates with crusts of bread and vegetable fragments, and bowls with remnants of breakfast cereal and oatmeal. Half a dozen of the small wooden delivery crates, still full of food, had been stacked up on one wall. Paul's visits had kept the kitchen at least sanitary. From the library, he heard Jim try out the "sit" command with varying amounts of severity in his voice.

When Paul returned, the puppy lay on her back and Jim was scratching her belly. "Look what she did—just flipped over on her own."

"I guess she likes you."

Jim looked down at the puppy as if trying on that possibility. "Perhaps she does," he said with quiet surprise.

Paul finished with the last of the plates, moving quickly because his day didn't allow for this detour. "I need to leave, but I'll try to come back tomorrow. She's housebroken, but you'll need to let her out often, and set out bowls of food and water."

"Wait—are you just leaving this dog here?"

"Yes, she's yours. Don't you want to keep her?"

"I never entertained the thought. I suppose so."

"Have fun with her," Paul said as he turned to leave. "And give her a name."

The next day was Tuesday, but Paul couldn't make the time to get to Jim's house as promised. On Wednesday, he stopped by a grocery store after work. Jim's odd diet would not work for the dog, and Paul half expected to find a plate with hot oatmeal and raw carrots set by the water bowl. Jim had seemed uneasy taking the dog in the first place, and Paul worried that he had overreached in trying to pull Jim out of his doldrums.

He bought a collar, a leash, a ball, and some meat scraps. Twenty minutes later, he stood at Jim's doorstep, a small bag in each hand.

"Have you fed the dog?" Paul said as Jim opened the door.

"Of course. She likes Corn Flakes."

"You know that dogs aren't vegetarians," Paul said as he pushed the bags into Jim's hands. "Is everything all right? You've let her out?"

"Relax—when my errand boy came by yesterday, I had him get some meat." He looked down at the puppy. "She knows where her food and water are, and I open the door to the backyard for her every hour or so. She sleeps on my bed with me."

Paul noticed that things did seem under control. The round little dog stood next to Jim, wagging her tail and looking up at him. Even Jim looked content. He wore fresh clothes—gray casual trousers and a white dress shirt without its collar and with the sleeves rolled up. His hair was damp and combed back, his face was shaved, and his horseshoe mustache was neatly trimmed.

Jim knelt to scratch the dog. "She's a fast learner. She comes when I call—sometimes."

"What do you call her?"

"Leviathan."

"Isn't that from the Bible?"

"It's the fire-breathing sea monster from the book of Job. Impenetrable scales on her back, fire streaming from her mouth, smoke snorting from her nostrils—don't you see the resemblance?"

Paul assessed the fat puppy looking up at Jim, her ears down and tail wagging. "A remarkable likeness," he said.

"Say, did I show you my Christian relic? I have a piece of the True Cross."

Paul knew that most of such relics were medieval frauds but was amazed that Jim owned so rare an artifact, real or not. Or that he would care to.

Jim walked down the hall into the library. "Oh, here it is." He picked up a crumbling cinnamon stick and put it in his mouth, where it stuck out like a cigar. He grinned.

Jim had returned.

కు

Paul stared at Jim's carpet as if it were the dim cobblestone alley, and he was back there, five years earlier, staring down at the motionless man. "I hit him once, just once. I didn't mean to."

"No one could say that it was intentional," Jim said.

"Yes, exactly." Paul was relieved that Jim agreed. It felt safe to breathe again. "If only he hadn't tried to be a hero. When someone stronger than you demands your wallet, you give it to him, right? Maybe I was just surprised, but when he hit me, I hit him back, like an instinct. It happened so fast—it couldn't have been more than five seconds from the time I collared him until he was on the sidewalk, just lying there, not moving. And then I saw the blood under his head, and I ran."

Paul drummed his fists against the arms of his chair, trying to calm his thumping heart. "I'm not sure why I'm telling you." But he did know. The memory continued to torment him, and he hoped sharing it with Jim might ease the burden. "The cops never connected me with the death. You do see that it was an accident?"

"Oh yes, but you need to decide how to make things right." Jim looked at Paul as he slowly stroked Leviathan lying next to him on the sofa.

Paul looked down. His hands shook slightly. "Prison." He breathed the word out, almost silently.

"That wouldn't be my remedy," Jim said. "I could talk for an hour about what's wrong with the prison system in this country. We've got the punishment part figured out, but that doesn't take us very far. It's like locking up someone in debtor's prison—how does a man pay his debts if he's in prison? And how would you right your wrongs to society if you were locked up?"

"I've been by his place."

"Whose place?"

"The dead fellow's. I've gone by lots of times. I found his name in the paper afterwards, and his address was easy to find—it's over in Boyle Heights." Paul heard a tremor in his own voice. He hated that weakness but forced himself on. "I've seen his wife, through the window. And his kids. He wasn't just a man, he was a father and husband, too. I don't know why I've gone there. Maybe I was hoping that something bad would happen, and I could jump in to be the guardian angel. Or maybe to scourge myself. I've committed the worst sin."

"You wronged a man and his family, and understanding that is where you must start. Forget sin. That's a religious invention—an offense against an imaginary God."

I wish I could see it that way, Paul thought.

"Is that why you stay in the church?" Jim asked. "Because you think you've sinned and the church can provide forgiveness?"

Paul didn't answer. His desperate need for absolution had made Samuel's description of Christianity enthralling two years earlier, and that remained an essential draw. He rubbed his hands on his thighs. "Well, I appreciate your hearing my confession."

"Just call me Father Jim." Jim swirled the teapot on the center table and poured two cups. "But seriously, this is a big load to carry. Talking helps, and if you'd like to talk more, I'm always here." He pushed one cup toward Paul.

Paul nodded. The brief talk had indeed helped. His telling of the story had begun as suddenly as a cloudburst, with the words spilling out almost on their own. He couldn't identify what had triggered it. The bottled-up memory had relentlessly harassed him for these five years but with the admission behind him, he felt unburdened—at least a little.

"Well, tell me how you and Leviathan are getting along," Paul said. The house looked about as well kept as normal. Jim too was back to his usual mismatched socks and uncombed hair.

Jim paused and Paul wondered if he would go along with the change of subject. "I appreciate the collar and leash—very thoughtful. But I don't think I'll need them. We'll just use the backyard."

"We could take her for a walk together."

"No, I don't think so. Standing on the patio when I let her roam around is about all I'm able to do. It's a strange feeling—I look at the back door and it's like I've fallen from a boat under sail, and it's pulling away, abandoning me."

"Let's just sit outside in the front."

Jim didn't respond as Paul picked up the collar and leash. He fastened the collar on the little brown puppy, picked her up, and walked toward the door. "Coming?" he asked.

Jim silently got off the sofa and followed, suddenly feeble as he shuffled down the hall with one hand brushing the wall.

"It's not like you're walking to the gallows. You'll like it out here in the sun." Paul sat on the top step, and Leviathan lay next to him on the warm stone. A gardener next door snipped at bushes.

A full minute passed before Jim made it to the steps, his hands out for balance. "This is not where I want to be," he said, his teeth clenched and a mild fury in his voice. He eased himself down to sit.

"Now you know what you've put me through," Paul said in a deliberately cheery voice. "Over the last couple of months, you've dragged me into your world. The last thing I needed was to become a freethinker."

Jim grunted, his eyes squeezed shut.

The breeze rustled the leaves on the trees and bushes. On the far side of Jim's hedge, people walked along the sidewalk and a horse pulling a wagon clopped by in the street. The smell of summer was strong—cut grass, compost, an outdoor brush fire, flowers.

"I smell something floral," Paul said. "Is that from your bush with the pink flowers?"

Jim squinted to the side and then shut his eyes again. "The smell is agave," Jim snapped. "The bush is crape myrtle."

"It's nice out here," Paul said as he reclined, propped up by his elbows.

"No, it's not nice out here." Jim's eyes remained shut, and his hands firmly gripped the step. "Talk to me so I can't hear all that noise."

"All right," Paul said loudly, "let's talk about the Ontological Argument."

Jim grunted again.

"It's quite old, isn't it?"

"It's credited to Anselm of Canterbury—twelfth century."

"Tell me about it."

Jim sighed. Apparently resigned to his fate and with his eyes still closed, he said, "First we define 'God' as the greatest possible being that we can imagine. Two: consider existence only in someone's mind versus existence in reality—the latter is obviously greater. Three: since 'God' must be the greatest possible being, he must exist in reality. If he didn't, he wouldn't meet his definition as the greatest possible being." Jim had graduated from gripping the step to hugging himself tightly.

"But you're not convinced," Paul said.

"Ha! There are many ways to attack this argument, but the most obvious flaw is that the first step defines an imaginary being. But in step three, we are now talking about beings that exist. The definition of 'God' from the first step can no longer apply."

Jim had relaxed a bit. His hands were fists in his lap, but his eyes were still closed. "Or, if you'd prefer, note that you can define a word to be anything you want, but it doesn't follow that that thing must then exist. There is no largest number, for example, and my imagination can't bring it into existence. And note that you can use the same reasoning to show that the *worst*-possible being imaginable must exist."

"So you don't think it's a strong argument."

"Actually, I think it's one of the more effective ones. Think of two types of arguments. The first type is so simple that it *obviously* has no errors. The second is so complicated that it has *no obvious* errors. The Ontological Argument is of the second type—it confronts people with things they hadn't considered before. It's complicated enough that there are no obvious errors. That's its strength—not that it's correct but that it's confusing."

Pleased that Jim finally had his eyes open but concerned that a lull in the conversation might break the spell, Paul said, "What other apologetics haven't we talked about?"

"There's Thomas Aquinas's list of five arguments. I'm sure you've heard of his First Cause argument."

Paul sat up and stared at the hedge in front of him. "Let's see: if something exists, it must have been caused by something else; but there must have been a First Cause to start it all; we call that First Cause 'God.' "

"And what response could you make to that argument?" Jim asked.

Paul had mulled over the atheist side of the debate before but never aloud. "Well, I suppose you could ask if God must also have had a cause."

"That's good. You're arguing for consistency—if things are in a chain of causes, and we add God to that chain, God must have had a cause, as well. Now, respond to that—give me the Christian rebuttal."

"I don't know," Paul began. "I guess you could say that God had no cause, that God isn't like the rest of nature."

"And the response to that is . . . ?"

"Um . . . that you're making up properties for God without evidence?"

"That sounds right. Science is ignorant of many causes, but we know of nothing that is causeless. Why should God get a pass?" Jim watched as Leviathan waddled over to lean against him. "When you consider an argument, think of the response the other fellow might have. This is not so you can win the argument but so you can find the truth. If the other fellow is right, change your position."

"Well, what's the next step in the argument, the next Christian rebuttal?"

"I can't think of an effective one—one reason I'm a freethinker." Jim scratched the puppy down her back. "What's amusing is Christians who state that the universe is too complex to just exist. It must have been created by a far more complex Creator . . . who just exists."

Jim looked more normal—as tense as a piano string but still an improvement over a few minutes earlier.

"Feeling better?" Paul asked

Jim's eyes snapped shut and his grimace intensified.

That was a mistake. "Sorry—forget I brought it up." Paul sat upright and spoke calmly and loudly. "We're talking about apologetics, about Christianity." He grabbed words to fill the void to hold Jim's attention. "Oh, have you ever considered what would convert you to Christianity—or re-convert you? Or is your mind made up?"

Jim took a deep breath. "I've considered that." More slow breaths. "To be intellectually honest, I must put my beliefs on the line. It's like a title fight in boxing where the champ puts up his title, and if he loses, there are consequences because he's no longer the champ. If I lose an argument, I need to find which beliefs are wrong and give them up. Too many people are shown that their arguments are flawed but never consider changing their beliefs to make them stronger. Instead, they just marshal their intellect to better justify their position."

Pink petals from the crape myrtle fluttered down in a light breeze, refreshing in the hot sun.

Jim said, "What would convert me to Christianity is the very evidence that Christians say they already have. The problem is that they satisfy themselves with the barest shadow of real evidence. Predictions, for example."

Leviathan had wandered into the bushes, pulling against the leash in Paul's hand. "Christianity claims hundreds of predictions have already come true," he said.

Jim opened his eyes again. "And when you investigate them, you find that the author of the fulfillment has read the prophecy, making his account suspect. Or you find that the prophecy and the fulfillment were both written after the events had taken place. Or you find vague claims that can be interpreted in lots of ways, depending on your bias."

Jim continued. "What I want in a prophecy is what anyone would want—a precise, unambiguous, and unexpected prediction about something important. The prediction must come before the event, and there can be no chance of bias in the report of the fulfillment. And every prophecy must be perfect—that is, we can't have one success out of a thousand tries. That's not much to ask of a divinely inspired book or of the creator of the universe."

Jim sprang to his feet. "I can think better inside." He trotted to the open front door. "Join me?" he asked from the hallway.

Paul scooped up Leviathan and followed Jim inside.

In the living room, Jim collapsed on the sofa, breathing deeply. "I haven't done that in a while." He held out his hands, and Paul gave him the dog.

"How did it feel to be outside?" Paul asked.

"Like I don't want to do it again."

"Aren't you ready to get back into society?"

"Perhaps. But slowly."

Paul sat in his chair and enjoyed its coolness. "You were talking about prophecy," he said. "Christianity has made end-times predictions. Those are forward looking."

"True, but Christians don't have much to brag about there. Have you heard of the Millerites?"

Paul shook his head.

"They're another Christian sect that sprang up in northern New York shortly before I was born. William Miller's group predicted the end of the world on October 22, 1844—bravo for making it precise. Many of his followers gave away everything to make themselves right with God and waited for the end. But October 22 came and went—nothing. Many walked away, wiser for the experience, but the sect continued. Some people just won't give up their comforting superstitions."

Jim drank from his teacup. "Since the early church, there have been lots of Christian prophecies of the end times. But when there are minimal consequences to the church for a false prophecy, the religion lumbers on, immune to common sense."

He carefully sipped the last of his tea, examining the contents of his cup several times as he did so, and then he swirled the cup and quickly inverted it on its saucer. He put the cup and saucer on the table and pushed them to Paul. "Turn it over."

Paul turned the cup over and saw the complex pattern the tiny fragments of tea leaf had made in the bottom.

Jim gestured toward the cup. "Foretelling the future by reading tea leaves is called tasseography. People have tried to predict the future by looking at animal entrails, the stars, dreams, and Tarot cards. Divining the future from the Bible is no better than those—we know because people have tried and failed. All civilizations would love to predict the future, to give some order to the chaotic events that plague us all. It's a universal desire, but that doesn't mean it's possible."

"Christianity would say you're demanding too much," Paul said. "That you want to eliminate the need for faith."

"That's just what they would say if their religion were fiction. I only ask for the quality of evidence all of us apply in every other segment of our lives. You don't use faith to design a building or learn French or set a broken bone. Faith is the worst decision-making technique possible. It's even worse than guessing—at least with guessing, you are open to change based on new information, but faith is immune to facts. I won't apologize for using reason and for demanding evidence.

"And that's the biggest clue that Christianity is false: that it's built on faith. Believing something because it's reasonable and rational requires no faith at all. Evidence gets the rational man into a belief, and contrary evidence gets him out of it. Scientists don't need a church service or revival meeting to recharge their belief that science works. If there were the evidence for God that we have for a thousand things we come across every day, religion would provide it. But that evidence doesn't exist, so religion celebrates faith instead. Faith is permission to believe something without a good reason. In what other area of life do we just believe something without a good reason? Would you marry someone you'd only heard rumors of and had never seen? And yet that is the relationship we're supposed to have with God."

Paul sipped from his teacup. "What happened to the Millerites? Did they fade away?"

"The religion broke into several sects. One became the Seventh-day Adventists."

"I didn't realize that group was so new."

"The nineteenth century was a busy time for Christian movements. Mormonism also came from that time, as did Christian Science, Jehovah's Witnesses, the Shakers, the Salvation Army, the Holiness movement. And that's just the big names. Religion seems fixed at any moment, but it's moving, like a glacier. We'll probably have a similar explosion of new forms of religious expression in this century. Not what you'd expect of the immutable truth, but exactly what you'd expect of a man-made institution."

∽

The supper dishes were cleared, and Athena set a cup of coffee on the dining table in front of her father. His face was hidden behind an open newspaper.

"Have you set a date for the wedding?" her mother asked.

"Not yet." Athena sat across from her mother.

Mrs. Farber slowly twisted her cloth napkin into a tight cylinder. "Come with us to church tomorrow. It'll be so nice to see your friends." Her eyebrows were raised as if she'd asked a question.

"No, thanks," Athena said quietly. She felt as if she'd smacked away the desperate hand of a beggar.

Mrs. Farber glanced at her husband, secluded behind his paper. "Tell us why you don't want to go."

"I've told you that the church has nothing to offer me. It's a poor fit." But it was more than that. Religion was a puppet show, and she'd peeked behind the stage and had seen the people who put it on. The illusion was gone.

"Dear, people at church have been asking about you, and I'm out of excuses."

Then don't make excuses, Athena thought.

Her mother tried another tack. "I've noticed that you read your Bible now. That's very nice."

"A woman can read too much," her father said from behind his paper.

Athena was about to tell her parents what she had discovered in the Bible's pages—the tribal violence, the treatment of women, the acceptance of slavery, the superstition—but that would have been no more productive than a chat with Father Mondegreen. Better to leave them confused than hurt.

"What must Paul think about you not going to church?" her mother asked. "Dear, you don't want to drive him away. You don't want to start over searching for a husband."

"Yes, Mother."

"Maybe you just have some doubts, and you'll return to the church later."

"Maybe."

Mrs. Farber looked toward her husband, but the newspaper was still in place. "And what are these meetings you keep going to?"

"It's the National American Woman Suffrage Association." Athena had already told her parents about the Movement, but they didn't seem to understand. "We have a suffrage rally in a month, and I'm writing letters to get people to attend."

"A public rally?"

"Of course."

"But someone could see you."

Athena sighed. "We're working for your rights, too, Mother."

"I have all the rights I want, thank you."

"We want a society where women are treated like full citizens. If you don't want to vote, you can at least want it for me."

Mr. Farber snapped the paper as he turned a page.

Her mother said, "Thena, it's as though you were working for my right to plow a field or dig a ditch. I don't want that. I like things the way they are."

"We want a chance to think for ourselves," Athena said. "Women have been fighting for decades, and they've been winning. We can already vote in four states."

"And you see the price they've paid," Mrs. Farber said, her voice shrill as it always was when she felt that she was losing an argument. "Hunger strikes, demonstrations, women thrown into jail. It's not lady-like. Politics is a filthy business—I can't imagine that you'd want to participate in that. After I had you, I had more than I could handle taking care of a baby and the house. It's as if you want to discard every privilege you have as a woman."

Her father dropped the paper and looked at Athena for a moment. "Don't you see how good you've got it? Women are on a pedestal—why would you want to climb down?"

"We're not on a pedestal," Athena said quietly. "We're in a cage."

Mr. Farber raised his voice. "I suffer not a woman to teach, nor to usurp authority over the man, but to be in silence." He seemed to have a Bible verse for every occasion.

Athena's mother's eyes were red as she reached across the wide dining table for Athena's hands. She couldn't quite make it, and Athena extended her arms to put her hands in her mother's. "What happened to my little girl?"

She's under a pile of rubble in San Francisco, Athena thought.

∞

Paul and Athena walked back to the Farbers' house after an afternoon stroll. Their conversation had been pleasant though a bit formal. To Paul their relationship seemed cooler since the reunion, more reserved and less intimate.

"My parents have been pressuring me to go to church," Athena said. "We had another argument this morning."

"Sounds rough. Do they harass you about it often?"

"During the week Father and I go to work together, and the talk is all about business. Saturday afternoon and Sunday are Mother's time to rule, and that can be a little more tense."

"You can tell them that you're slowly getting back into city life."

"That argument isn't working anymore. But why should it matter? I'm almost twenty, and I can make my own decisions."

Athena's lack of church attendance didn't trouble him, but her new independence did. He wasn't sure he wanted a relationship where his leadership position would be in jeopardy—it just wasn't the way things worked. It might do for some men, but not for him. And why should he make the concession?

Thinking of Samuel's advice, he said, "You're still working on your voting rally?"

She tisked with her tongue. "You don't like that I'm involved with the movement, do you?" Her tone wasn't angry, but firm.

"Well, not really." Things were so much easier before she changed.

"Yes, I'm working on the rally. We've been over this. This is a rights issue, Paul, plain and simple, just like freeing the slaves."

"Now that's an exaggeration. Women aren't enslaved like the Negroes were."

"But Negro men can now vote! I'm not saying that women are treated like slaves, and I'm not saying this is as big an injustice. But it's still an injustice."

They were almost at the Farbers' house. Paul took a quick breath. "Thena, look, I don't want you involved in this. If women happen to get the vote, let them. But can't someone else do it? Don't you have better things to focus on?"

"My name isn't 'Thena.'" She dropped his hand. "And suppose women do get the vote. Would you allow me to exercise the right? Would you allow me to go to college?"

"Well, I think we can decide that when necessary."

"You're just like my parents!" She picked up her skirt and strode the few yards to her house. "Goodbye." She pounded up the stairs without looking back.

Should he charge after her? Should he demand that she return to discuss this matter? But she was inside and the door had slammed shut before he had any response.

After adjusting to Athena's return, had he now lost her again?

℘

Paul sat in a chair at a square wooden table on the patio in Jim's backyard. The lazy and overgrown yard now looked like a military parade ground. Dark mulch evenly covered the ground between the bushes, pruned almost to skeletons.

Jim came out with a tray holding two glasses and a pitcher of iced tea. Leviathan trotted behind him.

"You've done some work," Paul said. The shaded patio and a bit of a breeze contrasted with Paul's agitated mind. The argument with Athena two days earlier was the worst they'd had, and it still consumed him.

"Leviathan needs room to run, so I hired some gardeners." Jim called to Leviathan and picked up a ball from the edge of the patio.

Paul watched the little dog rampage across the yard as Jim tossed the ball several times. Paul was about to break the silence and attempt some small talk when Jim spoke. "I must thank you for pushing me. My hibernation had become so natural that I couldn't see how distorted it was."

"You've prodded me," Paul said. "I'm happy to reciprocate." After the argument with Athena, he had stared at the closed door for many minutes before making the long trip home. He considered knocking on the Farbers' door to find some compromise but lost his nerve. Questions about his dignity and the role of a husband nagged him.

"You know what I'm most looking forward to?" Jim asked. "Going to the library. You can't imagine how frustrating it is to send an errand boy for the correct book on electrical engineering or physics when he hardly knows those disciplines exist. It's like assembling a watch with chopsticks."

"When will you go?" Paul had gone back to the Farbers the next day, and she returned his ring.

"I can't be sure—I make a little progress every day. Even now I feel a little off balance out here. So far, I've subdued my yard, mostly, and have opened my gate to watch the traffic. I tell myself that it's invigorating, not intimidating. Perhaps I'll conquer my neighborhood before Robert Peary has conquered the North Pole."

Paul held his glass with both hands and enjoyed the coolness of the tea. "Tell me, what do you think of women's suffrage?"

"I favor it."

"It doesn't violate the natural order?"

"The 'natural order' is carnivores eating herbivores—that kind of thing. Evolution isn't the basis for voting rights." Jim launched into a short speech on the other changes he wanted in society—equal pay for equal work, prison reform, the need for pure food laws, and so on. He seemed quite the radical.

Paul saw that he would find no ally here in his squabble with Athena and fell back on the reason he had come. "I've been rereading the Bible with a new eye."

"And what do you think?"

Paul looked away for a moment. "The Bible seems just like a history book of ordinary people, and that includes God's role. He's like a great king with great passions—He's compassionate and then cruel, He's generous and then inconsiderate."

"You can make the Bible say just about whatever you want," Jim said. "Most people use it simply as a mirror to reflect their own beliefs. When it suits them, they'll quote the Bible saying that you should love your neighbor, and in a different situation they'll remind you of the time when God commanded the Israelites to destroy whole cities and everyone inside. The Bible tells you nothing when you use it like a hand puppet to make it say what you already believe. But when it tells you something you don't want to hear but know to be true, then it's valuable."

"You're saying there's something useful about the Bible? You never said that before."

"You didn't need to hear it before. My complaints are directed at taking mythology as history. The Bible holds the wisdom of a civilization, and it's not surprising that it says things that are valuable today."

"Like what?" Paul sipped his tea.

"That's for you to decide. Weigh them yourself. The Bible is ambiguous, and you must use your judgment to make sense of it. That's why there are hundreds of Christian sects—because the Bible can be interpreted in so many ways. But if you must be the judge of what the Bible says, that ability to judge is where the answers come from, not the Bible. Cut out the Bible middleman."

"The Christian will say that, with the Bible, they have the word of God," Paul said.

"And yet at every step of the way we see humans—from the pastors in the pulpits to translators, historians, and through the copyists back to the original authors. Humans, every one. The Christian can imagine that God was there at the beginning, but there's faint reason to think it's true."

"Christians find a lot of life's meaning in the Bible."

"If you want meaning in life, assign some meaning. If you want to feel important, do something important. It's your life; don't let someone else determine its meaning."

Jim put Leviathan down, and she dropped her ears and wagged her tail furiously, which Jim took as a request to play again. He picked up the ball and walked onto the lawn. "Did you notice that the Bible's authors wrote only of the middle-sized world? Just the kinds of things that we see and understand in our everyday lives, from mustard seeds to mountains. But science has told us so much more."

Jim's hand swept the sky. "In the first chapter of Genesis, the Bible says, 'God also made the stars.' That's it! That's all the Bible says about the vastness of the universe, about the *billions* of stars out there. Think what a waste an entire universe is if the goal was simply to build one tiny home for humans. We know of too much to hold the conceit that Man is the purpose of this vast project.

"Here's my take on Christianity," Jim chuckled. "Imagine searching for Easter eggs in a dark room. Now, imagine searching for Easter eggs in a dark room in which there are *no* Easter eggs. Finally, imagine searching for Easter eggs in a dark room in which there are no Easter eggs, after someone shouts, 'I found one!' That's Christianity. And did I mention that an egg is actually your ticket into heaven, and without one you burn in hell?"

"You don't mind if I play the skeptic, do you?" Paul asked.

"I insist. You shouldn't take anything on faith—not the Bible, not religion, and not what I say. I can even use the Bible as a mirror to argue my point. It says, 'Test everything and hold fast to that which is good.' Faith is necessary to carry you over a gulf of insufficient evidence. But if you don't have enough evidence, why try to leap across the gulf? Simply admit to yourself that you don't have what you need to make a conclusion."

"But you use faith yourself," Paul said. "You don't know for certain that the sun will rise tomorrow. That you believe it will rise shows faith."

"I *trust* that the sun will rise tomorrow," Jim said. "Trust is belief in accord with evidence, and faith is belief despite a lack of evidence. When you *trust*, new evidence can change that belief, but when you believe on faith, you're immune to new evidence. 'Trust' and 'faith' are two useful words, but don't confuse them." Jim threw the ball again. "But I interrupted you—you were saying?"

"I don't know much about science," Paul said, "but I do know that it changes. It's often wrong. What's true today isn't true tomorrow."

"Science gives us an approximation of the truth, nothing more. Science is built on a body of facts that changes, and that's its strength. Christianity is built on a book that never changes, and that's its weakness. Christianity's ancient and unchanging foundation may be reassuring, but that hardly argues that it's trustworthy or relevant.

"Let me show you something." Jim walked into the house. He returned with an atlas that covered most of the small patio table when he opened it. After some leafing through the pages, he turned the book to face Paul.

The heading read "World Religions," and the map used hatching and shading to show the regions dominated by different religions—Roman Catholicism, Eastern Orthodox, and Protestantism, as well as Hinduism, Buddhism, Confucianism, Taoism, Jainism, Sikhism, and others, most of which were new to Paul.

"Imagine an equivalent map of science," Jim said. "Here, scientists believe that the earth is at the center of the universe." Jim's finger circled the Americas on the map. "But over here, scientists believe that the earth revolves around the sun, and the sun and all its planets are in an insignificant corner of an enormous universe." Jim circled Europe and Africa. "Naturally, the first group thinks of the second group as heretics, and they have fought wars over their opposing beliefs."

Jim looked up and said, "That's ridiculous, of course. Whether a scientist is Protestant or Hindu or Sikh, he should get the same result from the same experiment. Once the evidence for a better way of thinking is available, there is no good reason to cling to the old idea, and the new idea sweeps the scientific world. Astronomy replaced astrology, chemistry replaced alchemy, and the germ theory replaced evil spirits as a cause of disease. Science is given to us by people, and they make mistakes, but it's our best window into how the world works."

"But only religion can answer big questions like 'Why are we here?' " Paul said.

Jim smacked the map. "And this shows that the religious answer to that question depends on where you are. If you live in Tibet or Siam, Buddhism teaches that we are here to learn to cease suffering and reach nirvana. If you live in Persia or Arabia, Mohammedanism teaches that we are here to submit to Allah. What kind of truth depends on location?

"Think about a church steeple with a lightning rod on top," Jim said. "The steeple proclaims that God exists, and the lightning rod says that it can reduce lightning damage. Which claim is true? Science makes truth claims, just like religion does, but science takes it one step further: it delivers on its claims."

Paul found himself engaged with Jim's ideas in a way that he hadn't noticed in church. Samuel's sermons touched the listener in a joyous way, not an intellectual one. It was a joy that faded on the walk home, like the euphoria he felt at a tent revival that he could only rekindle with another tent revival. "But is science the only path to truth?"

"I don't see it that way," Jim said. "We have Shakespeare and Euripides, we have Voltaire and Plato, we have Rembrandt and Michelangelo, we have *The Wealth of Nations* and the U. S. Constitution. None of these is the last word in its field, but each makes a contribution."

"It's frustrating that nothing is definite," Paul said. "That you can't say, 'This is certainly true.' "

"Agreed, but that is Mankind's lot. 'God did it' is definite, but it explains nothing. It's the presumption, not the conclusion. We should reason our way to the conclusion, following the facts where they lead. If the facts strongly point to God's existence, we must accept that, but if the facts are merely rationalized to support a presumption, we deceive ourselves."

Paul poured himself more tea. "Why hasn't science replaced religion if science explains reality much better?"

"Here's how I see it," Jim said. "Imagine assembling an arch. An arch-shaped scaffold is first built, the stones are laid, and then the scaffold is taken down. Once the stones of the arch are in place, they support themselves—they don't need the scaffold. That's how religion works. Superstition in a world before science was the scaffold that supported the arch of religion. Science has now dismantled the scaffolding of superstition, but it's too late because the arch of religion is already firmly in place."

Paul said, "I understand, though it still seems that reason should easily win out."

"Keep in mind that we have pretty much the same brains as people who lived in the Bronze Age. We're not inherently smarter, and we're still susceptible to superstitious thinking. Christianity works only if you believe it will work, like a placebo. I don't need faith to benefit from an electric fan or light. They work whether I believe in them or not. Christianity can have a real benefit—it can bring comfort and hope—even if it's based on nothing. It's satisfying, like a piece of cake, but you fool yourself if you think that it's nutritious."

Paul said, "Evolution and the effectiveness of science seem so implausible that they can succeed nine times and not be believed the tenth time."

"And God's existence and the effectiveness of prayer can *fail* nine times and still be believed the tenth time."

An issue returned to tickle Paul's mind, one that he had brushed away before, but he felt comfortable enough to admit to it now. "Samuel says I mustn't talk to you." Only once the words were out did he realize how impotent they made him look and how much they had burdened him.

"Why not?" Jim asked. "Am I a serpent tempting you with the fruit?"

"I do feel like I've eaten from the Tree of Knowledge, but it's more that he thinks that I've outgrown you, that you have nothing to teach me." Paul hesitated. It had been one thing to act, to continue to visit Jim after Samuel forbade it. He had done that almost without thought. But he had never brought his rebelliousness to the front of his mind.

"I'd say that's for you to decide," Jim said.

"I was thinking of what held me in Christianity. It seems that people cling to religion with two hands, one of intellect and one of emotion. I had a solid hold with both, but no longer. With the intellectual connection gone, I feel like I'm up in the air with my feet dangling, barely hanging on. The hand of emotion may be strong enough for lots of people, but I don't think it will be enough for me."

"Good analogy. Makes sense."

Makes sense, but it doesn't give absolution for murder, Paul thought. "I've got to think on my own. I can't believe something just because Samuel told me to." By putting it into words, the rebelliousness suddenly became deliberate. He looked up at Jim for some assurance that he'd done the right thing, but Jim said nothing.

Paul had seen Samuel in many emotional situations. Parishioners came to him for advice in the face of infidelity, temptation, theft, and other crimes, both legal and spiritual. Neighbors and government officials had confronted him with matters both small and large. Samuel had a broad and effective palette of responses to these challenges, but for disloyalty, which this would surely be in Samuel's eyes, he only had rage. Paul knew he had steered onto a dangerous road.

Chapter 12

A gray morning light shone through the window behind Samuel. He stood with both hands on his desk, looking down at a half-page advertisement in the previous day's *Evening Express*. A large headline read, "Reverend Samuel Hargrove, A Moral Man for Immoral Times." Samuel's unsmiling photograph and his brief list of the city's corrupting elements completed the ad.

Looking at the photo, Paul remembered the long process with the photographer. Samuel had wanted to show a generous portion of sternness tempered with a bit of saintly kindness and had needed two sessions to get a look that satisfied him.

Samuel rubbed the ad absently as if making sure that it was fixed. "This was expensive," he muttered. "It shouldn't have been necessary."

Paul noticed the telegram from Representative McLachlan, Samuel's political mentor, still on a corner of Samuel's desk. McLachlan had sent the blunt telegram about ten days earlier saying that he expected more press, which had ignited a panic of activity in what had been a leisurely campaign. In the previous week, Paul had pasted up posters and delivered pamphlets throughout the district. He wondered where the money for all this came from.

The polling stations would open soon. Chatter from the "Hargrove for California Assembly" volunteers drifted through the closed door from the sanctuary, where they picked up their campaign signs and received their assignments. "Any ads for Henderson?" Samuel asked.

Paul's day had started an hour earlier when he bought the four morning newspapers and scanned them for anything about either Samuel or his Democratic opponent, Frank Henderson. "I checked all the papers." He tossed them on the desk. "Nothing."

Samuel eased into his chair, picked up a Henderson pamphlet that Paul had discovered a few days earlier, and unfolded it next to his own newspaper ad. He scanned both documents slowly, and then he slapped the desk. "No, I'm still convinced," he said, as if disagreement were inconceivable. "He's too focused on shallow issues." He jabbed at the promises on Henderson's pamphlet. "Sewage? Electricity? Bad smells? He's gone down a rabbit hole—these aren't the things people care about."

"I've heard that he knocked on every door in the district."

"Like a salesman. That's undignified. That's not how people want their representatives to act."

Paul had heard comments from some church members, and he wasn't so sure. While Henderson had been visiting the voters, Samuel was finishing two months of sermons that he wanted given in his absence during the legislative session.

"Let's take a look at the polling station at the post office," Samuel said as he stood.

Paul picked up his overcoat and hurried after him. They exchanged greetings with a cluster of cheerful volunteers and walked outside. A cloudy sky hung over them and the road was wet, though the rain had stopped for the moment. As they walked to the post office, Samuel did most of the talking, re-examining the strengths of his own position and the weaknesses of his opponent's.

At the post office, a short queue was already curving outside a door with a sign that read, "Vote Here." Samuel paced along the sidewalk for less than a minute when he called out, "Bob!"

Bob Parks, a spry haberdasher of about sixty and a long-time church member, was leaving the polling station. "Reverend—I didn't expect to see you here." He seemed startled, as if caught in an indiscretion.

"Just thought I'd stop by," Samuel said, smiling, as he clasped Parks's hand in both of his and shook it vigorously. Parks tipped his hat and walked off.

Samuel looked over the crowd deliberately now, smiling at strangers and walking with an eager spring in his step. He spotted another familiar face when Bill Mason walked out. He was also a church member, heavy-set and unemployed. Samuel gave another enthusiastic greeting and handshake.

"Reverend," Mason said in reply and walked off.

Shortly afterwards, another member, a man who worked in a grocery store. He seemed busy and walked off quickly.

Another minute passed and Samuel put a hand on Paul's shoulder and gestured toward the side street. "Get me a wooden box. Maybe a small crate—something to stand on."

Paul found a sturdy box in an alley.

"Yes, that'll do." Samuel walked to the end of the line of men waiting to vote, set the box against the side of the post office, and stood on it.

"Immorality!" Samuel thundered.

The men standing in line looked confused and stopped talking.

"Immorality!" Samuel said again, a little bolder this time, as if pleased with the response and keen for a repeat. "Society's dark stain— that is what burdens the soul of the Christian man today. If I may impose upon a moment of your time, gentlemen, I would like to share some thoughts on immorality and the problem that it presents to society today." Samuel bestowed the sermon with his usual strong voice, subduing the street noise and injecting the phrase "I, Reverend Samuel Hargrove" every minute or two. His talking points were the list of social evils from his ad—drunkenness, gambling, prostitution, women's suffrage, and so on.

Paul stood against the wall, just a few feet from the men in line, and sensed their eyes on him. His arms felt awkward, and he held his hands in front, fig-leaf style.

Samuel's audience initially listened as if in church but gradually regained their courage and returned to talking among themselves.

After about ten minutes, a uniformed postal worker came out and walked awkwardly around Samuel. Samuel continued talking. The postal worker finally waved his hands and said, "Excuse me sir, but we've had some complaints. Could you perform elsewhere?"

Samuel glared at him. "I'm exercising my free speech rights, my friend," Samuel said and continued as if the man weren't there.

The postal worker stood for a moment, recovered, and walked back inside.

Paul wondered if someone with more confidence and power would come out next to confront Samuel, but Samuel soon found a stopping point and wrapped up his critique of the city's ills. The men in line politely grunted in approval as Samuel walked off.

"This is a Republican town," Samuel said, and he pulled a cigar from his pocket.

Paul wondered if Samuel might want to preach at another polling station and didn't want to ask in case it gave him ideas, but Samuel's direction made clear that he was ready to return to the church.

"If Henderson had simply stood up for his position and debated," Samuel said as they walked, "we could have truly shown the voters their choices. We could have won this election weeks ago." This had been a frequent topic for Samuel lately. Early in the campaign, he had counted on a public debate with good press coverage to solidify his position, but the Democrat's polite but unambiguous refusal had infuriated Samuel and left him scrambling to find alternative sources of publicity.

Later that afternoon, Paul and Samuel went to Mrs. O'Brien's house. She had volunteered to host an election night party.

The sidewalk was wet from rain, and soggy bunting hung from the edge of the roof. Mrs. O'Brien greeted them at the door. "It's so exciting!" she said to Samuel. "Are you nervous?"

"I'm ready to accept the Lord's decision," Samuel said as he walked inside.

In the house, guests held flutes of lemonade. No party attended by Samuel would serve alcohol.

"And here's Representative Hargrove," shouted one man from a chair across the living room, and all eyes turned to Samuel.

"You got my vote, Reverend," said another, patting Samuel on the back.

"And mine."

"Sacramento or bust!" said a woman who shoved a glass into Samuel's hand.

Someone shouted, "For He's a Jolly Good Fellow," and the twenty or so guests joined in an enthusiastic performance of the song.

As the applause died away, Samuel moved next to the fireplace and faced the group. After thanks all around, he said, "You are the reason I do this—why I serve as a pastor and why I hope to win this seat in the

Assembly. You are my strength. And know this: win or lose, the church continues as strong as ever. The legislative session only lasts for two months, so I won't be gone long. I'll be as close as a mailbox." Samuel turned to look at Paul and said, "And during my absence, the church will be in good hands."

℘

The rain clouds were gone the next day and the morning was clear and bright, but Paul's mind was churning. His imaginings took hold and he saw himself in the church, at the pulpit, alone and without Samuel, staring out at the crowd, feeling the familiar fear like an anaconda twisting itself around him, squeezing him so he couldn't breathe. And then the dark wooden church dissolved into the new church, cavernous and sterile and bright, with face after sullen face staring at him, thousands of them it seemed, all unblinking and judgmental.

The clang of the trolley bell brought him back to the present. He put his newspaper under his arm, stepped off the trolley, and walked two blocks to a door under a sign reading "Farber General Store." The name was a relic from the establishment's early days as a one-room store on the outskirts of town. It still held a little of everything, but it had expanded to become a popular full-service grocery store. Los Angeles had grown up around it as well, and the "great white store," the enormous new Hamburger's department store, was just a block away.

In the three months since their breakup, Paul hadn't seen Athena, but he had thought about her many times. He reviewed his actions and his feelings for her often. Samuel's anti-feminist stand had been comforting but now seemed backwards and primitive. Paul followed the story of the suffragist cause in the paper and had felt his sympathies grow.

He passed the produce stands and walked upstairs to what had been a separate apartment but which now served as the store's office. He stopped at Athena's desk, in a corner and hidden behind tall filing cabinets. A wide ledger book lay open in front of her.

She turned from it to face him and looked startled and then vaguely pleased. "Good morning, Paul." Then she glanced at the newspaper under his arm. "You've seen."

"Yes. I'm sorry."

Athena stood and held out her hands, and Paul took them. He noticed that she had no engagement ring and that she looked as pretty as he remembered.

She gave his hands a squeeze and let go. Paul opened his newspaper to show the headline: "SUFFRAGE REJECTED."

"Yes, I've read that one," Athena said. "And the *Herald* and the *Examiner.* I thought that the vote would at least have been closer."

"People will come around. I never even knew women wanted to vote until you told me, and then I thought it was wrong, foolish. But I understand now."

"I'm glad you've come around." She smiled, but the smile faded. "I was hoping to celebrate, but this feels more like a funeral. We had such high hopes after our rally in September—lots of good articles, and some positive editorials. But we didn't even win the vote here in Los Angeles, let alone the state. Father's been gloating about this all morning. At least my parents should leave me alone now."

Athena sighed as she sat down slowly but then straightened and put her hand on the newspaper. "I've been so focused on the referendum that I never looked—what happened with Reverend Hargrove's election?"

Paul saw again the image of his speaking to the crowd, but it vanished without emotional impact. "He lost, too."

෪

Hammering gently to avoid disturbing Samuel's work, Paul tightened up the framing around the window in the office as the pastor handled his morning correspondence. The old building was built as a stable, with little concern for keeping out the weather. The original clapboard had been fortified with lath and plaster on the inside walls, but cold and windy days like this one exposed its cracks and put maintenance at the top of Paul's agenda.

Three weeks had passed since the election loss, and Samuel treated it as a failure, an embarrassment, something he didn't want to discuss. He acknowledged a sympathetic pat on the back or the wish for better luck next time with a tight smile or a curt "Thanks," and parishioners learned to avoid the subject. Whether he thanked his campaign volunteers, Paul never knew.

The creaking of Samuel's chair, the scratching of his pen, and the puffing on his pipe made a dependable background sound as Paul worked on the window. But with the rustling of a newly opened letter, that changed.

"They can't do this," Samuel said after a moment. He repeated himself several times as he burrowed through files in a drawer, pulling out papers to put in the center of his desk.

Paul knew enough not to intrude when the boss was upset.

Samuel dropped his pipe into the ashtray, leafed through the stack, and stood to pace his office. After a few quick circuits, he picked up the pipe, sat down, dropped the pipe again, and said, "I'll sue them, by God, I'll sue them."

That was the most blasphemous thing Paul had ever heard Samuel say, but his swearing quickly became worse.

After a minute of exercising his profane vocabulary, during which he wrestled with the offending letter like a cat worrying an indestructible mouse, he said, "Paul! I need you to get to the work site, now. Keep everyone there, and keep them working. I'll be there in less than an hour."

"What's wrong?" Paul tossed his hammer to the floor.

"A misunderstanding. Something we must resolve quickly. Just keep everyone working."

Paul grabbed his overcoat as Samuel hurried him out. They left the building together, Samuel going west into town, and Paul heading in the opposite direction toward the construction site.

An icy gray sky hung over Paul as he trotted the short distance. When he arrived, the site was vacant. He searched for any clue that the workers had left temporarily but saw nothing—no tools, no coats, no bags with lunches. It was a workday, the Tuesday before Thanksgiving, and yet the site was abandoned.

Tarps had been tacked into place as a temporary roof to keep out the November rains. Some had come loose, hanging down and flapping in the strong wind. He pulled up his collar against the cold. There was nothing to do but wait for Samuel.

He strolled the church floor and looked up at the towering roof beams, four stories tall at the peak, that had been installed the previous week. On the day that the last of the twelve arch-shaped timbers was set in place, with the horizontal ridge piece acting as a spine, Samuel had come out to examine the work. That had been his first visit on a workday, and he took the opportunity to give a little speech. He thanked the workers and then, with his voice rising in power and volume, he moved on to an extemporaneous sermon exploring the faith of Jonah. The workmen stopped to listen, and many took off their hats. As it became clear that instead of Samuel's promised "few words," he was taking the new church out for a spin, they sat.

After about ten minutes, the foreman, who had checked his watch several times, walked over to Samuel. Not bothering to wait for an opening, he said in his own loud voice, "Reverend, if you want to idle these men any longer, you'll have to pay for the privilege."

Samuel brought his remarks to a quick close.

The whistle of the wind returned Paul to the present. The sharp snap of the canvas on the roof beams gave the impression of a ship under sail, which was appropriate since the curved church roof had been designed to represent an overturned boat. The redwood beams had seemed magnificent when they were being installed, but looking up at the roof now, the flapping tarps seemed like flesh clinging to the bones of an enormous rotting whale.

Samuel pulled up in a hansom cab. Paul was sitting on the church's short stone wall and didn't stand.

"Where are they? Where are the workers?" Samuel asked as he trotted toward Paul, looking around piles of lumber and stone as if he expected the workmen to be hiding. "I told you to keep them here." His face was red and sweaty, and his jacket pocket bulged oddly.

"They were gone when I got here."

Samuel's shoulders sagged as he slowed to a walk. He seemed about to say something but instead eased himself onto the wall next to Paul. The wind turned slightly to come from upriver, bringing the smell of the meat packing plant, while the tarps fluttered and twisted from the ribs above.

Samuel sat silently, squirming occasionally as if wrestling with his choice of words. Finally he said, "We're out of money. We've been running on credit here for over a month."

Paul's head jerked to the side to stare at Samuel, and his fingernails dug into his palms.

Samuel paused as if gathering strength. "The construction company won't extend any more credit. They pulled the men to work on another project. I've tried for bank loans but they say we're not creditworthy." He patted his jacket pocket. "I hoped that some cash would keep the men working. This is all that we had in the bank." He looked down at the undignified bulge and straightened his coat to minimize it. "They only had small bills," he said.

"You never said we had financial problems."

Samuel slumped over with his elbows on his knees. "No, I wanted to shield you. The donations have dropped more than I expected. A win in the election would have boosted my profile, giving us a bigger Sunday attendance and more income—problem solved. That was the lesson from the prophecy, that good press means more people and more donations."

Paul finally understood. "You gambled."

"What did you say?" Samuel turned to face Paul, looking as if he'd been jostled awake.

"You acted like a gambler." Once the words were out, more came easily. Gambling was high on Samuel's list of vices. "You needed money, so you bet most of your available cash on the legislative seat. One big win and you could leave the track happy." Did the financial problem put his position in the church in jeopardy? He didn't particularly care.

"Now see here—"

"I do see. In fact, only now do I see clearly. You squandered the money that was entrusted to you by members of this church."

"You have forgotten your place, mister!"

"I believe my place is to do right by the members of this church, the people who pay my salary."

"I pay your salary! And I rescued you from the street. God only knows where you'd be if not for me."

Paul felt his instincts engage, bringing a whisper of rage and the familiar feeling of power and invincibility that came with it. He stared Samuel in the eye. "That's not the topic."

"You, sir, are on thin ice." Samuel held out one of his large hands and slowly crushed an imaginary egg. "I have your career and your very future in my hand. Don't push me."

Paul stared at the ground so Samuel couldn't read his face. He squeezed his fists tight and slowed his breathing. Samuel rarely played this card but didn't hesitate when it was convenient. Shortly after Paul arrived in the church, awash in the delight of honest work and a purpose in life, he had confessed the murder to Samuel. At the time, it seemed an honorable payback—Samuel had reached out to him, and the confession was Paul's gift in return—but now he cursed that moment of exuberance.

As if to restart the discussion on a more conciliatory note, Samuel said, "Anyway, I was investing in the future."

Paul wondered if Samuel was investing in the church's future or his own. "How much will this investment cost?" He had asked the same question at the beginning of the project, but Samuel had dismissed it, telling him not to worry.

This time, Samuel looked at him as if sizing up an opponent and then snapped, "Seventy-eight thousand dollars for the land and all construction costs."

"And how much has been paid?"

"Almost twenty-three thousand."

"So we're obliged to pay—what is it?—another fifty-five thousand dollars?"

"I'm aware of the difficulty!"

"How will we find that?"

Samuel slapped his thigh. "Why is it me who does everything? The elders aren't raising the money, it's me up there in the pulpit doing the work. And you—you had the chance." He jabbed his finger toward Paul. "If you'd pulled in that atheist, we'd have no money problems."

"You mean Jim? You think Jim Emerson would have paid for the new church?"

"It would have been pocket change for him."

"Is that why you had me find him? I was your tool to get him to join the church and give you money?"

"That wasn't the goal, but it would have been nice if you had converted him. But you couldn't."

"Neither can you."

"Whose side are you on? I know the man. Someone who is too afraid to leave his own house is not much of a challenge."

"The man is unbeatable. He has a fierce intellect. Trust me—you can't defeat him."

"So now I'm to take *your* counsel?" Samuel stood slowly and deliberately, as if stoking a fire to build a mighty head of steam. At his full height, he turned to face Paul. "We'll see who's unbeatable—and so will the rest of the city. I need an opponent for the next debate. Let's make it Jim Emerson."

ॐ

Paul spent Thanksgiving with Virgil, a quiet and happy respite from Samuel's petulance in the aftermath of his financial crisis, and he spent Friday and Saturday away from the church visiting housebound parishioners, catching up on this duty after shortchanging it when work on the new church building took his time. This gave him the chance to push away his feelings of betrayal at Samuel's hidden money transactions.

Sunday was the last three-service day. Attendance at the third church service had dropped embarrassingly low since Samuel initiated it five months earlier, and he quietly put it out of its misery with a brief cancellation announcement.

On Monday, Paul arrived at the church to find Samuel in a new mood.

"Come in, come in," he said as he beckoned Paul into his office. "Look what arrived today."

Paul took the letter that Samuel held out to him. It was from Jim. "Dear Reverend Hargrove," it began. "I would be honored to participate in your apologetics debate April next."

When Paul finished reading the brief letter, Samuel said, "I was pleased that Mr. Emerson could find time for me in his busy schedule."

He leaned back in his chair with a broad, comfortable grin. "Frankly, I didn't expect him to accept, but now if he backs out, I win."

"That'll be quite a show," Paul said. "You've never had such a formidable opponent."

"Not at all." Samuel brushed away the idea with his hand. "You've told me how effective our apologetics arguments have been."

"Well, I hope I've been clear about that." He had not been entirely honest about how poorly he had done against Jim. In fact, after Samuel's scolding from his first few failures, he had simply told Samuel what he wanted to hear. "Jim has a response to everything. You mustn't underestimate him."

"No chance of that—I've worked with him, and I know how he thinks." Samuel leaned back into his chair. "And I've become a much better debater since we met last. Anyway, outside of his safe and cozy house, he won't be in any condition to debate."

The smart money was still on Jim. Nevertheless, Samuel had a good point—Jim might be fragile outside his house. Paul worried about Jim, and the entire debate felt like a bitter fight between family members.

"But there's a second part to this debate." Samuel leaned forward with his arms on the desk. "Apologetics is what sets this ministry apart, and this is a chance to educate. Why have just one debate? Let's have another one—a warm up, a demonstration, between you and me."

Paul tried to analyze Samuel's broad smile—was it warm or cunning? He dropped the letter onto the desk and retreated to his chair.

"This fits nicely with your work this year," Samuel continued. "You've had some debating practice, and you're getting over your nerves. Let's show that—you play the atheist. You know the arguments. It'll just be good-natured sparring."

Did Samuel see through him? Was Samuel setting him up for a public comeuppance? Paul's heart rate rose as if he had been sprinting and he rubbed his hands on his thighs. "I'd rather not."

"There's no pressure, because no one expects you to win. In fact, no one *wants* you to win. It'll be good practice for you and a chance to teach the church."

Paul paused to turn his emotions into coherent words, to build an effective argument. Perhaps throwing himself at Samuel's mercy would change his mind. "This is just not something I can do."

"We won't have our debate for a few months—plenty of time to practice. Besides, most of the debate is reading your opening and closing remarks. You'll have those prepared ahead of time—easy."

Easy for you, Paul thought. The bravado that had let him confront Samuel the previous week had vanished. *Please don't do this to me,* went a little prayer cycling through his head like an incantation. "Let's find someone else. I don't think well on my feet. I can see myself standing there, unable to form any kind of rebuttal." More precisely, he could see himself standing there in front of hundreds of disapproving people, feeling like he were drowning.

"You've got to jump into the pond to learn how to swim." Samuel's voice was harsher. "Let's turn this weakness into a strength."

Paul felt drained. He held up his hands to gesture but dropped them into his lap. He leaned forward and opened his mouth to speak, but no words came.

"Good," Samuel said, slapping his palm on the table as if completing the bidding for an auction item. "That's settled." He reached for an unopened letter from the small stack of mail on his desk.

Paul shuffled out and sat in a corner of the sanctuary. With pen and paper, he focused on his opening presentation for the rest of the day, and the next, and the next. He knew the arguments well, but his brain felt like it was in quicksand, with all its energy spent staying afloat and none remaining to think. Still, an argument took shape, little by little. If Samuel wanted an atheist argument, he would give his best.

After he had worked for three days, Samuel asked to see what he had accomplished.

Paul followed Samuel into his office. Samuel had bought three new candles, and the office was filled with their floral scent. No gentle suggestion of a garden—this smell was overpowering.

Paul stood in front of the big desk and read his presentation. From a debating standpoint, tipping his hand to his opponent was the worst possible move. Samuel had made this point himself several times. But the debate would be just a demonstration, and Samuel could win whether he knew the argument beforehand or not. Paul worried instead about the inevitable critique as he studied Samuel's face for clues. When Paul finished, Samuel smiled and applauded for a few seconds. "Well done. In fact, I'm a little surprised at some of those arguments—very clever. You see there, you read your speech easily."

"An audience of one doesn't count."

"Nonsense—I'm the toughest critic, and I say you did fine."

Samuel sent him on his way with some suggestions, and Paul left the office still smelling the suffocating candles.

℘

On Sunday, Samuel stood in front of the congregation and made the debate official. "Friends, we have planned a special event. This ministry has an apologetics debate every spring to show the strength of our Christian faith and its intellectual foundation. On Wednesday, April 3, I will debate someone whom many of our older members will remember, Jim Emerson."

The reaction was immediate. Samuel let the buzzing build as it ran through the congregation, and people turned to their neighbors to share information about this new opponent.

"Yes, friends," Samuel said over the noise and then paused as the talking subsided, "this man who was a fellow sojourner twenty-five years ago is now an atheist and an enemy of the faith. He dismisses what we all know to be true. I suppose it's easier when an atheist is a stranger, but when he's a former friend, a former brother in Christ, then it hurts a little more." Samuel paused stiff-armed, with both hands on the lectern. The image of a sideshow barker came to mind for Paul. "I encourage you to invite your friends to this event—anyone who wants to see what makes this church special, who wants to see truth triumphant. We don't just claim the truth of the Bible, we prove it!"

Heads nodded confidently as the crowd murmured its approval. Paul imagined his friend up on the podium, a frail intellectual blinking out at the hostile crowd, swept away by Samuel's bullying.

"But the debate this year has two parts. A month before, on March 6, we will have a demonstration debate. This time, I will debate someone you all know well. Paul Winston, our associate pastor, will take the atheist side." Samuel gestured to Paul, who stood and smiled weakly, and then retreated to his seat.

Samuel took as his sermon the story of Elijah challenging the priests of Baal in a contest to see whose god was real.

A part of the story that Samuel omitted came to Paul's mind. After Elijah won, he had his competitors executed.

℘

Jim rested his hand on Paul's shoulder and said, "Just one more time." With Paul as his companion, he'd already crossed busy Bellevue Avenue half a dozen times as part of his self-designed agoraphobia recovery plan. He had tired of crossing at the intersections and now was testing himself by crossing in the middle of the block.

Two decades of solitude had made him a poor judge of vehicle speeds, however, and Jim had foolishly darted out into traffic several times. Paul had been obliged to follow, calling out apologies to honking automobiles and shouting teamsters. To Jim, this seemed a lark, and he laughed at the close calls, but Paul was sweating.

"I think we should take a rest," Paul said, and he guided Jim to a bench a few yards away. A smoky automobile chugged past, and a traffic policeman whistled at the intersection.

"So—tonight's the big event," Jim said. "How are you feeling?"

Paul's pulse shot back up. "No change—I'm as nervous as ever." In fact, his anxiety about the debate had worsened. During the Christmas season and through January and February, he had kept himself busy by securing the building site, conducting his pastoral duties, and maintaining the old church. But the anxiety of the impending debate had kept him awake with worry the previous few nights, and he felt empty. Oratory didn't play a large role in the life of a thief. Before the church, he had felt confident and invincible at the thought of a challenge, but this paralyzing fear made him feel hollow.

Maybe it's best to turn anxiety into action, Paul thought. "On that topic, perhaps we could revisit one or two arguments," he said as he took some notes from his inside jacket pocket and thumbed through them.

"No!" Jim chuckled. "No more. We've been discussing these arguments for months. You're stuffed—any more and it'll be like sprinting with a full stomach." Jim turned to Paul with a solemn face. "But even though this won't be a serious debate, let me stress one thing. Your primary goal in any discussion or even a debate must not be to win or even to defend your position. It must be to find the truth. If the other fellow points out where you're mistaken or gives you something you haven't considered, be grateful. He's done you a favor."

Paul swiped at his side where sweat trickled down, and he groped for a change of subject. "I'm still amazed that you promised to debate Samuel," he said.

"I hope I'll be up to it. This is part of my preparation," Jim said as he embraced the traffic with a sweep of his hand.

"But the church won't be filled with horses and automobiles."

"True—people are my vulnerability. As with you."

The two friends sat for a short while and then returned to Jim's house along a route made longer with Jim's frequent street crossings.

Instead of walking to the front door, Jim turned to the small stable. As far as Paul knew, Jim had never kept a horse. Jim flung open the two large doors and turned to face Paul. "What do you think of this?"

Paul saw the shining back of a new automobile, without mud or exhaust traces on the body. He ran his hand along the top of the leather seats as he slowly walked around the marvelous machine, but he stopped at the front. "What's this?" Strewn over a canvas sheet on the dirt floor were the components of the engine, neatly laid out. The piston with its connecting rod was the only part Paul could identify. "Did it come like this? Is it broken?"

"No, no—it arrived here under its own power. I just can't keep my hands off a new toy, and I took it apart. You can't operate something properly unless you know how it works."

"Will you be able to put it back together?" This looked like quite a complex jigsaw puzzle.

"Oh, I think so. I've already done it once."

Paul walked outside and took out his pocket watch. He had two hours until the debate, and he was not eager to return to the church. Talking with Jim would be a good way to ignore his anxiety.

Jim turned to the house without comment as if Paul's following him in was obvious, as if he knew that Paul needed a sanctuary. Paul wondered if the street exercise had the same goal.

In Jim's library, he noticed the chessboard. For the previous six months, he'd watched the pieces move about, slowly dwindling in number. "Is your game almost finished?" he asked.

"This is the end game. I have the clear advantage, and I expect that he will resign on his next move."

Paul noticed something odd about the board. Jim now had a second queen, tall and elegant, made of polished black wood. It stood out from the original dumpy and worn pieces. "Where did that one come from?"

"I took that piece from a different chess set. When you advance a pawn to the last row, it becomes a queen, the most powerful piece. A tricky thing to pull off, but satisfying when you can do it."

Jim gestured for Paul to sit and then put the kettle on to boil.

Paul was rubbing his hands on the arms of the chair when Jim returned from the kitchen. "This debate!" he said. "I can't wait for it to be over. What a birthday present this is."

Jim stopped and stared at Paul. "Today is your birthday?" Jim asked as he slowly made his way to the sofa.

"Yes. Can you believe it? And the thing I dread the most—"

"How old are you?" Jim's stern voice surprised him.

"Twenty-six."

"You were born on March 6, 1881?"

"Yes." Paul had no idea what Jim was getting at.

"And were you born in Los Angeles Infirmary?"

"I don't know exactly where, but I was born in Los Angeles."

Jim fell back into his sofa as if he'd had the flash of insight for an astonishing new invention. Or a terrible realization. Emotions played over his face as if it were illuminated by a flickering fire.

Paul couldn't imagine what was on Jim's mind, but he sat and waited for Jim to compose himself.

"I know now," Jim said finally. "It all makes sense." He turned to Paul, his face stony. "Listen to me. March 6, 1881 was an important day for me, too. I was with Jenny on that day when she gave birth to her firstborn. It was a boy. It was you."

This was not believable. "How do you know it was me? There could have been other boys born in Los Angeles on that day."

"Not given up for adoption. Not taken in by Sam Hargrove. Let me give you the whole story. Jenny was with child, and that got her expelled from the church. I was out, too. Her father and stepmother insisted that she move to a girls home near San Diego. Actually, the stepmother insisted; I don't think her father had much say. But since Jenny was already shunned by her community, I'm sure that hiding her away was not to minimize social embarrassment to her but to the stepmother.

"Jenny was lonely, and I visited her often—unlike her family. When she was due, she returned to Los Angeles with a new name, and Genevieve went from Jenny to Vive. Once she had the baby, it was taken away immediately—again, at her stepmother's insistence. She cried for days. They promised that it would be adopted into a good family, but Vive had no confirmation and was never sure. She got on with her life, but she carried that loss daily."

Paul struggled to grip this new reality as the tea kettle screeched in the kitchen. Could Jim be right? "Then who was my father?" Before the words were out, the answer came to him. He pointed at Jim. "It was . . ."

For the first time since he began the story, Jim's earnest face broke into a smile. "Me?" He laughed as he trotted into the kitchen. "Oh, no—not me. It was Sam."

Paul felt dizzy. What insanity was this? Reverend Samuel Hargrove his father—what would cause Jim to invent such a tale? Mrs. O'Brien's story about Jim and Jenny contradicted him, too. "But it was you. You told me yourself that you and Jenny were expelled together. Why would that be if it was Samuel's fault?"

"I ought to know if I was the father of Jenny's child," Jim said as he returned to his seat. "Sam and I fought for Jenny's attention back then, but Sam was the one who got her into trouble. She told me herself. Sam put the blame on me and got both of us expelled from the church to save himself."

"You could have told the truth to the church."

"I did, but Sam was ahead of me. He whispered his story into the ears of the elders. I knew what he did to Jenny, but I had no interest in tattling on him so I said nothing. By the time I was forced to defend myself, the jury was tainted and my story sounded like the denials of a guilty man."

Paul fell back into his chair, winded, and squeezed his head with his hands. He had yearned to uncover information about his parents his entire life and had now tripped over it. Jenny and Samuel as his parents—the idea still seemed preposterous. He could feel his heartbeat. "Why hasn't Samuel told me? Does he know?"

"Of course he knows. He's kept it a secret out of embarrassment, I'm sure. A pillar of the community whose reputation is built on living the righteous life can be brought down overnight by the scandal of a child out of wedlock. Out of all the street toughs in Los Angeles, why do you think Sam picked you to work in his church?"

That had indeed seemed remarkable, but Paul had always thought of that happy situation as simply Providence. And yet Jim was right. What else could explain Samuel's rescuing not just anyone but the son of his paramour? Paul thought back to clues in Samuel's behavior—how he ferociously defended Paul against the complaints of church members in his early months with the church, even while Paul had still been difficult and rebellious. And how Samuel would criticize his personal life in a way that an ordinary boss would not.

Paul rose slowly from the chair and walked to the bureau. He had passed the large framed portrait labeled "Genevieve" many times, never knowing that the sweet face was that of his mother. He reached out slowly with both hands and picked it up. The old-fashioned coil of hair on the top of her head reminded him of the princess mother's crown from his childhood fairy tale.

"She named you 'Wendell.' "

"That's my first name!"

"And Paul is . . . ?"

"My middle name—that's what I was called in the orphanage. But why 'Wendell'?"

"It's not a family name. It comes from a German name for the tribe of the Vandals, and it means 'wanderer.' It's as if she had an idea of the life ahead of you."

Jim walked over and stood behind him. "Paul, this is important. She never knew about the orphanage—you must understand that. Only just now, when I realized that the baby was you, did I know that you hadn't been adopted. Nothing stood in her way when she was determined, and if she had known, she would have come for you. She just didn't know—you can't blame her."

Paul wanted to agree. "Tell me what happened later," he said. He cradled the portrait, trying to recast the familiar face into the role of mother.

Jim paused and returned to the sofa. "The month after you were taken away was rough for her. But she was strong, she found her way out. You know most of the rest. We were married a few months later in June. She would have been happy to leave town, but her father lived here, and I needed to stay because of my work. We bought this house about a year later. We were ready for a family soon after, but she died in childbirth with our first. You would've been about three at the time."

"I'm so sorry." Paul could easily understand Jim's loss, as he had experienced much of that himself when Athena had been presumed dead during the summer. He thought of the young mother and the boy that he had been, separated forever but each wanting to know the other.

"You can be sorry for both you and me now," Jim said. He walked to the bureau next to Paul, opened a drawer, and pulled out a small round pillow embroidered with a pink heart. It was about the size of a flattened muffin. "I have plenty of mementos of Vive. Maybe you'd like one?" He handed the pillow to Paul.

Paul put the portrait on the bureau and took the pillow with both hands. "What is it?"

"It's a pin cushion. Your mother made it."

Paul set the pillow on the bureau in front of the portrait and carefully turned it so the heart was right side up. "And her parents? What happened to them?"

"They've died. The stepmother as well. But you have me—technically, I guess I'm your stepfather. I must say, I like the idea of a stepson—Vive's son. And now that I look for it, I do see your mother in your face."

Paul thought back on Samuel's actions. He might have too strong a taste for power to be the perfect man of God, but this kind of treachery was hard to believe. "I never imagined Samuel lying like that."

"Surprised me as well. Betrayed by a friend—I raged at the injustice. And, of course, because of Sam, I've been locked away in my own purgatory for a couple of decades. But why focus on the bad when there is so much good in life? Being with Vive was so joyous, so incandescent, that I could die without regret tomorrow."

The memory had aroused a gentle smile on Jim's face, but it vanished as he continued. "One thing I'll never forgive is how Sam treated Jenny. Anyone can make a mistake, but he just ignored her. No apology, no amends. He never visited her when she was alone in San Diego. She was an inconvenience, so he discarded her like a soiled handkerchief. He probably conjured up God's forgiveness and figured that was enough." Jim sounded like a prosecuting attorney making an appeal for the death penalty. "Perhaps seeking you out was his penance."

"I wonder how he found me."

"Sam was always good at cultivating allies and useful friends—reporters, politicians, police. I imagine it was through one of his connections."

It was indeed odd that Samuel found him only hours after his first encounter with the police. And what were Samuel's first words to him? They were memorable: "I've been looking for you."

He slowly turned his mother's portrait to face it away from his chair and then walked back and sat down with a new feeling rising in his chest, a focused clarity that pushed other issues into the background. "Growing up, I was frantic to know where my mother was and who disposed of me at the orphanage. But now I know." He said the words reverently, as if the idea were incredible, a sparkling jewel that he could examine in the light by simply speaking the words.

Now he knew. Vive was the mother who wanted the best for him, who cried when he was taken away and who would have rescued him if she had known the truth—the princess mother that he thought about daily in the orphanage. And Samuel was the person who wasn't particularly troubled by destroying a girl's honor, who was willing to let a friend take the blame for his villainy, and who didn't bother to even inquire into the welfare of his own son. Or perhaps Samuel did know the facts and simply let Paul rot in the orphanage to avoid the inconvenience of a child.

A thought burst into Paul's mind. "I might have grown up here!"

"I wish it had happened that way."

The new feeling grew, and the sense of power and control grew with it, fueled by his realization of the childhood that was taken from him. "I think back on my life in the church," he said, smiling. "I thought I'd earned my place. I felt like I'd done a good job—but doesn't that make me the biggest fool? My position in the church was given to me. It was like a prince imagining that he's earned his royal station."

His mind filled with a focusing fury, and now that he knew who to blame he was startled to realize that he could think easily of the orphanage. He thought back to the time when they wouldn't feed him. To the time when the warden had humiliated him in the dining hall, giving him his terror of speaking in public. To the many times when bullies had mocked him, humiliated him, beaten him.

The image came to mind of a fireman turning the wheel on top of a hydrant. With each turn, the water came out stronger and stronger. Deep in his chair, Paul silently sifted through memories and weighed injustices. Jim didn't interrupt.

Paul pulled out his pocket watch. "It's time." He thought what a curious bit of luck it was that the very man he was then most eager to confront had himself arranged a meeting in less than an hour, and a public one at that.

The two men stood. Jim put his hand on Paul's shoulder. "Good luck tonight. Just relax, and remember that it's not a real debate."

Paul picked up his mother's pillow and strode toward the door. "It is now."

Chapter 13

Paul hadn't seen the church this full since the weeks after the earthquake. He watched Samuel stand from behind their shared table and stroll to the podium as applause rang in the packed church. The thought that Samuel would be pleased at the turnout reflexively popped to mind, but Paul pushed it away. He no longer cared what pleased his father.

At the podium, Samuel smiled and breathed deeply as if savoring the aroma of praise and finally raised his hand to quiet the crowd.

"Thank you, friends. It is a delight to see such interest in this apologetics debate—this defense of our position. Nothing can be more fundamental to the serious Christian." Samuel extended an open hand to the white-haired man on his right. "I want to thank Mr. Paisley for again being the debate moderator, and, of course, to our own Paul Winston for acting as my opponent." Samuel gestured in the other direction. "Paul knows well my dictum that a man can't understand his own position without understanding his opponent's, and he will be putting that into practice tonight." Samuel smiled at Paul and said, "I just hope he goes easy on me." He turned back as light laughter rippled across the crowd.

Paul was unmoved by the jest and gave no reaction.

Samuel opened with his standard presentation, which Paul understood well. He didn't know exactly what mix of arguments Samuel would select, and Paul imagined him planning his presentation as if he were a chef planning a meal—a starter of the Cosmological Argument, perhaps, with the Design Argument as a filling entrée. A quick palate cleanser of the Ontological Argument, and we could finish off with the accuracy of the Bible. But no matter what meal Samuel served up, Paul was eager to play food critic.

Paul jotted "Truth of the Bible" as Samuel developed his first point. Uninterested in the predictable argument, Paul pulled his mother's heart pillow out of his jacket pocket. Holding it surreptitiously under the table, he admired the delicate needlework and imagined her sewing it.

"Pascal's wager," Paul wrote a few minutes later, as Samuel argued that the wise man bets on God. Paul looked out over the audience. The crowd didn't intimidate him—at least not yet. He noticed the reporter from the *LA Times* who had inadvertently boosted Samuel's career almost a year earlier and wondered what he would write this time. He probably expected to see a game of chess. Paul hoped to show him a prize fight.

"Design," Paul wrote, as Samuel talked about the marvelously complicated world God had created. Paul imagined himself rebutting each of Samuel's points: *your cheerful but naive view of the world ignores disasters, disease, and the like . . . mere complexity doesn't demand a designer . . . Charles Darwin's errors are irrelevant to what biologists now say about evolution . . . your argument is a deist argument that supports Hinduism as much as Christianity.*

He noticed Mrs. O'Brien sitting in an aisle seat with her coat neatly folded in her lap. She'd never shown an interest in the intellectual side of Christianity, and Paul wondered if she was here only because he was speaking.

"Ontological," Paul wrote, as Samuel briefly sketched his last argument, another predictable presentation. At the left side of the church, near the front, Athena sat with her parents. She smiled when she saw him looking her way and raised a hand with fingers crossed for luck. Surprising—he hadn't seen her since that visit to her store back in November. Paul nodded slightly in reply, but he didn't feel like he needed luck anymore.

And there was Jim, sitting in the last row—surprising, since Jim hadn't indicated that he was able to be in Samuel's church yet. He looked comfortable enough, as if he were the music teacher at a pupil's first public recital. Paul hoped to give him what he came for.

A few minutes later, Samuel concluded his opening statement. "So you can see that it is the man who denies God who is using faith, and it is the man who acknowledges Jesus as his savior who is following the facts. We are safe to trust in God's goodness." Samuel waved like a politician as he left the podium, swept along by enthusiastic applause. As if unable to resist a brief curtain call, he shouted out, "The Bible makes it clear: 'Praise the Lord, for the Lord is good'!" The applause surged like a fire driven by a blast from a bellows.

Mr. Paisley stood as the applause faded. "We will now hear the opening statement of Reverend Hargrove's opponent, Paul Winston, who will speak to the negative side of tonight's question, 'Does God exist?' Mr. Winston, your twelve minutes begin now."

Paul put the heart pillow in his jacket pocket and walked to the podium. The applause seemed friendly but distant, and electric spotlights in the rafters made the audience hard to see. He looked out into the indistinct crowd and felt a surge of invincibility, a little like the warmth from a drink of whiskey, but clarifying to the mind and far more intense. He wondered why public speaking had ever terrified him.

He pulled out the papers from his inside jacket pocket, unfolded them onto the podium, and looked down at "Opening Statement" handwritten in pen and underlined at the top of the page. He scanned the sheet. The audience was quiet, waiting for him, as he turned to the next page.

No—this wouldn't do. It was too timid. Samuel had no doubt already considered his rebuttal—maybe even written it. Any points that had been novel to Samuel on his first hearing would be no longer. He noticed that the hand holding the page was shaking.

"The Lord is good," Paul began, picking up from where Samuel left off. He hesitated but then felt his confidence harden. "Reverend Hargrove tells us that the Lord is good, but does the dictionary agree? We must use words according to their meaning." Though he had never practiced public speaking, he did have an excellent role model. He lifted his chin as he had seen Samuel do and spoke to fill the church. "Here is what God commands about cities that refuse to submit to the Israelites: 'But thou shalt utterly destroy them; namely, the Hittites, and the Amorites, the Canaanites, and the Perizzites, the Hivites, and the Jebusites.' " Paul paused here. "You and I know what 'good' means. If you were a king or a general and you ordered the destruction of all those tribes, would you be considered good?"

Paul thought how interesting it was that a directed rage could turn a lifelong debility like his fear of public speaking into a trivial nuisance. "But you might say: this was wartime, and the rules were different. Yes it was wartime, but the Israelites were the invaders, displacing Canaanites from land they had occupied for centuries. And tell me if this sounds like what a good and wise leader commands during wartime. God tells the Israelites to destroy the Amalekites: 'Spare them not, but slay both man and woman, child and infant.' "

Other Bible passages came to Paul's mind, memorable for their barbarism. "Moses tells the Israelites that they must kill all of the Midianites, with one exception: 'All the girls that have not known a man by lying with him, keep alive for yourselves.' Ever wonder why Reverend Hargrove never made that the subject of a sermon?

"God said, 'I am a jealous God, punishing the children for the sins of the fathers unto the third and fourth generation.'

"God said that if a friend or relative encourages you to worship other gods, 'thine hand shall be first upon him to put him to death.'

"God said, 'To me belongeth vengeance and recompense.' "

A baby cried somewhere in the back.

"God may exist, and He may be powerful, but the word 'good' can't apply to a being who acts like this."

Paul glanced over at Samuel and saw him scribbling his rebuttal. Samuel scowled at him and shook his head. Samuel didn't like surprises.

Surprise!

Paul turned back to the audience and nodded, and then the magnitude of this stunt hit him. Samuel deserved all that Paul could hit him with and more, but his father's face showed him that there would be costs. Paul had turned down a one-way street but probably could still retrace his steps at this point.

No—he had to press forward. "We're also told that God is just and merciful. But what kind of justice is it that punishes someone in hell forever, regardless of the crime? Our courts use proportionate justice, letting the punishment fit the crime. Can't God do that? And how could we offend God if we act imperfectly, just as He designed us to? If He insists on taking offense, He could simply forgive like the parable of the Prodigal Son tells us to. But no—for God, forgiveness comes with demands. From the thousand religions around the world, we must pick exactly the right one, and those of us who make a mistake burn in hell.

"We know what justice is, and this isn't it."

Paul folded up his papers and put them back in his jacket. He knew he had more time, but he had just one more point to make. "I wondered for a long time why the Ten Commandments have room for 'don't covet' but no prohibitions against slavery, rape, or killing every person in a tribe down to the infants. And then I realized that they weren't crimes—they were tools. They were the tools by which the Israelites conquered Canaan."

Paul paused and looked over the silent and somber crowd. Someone coughed and it echoed like a gunshot. "Does the Bible reveal the unchanging morality of an all-good God? Have we moderns fallen away from the truth by prohibiting slavery, rape, and the murder of children? Of course not. The Bible was written by ordinary men and records the history and rules of an imperfect civilization. If you understand the Bible in that way, it makes sense, but when you imagine that there is an immutable God with an immutable morality, you tie yourself in knots justifying it. Reality is explained much better with the assumption that there is no God."

Paul touched the jacket pocket with the heart cushion. "Imagine that the God of the Bible really exists if you must, but don't tell me that he's 'good' or 'just.' The dictionary doesn't permit it." He left the podium.

℘

Back behind the table and away from the glare of the spotlights, Paul looked over the audience. When Samuel had spoken, the audience had been happily engaged, like a cobra following the comforting swaying of the charmer. Their cheerful warmth was gone now, replaced by the stunned look of people who'd been slapped.

As Paul sat, Mr. Paisley got to his feet and began clapping. The audience supported him with scattered applause.

Samuel leaned toward Paul and hissed, "What was that? You changed your opening." He squinted and the cheeks above his beard were flushed.

You wanted a debate. You got one. Paul examined Samuel, the man he had worshipped and feared for the past few years, and shook his head. It was like seeing Santa Claus in street clothes. Samuel was an ordinary and very fallible man, never worthy of worship and no longer fearsome.

Mr. Paisley stepped to the podium. "And now we will hear the first rebuttal. Reverend Hargrove, you have eight minutes."

"This is not how it was supposed to go." Samuel glared at Paul and collected his papers. As he stood, he snapped his knees to shove his chair back, and it scraped loudly.

In the short trip to the podium, his demeanor changed back into that of the confident showman. His posture straightened, and his smile returned. "Well, Paul gave us quite a performance," he said in his strong voice, and he chuckled as he faced left to Paul. He laid his papers on the podium, shuffled through them, and flipped one page over to glance at the notes he had taken. He put first one page on top and then another.

Long seconds passed. What was Samuel up to?

"Mr. Paisley," Samuel said finally, with more shuffling and flipping, "with your permission, I'd like to suggest a change in format. I should have seen earlier that this rigid debate structure wouldn't allow us to explore these issues properly." He extended his left arm back at Paul. "And of course I must beg Paul's indulgence in this change. I propose we move to a more informal discussion format—just a chat at the table."

Mr. Paisley rose. "As long as Mr. Winston accepts the change, I see no problem."

Samuel turned to Paul, and Paul responded with an outstretched palm and a nod. He could take whatever Samuel wanted to dish out.

"Please proceed, Reverend Hargrove," Mr. Paisley said.

Samuel strode back to the table, and the genial face turned hard again. Once seated, he began. "God is not good, you say. That's a bold claim, but the Bible itself says that God is good."

"Then the Bible is wrong."

A few fragile chuckles rippled through the audience.

"Excuse me?"

Paul projected his voice so the audience could hear. "I'm simply asking that we not throw the dictionary in the trash. Don't say God is good if he does things that would be bad if you did them. If you killed an entire population including infants, you could not be called good. If you had the power to eliminate slavery but didn't, you could not be called good."

"Things were different back then."

"You're saying that slavery was morally acceptable? That killing babies was okay?"

Samuel smacked the table. "Well, aren't you the arrogant mortal!" He paused to look out at the audience, then folded his hands in his lap and continued in a quieter voice. "God said, 'Where wast thou when I laid the foundations of the earth? Declare, if thou hast understanding.' God said, 'As the heavens are higher than the earth, so are my ways higher than your ways, and my thoughts than your thoughts.' It's presumptuous of us to judge God. He knows more than you do—maybe those babies needed to die."

Paul repeated Samuel's words, "The babies . . . needed . . . to die," and gave them a moment to have their impact. "So each child would have grown up to be a tyrant or a murderer? Didn't Amalekites ever grow up to be dedicated teachers or loving parents?"

Samuel turned to face Paul more squarely and leaned in. "If I were omniscient and killed someone about to assassinate the president, I would be doing a morally good act. If God says that the Amalekites were bad, that's good enough for me."

"Why is killing the cleverest solution that God can come up with? He seems to have had no more imagination than Bronze Age desert tribesmen from three thousand years ago—almost as if they invented Him. God could have kept the Amalekites from harassing Israel by building a wall or keeping them in place with a flaming sword like with the Garden of Eden. He could have transported them somewhere else in the world or built them an island far away. He could have made them nice or made their women barren a century earlier or turned them into birds. But no matter—if you want to call God unknowable or un-judgeable, I can accept that. Just be consistent. If God is beyond human definitions, don't use them. If you can't understand God's actions when they look bad, why flatter yourself that you understand them when they look good?"

A blotchy redness had crept across Samuel's cheeks and nose. "You obviously don't understand. God's actions are good—they just are. That's as fundamental a truth as we have." The gas lamps hissed faint-ly.

"So God isn't constrained to follow his own standards?"

"Of course not. God is God. His actions are the very definition of good."

"That's where you're mistaken. 'Except when God does it' doesn't appear in *Webster's* definition of 'bad,' so if the stories of God's mur-derous actions in the Bible are to be believed, a 'good' God doesn't exist."

Paul's arguments were built so closely on Jim's that he felt as if Jim were sitting next to him. He continued, "When you judge some of God's actions as good and others as beyond our understanding, you judge the Bible with your own standard. Our sense of right and wrong comes from ourselves, not from the Bible. People prove this when they rationalize the Bible to make it fit their moral standards rather than change their moral standards to fit the Bible—they beat the copper of the Bible on the anvil of their morality, not vice versa."

"Moral standards are not arbitrary!" Samuel's agitated head move-ment dislodged the hair that normally covered his bald spot, and it stood up from the side of his head like a hand. "We don't pick them like a suit of clothes and then discard them for the newest fashion. There's an objective standard of good and evil—morals represent a universal truth. You can find primitives in the middle of Borneo or the Congo that know that murder is wrong. How is that possible? The Christian has an answer: God. God put that wisdom in the heart of every man."

"Let me offer a better answer: instinct. We're all born with it. Moral instinct and social convention explain the morality that we see quite nicely—sometimes heartfelt and touching, sometimes blundering and callous. Natural explanations are sufficient. Are we seeing God's universal moral truth or simply universally held moral instincts? They look very similar, but the latter is natural and easy to imagine. What is more likely?—that's what we must ask ourselves. There's no need to invent a God to explain what we see."

"Answer me this," Samuel said. "Are there moral absolutes? Are some things just wrong?"

"I know of no moral absolutes." A few voices objected from the audience.

Samuel sat more erectly, as if building himself up to pounce. His smile showed his teeth. "So, according to you, anything is allowable? With your history as a street criminal, I could imagine you saying that, but I would have thought that the church convinced you different. Perhaps I was wrong."

Now it was Paul's turn to feel slapped, and the insult fueled his rage. Still, he had to remain in control or he would undercut any points he had made with the audience. "I see no moral absolutes, but that doesn't mean that there are no morals. We're all humans, and we have a shared moral instinct, but the idea of moral absolutes is ridiculous. We see that in our own country's history. Slavery was morally acceptable, and now it's not—we have veterans of the war that made that change possible in this very audience. Eating pork was wrong in the Old Testament and polygamy was acceptable; now it's the other way around. Alcohol is now morally acceptable, but many in this church argue that it shouldn't be. Denying women the vote has been moral; perhaps it won't be."

"Gentlemen," Mr. Paisley stood at the far side of the podium, gesturing to his pocket watch.

"Morality is impossible without a standard," Samuel said, speaking louder and turning away from Mr. Paisley.

"Gentlemen," Mr. Paisley tried again. "I must ask you to move to your closing arguments."

Samuel spun around in his chair. "I will not be silenced in my own church!"

Under Samuel's glare, Mr. Paisley made his way back to his chair.

Samuel looked out at the audience, then at Mr. Paisley, then back.

Making an apology was not one of Samuel's strengths, and Paul guessed that he wouldn't bother cobbling one together this time.

After a moment of hesitation, Samuel regained his balance. Facing the audience, he said in a controlled tone, "I would like to explore one more idea with Paul here, and then Mr. Paisley is quite right that we'll need to move to closing remarks." Samuel's face was again relaxed and confident, and Paul guessed that Samuel had seized upon his signature argument, the one that never failed him in his many public debates.

"Paul," Samuel began in a gentle tone, as if talking to a child, "I'm sure you know of the laws of logic—the Law of Non-Contradiction, for example. The statement 'this is a rock' can't be both true and false at the same time. Would you agree that a mind is required to hold these laws, that they can't exist by themselves?"

"Yes, a mind is required to hold them."

Samuel smiled and nodded slowly. "And you know that Man has not been around forever. There was a time in the past when Man didn't exist." Samuel stroked his mustache.

"Agreed."

"So before Man, what mind was there to hold the laws of logic? Or would you say that before Man something *could* have been a rock and not-a-rock at the same time?"

Paul imagined the gears turning inside Samuel's head. Samuel might see himself nudging Paul to a narrowing part of the paddock, where the sides close in gradually until *slam!* a gate drops behind to trap him like an animal.

"The laws of logic and logic itself are not the same thing," Paul said.

"Pardon?"

"You agree that gravity existed before Isaac Newton discovered the Law of Gravity?" Paul asked.

"Of course."

"Then you see the difference. You need a mind to hold the Law of Gravity. But no mind is required for gravity to exist. You need a mind to hold the ideas of 'September' or 'ten o'clock,' but no mind is required for time to exist. And you need a mind to hold the Law of Non-Contradiction, but no mind is required for logic to exist."

Samuel was like a pinwheel, spinning merrily, that a child stopped with a finger. Paul enjoyed seeing his antagonist brought up short. Samuel's mouth hung open, empty of words for once, but after a moment, he recovered. "All right, then, where do the laws of logic come from? That's the flaw with the atheist's worldview. He can't answer this, but the Christian can—God did it."

"And where did God come from?" Paul asked. "What created God?"

"God has always been here, of course. God just exists."

"Then there's no problem with logical laws just existing. If you can have a fundamental assumption about reality, then so can I."

This was the point in the argument where Samuel would normally smile in a saintly way at his befuddled opponent and, in a gesture of Christian kindness, avoid humiliating the man but instead gently point out his errors.

"But God explains it!" Samuel said, his voice in a higher register.

Mr. Paisley stood, as if ready to test his courage again.

" 'God created logic' is a statement, not an explanation," Paul said. "It simply relabels 'that which we don't know' as 'God.' It's no more useful than 'fairies created logic' or even 'it's magic.' In fact, it's no more useful than 'I don't know.' "

"Gentlemen," Mr. Paisley tried again. "The schedule demands that we move to closing arguments."

Samuel opened his mouth as if he were about to try his luck again with 'God explains it' but said nothing.

Mr. Paisley seemed comfortable taking charge again. "Reverend Hargrove, if you will give us your closing remarks? Five minutes, please."

Samuel turned to Mr. Paisley, then Paul, then the audience. His face showed irritation and anger, and Paul imagined more gears turning, with Samuel quickly considering and discarding his various options. "We'll discuss this later," he whispered hoarsely to Paul as he stood.

Paul scanned the audience as Samuel walked to the podium. Some people leaned on the pew back in front of them, hands clasped together, and many brows were knotted. One man rubbed the side of his head as if in pain.

Samuel looked out at the audience with a smile. "Well, hasn't Paul given it his all? I'm quite pleased. Let's show our appreciation for his enthusiasm." Samuel led the applause, which seemed to liberate the audience. The applause grew, and worried faces relaxed.

"We've had a spirited little chat here," Samuel said, "but let's consider this topic seriously now. The truth is that the atheist outlook is impossibly dismal. After death, there is nothing. No heaven, no reuniting with friends and family who've passed on. In this view, your dear mother or husband, departed but still beloved, is just gone. Forever. What happens to the human soul is what happens to the bird or fish that dies—nothing."

Paul shook his head as he wrote on a clean sheet of paper.

"And consider the big questions in life," Samuel went on. "Questions such as, why are we here? What is the purpose of our lives? Christianity answers those! The atheist bobs along on the surface, untethered and ungrounded, unsure of anything and determined to invent whatever morality he chooses."

Samuel paused, looked above the congregation, and smiled at something that only he could see. "I grew up in a small town in southeastern Ohio—hilly country. God's country. Our town had two whitewashed churches, each with tall, narrow steeples. I remember climbing the hill behind our town one fall day and looking down. The colors in the maples, hickories, and buckeyes were stunning, and the two steeples peeked up through the trees. I must have watched for an hour—seeing my neighbors going about their honest toil, marveling at the clockwork precision of how Man and Nature fit together to make a working, godly community. And then the bells in the Methodist church rang." Samuel hesitated and then rubbed a cheek. "I tell you, that's what heaven sounds like."

The imagery of Samuel's words and the music of his voice captured Paul as they usually did. He shook his head to break the spell.

Samuel continued. "Friends, this is what the atheist has lost by giving up Christianity: honest American values. Christianity is the sigh of the impoverished woman, the heart in a heartless world, the soul during soulless times. I have Jesus every day to lean on when things are difficult and to praise when things go well. I can't imagine life any other way." Samuel's voice had softened, but he now returned to his sermon voice. "And Jesus gives us His promise of life after death."

Samuel used the last of his time to lovingly sketch the wonder that he saw in Christianity, from the vastness of the universe in space to the universe revealed through a microscope.

Paul leaned forward on the table, eager for his turn at the podium, and he pumped up his rage by replaying the discussion he'd had with Jim that afternoon. Samuel was the traitor who let Jim take the rap. Samuel was the rogue who discarded Paul's mother. Samuel was the father who abandoned him to Mr. Dammer and the orphanage.

As Samuel finished his remarks, the audience looked relieved—their man was back in charge, and everything was right with the world. Their applause was loud and long. To Paul, it seemed to turn defiant as they looked at him.

Paul hoped to shake that up a bit when he took the podium. He pushed his chair back and stood at his place behind the table. Mr. Paisley also got to his feet.

The applause quieted, but Samuel remained behind the podium. "I believe we've run a few minutes long," he said, "but I do want to thank you for your patient attention. I hope this event has been informative."

"Reverend," Mr. Paisley said.

Samuel held out his arms. "God bless—"

"Reverend! We have one more presentation."

"Thank you, Mr. Paisley," Samuel said with a wave in his direction. "I'd prefer to end right here. I think we've explored all that we came for."

"The rules of the debate say that Mr. Winston is entitled to the last word. You had the opening remarks, and he gets the closing."

Samuel chuckled, "I'm sure Paul has had enough for one evening." He turned to Paul.

"Not at all," Paul said. "I'm ready."

"Now Paul, I know how difficult public speaking is for you. You don't want to embarrass yourself."

What a pathetic ploy. No more Marquis of Queensberry rules now—this was a brawl. "You're considerate as always, Reverend, but I'd like my time."

Mr. Paisley said, "Mr. Winston, five minutes, please."

Samuel whirled from the podium and stomped back to Paul. He put a hand on the corner of the table and leaned in. The rage was barely contained in his hushed voice. "You're out of line, mister, and you've done more than enough for one night."

"I've got a lot of catching up to do." Paul turned to walk to the podium, but Samuel straightened and took a step to put himself in Paul's way. The man in Paul's path outweighed him by a hundred pounds and stood six inches taller. The mental image of Samuel falling to the floor like a side of beef flashed to mind. *Go ahead—take a swing.* Paul's hands curled into fists at his side, and he felt a smile cross his face. "Let me pass, sir."

Samuel's clenched teeth distorted his words. "I never move aside for traitors."

Paul could always have won the physical argument, and now he could win the intellectual one. "I always do," he said as he nimbly slid past, leaving Samuel spluttering behind him.

Paul took the podium and shaded his eyes from the glare of the spotlights to look over the crowd. Mrs. O'Brien hugged her coat to her chest. Mr. Farber looked stern as he held his wife, and Paul was unsure what he saw in Athena's face, but it wasn't the displeased look that he expected. The reporter, perhaps the only person not looking at him, was hunched over and writing.

For the first time in the debate, Paul smiled. He had something to say, he had the podium, and the audience couldn't do much more than run away. The room was silent. Everyone seemed expectant, including the fussy baby. A line from an ancient Chinese poet came to mind, something he had read in a book of Jim's: "The slave is now the executioner."

⅋

Paul laid his notes on the podium and grabbed its edges, smooth and rounded after thousands of sermons. "Reverend Hargrove tells us that the atheist outlook is dismal. But how is this relevant? Is it possible that the agreeability of something bears on whether it's true or not?

Since a world without earthquakes is more pleasant than one with them, perhaps he imagines that earthquakes don't exist.

"Are we not adults here? Don't we need the unvarnished truth? Wishing doesn't make it so. That a believer might be happier than an atheist is no more relevant than the fact that an opium addict might be happier than a sober man. What do we think about the man who rejects reality to cling to comfortable myths?"

He considered the sound of his voice. Not Samuel's rich baritone, but not bad. It carried well over the hiss of the arc lamps and the shuffling and creaking from the pews. He also noted that if Samuel hadn't pushed him, he would never have discovered how intoxicating public speaking could be.

"Reverend Hargrove would also have us consider life's big questions. I grant that Christianity can answer those questions, but so can anyone. There are people around the world in different societies congratulating themselves right now for having the correct answers—quite different answers than what Reverend Hargrove would give us. Why should I think his answers are correct? Why trust *any* answers gotten through some ancient book or what one imagines as God's voice?

"Reverend Hargrove tells us that the Christian has a reliable and unchanging source of morals but that atheists invent whatever morality suits them. But it's the Christian who must justify the Bible's slavery and rape and infanticide. And if he does reject the evil in the Bible that was clearly supported by God, he must invent a reason why *any* of it is supernaturally inspired and should rule their lives today. The Bible is no help in deciding that 'love your neighbor' is important but 'save the captured virgins for yourself' is wrong, since it says both.

"In fact, it's not the atheist but the Christian who is untethered from what he knows to be true—that killing every last man, woman, and child of a neighboring tribe is just wrong. That's what happens when you get morals from the diary of a desert tribe that lived 3,000 years ago. Atheists are not bound by the errors in an ancient book but are free to follow their natural sense of right and wrong."

Paul looked down at his notes. "And finally, Reverend Hargrove would have us equate Christianity with 'honest American values.' I wonder if he has read the United States Constitution, a national charter remarkable for being the first to exclude religion. Reverend Hargrove is entitled to free speech tonight, and so am I, but it's the Constitution that gives these rights, not the Bible.

"And the Declaration of Independence makes clear what our country is built on. It says that governments derive their just powers from . . . what do you think? From God? No: 'from the consent of the governed.' Authority comes from us, from 'we the people.'

"Reverend Hargrove thinks that he's preaching American values? Not if he wants to replace the strong and independent American character with dependence and the childlike acceptance that religion demands."

Paul glanced back at Samuel. His arms were crossed, and he stared back, unmoving. He had abandoned the subtle, "That's enough; rein it in" gestures from before. Paul turned back to the congregation and said, "If we make any claim to being rational adults, if we reject the idea of acting as mindless sheep, we must follow the facts where they lead. We must ask ourselves, what is more likely—the supernatural answer or the natural one?

"For example, why is blasphemy a sin? Is it that God needs man to uphold his honor? No, a god that needs us to defend him is hardly a god.

"Why was Jesus introduced to mankind less than two thousand years ago if faith in Jesus is required for heaven? Did the Jesus part of the plan simply slip God's mind? No, this is what an evolving religion looks like—a perfect and unchanging God would have shown his perfect and unchanging plan from the beginning.

"Why was this congregation lucky enough to have picked the correct religion out of the thousands of invented ones? Is it that Christianity is the one true religion? No, if foreign believers tend to embrace the religion of their culture simply because they grew up with it rather than because it's true, that analysis also applies to Christians.

"Why is faith so necessary to Christianity? Is it that God wants to test us, so He deliberately provides flimsy evidence for His existence? No, faith is just a stand-in for a nonexistent god."

Paul shielded his eyes and looked over the audience. Was he reaching them? One man squeezed his head. Another, perhaps feeling trapped in the middle of his crowded pew, had turned his body at an angle and stared to the side. A woman stroked the hair of the boy sitting next to her without taking her eyes off Paul. He saw brief whispers between neighbors, arms crossed, frowns. Maybe his criticism was too harsh for them to accept. Or maybe they were not willing to be woken from their dream. He had the podium, but the silent rejection from the people, most of whom he knew well, was personal.

He shook his head. "I wonder if I'm wasting your time," he said and scanned the audience again. "I wonder if anyone cares. There's only a couple of minutes left, but for the few of you who might find this useful, let me suggest how the clues to the fiction of Christianity are apparent within Christianity itself. I'll continue with faith.

"Faith makes clear that there's nothing there. Defending an invisible God and celebrating faith is exactly what a manmade religion would be forced to do. Faith is always the last resort. If there were convincing evidence, Christians would be celebrating that, not faith. Faith is the excuse people give when they don't have a good reason. Believing something because it is reasonable and rational requires no faith at all."

He looked down at his notes for his next point. "Imagine what would happen if we categorized Christianity as an adult activity, like smoking, drinking, or voting—things that you must be mature enough to handle wisely. Christianity would die out within a few generations. Christians must be indoctrinated as children, while they're moldable and before they develop skepticism to crazy ideas, the skepticism that all of us use to reject the other fellow's religion. What kind of truth can't be taught after people are mature? Obviously, a very poor stand-in for truth.

"Lastly, the Ten Commandments themselves show that the emperor has no clothes. The Israelites came into the Promised Land following the one and only true god, but God said in His first commandment, 'Thou shalt have no other gods before me.' Why warn the people to avoid the invented gods in this new land? Who would even consider worshipping a make-believe god when he was cared for by the very Creator of the universe? The only explanation is that the other gods were actually tempting, that they looked similar to the Israelites' god because they were *all* just various Canaanite gods—in other words, all invented.

"Any of us who care about reality must soberly pick the likelier of two worlds. One world has the Christian god, who doesn't bother preventing earthquakes, who answers prayers as reliably as a jug of milk, and who competes for followers with a thousand other gods—imaginary gods. The other world is the same, except that *all* gods are imaginary. Which world are we living in? Which is more likely? God may exist, but there's no reason to think so. Religion is what you invent when you don't have Science. Let's live in the real world and not one of make believe."

℘

The chatter on the far side of the office door quieted as the audience gradually filed out. Paul sat alone in his usual seat opposite Samuel's desk and considered the evening. By the end of the debate, Samuel had been shot, gutted, and skinned. Paul didn't worry whether the audience enjoyed the show or not, but he felt satisfied.

He looked around the familiar office—the deep Oriental rug, tidy bookshelves, impeccably clean desk, thick perfumed candles. It was familiar and unchanged and yet things were different. He was different. Wonder had filled him every time he had entered before, but now the room seemed provincial and confining. The framed articles now looked dingy, the needlepointed Seven Virtues on the wall looked amateurish, and the busts looked pompous. He pulled at his tie, undid his top button, and slouched in the chair.

What had he seen in Athena's face? She had looked almost pleased. Could she be in agreement? That would explain why she stopped coming to church. He thought back to the last time he saw her at her desk. She had worn a narrow-waisted dress and didn't seem to be wearing a corset. He imagined hugging her to find out.

One memory did ache, that of Mrs. O'Brien leaving the church and looking back at him as if disappointed, as if he'd broken a promise. He had no desire to hurt his friends, her most of all.

The door knob tipped with a hand on the outside—Samuel's hand. Samuel would make his predictable bold entrance, and the final act of the evening's performance could begin.

"No, I don't know what's gotten into the boy, but I'll find out." Samuel's voice on the other side was weary. "Things will be normal by Sunday, don't you worry." Mr. Paisley said good night in response. The knob didn't move as steps receded in the quiet church. Finally, the door swung open and Samuel entered.

Samuel hurled the door shut. He took a step closer, hands on hips, and his mouth opened and closed as if he were chewing the words he was preparing to deliver. When the words finally came out, they came out loud. "I'll tell you what you're going to do," he said, with cheeks flushed and hair unsettled, as if he'd just run up a flight of stairs. "You're going to go visit every single person who was in church tonight and apologize for your behavior. For penance, I should make you crawl to each one on your hands and knees."

Paul remained slouched in his chair, returning Samuel's stare.

"Are you listening to me? Do you understand what you've done? The trouble you've caused?" Samuel was shouting, the joy and confidence of his sermon voice now discarded. "A man's reputation takes years to build, but a stunt like that can undo it in a moment. And who knows what that reporter will write. How could you have been so stupid? This wasn't a game—this was our chance to boost our reputation and restart construction on the new church. God only knows how we'll finish it now."

He flung his hand toward the door. "And I noticed Miss Farber in attendance. She can't find time to come to church, but she can make it here to see your little song and dance?"

Paul crossed his arms, never breaking his gaze.

Samuel swung his hands in frantic circles. "Sit up when I talk to you!"

Paul leaned forward slowly and got to his feet. How had he not seen it before? Samuel had precisely the stature that Paul granted him and no more. Samuel had been the image in the barbershop, reflected back and forth between opposite mirrors to create an illusion that extended into infinity. But now he looked at Samuel instead of the illusion, and he saw . . . just a man. No infinite progression, not even a particularly impressive man, but only a jealous earl protecting his tiny fiefdom.

"You made me look like a fool out there!" Samuel said.

"You didn't need my help with that. Use foolish arguments and you look like a fool."

Samuel's face showed a noiseless snarl and he swung at Paul, hitting him just below his left eye. Paul saw the punch coming only when it was too late. He took a half step back and blinked to regain his balance. Stars swum in his vision. That hurt—Samuel's ring had connected with his cheekbone.

For an instant, the image came to mind of Paul raining blows on Samuel—a left uppercut, then a right cross and then another; Samuel's face bloodied as he takes a wild swing; Paul ducking underneath and delivering a shin to Samuel's groin; Samuel blubbering and collapsing to his knees; Paul grabbing Samuel's head and giving him a knee to the jaw; Samuel biting his tongue and blood gushing from his mouth as he flops over; the rich carpet darkening around Samuel's mouth as he coughs and gurgles.

Instead, Paul reached up to touch his wound and felt blood, warm and wet. He'd had his guard down, but that wouldn't happen again. "I'll let that one go, but touch me again and you'll regret it." Hands at his sides and eyes on Samuel, he extended his chin, making an easy target. Samuel looked as if he considered the possibility, then the will drained from his eyes and he stepped back.

Paul held his ground and smiled. "Let's see . . . four weeks from now—I really must mark my calendar. I don't want to miss the debate with Jim. I destroyed you out there, and if I can do that, imagine what Jim will do."

"You really weren't putting on an act, were you? You really buy into this atheist rubbish?" Samuel's head jerked forward. "Wait . . . that atheist has been training you! You've been planning this, the two of you—don't think I didn't see that snake tonight, lurking in the back. I told you to stay clear of him, but you went to see him anyway."

"I'm not a pawn anymore, and I have Jim to thank for that."

"I don't know where to begin." Samuel's voice was imploring, and he glanced around as if looking for advice from the busts in the bookcase. "You've humiliated me in public, you've shown disrespect for the church, you've ruined our chances to restart the new construction, and now you've violated my explicit directions to ignore that man."

"I hope you're not expecting sympathy."

"You're still just a street hoodlum, aren't you? So much potential, but you haven't changed." Samuel shook his head slowly. "Well, if you're leaving, then get a good head start. I'll visit the police department tomorrow. I have some information that I'm sure they'll find interesting." Samuel's face had become energized but calm, with everything said except for the word "Checkmate."

"That so?" Paul raised his eyebrows as if helping a toddler. "And perhaps I have information that the congregation will find interesting, Father."

"What did you say?"

"I said, *you are my father.* I know all about Jenny and what you did to her."

Samuel mouthed a response, but nothing came out. "No," he began and then cleared his throat and continued a little stronger, "What nonsense—that was Jim."

"You sought me out! You didn't pick just any criminal to save for Jesus—you were looking for your son. You helped me just to ease your guilt. Well, let me tell you, you have a lot to feel guilty about."

Samuel turned and walked slowly to his chair, dragging his hand on the desk for support. "No, that was Jim." His voice was almost a whisper.

"Let's let the congregation decide." Paul stepped to the desk.

Samuel seemed unsteady even in his chair and his head tipped to one side. "No," he began.

Paul raised an open hand and smacked it onto the desk with his entire body behind it. The busts rattled on the shelves. "It was you!" He felt no pity as he looked down at the shapeless man slumped in the chair. "Can you imagine what it was like growing up in an orphanage? Calling that home?"

Samuel hugged himself, his hands rubbing his upper arms. "I thought you were adopted, maybe."

"Well, I wasn't. You can't imagine the life I had. It was an unforgettable horror—the bullies, the indifferent staff, the sadistic warden," Paul said. "But why trouble you with my past? It didn't inconvenience you, so why should you care? And I just discovered that my mother's dead. She died twenty years ago—but perhaps you don't care about that either."

"It was so long ago." Samuel put his elbows on the arms of the chair and pushed, but one slipped off. He tried again with his hands. "I was younger than you are now."

"So that excuses you?"

"I gave you a job, cleaned you up. Surely that counts for a lot."

"Yes, you're a goddamn saint. Why didn't you come for me when it mattered?"

"I felt bad . . . I wanted to, but I couldn't take you. I was married."

"So doing right by your son would have been an inconvenience."

"I had a church and I had my reputation," Samuel said. "I assumed you were being taken care of. That was the job of the orphanage."

Paul shook his head.

"It wouldn't have worked," Samuel said, his voice quiet and whiney. "Bea would have figured it out. But after she died, I wanted to find you, make sure you were okay, help you out a bit. The church was big enough then for me to give you a job."

Paul felt the blood from the cut under his eye dripping down his cheek. A drop fell onto Samuel's desk.

Samuel extended his palm. "I reached out to you. I wanted to make amends."

Paul wiped his cheek and glanced at the blood on his hand. "I'm leaving," he said, and pushed away from the desk.

"I need you to help rebuild the ministry. As a team, we can do this, father and son. I need you by my side."

Paul shook his head.

"You're not going to tell anyone?"

Paul realized that he was free, as if standing in front of a door that had never been locked. It didn't matter anymore—the argument, Samuel and his petty concerns, the past. He was free of it all. It was as if he were a marionette suddenly rid of his strings. He looked down at Samuel. "Goodbye," he said as he turned to leave.

Chapter 14

Paul slept in late the next day, a Thursday. Being unemployed had its advantages.

It was almost noon when he left home. He wanted to celebrate the results of the debate with Jim, since Jim had made it possible and was one of the few who would appreciate it. He was also eager to get Athena's reaction, though not so eager to see her parents. He had read displeasure in their faces during the debate.

Jim's car was on the cobblestone drive, parked at the front door. He'd never seen it out of the garage before or in working order.

He walked in after Jim's customary greeting. Leviathan ran up barking and wagging her tail.

"Wow—that's quite a shiner," Jim said. "What happened?"

Paul touched his left cheek. His eyesight was fine despite the black eye, but the cut hurt. "Yeah—ran into a door last night in the dark. Stupid." He didn't feel like getting into the details of his argument with Samuel.

Jim came over to take a closer look. "You need to keep away from such dangerous doors." He walked into the kitchen. "Excellent performance last night," he said as he filled the tea kettle.

"You gave me the ammunition." Paul knelt to pet Leviathan.

"And you used it effectively."

After half a minute of silence, Paul volunteered, "I've left the church."

"Yes, you burned that bridge pretty effectively last night. Have you decided what's next?"

"I don't know," Paul said. He hesitated before putting forward an idea that was only half coherent. The words came out deliberately as he chose each one. "I thought that maybe I might stay here, with you," he said and then quickly added, "if that's okay."

Jim finished his preparations in silence. A minute later, he set the tray onto the center table and carefully swirled the teapot. "Staying here—that's a great idea. However, I had been planning a bit of a driving trip."

"I saw the car out front."

"That's what I'm taking." Jim gestured to a small stack of boxes and suitcases in the corner by the bookshelves. "And Leviathan, of course, but she doesn't add much weight, despite her name."

"How long have you been planning this?"

Jim poured two cups of tea. "A few weeks."

"You didn't tell me."

"You've been pretty anxious the past month, so I thought you had enough to think about. I've been driving around town for practice and I've assembled the car twice, so I know how to repair it. Now seems like a good time."

"Where are you going?" Paul asked.

"I don't know for sure. I'm prepared for walking in the mountains, and I'd like to see some of the natural wonders I've read about—the Grand Canyon or Yosemite, maybe."

"Are there roads?"

"There are auto trails, and stagecoach roads still exist, but I may leave the car to visit some sites by train. Or even put the car on the train—that's how it got out here from Michigan."

"But you've got to be here for your debate with Samuel."

"No, Sam won't want to go through that again. I'm sure he'll quietly cancel it. I think you've convinced him that apologetics isn't what he should build his church on. I had first planned on traveling for just a week or two, because I needed to return to face him, to close that chapter for good. But you closed it for me last night—I almost felt sorry for Sam. Seeing you beat him was healing for me, and I feel unburdened from something I didn't realize I was carrying."

Twenty-four hours earlier, Paul had been within the church—precariously, to be sure, but he had a job and an identity. An hour earlier, he had a flimsy plan for his future: to adopt Jim as his mentor instead of Samuel. Now, nothing. "Your trip sounds interesting," he offered. "I've got a little free time myself right now."

Jim studied the contents of his cup. "Paul, I've thoroughly enjoyed the—how long has it been?—nine months that we've had together. You've become a fast friend. You're the only family I have in this half of the country, and I've only known that for a day, but I think that your living with me here or our traveling together would not be fair to you. That's not what you need. I don't want you to be like me; I want you to be yourself."

"I don't know who that is," Paul said.

"You had to get through the debate last night on your own. I couldn't do it for you, and I can't tell you what you should do next. Only you can. But you have a sharp mind. What about becoming a teacher or journalist? You could be a writer or speaker—another Robert Ingersoll. Or what about college?"

The two friends talked about college and careers, and Paul felt a little less abandoned.

Jim said, "You're welcome to stay here while I'm gone, if you'd like. You've still got a lot more books to read." He gestured toward the bookshelves.

The loan of a mansion would otherwise have delighted Paul, though now it seemed like a consolation prize. "That's great. That's very generous of you."

Jim finished his cup and looked at the clock on the bureau. "It's getting late, and I'd better pack up the car. I'd like to have a few hours of daylight, and I don't trust those car lights."

"You're leaving today?"

"Nothing like jumping into an adventure with both feet."

Jim was an overwound toy, his excitement apparent in his quick movements and cheery face. Only now could Paul see past his obsession with his own future to see Jim's new passion. How could he have been so selfish? Jim picked up a box and a suitcase, and Paul carried the rest.

They put the luggage in the car's back seat, and Paul said, "Samuel deserved what he got, but I regret putting the congregation through that ordeal. Many people seemed hurt."

Jim took a moment and then said, "Imagine this situation. You're in the lobby of a hospital, and there's a wishing well. You see a little girl walk up and throw in a penny. She's wearing a hospital gown, so you know she's sick. If you had to guess, her wish was probably to get well, and she surely felt better after throwing in the penny, as if she took a happiness pill. The benefit was all in her head, but it was a benefit just the same. Now, who would interfere with that? Who would tell her that the wishing well really doesn't grant wishes? There's no harm."

Paul said, "But she's a child, and she can believe childish things. She presumably has a family to protect her from reality."

"Exactly, which is why believing in wishing wells as an adult is a different situation. A responsible adult wants to see reality clearly to make responsible decisions. Reality is better than delusion. That's the problem I see with Christianity—it keeps the flock childlike and stunted."

Jim leaned over from the front seat to fit the luggage better. "And who can suppose this is harmless—that the Christian belief is just a curious and innocent little practice without any consequences? Once the mind's drawbridge is down to let in one kind of magical thinking, like the idea that supernatural things will happen if you pray for them, politicians and charlatans will push more bad ideas past your defenses."

Paul thought about Mr. Bradshaw's obsession with quack cures and money-making schemes. "What would you replace Christianity with?"

"I don't know if 'replace' is the way to look at it. When a man has smallpox, you don't replace it with anything. You cure him and send him on his way."

Paul scoured his mind for more activities that needed doing, for some vital task that must take place before Jim left, that would delay the departure, but he found nothing. "But Christianity isn't all bad," he said. "It can give people identity, community, and tradition. It encourages charity and kindness."

"Nothing wrong with those," Jim said as he lifted Leviathan onto a blanket on the passenger seat. "The problem is with the supernatural component of religion. Religion gives bad reasons for doing good things, when there are so many good reasons. All the good of religion can be found elsewhere."

Back in the house, Jim opened the closet door. "It's getting cold out there," he said as he pulled out a tan duster and put it on. "This is too important to let someone else decide for you. You must think for yourself." He pulled a pair of goggles over his head so they hung around his neck. "But you know this now."

Jim headed toward the door but stopped. "Almost forgot," he said as he returned to the library. At the bureau, he picked up the new black queen from the chessboard, the tall and elegant one, and gave it to Paul. "My chess game is over. This is for you."

℘

Paul walked through the quiet house and found an envelope on the kitchen counter, where Jim said it would be. He examined it for a moment and pulled out a single typed letter. Unfolding it, he found five new bills.

He could hear his breathing as he turned the top bill over several times and then examined the other identical notes front and back. He read out loud, "This note is legal tender for one hundred dollars." Finally satisfied that they were what they appeared to be, he whooped and grabbed the stiff bills, fanned them like playing cards, held them to his face, and breathed deeply. That was the most cash he'd ever seen in one place. It was a year's salary for him—or had been, up to a day earlier. He carefully laid the bills, Lincoln side up, in a row on the counter and read Jim's letter.

It explained that the money was his to use as he liked but noted that it would pay for a lot of college and suggested that he use it for that purpose. It went on to encourage him to live in the house if he wanted to, treating it as if it were his own. "Stay as long as you like," it said. It concluded with a list of practical matters: where the kerosene was kept and how to refill and light the heater, when the ice man and laundry service came, how to contact the handyman for maintenance issues, a request to take in the mail and forward it to him periodically, Jim's promise to keep Paul updated with his adventures and where he could be reached, and so on. Last in the list was a request that Paul tell Jim how he was managing his new life. At the end, it was signed in blue ink, "All the best, your loving stepfather, Jim Emerson." He wanted to rush out the front door to shout his thanks, even though he knew Jim wouldn't be in sight.

The possibilities overwhelmed him, and he wandered back into the library feeling lightheaded. He could stay in this mansion, free of charge, as long as he liked. He walked past the bookshelves, touching the spines of the books with his fingers as well as his eyes. There were books on physics, chemistry, and engineering, which didn't interest him—not at the moment, anyway—as well as more intriguing titles on geography, history, philosophy, art, and sociology.

Books had been rare and precious things to Paul. A sympathetic matron at the orphanage had encouraged his reading interest with her own children's books. Once he was out and on his own, he would sometimes pass as a student to spend a day at the University of Southern California library, even borrowing books without permission on occasion, and he bought the occasional classic work for his own small collection. But now there was no admission requirements and no closing time. He could travel through history or around the world without leaving this room.

Paul pulled off a biography of Sir Richard Burton, the first outsider to visit Mecca. Next, a book on ancient Egyptian art. Then an atlas. Only when the light became dim did he realize how late it was. It was past five o'clock, and he had been lost in books for hours. He'd had no lunch and realized that he'd given no thought to planning his evening in this familiar yet strange house.

In the kitchen, he rummaged through the pantry and ice box, fixed himself a dinner of boiled wheat and a cheese sandwich, and made a note to buy some food that was more to his liking. Money wouldn't be a problem. He put one of the hundreds into his billfold and hid the others under a serving platter on the top shelf in the cupboard. The next day, he could give notice at his rooming house and get his clothes. And of course he needed to visit Athena to see if their relationship could be revived.

Jim's house had electric lights, but Paul had to feel for the switches as he made his way up the dark staircase and into unfamiliar rooms. The upper floor had one master bedroom, two smaller bedrooms, and a bathroom. Jim's big bed was bare with neatly folded sheets lying on top—an invitation to sleep there—but this felt oddly intrusive. Before he left to pick another of the bedrooms, he noticed Jim's diploma on the wall. "Bachelor of Science," it said, from the Massachusetts Institute of Technology. Going to college himself was not what life had prepared him for, and yet Jim's confident suggestion made it seem almost reasonable.

Paul retrieved his mother's portrait from the library and set it on the dresser in his new bedroom. He put her needlepoint pillow and the chess queen next to it. Emptying his pockets, he found his remaining "Assistant to the Pastor" calling cards and tossed them into the waste basket.

In bed with a book on the Spanish conquest of the Americas, he paused to review the events of the day. A grand house, rent free, and money enough to leisurely consider his options—it was like being in an endless meadow with good hunting in any direction. He almost had too much choice, and his mind spun to think about it.

He thought back on the shackles he'd left behind. Only in the intensity of the debate had he finally seen the world through godless glasses. He'd been a misfit within the church, but the defect wasn't with him but rather his belief.

The medieval Christian constraints were gone. He felt a door to the twentieth century swing open, and he entered a rational world governed by intellect and logic.

℥

Floyd Paisley paused outside the church. Though head of the board of elders, Paisley worked best with Samuel Hargrove when Samuel was on target and he could applaud, assist, or get out of the way.

This would not be one of those meetings.

The debate with Paul Winston the previous evening had clearly been a mistake. Samuel had been overmatched and embarrassed. His unwavering confidence was normally an asset, but this time that inflexibility eliminated thoughtful responses and he came across as petulant.

With a deep breath, Mr. Paisley walked through the church and on to Samuel's office. Inside, newspapers were strewn on the carpet and Samuel sat behind his desk with that morning's *LA Times*.

"We agreed that I'd come by," Mr. Paisley said.

"Look at this." Samuel smacked the paper. "And on the front page too. Have you read it?"

Mr. Paisley shook his head.

"It says I was outclassed. That it was obvious to everyone in attendance. Was that how you saw it?"

Mr. Paisley cleared his throat, but before he could compose an answer, Samuel spoke again. "Listen to this. It says 'Reverend Hargrove came in like a clipper ship, proud and full of wind, but was listing heavily and taking on water by the end of the evening.'" Samuel scanned down the page. "I'm a 'pompous tent preacher.'" More scanning. "And a 'tired horse whose racing days are behind him.'" His head snapped up as if Paisley needed to answer for this insult.

More throat clearing. "Sam, we need to put this behind us. I'm sure I speak for the entire board when I say that we're fully in your corner. We need to look forward and plan for the future."

Samuel glared.

"Let's start with Paul," Mr. Paisley said. "He's our biggest problem. It's an embarrassment to have our assistant pastor act like that."

"Not a problem anymore. Paul is gone."

"Just like that?"

"We had words. He's gone."

Mr. Paisley strode to the guest chair and sat. "Well, that's the answer, isn't it? He was a bad element, and you've expelled him. He was a splinter in the body of the church, and now that he's gone, the church can heal."

The rage in Samuel's face drained away and he slumped back into his chair.

Paisley waited for Samuel's response but he was silent. "What's the matter?" Paisley asked. "That's the answer—Paul was evil and we're better off without him."

Samuel gazed down at the newspaper. "It's just that he was an important part of the church for me."

"Of course, but hard-working young men are easy to find. We can get you a replacement next week. A month from now, you won't know there's been a change." Mr. Paisley paused to give Samuel the chance to agree, but he sat, staring. "All right then, let's talk about what you have planned for this Sunday."

"I haven't given that much thought."

"People will need reassurance on the debate, so you'll need to address that in the sermon. But Paul's leaving makes that much easier. Let him take the blame—throw him to the wolves."

Samuel grimaced.

"I don't understand. It's like you care for him after what he did." Mr. Paisley leaned forward and lowered his voice. "Sam, your own man humiliated you. Everyone will be concerned. For the good of the membership, show them that you're in charge, that the church is in good hands."

Samuel wiped the newspaper. "Why did he have to write this?" he said and resumed his rage at the article. And then back to his odd concern for Paul.

Samuel continued his ruminations through these topics, but Mr. Paisley interrupted, "I came here to check on Sunday's service. I want to make sure you're alright. Can I do anything? Do you need help with the sermon?"

"I'll be fine."

Mr. Paisley eventually gave up and left Samuel to recover in his own way, but Samuel's assurance wasn't reassuring. Mr. Paisley considered calling a meeting of the elders, but that would've shown a lack of confidence in Samuel. He walked slowly from the church, wondering when things would be the same again.

On Sunday, half an hour before the first Sunday service, Mr. Paisley found Samuel in his office staring at his sermon. Normally a tidy list of points fit neatly on a single sheet, but this sermon seemed to be pages long, scattered across the desk, with a flurry of cross outs and additions. Even from across the desk, he could see that the handwriting was no longer confident and looked as if written by different people.

Samuel didn't look confident either. "Sam, did you sleep alright last night?"

Samuel's eyes were sunken and nervous. "I couldn't sleep." He gestured at the pages. "I was worried about this. I've spent days, but I don't know what to say. Everyone's counting on me and I bungled the debate and we can't pay for the new church building. Paul's gone now, and they'll blame me for that. It's too much to expect."

Samuel's voice had a childish tone he had never heard before. Mr. Paisley sensed disaster ahead. "You'll do fine."

Samuel slowly picked up different sheets of his sermon, put some down, and rearranged others, apparently unable to find the order. Mr. Paisley did what he could to help, and they left the office just before the service began.

The church was full, doubtless because everyone was eager for comfort, for a return to normal. Mr. Paisley looked around and saw many who seemed to be anxious and off balance. He felt drained.

Samuel began the service without incident, but as he listlessly took the podium for his sermon, Mr. Paisley felt like he was back in the debate. He held his breath.

"Friends, let us consider the lessons in the story of David." Samuel's voice was a quiet monotone as he recounted David's life as a shepherd and the king's armor bearer. He passed through the story of Goliath in a few sentences and then crafted an elaborate picture of David's life as a king and God's anointed. Next, the story of Bathsheba, the wife of one of his soldiers, and how David committed adultery with her. David first tried to cover up his sin, then ordered her husband killed, and then married her.

Samuel's voice had grown stronger. "He forced himself on a woman, and he murdered a friend. But was God fooled? Certainly not, and He punished David by . . . by taking his son." His tone was reverent, and the true meaning of the story seemed only to have just then burst upon him. "And yet God saw fit to favor him again. And that's the lesson: that God's patience and mercy are infinite, even though it's clear that we're unworthy.

"Friends, when we examine our souls honestly, we see the flaws. I certainly do. I see sins that I shudder to remember." Samuel's voice was shaking and Mr. Paisley leaned forward. "Indeed, sins that make me question whether I'm worthy to continue as God's messenger." A long pause as Samuel slowly turned one sheet of paper, then another, then another. Mr. Paisley strained to hear what Samuel said next. "I can't." Samuel slowly turned and took small steps back to his chair.

Long seconds passed before the pianist took control. The audience slowly reached for their hymnals, and everyone stood to sing except Samuel. The hymn over, two ushers stood with offering plates, awaiting Samuel's signal. More silence. Finally aware of his cue, Samuel stood and, not bothering to walk to the podium, gave a mumbled benediction. He turned and shuffled to his office and closed the door.

80

The morning after Jim's departure, Paul awoke to the dawn, a foreign experience for someone accustomed to waking in a windowless room. The bedroom was cold, and he pulled the blankets tight around his neck. He'd never experienced Jim's house this cold before, but of course he'd never been here so early on a March morning. His own apartment was a shack by comparison, though it did at least have a radiator that kept it warm.

Once out of bed, he pulled on his clothes and refilled and lit the kerosene heater, cursing himself as he shivered for not refilling it the night before. A little warmer with the heater on, he found his breakfast and returned upstairs to tidy up. In the bathroom, he saw that his black eye was unchanged. He'd need to explain away the ugly thing to Athena that evening—a small annoyance, to be sure, but he was eager to see her again to see if his hunch was correct.

He toured the house again, in full daylight this time, as he imagined himself living here as a man of letters, even a man of leisure. Fired with a vision of his new life, he took Jim's house key and stepped outside.

The bright sun that had woken him hid behind clouds, a light breeze blew, and it was cold—very cold. He returned to the house and found a sweater and a tight-fitting overcoat in Jim's closet. Back outside, he could see his breath but trusted to brisk walking to warm himself up.

At his rooming house, he found the landlord and gave notice that he was leaving. The landlord said that because of some obtuse contractual clause, Paul was obliged to pay through April. Nothing to be done for it, he figured, and he went up to collect his clothes.

Back in his new home with groceries, a newspaper, and his clothes, Paul made lunch and settled down with the newspaper. He missed the activity of Jim and Leviathan, but he looked around the familiar library and felt at home.

He took Jim's spot on the couch, opened the *Los Angeles Herald* as if it were a Christmas present, and turned to the help wanted section. It was short, surprisingly short. Discouragingly short. In fact, less space was taken up by help wanted ads than ads for property and businesses for sale. Eliminating the jobs reserved for women, he found little of interest. Some were beneath him—delivering newspapers, selling novelties, or distributing circulars. Some required skills he didn't have and didn't particularly want to have—barber, iron or brass worker, blacksmith. And the remainder he could imagine himself stuck in for the rest of his life with no chance of advancement—mule skinner, wagon teamster, pick or shovel man, stable man, brick layer, mucker. He wasn't above working hard for a living, but he wanted to exercise something more than his muscles.

He tossed the paper on the floor. It was naive or even childish to expect to find something the first day, but somehow he had expected it anyway. He felt alone in this too-quiet house and got up to pace. What kind of job did he want? Maybe a government job, or a job in a big company? A desk job—that's what he needed. Something where his contribution would be intellectual. Unsure of how to proceed, he set aside his career plans. Perhaps that evening Athena could be a sounding board.

He spent the afternoon lost in Jim's books, paging through titles that caught his eye and stopping to read interesting sections. Once the light faded, he went upstairs to bathe and put on clean clothes.

Two days had passed since the debate, and he longed to hear Athena's reaction. He grabbed his sweater, coat, and hat on the way out to the trolley stop. By the time he arrived at the Farbers' house, on the opposite side of town from Jim's house in Angelino Heights, it was almost 6:30. He hoped the Farbers hadn't started dinner.

Athena's father answered the door.

Paul took off his hat. "Good evening, Mr. Farber. I was hoping to see Athena."

Mr. Farber stepped squarely into the doorway. "No, I don't think so."

"Is she not here?"

"She's here. I'd just rather you not see her."

Paul felt his energy drain away as if he'd made some faux pas. "Can you tell me why?"

"You think that after Wednesday night's performance you'd be welcome here? This is a God-fearing home. That child has turned from the church enough already, and we certainly don't need your contribution."

The thought flashed through Paul's mind that he could just call his role in the debate a bit of overexuberance. He was playing a part—had that been unclear?—and he could apologize for any unintended offense. But Paul's disdain for Christianity had been unmistakable in the debate, and he wouldn't be dishonest now about his position. "Could I see her just for a minute?"

"You made your position quite clear. Let me make mine clear: stay away from my daughter."

Paul suddenly felt embarrassed by his black eye and turned his head slightly to the left and held his hand up to cover as much of it as he could. Now *he* was the villain?

"This is a Christian home. Your corruption isn't wanted here." The door closed, and the deadbolt thumped into place.

♋

Paul stood by a bench Saturday morning, bundled against the cold. This was the rendezvous point where he and Athena had often met after her work day, a block from the store and safe from Mr. Farber. Paul fanned the embers of his feelings for Athena, hoping that she might also want to rekindle their romance and that she would think to find him here. He idled away the hours thinking what he would say, wondering how she might be planning to slip away to meet him. Or even if she wanted to. He left his post cold and hungry after the sky was dark. The day had been a waste.

He picked up several newspapers on the way home but again found nothing in the want ads, as if he were sifting through mine tailings. Contacting companies directly—that's how he needed to do it. Back home, he spent the evening drafting a letter with his qualifications and interests.

The next day was Sunday—a good day to sleep in. After a little more work on his letter, he left to roam downtown to find companies in which he could see himself working. He jotted the names and addresses of those that looked promising and by mid-afternoon returned home.

On Monday, he planned again to wait for Athena, but he first stopped by a store with a telephone to look for businesses in the telephone directory. He paged through the listings of art suppliers, automobiles, banks, bakeries, barbers, bicycles, brewers, brick manufacturers, and so on, imagining with each company what job he might find, and adding to his list the names that seemed promising.

When he got to meat packers, he stopped at one listing as if he'd walked into a glass door. "Swift & Co.," it said, with an address just a block from the river. That was where he had killed that man. He'd deliberately been there late in the day because he'd heard that the managers came out later than the hourly employees, and he wanted to rob a rich manager. If they now had a job opening that he could fill, it might be a manager's job, maybe even the dead fellow's job. Maybe after five years it was still open. Vacant. Unfilled. Maybe they'd give it to him—give him the job of the man that he had killed.

He closed the directory and looked up to see if anyone was looking at him. They might have read his crime in his face—but no, of course not. His face was hot as he wiped his forehead, and he tried to empty his mind as he left.

He spent the rest of the day sitting on his bench with his head pulled down into his coat, and again his cold vigil ended without success.

On Tuesday at midday, while puzzling over alternative ways to contact Athena and wondering if her absence was deliberate, he saw her walking toward him.

"I've been trying to find you for days." He held open his arms, afraid that he might shoo her away.

She stepped close, and he embraced her. Stuck in Jim's house, he'd not realized how much he missed human contact. "You've been locked away, Rapunzel." Paul leaned down to inhale the smell of her hair.

"Father's been extra protective," she said. "I heard that you came by on Friday, and I thought you might be here. You must be freezing." She reached up to touch his cheek. "Oh, no—how did you get that?"

The skin around Paul's left eye had turned greenish. He'd seen plenty of bruises and understood the healing process, but his face was now uglier than ever. "Oh, just ran into something," he said and gestured for her to sit on the bench, positioning her so his eye would be more hidden. "Thanks for coming to the debate."

"My parents made me go. It was something of a compromise—I listen to the debate, and then they let me decide to attend church or not. They thought it would be convincing, but it wasn't quite what they had in mind. You certainly weren't subtle."

"What did you think?" Paul asked.

"I thought it was great—were you in earnest?"

"I was. I'm an atheist now, though I only fully realized it at the debate. But what about you? I thought we were irreconcilable."

"It seemed like that, at least on the suffrage issue." Athena pulled her fur collar tighter.

"Oh that. I'm past that—sorry. But what about Christianity?"

"I pretty much lost that belief at the monastery."

Paul felt his heart beat faster.

She said, "All that I've read since has only pushed me farther away. My loss of faith in the rightness of religion allowed me to lose faith in the rightness of society's treatment of women. I must say, your arguments in the debate were terrific."

"I don't suppose I convinced anyone."

"Someone who wasn't argued into a belief isn't easily argued out of it."

He loved this girl's wisdom. "Did you hear how church went on Sunday?"

"My parents told me. Reverend Hargrove seemed confused, distracted. He compared himself to King David."

"So he's a king now? That's bold."

"And what about you? Are you looking for a job?"

Paul told her about the ups and downs of his job search, the loan of Jim's house, and Jim's encouragement to go to college.

"College is what I want, too," she said.

"What do your parents say?"

"They treat me like a child again, and they weren't happy with my suffrage work. I guess they think they're losing their little daughter or I'm straying from the straight and narrow, so they're pulling me closer. It's suffocating. I'd go to church if there were a reason to believe that the myth is actually true. Christianity would be a lot easier if God just came out of hiding and showed himself."

"The invisible and the nonexistent look very much alike," Paul said. "Either God doesn't exist or He's very secretive."

"God didn't seem to be shy in the Old Testament. Now he doesn't appear at all, just like he's a fictional character."

"Reverend Hargrove says that an obvious God would rob us of our free will, that we'd have no choice but to believe in him."

Athena said, "I know that you exist, and that doesn't damage my free will."

"We're told to puzzle out His existence from ambiguous clues."

"And we're punished if we get it wrong. When I was at the monastery, the abbot said that the same question of existence is asked about the Buddha."

"What do they say?"

"That the Buddha exists for those who need him to exist, and he doesn't exist for those who don't need him to exist."

"Maybe that's the way it is for Jesus too, except that Christianity just doesn't admit it." Paul took her hand in both of his. "What about us? Do you want to see me again?"

"Yes, of course."

"I'm not welcome at your house."

"They'll come around. Patience."

"We could . . ." A crazy idea formed in Paul's mind. "We could elope."

She tilted her head and frowned. "Silly—we're not even engaged."

He took her hands in his. "We can get married and live in Jim's house until we find a place of our own—it's like a palace. That'll get you away from your parents' control."

"Oh no—I can't do that. It would hurt them."

"But they're hurting you. They're keeping us apart."

"It won't last. That kind of emotion will burn itself out."

"How long then?"

She sighed. "It frustrates me, too—maybe a month, maybe longer."

"Maybe never."

"Be patient. If I walk out, I hurt my parents, and I'd be on my own. I'd lose my job at the store. And there goes college—I can't pay for it."

Paul remembered Jim's gift. "But I can! Jim left me money for college. We could use it for you."

"That's sweet, but that's for your college." Athena looked at her wristwatch. "I can't stay any longer or Father will suspect. Look, I want to get married, just not yet. I want to help get women the vote, and I want to go to college. With a degree, who knows what I could do."

"But this wasn't part of our plan."

"I know, and I'm sorry, but I have a lot I want to do before I have a family."

Paul began to protest, but Athena put a finger to his lips. "I'm late, and I must get back. It will work out—have patience."

"When will I see you again?"

"I'll write to you when I have news."

He gave her Jim's address. She squeezed his hand and was gone.

∞

The next day Paul put on his suit to call on some of the companies on his list. He visited seven companies, a quarter of his list, and three asked for a formal letter of application.

He spent the rest of the week visiting companies during the day and writing the required letters at night, wearing a sweater and scarf in the chilly house. He considered typing the letters but rejected that as too tedious, and he wrote them carefully in pen as Samuel had taught.

The letters were finally out, and he had a Sunday to relax. The only chore that remained was to wait—wait for replies to his letters and wait for updates from Jim and Athena.

Monday blurred into Tuesday which blurred into other days. Forced to do nothing else, Paul found his reading gradually wither from delight to burden, like a diet of cake. He thought back on Jim's solitude here.

Jim had been a secular monk for over twenty years and loved the independence, but the long and unstructured days weighed on Paul. This new life began to feel like prison.

When not reading or going on errands invented mostly to change his surroundings, he sometimes imagined himself working in one of the companies he'd written to. Who would he work for and compete with? There would inevitably be other workers who would look down on him, denigrating his background or lack of experience. Younger men might be promoted over him, and he would need years to earn his place, slowly rising within the company. Maybe he wasn't cut out for work in a big company after all.

No—this thinking was unhealthy, and he had to give any job a chance. That was, if he got one. The newspapers made clear that the job market was weak and had been for months. He cheered on the economy but found himself the fan of an uninspired team. The stock market was falling, the San Francisco earthquake recovery effort continued to hobble the money supply, and job openings were scarce.

Perhaps college then? The idea of a degree like Jim's enticed him, but the road to a degree seemed to stretch on endlessly—years of classes plus remedial work before he could even enter. He would be in class with students much younger than himself—rich kids coming from education and luxury. His two years working for Samuel seemed like a career, but these unbroken years of college seemed like a lifetime. And to what end?

Walking became a retreat. It helped him think, though sometimes it helped him to stop thinking. The cold snap eased, and a light jacket was enough to keep him warm. He wandered through all parts of town while avoiding Second Street near the church.

When he returned from a walk, he would always check the mailbox after first crossing his fingers for luck. Often, it was empty. Every few days, he'd find a letter for Jim. One day, he discovered the first letter addressed to him, a reply to one of his job applications mailed the week before. His heart fluttered, and he dashed in to open it—a letter from the Los Angeles Brick Company. He let out his breath as he read, "While we were impressed with your credentials, we regret to inform you. . . ." He scanned it for subtle messages, but it seemed clear that they simply weren't hiring just then.

Two days later, he received a letter from Athena. He reread it many times though it was little more than a heartbeat saying that she had nothing to say. With no way to reply, let alone see her in person, it was a poor surrogate.

On one of his rambling walks, he realized that his route would take him past his old apartment. It was already an hour past sunset, and he decided to eat dinner and sleep in his old place. It was still his for another six weeks. He could pick up a few more things and return home the next day.

He'd become accustomed to Jim's spartan way of life and was surprised at how pleasant his apartment felt—so warm that he was comfortable without his jacket. After dinner, he scanned his bookshelf and discovered old favorites that he had forgotten amid Jim's scholarly works—books by Twain and Poe, Jules Verne and H. G. Wells.

He felt a bit like a tycoon who had an apartment in the city as well as a country house. Back home the next day after a leisurely morning, he checked the mailbox to find another rejection and finally, after close to three weeks, the first letter from Jim. He tore it open. Jim was in San Francisco—or had been two days earlier. He and Leviathan had traveled without car trouble, Jim enjoyed the scenery of the coast road, and they'd spent some nights in hotels and others camping on the beach. He described the desolation in the burned-out center of the city and the vast cities of tents in the parks. He concluded, wishing Paul good luck with his search and giving a temporary address for mail.

The letter was everything Paul expected but nothing he needed. He was pleased that Jim's trip was proceeding nicely, but he had hoped for some wisdom to help him see his path.

Paul replied with a detailed summary of his difficulties finding a job, his doubts about college, and the Farbers' injustice in keeping him from Athena. After reading it, he tried again with a shorter, more businesslike letter. He wouldn't complain to the man who had given him so much and who had transformed his life. If not for Jim, he'd still be in the church.

The next day he took the trolley to the University of Southern California to face this demon. He coaxed a tiny flame of optimism.

He found the Admissions building and was ushered in to see an unsmiling woman behind a desk.

"What can I do for you?" Her words were more accommodating than her demeanor.

"I'm interested in attending USC."

"How many years of schooling have you completed?" She had an odd habit of nearly closing her eyes as she spoke.

Paul felt his face flush. "About six years, but I've read a lot on my own."

She sighed. "And what degree do you hope to complete?"

"I really don't know. I guess I haven't thought that far."

"College isn't for everyone," she snapped, eyes fully open. She paused and Paul imagined that she was calculating how to most quickly end this interview, then she took out a sheet from a drawer and pushed it across the desk. "These are the entrance requirements for all students. There are no exceptions. In your case, I would guess three years of full-time remedial work before matriculating as a freshman and then another three years to graduate with a degree. And know that you will be close to ten years older than most of your fellow students."

She clasped her hands on her desk. "Know also that students as ill-prepared as you rarely complete the remedial coursework."

Paul waited for more, but the meeting was apparently over. He took the long list of required courses, mumbled his thanks, and walked out. At the trash bin down the hall, he discarded the paper.

As the weeks reluctantly unfolded, he spent more time in his rooming house and rationalized that he needed to get some use out of it since he was paying for it. He would idle away his time, finding excuses to run some small errand, losing himself in the newspaper, or reading his fiction, and then return to Jim's house to check the mail and deal with his reading. He felt an obligation to Jim to use the library wisely, but his drive was gone.

Paul received more we-regret-to-inform-you letters from local companies. He still had applications in process, but he slowly understood that finding a job would be harder than expected.

The lonesome vacation was becoming more difficult. Reading would hold his interest for a bit, then he'd worry about a job and critique his list of companies and try to add to it, then he'd take a walk and revive the option of college. It was as if his ship had sunk and he were flailing in slow motion, first toward one bit of flotsam, then another, then another, and finally back to the first.

Driven one afternoon by frustration at his aimless study and unclear future, he left Jim's house and headed east with no goal other than a change of scenery. He crossed the river on Alhambra Avenue, passed the train yard, and turned south through the residential area of East Los Angeles and Boyle Heights. Only when he passed the cemetery did he realize that he was walking with a destination.

His pace slowed as he walked a familiar street he had first visited five years earlier, a street on which he didn't feel welcome, on which he was a voyeur. He crossed to the far side and slowed his walk further. At a tan colored house, he saw two children sitting in a dirt yard with little grass. A woman—the widow—watched from inside. She looked as he remembered her, or perhaps a little older. The house was small and more tired looking than its neighbors.

A thought came to mind. He could offer to repaint the house. That chore was clearly past due, and he had the money for paint and time to do the work. Giving back to the family that he had wronged, if only in a small way, would feel good. But she would want to know why. He could say that he was from a church—but did he need an excuse, especially a religious one, to do someone a good turn?

Maybe she'd bring him a cup of coffee as he worked, and they'd chat as he took a break. She'd say how pleased she was that he was helping, and he'd say that he was happy to help someone in need. Perhaps she'd volunteer, "Things have been so difficult since my husband died," and he would get his chance to say, "I'm sorry to hear that, so very sorry."

With a deep breath, he turned back. He would just knock on the door, say that he noticed the need for some work, and offer to paint the house.

When he was halfway across the street, the widow turned to face him. Her vacant expression became alert, and he imagined her responding with a dozen suspicious questions.

The familiar out-of-control drowning feeling returned, and he quickened his pace, looked away, and strode purposefully along the sidewalk, pushing the tan house away as just another uninteresting house in a distant neighborhood. At the corner, he turned and headed back toward downtown as his pulse gradually slowed.

Back on the west side of the river, he retreated to his rooming house where the last of his anxiety vanished and he felt safe. Revisiting the consequences of his crime made clear that he needed rules. To someone lost in a sea of possibilities, constraints felt like a comforting blanket. They were the trolley rails that kept him on a safe path.

℘

Mr. Paisley reached for the door but pulled back when he heard whistling from Samuel's office. The haggard Samuel Hargrove that he had helped back to his apartment three days earlier after the odd sermon had been in no mood to whistle. He knocked.

"Yes, come in." It was Samuel's voice.

Inside, he found Samuel in paint-spotted work clothes. The rug was rolled up against the bookcase and tarps protected the floor and desk. A crate on the rug held the wall hangings—the framed articles, awards, lithographs, and the Seven Virtues needlepointed by his wife. Samuel held a paint can and brush and was halfway through painting over the red wall with pale yellow.

"You seemed to have recovered from the debate," Mr. Paisley said.

"Oh that—I really haven't thought about it. The lesson from the debate was that my focus on apologetics was misplaced. No, not a lesson—a blessing."

"That's a radical change."

"But a change for the better, I think. It was a prideful diversion that I regret. It distracted me from opportunities to help others."

If it wasn't the debate, then what had caused Samuel's startling behavior on Sunday? Mr. Paisley was about to ask when Samuel said, "Floyd, I need to come clean on something that happened three months ago." Samuel put down the can and brush. "I took close to four hundred dollars from church donations and spent it on my Assembly campaign. My hope was that I would win and that publicity would increase donations to more than cover it, but win or lose, it was wrong to do without permission. I want to explain all this to the board, and I'll accept their judgment. I'll also recommend that we drop our annual debate."

Samuel had never treated board approval as more than a formality before. Mr. Paisley struggled to respond, but all that came out was, "I see you're redecorating."

"Yes, I'd like a simpler life. I'm getting rid of the framed things." He gestured at the crate. "Wouldn't you know it—they left shadows on the wall like they were still there. I had to paint." Samuel walked over and picked up the Seven Virtues.

"But you'll put them back up?"

"Oh, no." Samuel chuckled as he laid it back in the crate. "And I'll get rid of this, too." He kicked the rug.

"That's an expensive rug."

"Indeed—several hundred dollars have been lying on my floor that could be put to work. Deuteronomy says, 'I have given tithes unto the Levite and the stranger, to the orphan and the widow, according to all thy commandments.' I want to be able to say that. I want *us* to be able to say that. And speaking of which, I have an idea for the new church."

Excellent—the moribund building project was weighing down their small church. "What do you suggest?"

"Sell it."

"*Sell?*" Samuel had practically imposed this project on the board. "You said the new building was God's will, that He would see us through."

"And I was wrong. Hard to imagine a man being so wrong, but there you have it. That money can be put to better use."

"How can we get our money out? That site can't be used for anything but a church—unless you tear down the work that's been paid for already."

"I know that Immanuel Presbyterian is looking to expand. Perhaps they'll buy us out."

"And if not?"

"Then I'll look for another buyer. The building project took us away from what counts."

"Which is?"

"Helping the needy—the poor, the widows, the orphans. Let's convene a meeting of the board of elders tomorrow. I'd like to get approval for this new direction." Samuel looked like a child eager to play with a new toy.

"Are you sure about this?"

"I've never been more so."

"This will take some getting used to," Paisley said as he steadied himself with the bookcase, "though I like the change. But what's gotten into you? What prompted this?"

Samuel leaned back against the desk. "Your boy Michael is, what, thirty-two now?"

"Thirty-three."

"And you have how many grandchildren?"

"Two, with one on the way."

"That's marvelous." Samuel smiled. It was a warm and honest smile, and it suited him. "I came from a close family. Bea and I couldn't have children, and since she passed, I've been missing family all the more. Helping others, maybe an orphanage, seems the right path."

Mr. Paisley shook his head. This was either a selfless move that would invigorate and strengthen the church or a foolish public admission of error that would destroy it.

&

The next morning, Paul wasted time with reading and household chores and then detoured to the Dresden part of town that had been his neighborhood before Samuel found him.

On the third floor of a rooming house, Paul found Virgil's name on the door where he'd seen it last. It had been four months since his last visit to the friend who'd shared so much of his childhood.

He knocked, and Virgil was in. After smiles and handshakes, Virgil explained that he was working part-time at the train yards, which gave him a lot of time at home.

Virgil's small apartment was as cluttered as before. His trousers were held up with suspenders and he wore an undershirt, and his combed-back hair was peaked in the center like the gable of a house. He offered a chair and a cigar, and Paul accepted both. The two men paused to light their cigars. As the smoke drifted up, Paul noticed that this was not the refined brand that Samuel had favored, but he had no interest in criticizing his friend's hospitality.

Paul filled in Virgil on his struggles with atheism and how he'd left the church. "It just isn't a fit. I don't believe anymore. I had an emotional approach before, but logic is my ruler now."

"Well, you're the philosopher, but seems to me that using logic to take care of your spiritual needs is like slicing bread with a hammer." Virgil took a big pull on his cigar and turned his head to blow out the smoke. "Anyway, it's a shame you don't have your job. You had a pretty good situation. Steady indoor work is nice, especially now."

"No work here then?"

Virgil shook his head. "Don't come back here. Get a desk job—use your brain, not your back." He pulled up a coffee can from the floor, set it on the magazines on the table, and tapped his cigar on it. "You're smart. You escaped. Since you've been gone, I smile every time I think of you. But if you came back . . . opium, gambling—you don't want to know what the gangs are doing now."

"But a fellow can stay away from crime. You have."

Virgil looked away. "How would you know?"

Paul hadn't come just to catch up with an old friend and certainly not to test him. They had shared so much that he didn't need to apologize or justify himself here. "I went by that house yesterday—the widow's house."

"Aw, now you shouldn't be doing that to yourself. That's just torture."

Paul mentioned his idea to paint the house.

Virgil laughed, which sent him into a coughing fit. He spat into the can. "She doesn't want her house painted, she wants her man back. Look—it was an accident. Let it go."

But Paul couldn't let it go. Hardly a day had gone by but something reminded him of the murder. "I had absolution in the church."

"Well, friend, in the real world, absolution is called 'prison.' "

"I've already spent a lifetime in prison, for no crime but being born."

"Then why keep punishing yourself? It was an accident—it's in the past."

And a family was hurting in the present. Absolution in the church had salved the guilt—but the church was no answer now. Paul saw no clear path.

But Virgil apparently did. He raised his eyebrows as he looked at Paul, as if he were waiting for the answer to an easy math problem. "You make up for your failures by being a good person, right?" he said. "Life is a balance scale—good things on one side and bad on the other."

"Where did that come from? You're not religious."

"Don't have to be. It's just fairness—everyone knows it. It's common sense. You've lived a good life if the good things outweigh the bad. So you've got a lot on the bad side—okay, then get to work on the good side."

There was something to that, and Paul considered Virgil's words. After a minute's silent puffing on his cigar, he moved on to another issue he wanted to unburden himself from. "I told you about Reverend Hargrove, the pastor in my church? I discovered that he's my father. All this time, even back to his pulling me out of jail, he knew he was my father, and he didn't tell me. He could have come for me at the Boys Home, but he didn't."

"So your father searched for you and took you in."

"Yeah," Paul said. "And he lied to me."

"After all this time, you found your father." Virgil pushed his hands slowly down his thighs and looked at the floor. "I wish I had a father."

ɛͻ

In the several days since his visit with Virgil, Paul's wandering thoughts had groped for friends and advisors, and he was increasingly harassed by an image from the end of the debate.

In the confused aftermath of the debate when Mr. Paisley tried to end the event, Samuel had leapt to his feet and demanded another re-

buttal. This created a spontaneous new contest, with Mr. Paisley arguing that the rules of debate were fixed. Paul had no interest in the outcome—the debate was over for him, even if Samuel got his rebuttal—
and was collecting his papers when Samuel saw him, accused him of
trying to slink away, and demanded that Paul wait for him in his office.
This suited Paul nicely, as he was eager to confront Samuel with his
secret.

Paul was walking to the office when he saw Mrs. O'Brien. She was
standing in the aisle of the church, hugging her coat and looking back
at him. She didn't look angry or judgmental but simply hurt. He looked
into her sad face for a moment and then she turned slowly and hobbled away.

Samuel deserved what he got, but Mrs. O'Brien was a good and loving soul who had been caught in the crossfire. Prodded by the memory
of her crushed expression and eager to get out of the house, he put on
his suit and left late one Saturday morning to see her. He'd hurt a decent person and wanted to apologize.

He had last visited Mrs. O'Brien's small house with the backyard full
of citrus trees in mid-February, but, as he put out his hand to knock on
the door, he felt as if he were reaching across a gulf much more than
two months wide.

The door opened. "Paul!" She reached up to grab his face and pulled
him down to kiss his forehead. "It's so good to see you. And you're
just in time—I was about to have dinner. Share it with me." She wore
her usual ready-for-an-outing clothes with a thick shawl.

Paul was glad that his black eye was finally gone. "I don't want to intrude."

"You couldn't if you tried, dear—you're the closest thing to family I
have. I bake a ham most Saturdays, but it takes me days to finish it. I
have plenty." She nudged him toward the dining room. "Sit. And get
yourself a plate and silverware."

Paul set a place for himself. The table had bread and a small plate of
steaming vegetables and lacked only the main course. He marveled at
the reception—he had no right to expect this.

Mrs. O'Brien came in from the kitchen with the ham, chatting all the
while about goings-on in the neighborhood and updating Paul with

who was doing what within the church community. Paul was content to play the attentive listener. Nothing had changed.

During dinner, Mrs. O'Brien provided most of the conversation while Paul puzzled how to bring up the big issue, his break with Samuel and the church.

"I've been thinking about college," Paul finally volunteered.

"That's a big change. Do you know what you'd do?"

"I haven't decided what to study. It's just an idea, anyway."

"Would you leave town?"

"I haven't figured that out either."

"I do hope you fit in. A new life can be hard, especially when you leave behind those who care for you. And I hope you'd go for the right reasons. Novelty can be attractive, especially to young people, but the excitement over something new vanishes quickly. And dear, if you're just running from problems, it's usually best to turn around and face them."

Paul pushed a scrap of potato skin around his plate with his knife. "I don't think you understand."

She put a hand on his. "Families squabble sometimes, even a church family."

"This is more of a family than you realize." Paul threw his napkin on the table. "I was raised as an orphan, treated like garbage and then thrown onto the street. But now I know why." He turned to face her. "Samuel is my father. He admitted it after the debate. That's why he took me in two years ago. He's the reason I spent an eternity in that orphanage."

Mrs. O'Brien took a piece of bread and artfully buttered it, shaping the butter until it was spread as evenly as paint. Finally she put it down. "Sounds like you have a right to be angry."

"You bet I do."

"Every parent is imperfect. I'm sixty-four, and I've seen a lot of them."

"Samuel must be more imperfect than most."

"We've all done things we shouldn't have," she said. "I've seen you two work together, and I've heard him talk about you. He genuinely loves you—I know he does."

Paul said nothing.

"Give him a chance to make amends. I've known him since he was your age, and he's a good man. Flaws and all, he will always be your father."

Paul picked up his napkin and folded it neatly. "I can't go back to the church. There's just nothing there—no intellectual foundation."

"I always knew you were smart. I couldn't follow half of the debate, but you sounded so forceful. You reminded me of William Jennings Bryan. But the church is much more than arguments and debate—it's community and heaven and forgiveness. All these years of Samuel's debates have changed my mind not a jot either way. Even if I were to accept all those fancy arguments against religion, my faith would remain. That's why it's called 'faith.' "

℘

Samuel turned his letter face down on the desk. "Yes, come in."

The *LA Times* reporter who seemed to have adopted the church for his newspaper came in and took the chair that Samuel indicated.

"It's been almost a year since your famous prediction, Reverend. Thursday is the anniversary of last year's earthquake, and we wanted to update everyone on the goings-on in your church."

More likely, this was an excuse to revisit the debate. This was the reporter who had written the scathing summary of the debate that had wallowed in Samuel's humiliation. He was probably eager for more of the same.

"I hear you've stopped work on your new church."

"That was the wrong project for us. We've sold that property, and another church has picked up construction."

"So, a bit of a retrenchment?"

"A redirection. We've sort of adopted the LA Boys Home. That's a better focus for us."

"An expensive detour, then."

"We made a mistake, and we corrected it." Samuel glanced at his bare floor. When rolled-up, that rug had reminded him of a snake skin. It was much better sold, with the money doing service in the orphanage.

"Let's talk about the debate." The reporter looked up from his notebook. "How do you think you did?"

"I don't much care how I did."

"You set up a debate, invited the city to watch, and you don't care whether you won or lost?"

"Not anymore."

"Come now, Reverend. This isn't the man who made a citywide reputation as a tenacious and unbeatable debater. I'm giving you a chance to air your side."

"We've dropped our annual debate."

"Apologetics has been the signature focus of your church."

"No longer."

"Then what do you ground your religion on?"

"On faith."

"Another retrenchment?"

"Another redirection." Admitting the true grounding of his belief—faith, not facts—came easily now, but this was a hard-won insight.

The reporter sighed and flipped through his notes. "I must say—abandoning the new building, the public defeat in the debate, the loss in the Assembly election. I would've thought that you'd have more to say in your defense."

"Looks like I won't be able to give you what you want."

"You have nothing for our readers then?"

"If your readers are interested in this city's poor treatment of her orphans, I have much to say," Samuel said as he stood. "It appears instead that you want to focus on the past. In that case, write what you will."

The reporter took the hint and left.

Samuel sat back heavily in his chair. He had brought this scrutiny on himself, but he wanted to put it behind him. One misstep in particular that he was eager to shake off was that confused sermon after the debate. Paul's discovery of his sin with Jenny and the possibility that he might make everything public had overwhelmed him. Even now he felt a bit like a fugitive because Paul could expose him at any moment. The anxiety was crushing, but he wasn't strong enough to go public and admit everything.

Surprisingly, the membership's response to the sermon hadn't been to chastise him but to interpret his veiled confession as humility. They hadn't punished him but praised him, and that hurt almost as much as if they'd found out the truth.

He considered the reporter's comment about the upcoming anniversary of the earthquake in—what had it been?—almost forty days since the debate. A lot had happened since then. Forty days of trials that had been painful but productive.

Awakened to his past, he'd visited Jenny's grave for the first time and admitted to himself how he'd wronged her. The choice between Bea and Jenny had been the choice between career and love, and love had lost. Perhaps his lifeless marriage to Bea was partial penance, and seeing the "Emerson" last name on Jenny's gravestone stung. He'd outmaneuvered Jim, but Jim had won just the same.

He'd also gotten approval from the board of elders for the redirection. Before the vote, Samuel and the board toured the Boys Home. Though it was fairly sanitary, everything was substandard—the food, the clothes, the overcrowding. The board voted later that day to select the Boys Home as their primary charity.

The church membership had gradually gotten behind the Boys Home project. A few members, captured by the idea of the grand new church, couldn't accept the change and left, but this was a small expense. Samuel mused that the church might never run out of good that it could do with this project alone—improve food, provide clothes, even add a wing to the orphanage.

This ordeal had one last task. He turned over the letter on his desk, his letter to Jim. He'd written several earlier drafts since the debate, all through gritted teeth, but this version finally felt right.

Dear Jim,

It's been more than 25 years since we worked so well together and since I wronged you with my false accusation. Perhaps I can be forgiven the recounting of the specifics since I'm sure neither of us needs reminding. This admittedly does nothing to correct the error, but let me assure you that I am very sorry. I can think back fondly now on our friendship and cannot conceive how I could have discarded it so selfishly.

I have appreciated only recently how wrong I was thanks to the help of Paul Winston. I believe you know our relationship.

I also want to thank you for your care of Jenny Christianson. You did for her what I should have done. With Jenny, the better man won.

Death prevents me from making amends to Jenny, and that fact will burden the rest of my life. However, I do have a chance with you. If a remedy comes to mind, I beg you to make that known to me.

When he finished reading, he signed his name to the letter.

℘

At home that evening, Paul found a letter from Athena in the mailbox. She began with some formalities and apologized for not writing more often. Then she got to her big news.

I've just begun an evening class in Algebra at USC! I checked a few colleges & that's an entrance requirement for the Sciences. Can you imagine me in an Algebra class? My parents can't & one reason I'm taking it is to prove that I'm serious about college.

You might not recognize me now! I carry my text-book wherever I go & study in my free time. My friends at the store make fun of me, but I don't care. I think now that a degree in English would be boring. Science or Engineering or Architecture interest me now.

I don't know what college I want to apply to. USC would be convenient—I walk there in 10 minutes. Maybe Berkeley—it would be fun to watch San Francisco being rebuilt across the bay. Or even Boston Tech, where Jim went, which teaches every kind of Science and Engineering I can imagine.

I must go—my first test is in 2 days & I must study!
With love,
Athena

She was right—he found it difficult to recognize her.

Two days later, Paul leafed through the newspaper as he ate his breakfast in the sunny library. A growing theme in the paper was the Thursday anniversary of the earthquake. Articles revisited the horror and destruction of a year earlier and talked about the rebuilding of San Francisco, which construction projects were running smoothly and which weren't, stories of life in the tent cities, and so on. An article with a local connection caught his eye—"LA CHURCH PREDICTED QUAKE." It told of Samuel's prediction, the short burst of national publicity, Samuel's failed run for California Assembly, the overextended attempt at a new church building and its sale to another church, and the humiliating debate six weeks earlier. It concluded, "Perhaps never in the history of our city has a house of worship so completely squandered a beneficence from God." He read the article a second time, then looked for the name of the reporter. It was the reporter he had invited, the one he had talked with on the church's sunny steps a year earlier.

He thought back on something he saw the previous day while walking. He'd heard church bells and, to satisfy idle curiosity, went closer. From a block away he watched the people in front of the church standing in the warm sun, chatting and comparing outfits. A trolley clanged its bell a block away, and a small surge of parishioners appeared a few minutes later. He smiled at the memory.

Paul returned his breakfast plate to the kitchen. He washed and dried everything and put things back in their drawers and cupboards. The last bit of milk went down the drain and the newspaper into the trash. He took down the serving platters and retrieved the four hundred dollars he had hidden underneath.

Upstairs, he put his mother's pillow in one jacket pocket and a stamped letter to Jim in the other. He picked up the black chess queen, admired its elegant lines, and set it back on the bureau and then picked up his mother's portrait. She had been the Princess Mother who had saved him during his early years, and he would reciprocate if he could.

As he left the house on Stageira Street, he found that the warm sun made his suit jacket unnecessary, and, for the first time in weeks, he had a long walk with a planned destination. With the morning sun in his face, he headed toward the river and the brick-paved Swift & Co. plant.

He toured the site as workers and delivery wagons went about their work, searching for the alley where he had accidentally killed that man five years earlier. He paused when he found it, feeling almost like he was at a consecrated site. He left feeling humble and meditative, as if he'd just left a prayer meeting.

From the meat packing plant, he walked south to the construction site where he had spent so much time the previous fall. He admired the massive arching timbers, and it felt good to see the site once again active with workers. This had been a team effort, and he'd been part of the team. It looked different in the warm sun compared to the last time, when a cold wind had whipped the tarps.

He felt like a compass that had been put away on its side, its arrow pointing in the wrong direction. But back in its natural orientation, it again pointed true. He knew where he needed to go next and walked a block to Second Street, a broad boulevard, and turned west, feeling the April sun on his shoulders. The Prodigal Son was going home.

Author's Note

If you enjoyed this journey, continue it at the blog, www.patheos.com-/blogs/crossexamined. I think of the blog as an energetic but civil critique of Christianity, and I'd love to see you become a regular reader and participate in the discussion.

You can contact me at crossexaminedblog@gmail.com.

From the time when I first wrote notes for this project until now has been over eight years, and I've had some great help along the way. I'd like to thank my friends from several critique groups: Dave Gardner, Ben Barrett, Raymond Wlodkowski, Roger Curtis; Lynn Knight, Gary Bloxham, Brita Butler-Wall, Lauren Basson, Kathy Gunovick, Malissa Kent; Loretta Matson, Elizabeth O'Connell, Jesse Rowell, Vivi Brown; Mel Clark, Kim Ritchie, Donald Gilbert-Santamaria, Chris McFaul, Gilla Bachellerie, and Donna Fitzgerald.

Others read the final manuscript and provided invaluable input: Chris Doerr, Keith Brown, Eliza Sutton, Paul Sager, Neil Gerrans, Jerry Schiffelbein, Paul Pardi, Marion Spicher, Randy Rumley, Jim Corbett, Paul Case, Gayatri Salunke, Andrew Jonsson, Robert Parham, Rob Townsend, Abby Weltman, Wendy Britton, Paul Hartman, and Jason Black.

I thank you all.

Made in the USA
Middletown, DE
03 February 2019